54732

Sanguinet's Crown

Also available in Large Print
by Patricia Veryan:

Some Brief Folly
The Wagered Widow

PATRICIA VERYAN

Sanguinet's Crown

G.K.HALL &CO.
Boston, Massachusetts
1986

Copyright © 1985 by Patricia Veryan

Published in Large Print by arrangement
with St. Martin's Press

G. K. Hall Large Print Book Series

Set in 16 pt. Plantin

Library of Congress Cataloging-in-Publication Data

Veryan, Patricia.
  Sanguinet's crown.

  (G. K. Hall large print book series)
  1. Large type books.   I. Title.
[PS3572.E766S2   1986]   813'.54   86-205
ISBN 0-8161-4028-6 (lg. print)

FOR LELIA,
who has waited with such
delightful impatience for
this book.

Author's Note

The Royal Pavilion at Brighton is impressive today and must have been even more so when occupied by the dashing gentlemen and lovely ladies of Prince George's Regency.

In setting some of the scenes of this tale in the Pavilion, I was unable to resist including some apartments that were actually not quite completed in June of 1817.

I beg the forgiveness of my readers for having strayed thus from strict chronological observance in depicting the Pavilion for those who have not been able to view it in person, and in recalling it to those who have.

Patricia Veryan

PART I

The Capture

Prologue

The May morning was bright and pleasantly warm. Tiny daisies starred the lush turf of the Sussex hillside, and chestnut trees, pink and white and red, were glorious in their new gowns. At the top of the hill the leaves of the cluster of birches were stirred by a gentle breeze, and on the level ground below, sunlight awoke a glitter of diamonds on the ripples of a stream and glinted no less brightly along three steel blades that rang and darted in deadly combat. An uneven combat this, for two men, broad of shoulder, long of arm, and having the grim look of merchants in death, battled a single adversary: a tall, lean young gentleman whose every movement proclaimed the athlete, and whose appearance branded him unmistakably as a member of that exclusive set known as Corinthians. He was clad with quiet elegance in buckskins and fine linen. His boots were mirror-bright, and his bottle-green riding coat a masterpiece of tailoring. He wore no hat, and dark hair, wet now with sweat, curled against a high, intelligent brow. In spite of his hazardous

3

situation there was no fear in the long, pewter-grey eyes. Rather, they danced with exhilaration, and he mocked and taunted his opponents as he parried and thrust, his footwork as skilled as the slender but strong hand that so deftly manipulated his small-sword.

Of the men facing him, one was very tall and wiry, with a narrow face, small cruel eyes, and a vindictive mouth. The other, heavy-featured and having an untidy mop of black hair, now attacked with the outside thrust under the wrist known as *seconde*. It was a well-executed manoeuvre, but the Corinthian countered as swiftly, and in a brilliant prime parade his sword beat down with devastating power, ringing loudly against his opponent's blade and smashing the weapon from his grip.

The black-haired man leapt out of distance, clutching his numbed wrist. "Almost I had you, Redmond!" he cried, chagrined. "Damn your eyes, I *almost* had you!"

Mitchell Redmond spun, lightning-fast, to deflect the wiry man's lunge, but it was very close, the steel whispering through his jacket. These two knew their trade, and he said, circling his own sword warily, "So you know my name. And someone has paid highly for your services, I think. Who wants me dead, my bullies?"

Frustrated because his blade had not struck home, the wiry individual snarled, "How many enemies have you got, eh?" He thrust even as he spoke, Redmond parried, and the swords

4

rang together and locked. The two men strained, eye to eye, foible to foible, and the assailant went on, "How many coves have you gone and . . . cuckolded, fine gent that you is? How much blood you . . . spilled, in all them duels of yours?"

Redmond was aware that off to the side the other ruffian was reclaiming his weapon. With an expert twist, he broke free. "And you think to even the score for them?" He laughed mockingly. "I'd not be spending your blood money before it's won, were I you."

"Wouldn't you, now?" The black-haired man rejoined the attack, coming in from the side, since Redmond was managing to keep a tree trunk at his back. The battle escalated in intensity, the swords flashing and ringing, the hired assassins grim and murderously resolved, Redmond alert and very fast, and still exhilarated by this fight. They were good. Both of them were good. But he was better. His main concern was not to allow either of them to get behind him. And so he parried and riposted, his blade a whirling glitter, his movements swift, graceful, and untiring as he defended himself and managed occasionally to snatch the offensive. Overconfident, the black-haired man thrust in *tierce*. The blade that should have spitted Redmond's heart was beaten aside. In a silver blur Redmond's sword came at him. The man dodged, too late, then reeled back to lean weakly against a tree, one hand pressed to his side, the fingers at once stained with crimson.

The disengage, however, left Redmond vulnerable for a split second. He had to resort to a desperate leap to avoid the wiry man's immediate attack. Inevitably, he lost the protection of the tree, but it did not matter because with one rogue disabled the fight would be fair now, and it shouldn't take more than another minute or two to end it.

He parried a thrust in *carte*, but as he essayed the *riposte*, he sensed that someone was close behind him. His reaction was so fast that his lithe sway almost averted the dagger at his back. He was hampered, however, by the need to counter the sword that menaced him, and the dagger struck home glancingly. Redmond gasped, and staggered, and the third attacker, who had left the horses to join his hard-pressed comrades, uttered a howl of triumph. His wiry friend lowered his blade, grinning broadly. Redmond recovered himself and whirled about, his drooping sword whipping upward. The joyous howl of the back-stabber became a scream. He grabbed at his slashed face and fled.

Belatedly, the wiry man leapt again to the attack. He found that, far from dying, Redmond seemed cast of quicksilver. The aristocratic features were pale now, the laughter quite gone from the narrowed grey eyes. Redmond mounted a savage attack and, released of the need to remain in the one location, was agile as a cat so that where the assassin's blade was, he was not. Driven back and back by this grim ferocity, the wiry man knew fear at last. "Will!" He cast a frantic glance to his sagging friend. "Don't just mess about there! Help me, for Christ's sake! Redmond's a madman!"

Redmond's laugh was harsh and without humour. His right foot stamped forward, his knee bent gracefully, and his blade thrust in *carte* to the full length of the powerful arm behind it. The wiry man shrieked, swayed, and went down, a spreading bloodstain brightening his shirt front.

"Will" swore, pushed himself from the tree trunk, and staggered away.

With reddened sword leveled, Redmond advanced, his smile striking terror into the heart of the wounded man who lay, propped on one elbow, helplessly watching.

"Now," Redmond murmured, "you've a free choice, carrion. You can die, or you can tell me the name of the man who sent you."

Chapter 1

Charity Strand's slight shoulders rose and fell in a deep sigh. Remarking this, her attendant groom shifted in the saddle and eyed her profile with a trace of anxiety. Mr. Best had served the Strands for most of his life, working his way up from bootblack to head groom, and his affection was as deep as his loyalty. He decided that Miss Charity's face, framed by the simple straw bonnet, was still much too thin. Her sister Rachel had persuaded her to have her hair cut short, so that the thick sandy braids no longer wound about the beautifully shaped head. Best wasn't sure that he approved of such new-fangled notions, but it was true enough that the fluffy curls lent a softer look to Miss Charity's delicate features. Even so, the fine eyes, somewhere between green and grey, appeared too large for her face, and the clear skin seemed almost stretched over the high cheekbones. Charity Strand had come a long way since her horse had fallen with her five years ago. For three of those years she had been trapped in a wheelchair, and although she had at last escaped that painful existence, she was far from being sturdy.

To Best's way of thinking, she would have done well to accept her brother's offer and make her permanent home at Silverings. Certainly, she knew that Mr. Justin and his lovely wife, Lisette, would have been nothing but pleased, for they both loved her dearly. The same could be said of Miss Rachel (though she wasn't a Miss any more, but was now *Mrs.* Tristram Leith). And no one could ask for a kinder young gent than Colonel Leith, even if he *had* been as good as cashiered after Waterloo! No, the problem was that little Miss Charity didn't seem to know where she belonged, poor lass. Forever drifting about from the old family home at Strand Hall, to Silverings, her brother's beautiful estate; or to Berkshire, where her sister and the Colonel spent most of the year. One would think as she be a old spinster lady, instead of barely two and twenty, and getting stronger and comelier every day now, bless her heart!

The object of these musings continued to look rather wistfully to the south, her eyes following the distant gleam of the river that wound for better than twenty miles to where Silverings spread graciously upon its banks. Justin and Lisette were away, of course, and the great house closed. It was because they were in Town, and she had preferred to remain in the country, that Rachel and Tristram had come down to be with her. And it was because Justin understood her fondness for their old family home that Strand Hall had been reopened for the month he would be away. They all had grown up at the Hall, Justin, Rachel, and Charity, but she was the only one who really loved the old house, and she yearned to make it her permanent abode. There was little chance she would ever marry, for she was neither pretty nor accomplished, and she had already planted a hint in her brother's mind that she planned to engage a chaperone and occupy Strand Hall year-round. She stifled another sigh. Her hint had not been well received. Justin, his blue eyes glinting, had said impatiently, "Oh, by all means, m'dear. I think it a splendid scheme. When you reach forty."

Best saw that second sigh, and he scowled. What was she thinking on, staring like that? Silverings lay that way. Was she remembering last year, when Mr. Justin had come so close to slipping his wind down there? Or were her thoughts drifting even farther away — to France and Brittany, and the terrors she had lived through at the hands of Claude Sanguinet? A rare lot of violence this slip of a girl had known in her brief lifetime. It wasn't good for her to brood on that Frenchy's wickedness! Wherefore, faithful soul that he was, Best coughed politely and observed that it was a "nice view from here. Will I be getting ye settled like, miss?"

Charity tilted her head a little and agreed that the view was lovely. "But I think it will be better from the top, you know."

Best had thought the same, but as he'd intended, his remark had broken her reverie, and she urged her mount up the hill once more. Satisfied, the groom slapped the reins against his horse's neck. Nosey started off with un-characteristic reluctance. Come to think on it, the old fool had been acting a mite odd since they'd started up here. Dang it all! He should've noticed! Best called to Miss Strand and dis-mounted hurriedly. It took but a moment to determine that the chestnut gelding had picked up a stone in his hoof, and another moment to dislodge it, but Nosey, irreverently named after the Duke of Wellington, still favoured the leg.

"Oh, dear," said Charity, "he does not go on very well, Best. Do you suppose he has taken a stone bruise?"

Furious with himself, the groom nodded. "I fear he has, marm. The more fool I, for not noticing. Cut his hock as well — see here."

"Poor fellow. You must take him home at once."

Best replaced the little knife he always carried, and eyed the girl uneasily. "I do be that sorry, Miss Charity. And this the first nice day we've had in a week and more. But I reckon as how we better get back, else I'll have Colonel Leith a-jumpin' down me throat." He grinned at this mild aspersion on the character of a man for whom he had the deepest admiration, and took back the reins Charity held for him. "I'll walk him, miss."

"Yes, do. And when you come back —"

Dismayed, he exclaimed, "Marm? Ye never mean to stay out here all alone?"

"No, pray do not look so aghast," she said, with a little trill of laughter. "We are less than two miles from home and this is Sussex, Best, not London."

"Aye, marm. And there be those across the water" — forgetting his earlier anxieties, he jerked his head in the direction of France — "as would hit out at the Colonel howsoever they might. And you being his lady's sister, they might just vent their spite on you!"

The fear that never failed to grip Charity when she thought of those terrible days in Brittany wrapped chilling fingers around her heart. She took a steadying breath. "It is almost two years now," she pointed out quietly. "I will not walk in terror of Monsieur S-Sanguinet forever." And knowing she had stumbled over speaking that dread name, she met Best's troubled eyes levelly and stretched forth an imperative hand. "My sketchbook, if you please."

The groom stared miserably at that frail little hand. "Mr. Justin would have my ears was I to leave you here alone, miss, as well you know."

"My brother," she argued with a faint smile,

"would be the last one to have me creep about, trembling at every shadow for the rest of my days." And knowing that this good man's balking was prompted by love for her, she teased, "I know you mean well, but poor Nosey looks most uncomfortable. And, my faithful friend, can you really suppose anything evil could transpire in our gentle Sussex — especially on so beautiful a morning?" Seeing him frown uncertainly, she hastened to urge, "Come — it may start to rain again tomorrow, and I have promised Miss Rachel a painting of the Hall that she may take with her when they go back to Cloudhills."

Reluctantly, Best detached a flat and rather battered leather case from his saddle and handed it up to her. "You'll not wander off, miss?"

She promised to go no farther than the brow of the hill. "So be off with you. You can walk poor Nosey home at your ease, and by the time you come back I shall have a splendid painting for you to admire."

Her eyes twinkled merrily at him. And after all, what she'd said was quite true. The Frenchy had frightened Miss Charity and her sister half out of their wits, done his best to murder Colonel Leith, and pretty near crippled poor Mr. Devenish, but that had been in France — which everyone and his brother knew was a place fit only for snails and serpents! Best looked around at peaceful fields, drowsing woods, and the musical hurrying of the stream.

England. Not even that ogre, Bonaparte, had managed to invade this dear old isle; what chance had a fumble-foot like Claude Sanguinet?

And so it was that, uttering a final stern admonishment that Miss Charity not talk to no strangers, Best took up Nosey's reins and started down the hill. "I'll be back in an hour," he called over his shoulder. "Or less, like as not."

Charity waved and rode on. If she knew Best, he would be back just as quickly as he could, and fond as she was of the groom, the opportunity to sketch without benefit of his critical and vocal appraisal of her efforts was enticing. She slipped from the saddle when she came to the brow of the hill, and tied the reins to a low-hanging branch in a copse of birch trees so that the mare might graze comfortably. The light was as good as she had hoped, and it was the work of a moment to spread the blanket on the damp turf and settle down with her sketchbook and colouring case.

With deft, rapid strokes, she sketched in the outlines of Strand Hall, the soar of its neoclassical columns, the deep welcoming terrace where Brutus was probably outstretched and snoozing at this very minute. She smiled, pleased with these first efforts. A long way off small bells were jingling erratically, a puzzling sound that was relegated to the back of her mind as she roughed in the pleasure gardens.

It was easier to draw the Hall than to get

Silverings onto paper. During the three months she had just spent there with Justin and Lisette, she had tried several times, without success, to capture the house bathed in the dancing light from the river that had given the estate its name. Her thoughts dwelt fondly on her brother. Dear Justin, so happily settled at last, so adoring his beautiful bride. Sometimes, when he did not guess he was being watched, she had caught him looking at Lisette with an awed wonderment in his eyes, as though even now he could not quite believe the depth of happiness that had been granted him.

"Perhaps," thought Charity, "I *do* have a chance to find love. Perhaps the day will dawn when a gentleman looks so at me. . . ." And at once she felt guilty even to wish for such a blessing when she had been given so very much. Two short years ago, her one prayer had been that the pain would stop. Now she was not only free from suffering, but she could walk and ride and lead a normal life (even though her dancing left much to be desired!). To ask the good Lord for more was pure greed.

The little bells rang louder and, intruding thus into her awareness, caused her brow to pucker. Bells? On a Thursday morning? And they had been chiming with that odd lack of rhythm since just a little while after she'd sat down. Curious, she set aside pad and pencils and stood.

Her scan of the surrounding countryside

revealed no logical source of the sound, but it could be coming from the northern side of the hill. She walked up through the stand of trees and, coming out into the sunshine, halted, appalled by the scene before her.

A man, his shirt most gruesomely stained and his attitude one of mortal fear, lay on the ground at the foot of the hill, one arm thrown up in a feeble attempt to protect himself from the blade that menaced him. The individual who held that glittering sword, far from showing any pity, stepped even closer, until the point of the blade cut into his victim's throat.

Paralyzed with shock, Charity heard a soft, gloating laugh. A cultured voice observed with cold inflexibility, "Very well, then. This world is overburdened with your kind!"

The sword was drawn back, the hand holding it now aiming in such a way as to make his murderous intent very clear. The wounded man gave a shriek and began to babble frantically, but his words were drowned by the scream that burst from Charity's throat. Running pell-mell, she called, "Do not! Oh, you *must* not murder the poor soul!"

"Damn and blast!" The swordsman spun to face her.

Still running, Charity beheld a slim gentleman whose expression fairly hurled wrath. He was much younger than she had at first supposed. Even in that taut moment, a portion of her brain registered the fact that he was excessively handsome, his hair thick and dark, his nose high-bridged and Roman, his features of an aquiline cast, and his chin firm. The mouth, however, she judged cruel, with thin lips compressed into a tight, angry line, while the eyes — Oh, heavens! Had she ever before seen eyes of such an icy grey?

His voice a snarl of rage, he demanded, "What in the devil are you doing here, madam?"

The question was as arrogant as it was stupid. Ignoring it, she stood before him and panted, "You *must not!* It would be cold-blooded murder!"

A twisted smile curved his mouth unpleasantly. He sneered, "Much you know of it. My gift to England, rather."

"Oh! How can you be so wickedly unfeeling?" And noting from the corner of her eye that the wounded man had managed to stand and was tottering away, she said, "Have you never heard of good sportsmanship, sir?"

"My God! A missionary!" The grey eyes, glinting scorn, flickered in the direction of the hilltop. "Where's your keeper, ma'am? You are surely not allowed to run loose?"

He was as brutal and ill-mannered, Charity decided, as he was good to look upon. She said haughtily, "One might expect a gentleman to apologize for swearing at a lady, rather than to rail at her."

"And one might expect a *lady* to be accompanied by a maid or a footman, rather than prancing like any hoyden into affairs that don't con —" He had turned about as he spoke and, discovering that his intended victim was making good his escape, uttered a cry of rage and started off in pursuit.

With a cry of her own, Charity sprang to throw her arms about him. "No! You shall not!" she cried, heroically clinging to him.

She discovered her mistake at once, even if she did not repent it, for despite his slender build, he was all steel. Her determined clasp was broken in an instant and so violently that she fell headlong. The Villain was stamping off after his prey; he wasn't running, as she would have expected, but that he fairly slavered for the kill she did not doubt. Starting to get to her feet, Charity saw that the wounded man had reached a cluster of trees, but even if his horse was tethered there, he could not hope to get very far, and when his merciless opponent came up with him, would have no chance to defend himself. Nor could she hope to prevail upon such ferocity, unless . . . She lay back and uttered a sobbing wail. Somewhat to her surprise, the Villain slowed and turned to scowl irresolutely at her. She moaned loudly. He hesitated, glaring after his departing victim, for all the world, or so thought Charity, like a wild beast deprived of its prey. The simile pleased her highly developed sense of the dramatic, but a moment later as he strode reluctantly towards her, she experienced a pang of fear. For only then did it occur to her that she was alone, far from help, with a man who would not balk at murder.

Coming up with her, he said grittily, "I suspect you mean to enact me a proper Cheltenham tragedy, no? What is broke ma'am? Your neck . . . at the very least?"

Oddly enough, those scathing words eased her anxieties. She lifted one drooping hand. "I will trouble you only to help me rise, if you please." And with a saintliness that would have astounded those who knew her, she murmured, "I have been rather ill, you see."

He snorted derisively, but his hand went out and gripped hers. She was surprised to find it cold as ice, and shot a searching glance at him. He was very pale, which was fashionable, of course, and probably merely indicated a life of debauchery.

His strong tug having restored her to her feet, he sneered, "I collect it must be a forlorn hope to enquire if you've someone to escort you home, ma'am?"

Home? She had no intention of going home. She'd scarcely begun her painting. He wanted to be rid of her purely so as to hunt down and slaughter his wounded adversary. Bloodthirsty wretch! Charity had always felt a deep contempt for dueling, but she was well aware that in spite of the efforts of the Bow Street Runners and other minions of the law, the practice continued. She knew also that it was governed by a rigid Code of Honour. It was scarcely to be credited that a man so obviously well bred as this one should ignore every precept of that Code, but credit it she must. To divert him from his savagery would, she decided, be well worth the sacrifice of a morning's sketching. Therefore, she abandoned the pithy indictment of his manners and morals that she had been about to dispense and instead said in a die-away voice that her groom's horse had gone lame and he was walking the animal home.

"The fellow should have his wits refurbished for leaving a lady alone out here," growled the duellist. "Have you a horse nearby, ma'am?"

She acknowledged, quaveringly, that she had, and that it was tethered at the top of the hill.

He grunted and, putting fingers to mouth, whistled shrilly. A horse neighed. Charity heard fast approaching hoofbeats and from around the curve of the hill came a magnificent black mare, galloping with a smooth, effortless stride that was a delight to behold. For a moment it seemed that she would trample them, but at the last instant she plunged to a halt and stood sidling and snorting beside her master. She nuzzled at him fondly, but then flung up her pretty head and danced away, eyes rolling.

"It's all right, Whisp," he said in a voice that surprised Charity. "Come now, quiet down." His tone becoming acid again, he asked, "Are you able to mount, ma'am? She's a trifle frisky, but —"

"Thank you. That will not be necessary. I am quite able to walk to my horse."

He shrugged, and instead of walking beside her as any gentleman would have done, thrust one foot into the stirrup. His decidedly stiff swing into the saddle was so at odds with the splendid mare that Charity again appraised him narrowly. He was white as death and when he lifted the reins she saw blood on his wrist. "Good heavens," she exclaimed, "you're hurt, Mr., er . . ."

"Pray do not weep, Miss, er . . ." he said harshly. "And my name is Mitchell —" He broke off, his jaw setting and his right hand gripping hard at the pommel.

Incensed, she cried, "Of all the nonsensical starts! Get down at once, Mr. Mitchell, so that I may —"

"I shall do no such thing. And if you do not hasten, ma'am, I shall leave you to your probably gruesome fate. I've . . . I've much to . . . do."

The words were as obnoxious as ever, but his voice had wavered and was less distinct. Running to keep up with the mare, Charity declared indignantly, "Never in all my life have I encountered so idiotic a creature! For heaven's sake, sir, would you prefer to bleed to death rather than suffer me to —"

"Oh, infinitely, ma'am."

Dumbfounded, she halted to stare up at him. The mare cavorted and danced. Her rider swayed easily and instinctively, winced, and again grabbed hard at the pommel.

"Mr. Mitchell," said Charity, torn between anxiety and exasperation, "if you will not allow me to help you, pray leave me and ride to the nearest inn. There is a delightful one a mile or so to the west, and —"

"And I shall repair to it, just as soon as I've seen you safely home."

She tightened her lips and threw an irked glance at the heavens. The man was all about in his head. But despite his stubborn stupidity he really did look very ill, wherefore she picked up her skirts and ran the rest of the way. She did not attempt to gather her belongings, hurrying instead to her horse. As she reached for the reins she glanced around and was just in time to see Mr. Mitchell topple from the saddle and lie in a motionless heap beside his Arabian.

With a groan, Charity ran to snatch up the small bottle of water she carried for her paints, then fairly flew back to the fallen man.

He lay on his right side and she sank to her knees beside him, opened his coat, and searched for the telltale signs of a wound. There were none. She took up his left wrist. The crimson streaks had crept down to his fingertips but the coat sleeve revealed no tear. Baffled, she pushed him over onto his stomach, finding it to be more of a task than she'd anticipated.

"Good God!" she gasped.

The back of his coat was slashed and wet with blood. She stared numbly for an instant, thinking, "In the back . . . ? Was he running away then?"

Recovering, she attempted to tear the jacket, but the cloth might have been made of iron, and she carried no scissors with her artistic supplies. The garment was very well tailored and fit snugly across his shoulders; to remove it by conventional methods would require quite some time and possibly more strength than she possessed. At this point, she remembered the duel. His sword had been restored to its scabbard and was a trifle difficult to come at, but eventually she succeeded in retrieving it. She held it gingerly. It had not looked nearly so enormous when Mr. Mitchell had held it. Now, it seemed prodigiously heavy, and the horrid thing was razor sharp. It was necessary that she proceed with great care lest she add to his woes by impaling him, but somehow, in struggling to rend the back of that once excellent jacket, she dropped the weapon and, grabbing for it, inflicted another long slash in the back of the unconscious man's pantaloons.

Two years ago, when poor Alain Devenish had been so brutally hurt in Dinan, she had done what little she could to help her sister nurse him and had frequently held the bowl while Rachel applied hot compresses to the wound in his thigh. That had seemed quite convenable. For some odd reason, the slash in

24

Mr. Mitchell's britches and the glimpse of the smooth flesh beneath did not seem at all convenable. Her cheeks burned and, laying the sword aside, she tried with the foolishness of panic to pull the severed edges of the fabric back together.

"What in . . . hell . . . ?"

Charity gave a little shriek. Mr. Mitchell's dark head was turning to her. "Do not move!" she shrilled.

"The devil I won't!" He tried to sit up, but abruptly subsided.

With her heart fluttering, Charity grasped the sword and completed her desecration of the jacket.

"Madam," said Mitchell, faint but determined, "whatever it is that you . . . attempt, desist!"

Whatever she attempted? What did he *think* she attempted? But she knew all too well! Horribly embarrassed, she nonetheless investigated further. His shirt was wet with blood and slashed from the area of his spine across to the left side, just below his shoulder blade. Still wondering how such a wound could possibly have been inflicted during a duel, Charity slipped the sword under the fine cambric, made a long slit, and laid the sword aside. She spread the shirt apart and stared, suddenly very cold. The gash was quite deep and had bled profusely, but it was not the wound that caused her heart to all but stop. The muscular back she gazed at was a mass of scars, the criss-crossing ridges leaving no room for doubt that at some time in the not too distant past this man had been flogged half to death. Very few crimes, she knew, could cause such punishment to be inflicted upon an aristocrat, and she shrank back in revulsion. Small wonder he had not wanted her help!

A derisive chuckle brought her eyes flashing to meet his. "Well," he sneered, "and what have you decided, Madam Prim? Did I murder my mother? Or violate my baby sister, perhaps?"

The words were as contemptuous as they were disgraceful. Her disgust of him flared, but there was a pinched look about the thin nostrils now, and for all their mockery, his eyes were dulled. Charity pulled herself together. Whatever his offence, he was injured and in pain.

She said quietly, "Both, I fancy. Only lie still, sir, and I shall do what I may to help you."

Chapter 2

Despite her limited experience in the actual treatment of wounds, Charity knew that it was imperative the bleeding be stopped as soon as possible. To this end, she appropriated Mr. Mitchell's neckcloth, formed it into a pad, and placed it over the wound. Peering over his shoulder to watch these procedures, her patient said, "That won't serve. You shall have to tie it." His eyes glinted at her with fiendish enjoyment. "You must now tear a flounce from your petticoat. If you will hand me my sword, I'll be glad to assist."

She ignored him, unwound the sash from her gown, and said with cool self-possession that if he could contrive to sit up, she would manage.

He sighed in disappointment, but complied. It was inevitable that she should come very close to him as she performed her acts of mercy. His body reminded her of her brother. Like Justin, he carried not an ounce of fat. The muscles rippled smoothly when he moved. The hair on his chest was thick and very dark. She averted her eyes, her cheeks hot.

Amused, he said, "You are blushing ma'am. But I'll say one thing for you, the sight of blood don't reduce you to blancmange, as it does most females."

"You are too good," she murmured. The blood was still seeping from under her impromptu pad, and there was only one way to stop it. "I'm sorry, but I must tighten this." Nerving herself, she gave a sharp tug at the sash she had wound about him. There was a hiss of indrawn breath, but not a sound escaped him. Despite this stoicism, when she asked him to put a finger on the knot she was tying, his hand shook and he stared down blankly at the makeshift bandage. She wondered uneasily if he would be able to climb onto the saddle, and had seldom been more relieved than when the thud of hooves announced Best's return.

The groom reined up and dismounted with a leap. "What on earth happened, Miss Charity?" he asked, running to her in considerable agitation.

"The lady was good enough to help me," said Mitchell, reaching for the remains of his jacket.

Charity thought, "He doesn't want Best to see his back." She reached around to assist him. "I chanced upon a duel," she exclaimed.

"A duel!" Dropping to one knee beside the injured man, Best moaned, "Oh, I knowed as I shouldn't have gone off and left ye, miss! Were there no seconds, sir? No surgeon?"

Charity frowned, wondering why she hadn't thought of such questions.

Mitchell answered a curt, "No." He turned to Charity. "I am most grateful for your . . . assistance, ma'am."

He did not look grateful. He looked haughty and vexed. Therefore, she responded with deliberate double entendre, "I am only glad that I reached you when I did."

His lips tightened, and he turned to Best and requested the aid of his arm.

The groom, who had watched this small exchange in some bewilderment, at once helped the injured man to his feet. Mitchell seemed dazed, and with no little reluctance, Charity suggested that they proceed to her brother's house so that he could rest.

"Thank you, ma'am. But I am already late." He whistled, and the mare that had been grazing nearby trotted over. Best guided Mitchell's left foot into the stirrup, then provided cupped hands to receive the right foot and boost him into a clumsy but successful mount. "My," Best murmured, stroking the mare's glossy neck admiringly, "she do be a prime bit o' blood, sir. Arab?"

"Obviously," said Mitchell, taking up the reins. "Now, could you direct me to a house called Strand Hall?"

Charity's heart dropped into her shoes, and Best looked at her in surprise.

Turning from one to the other, Mitchell drawled a sardonic, "It *does* still stand, I presume?"

"It did two hours since," Charity replied. "Strand Hall is my brother's principal seat, Mr. Mitchell. Please collect my belongings, Best, and then we can take —"

"If you will rather be so good as to direct me," Mitchell interpolated. "As I have said, I'm in something of a hurry."

How insufferable he was! Charity was very tempted to inform him that no one at Strand Hall waited in breathless impatience for his arrival, but it dawned on her that Tristram might be expecting him. "In that case," she said in her calm way, "I shall ride with Mr. Mitchell, Best. You will not object, sir, if my groom takes the time to aid me to mount?"

Mitchell scowled and did not respond to this deliberate provocation. His irritation communicated itself to the mare, and she danced about nervously so that for a few minutes he had to place all his concentration upon staying in the saddle. When he glanced up, the girl was mounted and waiting, a look of saintly resignation on her face. He didn't want her. Thanks to her confounded interference, his chance to identify the man who'd sent the murderous trio after him had been foiled. Besides, he felt like hell, and the dread of toppling from the saddle and again being forced to submit to her martyred airs, scourged him. If Whisper would just behave herself for once! He yanked on the reins with unnecessary violence. It was not a touch Whisper knew, and she snorted and stood trembling. "You damned gudgeon!" thought Mitchell remorsefully, "now see what you've done!" But before he could comfort his beloved mare, Miss Prim was saying in her soft and confoundedly sanctimonious voice, "You will spoil her mouth if you treat her so, Mr. Mitchell."

"Mr. Mitchell!" The foolish chit didn't even know his name! And choosing to forget that his own halting words had given her the wrong impression, he snapped, "Might we perhaps start today?"

Without another word, Charity guided her horse down the hill and across the meadows towards the belt of woodland that marked the start of the Strand preserves. She set a steady but not fast pace and, ignoring Mitchell's smothered mutterings of impatience, waited for him to fall from the saddle.

She was still waiting half an hour later when they followed the winding drivepath up the slope and stopped in front of the Hall. A stableboy sprinted to take the horses, his eyes becoming round as saucers when he noted Mitchell's bloodstained rags. Not waiting for assistance, Charity kicked her little boot free of the stirrup and jumped down. Mitchell had kept his back ramrod straight during the ride; she watched to see how his arrogance would dictate that he manage the dismount. Instead of swinging down in the customary manner, he tossed his leg up over the mare's mane and slid down gracefully. She saw the sheen of sweat on his brow and around his mouth, but he gave not the faintest indication of discomfort, staring instead at the great house for a moment before remarking in an awed and quite unaffected way, "What a jolly fine place!"

The front door opened and the butler came out onto the terrace, his slim figure as immaculate as ever, his hair a silver gleam in the early afternoon sunlight. His pale blue eyes shot to the unexpected visitor and widened, and immediately his attention flashed to Charity. She

31

looked strained, and there was blood on her gown. He asked in sharp anxiety, "Are you all right, miss?"

"Yes." Grateful for the solicitude, she smiled at him. "I am perfectly well, thank you, Fisher. But this gentleman has had some — er, trouble. This is Mr. Mitchell —"

"Redmond," Mitchell finished. "Has my man arrived?"

Charity blinked. At breakfast neither Tristram nor Rachel had mentioned the imminent arrival of a guest. Fisher, however, seemed not in the least surprised, and advised that Mr. Redmond's chaise had indeed arrived and his valet awaited him above stairs.

"Redmond . . . ?" thought Charity, her brow wrinkling. "Now where have I heard that name before?" And then she gave a gasp as Redmond had the effrontery to ask, "Who else is here?"

Fisher hid his own surprise admirably. "We have no other guests at present, sir."

Redmond scowled as he strode confidently across the terrace and came near to colliding with the doorjamb. Charity was mildly disappointed when Fisher caught him at the last instant and guided him through. "Easy, sir," he said gently. "May we hope Sir Harry and his lady plan to join us?"

Charity smothered another gasp. Sir Harry Redmond had been believed killed at the battle of Ciudad Rodrigo, but had been found alive days later and had surprised everyone by surviving his wounds after a long convalescence. Dimly, she recalled that there had been some scandal involving Sir Harry, but just what it was eluded her, and she wondered uneasily what could possibly bring such a celebrity to this quiet corner of Sussex.

Mitchell Redmond, meanwhile, having firmly denied the possibility of his brother's arrival, had drawn away from the butler's supporting arm. "Have my man down here, if you please. He will assist me."

Fisher beckoned to a hovering parlourmaid and sent her scuttling up the stairs in search of Mr. Redmond's valet.

Charity murmured, "Is my sister from home, Fisher?"

Having vainly attempted to persuade Mr. Redmond to sit down, the butler said, "They went out for a drive, miss."

Redmond said autocratically, "I must see your master directly he returns."

With difficulty, Charity restrained herself from sweeping him a low and royal curtsey. The arrogance of the creature!

There came a flurry of volubility from the stairs, and a plump gentleman's gentleman, very black of hair and eye, and very white of skin, ran down to them. Charity had been expecting someone as supercilious as his employer and was amused by this excitable individual who fluttered about Redmond, wringing his hands, uttering a spate of Italian lightly interspersed with English, and having many references to someone called "Mama Mia."

Redmond looked suddenly exhausted, as though his strength had stretched only until this moment. Wearily, he muttered something in fluent Italian. The valet glanced at his master's back, groaned, and clapped a hand over his eyes, then slipped out of his own discreet coat to throw it around Redmond's shoulders.

"A thous' pardons, signorina," he apologized, casting an anguished look from Charity to his shirt sleeves. "I am indecent. But Signor Mish-hell" — he shrugged, a gesture that involved every inch of him — "have mos' the need-a. You forgive, *si?*"

Leaning heavily on his arm, Redmond said, "Miss Strand, this is Antonio diLoretto, my man. Miss Strand, er, cut off my garments, Tonio. And, ah, tied me up."

There was a whimsical gleam in his eyes, and the tug at the beautifully shaped lips enhanced his good looks to a degree that Charity found deceptively unfair even as she wondered that she'd thought his mouth thin and cruel. DiLoretto left her little time to recover. Abandoning his hold on Redmond, he bowed so low that his pomaded curls all but brushed the carpet. With impassioned voice and dramatic gestures he came near to sobbing as he exploded into a flood of mingled English and Italian, his speech so rapid that Charity caught only the words "art," "life," and "feet." The monologue ended as abruptly as it had begun. In the midst, or so it seemed, of a death scene that would have made Edmund Kean envious, this droll little man spun around, seized his employer once again and said with brisk authority, "We now uppa go stairs."

Charity closed her parted lips. "What on earth do you suppose he said?" she asked Fisher, as the oddly assorted pair disappeared along the first floor landing.

"Something to the effect that he is your slave forever. That his heart will break if you do not allow him to sacrifice his life for you, and that, meanwhile, his soul is at your feet. I think," replied the butler.

"Good gracious!" With one hand on the banister, she asked, "Did you know that Mr. Redmond was coming today?"

"I had no idea, miss. But" — he hesitated — "when his man said they were expected, I assumed Mr. Redmond must be acquainted with Mr. Justin or the Colonel. I hope it was in order for me to —"

"Don't be silly, of course it was. And I fancy he must know my brother-in-law, because of the way he asked for him just now. Where have you put him?"

"The green room, miss. In view of Mr. Redmond's injuries, I fancy his man had best stay with him. Would you wish that I send for the doctor?"

"Yes, please do." Charity said uneasily, "I hope this business will not upset my sister."

Fisher's thoughtful gaze drifted down her rumpled gown. Following his eyes, she exclaimed, "Oh my! I must hurry and change."

Fisher said with a twinkle, "Yes, miss. I fancy the sight of you just now would be a *decided* shock for Miss Rachel."

"And we must allow nothing to alarm her at this particular time, must we, Fisher?"

They exchanged understanding smiles, then Charity started up the stairs. She had taken only a few steps, however, when a rapid pounding from below was followed by a startled exclamation from Fisher. Charity turned back, having first taken the precaution of clinging to the rail.

A tawny tornado galloped full-tilt up the stairs. Tongue lolling, powerful paws flying, ears back, the large grinning bulldog tried to jump into her unavailable lap, rebounded down three steps, gambolled up again, succeeded in wiping his long tongue around her chin, turned around in midair, landed heavily, and stood stock-still. He had caught a new scent.

Charity, who had been angrily adjuring the dog to "behave," glanced at Fisher in amazement. "My heavens! I do believe he is obeying me."

"Perhaps," suggested Fisher, straightening

the cravat that had become disordered when he was flung against the wall, "he knows that —"

His words were cut off. With every indication of a dog defending his mistress against a murderous threat, Brutus hurled his challenge up the stairs. Charity threw her hands over her ears and commanded the "bad dog" to be quiet. Fisher added his own exhortations to the din, and two downstairs maids joined in the howl for silence. Brutus quite enjoyed it, but he tended to become bored very rapidly, and, deciding that enough was as good as a feast, ceased his roars and trotted sedately down the stairs and across the hall towards the kitchen.

The humans sighed with relief. Fisher signalled to the maids, and they departed. Charity wondered uneasily why Brutus had taken so violent a dislike to Mitchell Redmond.

Charity's abigail was putting the last deft touches to her hair when the door opened and Rachel entered. No one, seeing them together, could have the slightest doubt but that they were related, but the likeness was manifest in the fragile build that was characteristic of all three Strands, in their mannerisms and grace of movement, rather than in any marked similarity of features. Rachel Strand Leith's hair was a light dusty brown, containing none of the red tints that caused Charity's locks to be termed sandy. A famed beauty, Rachel had a shapely figure that was just beginning to betray the fact that she carried her first child, but if anything, approaching motherhood lent a deeper radiance to the delicate features, only a slight trace of fatigue marring her loveliness.

Just now, her deep blue eyes clouded with anxiety, she hurried to Charity saying, "Dearest? What is this I hear about your having become involved in a duel and arriving home covered with blood? Are you all right?"

"Oh, but how vexing of them to worry you so!" Charity stood to hug her. "I particularly wished to spare you any alarm." She dismissed her abigail and when the girl had left them, asked, "Was it Best told you such stuff? I vow he gossips like an old woman!"

"No, it was not Best." Rachel allowed herself to be guided to the sofa in the adjoining parlour. "And I'll not betray my source of information, so never try to worm it out of me. Come, Charity. Sit here beside me and do not try to fob me off with fustian, as Fisher did."

Seating herself obediently, Charity explained, "All I did was try to help a — er, gentleman, who had been hurt in a duel." She knew her hesitation had been noted, and added resignedly, "Oh, very well. I'll own I had sooner describe him as a boor, for a more arrogant, ill-mannered, ungrateful wretch I never met!"

"Mitchell Redmond?" Considerably astonished, Rachel exclaimed, "Why, he is the very nicest boy. I've not seen him for years, but as

I recollect he was so well featured as to take one's breath away."

"And still is. Though not nearly so handsome as your Tristram. And I hope you may not be disappointed when you meet him, for I can assure you that his disposition does not at all equate with his looks. Unless you could like an acid-tongued cynic."

Rachel was quite aware that her sunny-natured sister very seldom took anyone in such deep dislike. Perplexed, she said slowly, "I've heard a few rumours, of course, but set little store by them. You know what the gabblemongers are. The Mitchell I knew was shy and gentle, and most shockingly absent-minded, which used to drive his poor brother fairly into the boughs. He was quite a scholar and always had that handsome head stuck into a book. Now they say he is become a rake, which I *cannot* believe! Why, I recall meeting him in Town once, just before Justin went out to India, and who should chance to trip past but Dorothy Haines-Curtis. She spent at least ten minutes simpering and fluttering and flirting, while Mitchell grew red as any lobster and was so aghast he all but sank through the pave! Justin thought it hilarious, but Mitchell was truly embarrassed to death."

Charity tried vainly to visualize Mr. Redmond in such a state, and asked dubiously, "Are you quite sure, love? His brother is quite well thought of, I know, for he was a war hero.

Could you be confusing them?"

"Heavens, no! No one could do so, for they are totally unlike. Harry is the dashing one. I think you have not met him?"

"No. But Justin says that Harry Redmond is a splendid fighting man, and Jeremy Bolster once spent ten minutes trying to tell me something about Sir Harry; it was to do with a false charge that had been levelled against him, I believe, but I couldn't quite understand it all. You know how Jeremy is." She paused, it becoming apparent that Rachel was not attending. She asked, "What is it, dear? You are not worried about Mr. Redmond?"

Rachel started. There *had* been something about Harry Redmond a year or so back. At the time she had been absorbed with rearranging Cloudhills and adjusting to her newly married state, but there had been quite a scandal, and she was *sure* it had to do with one of the Sanguinets. Apprehension touched her, causing her heart to flutter, but she did not mean to worry Charity over such vague trifles and so responded hurriedly, "How rude of me to go wool-gathering! No, I was thinking about Tristram."

"I might have known," said Charity, laughing at her. "And what has he been doing to bring so troubled a look?"

Rachel's blue eyes softened as they always did when she spoke of her husband. "Nothing really, except" — she blushed faintly and looked away — "these late weeks he has been a touch uneasy, you know. Which is so silly, because although I was a little unwell just at first, I am healthy as any horse."

"Cart-horse," amended Charity with a twinkle, but she was less amused than she seemed. Her large brother-in-law was, she knew, desperately afraid. His courtship of her sister, at a time when Rachel had been betrothed to that horrid Claude Sanguinet, had been as perilous as it was unorthodox, and had not only almost cost him his life, but had resulted in disgrace and social ostracism for them both. Despite such an unfortunate beginning, their marriage had been blissful, marred only by Tristram's dread that the fulfillment of his hopes for children might also take from him his beloved wife. He had come near to fainting with shock when Rachel had gently broken to him that she was in a delicate condition, and he had subsequently guarded her with ill-disguised apprehension. It was true that the early weeks had not gone very smoothly. Nonetheless, Rachel had always enjoyed excellent health and when her time came would doubtless present her husband with a sound and beautiful baby. If Mitchell Redmond's arrival could turn poor Tristram's thoughts in another direction, thought Charity, the wretched creature might serve a useful purpose after all. "I wonder," she murmured, "what brought Mr. Redmond here."

"I fancy Tristram will find out just as soon as Dr. Bellows has gone. I was so startled to see his chaise in the yard. And you shall not fob me off any longer, Charity. What *is* all this about a duel?"

The Honourable Tristram Leith's swinging cavalryman's stride slowed as he rounded the corner of the first floor hall. Dr. Bellows had paused outside the green guest chamber, a puzzled expression on his face as he stared at the closed door. The little doctor was, in fact, so lost in thought that he jumped violently when Leith came up with him to enquire, "Have you finished with our guest, sir?"

"Goodness me!" exclaimed Bellows, almost dropping his bag. "How you do creep up on a fellow, Leith!" And peering up into the smiling countenance of the young man who dwarfed him, he said with less heat, "I have, but — he's a peculiar fellow. D'you, ah, know him well?"

"Don't believe I've ever met him. Is he very bad?"

"I wonder . . ." murmured the doctor inexplicably. Then, as if recovering his wits, he ran a hand through his thinning, reddish hair and drew Leith a few paces along the hall. "Bad? Oh no. Nasty cut. Lost some blood. I had to perpetrate some of me famous embroidery on the poor chap, which he endured bravely enough. All in all, it's more painful than serious. Funny, though." He pulled at his lower lip and muttered half to himself, "That back . . ."

"Back?" echoed Leith, curious. "I'd understood Mr. Redmond was hurt in a duel."

"What? Oh — likely you're right." The doctor smiled absently, said his farewells, promised to call tomorrow, and hurried off.

With the odd feeling that they had been talking at cross purposes, Leith watched the little man stamp down the hall, then turned and quietly entered the bedchamber.

Redmond lay on his side. His lean face was pale and had a look of exhaustion, but he heard the door open, and his long grey eyes watched the visitor levelly.

There was a trace of guardedness about that steady stare, and again conscious of being caught in an unexpected current, Leith said, "I was told you wished to see me directly. Shall it tire you if I come in now?"

"Probably," Redmond answered. "But I must talk with you, as you should be aware."

Puzzled by the note of impatience, Tristram drew up a straight-backed chair and straddled it. "If you mean by reason of your turning our lands into a duelling ground . . ." he said with his friendly smile.

Redmond's lips twisted sardonically. "I take it you have noted that I am, most uncomfortably, lying on my side."

"Yes. Dr. Bellows informed me that you had

suffered a cut on your back."

"Did he?" In a bored tone but with his eyes very intent, Redmond drawled, "May I ask what more your estimable physician had to impart?"

"That the wound is not serious. And he will come and see you tomorrow."

Redmond watched him thoughtfully. He'd heard that Justin Strand was a man of driving energy and likeable but uncertain temperament. The mental image he'd formed did not match this poised young giant whose deep voice was a lazy drawl, and who must have been very good-looking before the right side of his face was scarred. Just now his expression was calm but there was reservation in the dark eyes and, amused, Redmond said by way of explanation, "I am very agile, you see."

Leith responded with courtesy, if not complete veracity, "And I am notoriously lacking in curiosity."

"Fustian! You're likely thinking I turned tail and ran."

It was said whimsically rather than in anger, and Leith responded with a grin. "I'll own the cut in your britches surprised me."

"Not so damned much as it surprised me!"

He looked indignant, but Leith eschewed the obvious question. "How you conduct your duels is —"

Redmond made an impatient gesture. "I have, as you're doubtless aware, conducted

44

several. However, I ain't yet so foolhardy as to take on three men at once."

"The devil you say! It was *not* a duel?"

"Very shrewd."

Leith stiffened, thinking, "Impertinent cub!" and wondering why he had expected to meet a mild-mannered scholar. With a veneer of frost on his voice, he said, "May I ask if it is your custom to wear a small-sword when you travel?"

"Scarcely." Quite aware of the changed tone, Redmond smiled faintly. "I've discovered, though, that in case of emergency a pistol can be fired only once."

So the man had been expecting trouble. Perhaps he carried valuables about his person. Leith asked, "Thieves?"

Surprised, Redmond turned painfully on the pillows and settled back with a cautious exhalation of breath. Good gad! If the man really thought it had been thieves, then he knew nothing and this must be handled very carefully indeed. "Have you another suggestion?" he countered, probing.

In view of the fact that this individual was apparently something of a duellist, Leith answered dryly, "I can think of several possibilities."

To Redmond that remark suggested that this man might be playing a deep game. In which event, he would brave the water after all. Watching for the reaction, he said a tentative, "I came here because I'd a letter from" — he

45

dared not say "Diccon" — "from the Trader."

Racking his erratic memory, Leith could recall no Trader. "Did you?"

"Concerning my father," Redmond went on.

Again, Leith's recollection played him false. Beyond a vague knowledge that Redmond's sire was a fine sportsman, he couldn't seem to put a face to the name, but it was very possible he was a friend of the family. "I, er, trust Sir Colin is well," he murmured hopefully.

That he had erred was at once obvious. Redmond looked horrified and exclaimed, "Hardly! He was murdered in '14!"

"Good God! How damnable for you! Do you know who did it?"

"Oh yes," said Redmond, a deadly glint in his eyes. "We know, my brother and I. I believe you are acquainted with Harry?"

Leith sighed and gave up. "I might be," he admitted wryly. "There's a deal I cannot remember, even now. Only bits and pieces, I'm afraid."

"Ah, is that the way of it? Must be beastly annoying for you, Strand."

"It is, indeed. But I see you mistake, sir. Justin Strand is my brother-in-law, and presently in Town. I am Tristram Leith."

"Oh, Lord!" gasped Redmond, dismayed by the pitfall he had so narrowly avoided.

Leith's expression became chill. He stood and said coldly, "You have heard my name before, I see."

Redmond considered him. Egad, but it was a big fellow. "I should have, I take it. I've been in Europe a great deal the last year or so. But I fancy the uniform became you."

"So you *have* heard of me!"

"No, I tell you." Redmond grinned. "But military is writ all over you. Cavalry? You've seen service, I gather."

Instinctively, Leith's hand lifted to his scarred cheek. "Yes. Boney gave me something to remember him by. I wound up on Wellington's staff, actually."

"Did you, by God!" Looking suddenly boyish without that cynical hauteur, Redmond sat up, flinched, swore, but asked eagerly, "Waterloo?"

"Yes."

"Jove — what luck! How I'd love to have been there! Invalided out, eh?"

"No."

Nonplussed, Redmond watched him. That flat denial could mean anything — even that he had been cashiered. He thought impatiently, "What stuff!" The man was the very essence of pride and integrity, and the last type the military would have kicked out. On the other hand, it did not do to jump to conclusions, as that silly little chit had done this morning when she'd caught sight of his own back. The muscles under his ribs cramped, and he thrust away the recollection. He was laid by the heels for the present, else he'd ride out at once and track down Strand. Or better yet, Diccon himself.

Instead, all he could do was wait to see what developed. An anxious frown pulled his brows together as in his mind's eye he saw again the letter that he had most dishonourably intercepted. It had been addressed to Sir Harry Redmond, Moiré Grange, Hants., but he'd recognized the untidy writing of the direction and had broken the seal with not a second's hesitation. The message had been very brief:

Harry —
    Claude S. is on the move at last. Meet me at Strand Hall near Horsham, in Sussex.
Tell no one.
    In haste —

Trader

Trader meant Diccon, of course, and that zealous and little appreciated guardian of Britain's well-being seldom erred. If Monsieur Claude Sanguinet was "on the move," there was no telling what devilment was brewing. One could but pray old Diccon reached Strand Hall before Harry got wind of it all!

Mitchell put out his hand and, with a transforming grin that caused Leith to revise his first impressions hurriedly, said, "Very glad to know you, sir. I'm afraid I impose on your hospitality, and I'll likely be a blasted nuisance for a day or two, but I assure you I'm a fast healer."

Taking that slim hand and surprised by the

strength of its grip, Leith, ever courteous, answered, "It will be our pleasure to have you with us. Is there anyone you wish us to notify?" And he was at once intrigued by the schoolboy guilt that was reflected in the handsome face of his guest.

"Oh, n-no," stammered Redmond. "No one at all. Thank you."

Chapter 3

"Well, I think it a very odd circumstance," said Charity, walking slowly downstairs beside her sister. "He has been here for three days, surely there must be *someone* in this world who cares about the man and would be interested in knowing of his whereabouts? Sir Harry, certainly."

"Perhaps he told Dr. Bellows," suggested Rachel, straightening the pink zephyr shawl about her shoulders. "On the other hand, he *is* a bachelor, and besides, it is possible that he does not wish to alarm his relations."

"I asked Dr. Bellows how he goes on, and he said that the wound is healing nicely." Charity frowned slightly. She had not slept very well with such a man in the house, although Tristram would make short shrift of any attempted knavery. If she had warned him. For perhaps the hundredth time, she wondered why she had said nothing to anyone of Redmond's shameful scars, instead allowing Brutus to sleep at the head of the stairs. There was little doubt that the bulldog had taken an immediate (and perfectly logical) dislike to Redmond, and would alert the household if the man dared to set one foot outside his door.

Rachel laughed softly. "Whatever are you pondering? You look positively ferocious."

"No, do I? I was thinking of that strange valet, diLoretto. He has the other servants properly in whoops, you know. Mrs. Hayward told me that he has a little song or line of opera for practically any situation that arises, and does not hesitate to render it, wherever he chances to be."

"Yes, so Agatha told me. But he seems a very pleasant kind of man. I hope —"

They had reached the ground floor and were starting across the entrance hall.

"Oh, dear," said Rachel, pausing. *"Now* what is Brutus about?"

The bulldog's frenzied barking did not contain the warning note he employed when strangers approached. His excitement was evidenced by ear-splitting squeaks and yips interspersed with his usual stentorian tones. The sisters halted and looked at each other uncertainly.

"You do not suppose Justin is come home?" said Charity.

There was no rumble of carriage wheels outside, however, and the door that opened was the one beyond the kitchen that led to the stableyard. Rapid thuds, accompanied by the click of nails, presaged the arrival of the dog, who hurtled at them from across the hall. Charity flung herself in front of her sister, shrieking, "Brutus! Down!" She had armed herself with a hastily removed slipper, but although she applied this impromptu weapon to the dog's nose with firmness, once more her chin was lovingly caressed by what seemed several yards of pink tongue. "Horrid . . . beast!" she spluttered, staggering back.

"Br-Brutus! You silly dashed pest!" There was laughter in the familiar voice.

With cries of surprised welcome, both girls ran to greet the newcomer.

"Bolster!"

"Oh, Jeremy! How *lovely* of you to come! Is Amanda with you?"

The broad shoulders of the man who strode across the hall were exaggerated by the many capes of the long drab driving coat he wore. He had snatched off his high-crowned beaver, causing straight yellow hair to tumble untidily across his brow. Beaming, he bowed over Rachel's hand, straightened, his hazel eyes aglow with pleasure at this reunion, and turned to Charity to be seized in an impulsive, improper, and fond hug that delighted him. His ruddy features became ruddier. "I s-say, Charity," he stammered, grinning from ear to ear and dropping his hat. "Here's a jolly f-fine welcome! Hey! Brutus! Give it here, you curst commoner!"

Brutus had no intention of relinquishing his prize and, with the beaver firmly gripped between his jaws, galloped jubilantly round and round the three people who pursued him, variously entreating, commanding, and threatening. Ears back, eyes narrowed, his powerful legs pumping, he tore up the stairs, collided with the two men coming down, and stiffened. It was the scent again! Fainter, but still beyond bearing. He crouched, growling around the beaver, only to be shocked by a voice like steel — a voice that brooked no falderal.

"Behave!" it proclaimed ringingly. *"Down, sir!"*

Charity, who had been about to berate the dog, was at once vexed that Mr. Redmond should presume to do so.

Brutus, however, dropped so abruptly that he slid down the next stair. Looking up at the tall individual who had spoken with such authority, he humbly laid his prize at the man's feet and assumed an air of fawning servility.

"Do not toad eat me, you clumsy leviathan," said Mitchell Redmond. "Be off with you!"

"Well!" murmured Charity.

Brutus grinned and wriggled his hips in the contortion that passed for a wag of his tail. His efforts were wasted, however, and he went dejectedly down the stairs.

Tristram Leith snatched up the battered

beaver and tossed it to its owner. "Greetings, Jeremy!"

"Thank you, Leith. Hello, R-Redmond. You here?"

"Evidently," drawled Redmond.

Bristling, Charity saw a matching indignation come into Rachel's eyes. There was no cause for Mr. Redmond to speak so cuttingly. Everyone loved Jerry Bolster, for surely a kinder, more chivalrous person never drew breath.

Leith crossed to shake his friend's hand. "This is well timed, indeed," he exclaimed. "You mean to spend a week or two with us, at least, I hope?"

"Oh, do say you will, Jeremy," urged Charity.

"Did you bring your wife?" repeated Rachel eagerly.

"No, as a matter of fact. That is to say, I left her in Dorset." He turned his amiable smile on Redmond. "With your cousins, dear boy. I fancy you know that Sophia has presented Camille with twins."

"Good God!" exclaimed Redmond, astonished. "I knew she was in a delicate condition, of course, but — twins!" For an instant he looked quite enthusiastic, but catching Charity's eye, he added, "I wish Cam joy of 'em. One brat is a devilish nuisance, let alone a pair."

Charity could have scratched the obnoxious creature. He must certainly be aware of Rachel's condition, and he was, besides being an unexpected guest, one for whom they had been compelled to summon the doctor, give lots of extra care, and prepare a special diet. They would have done as much for a horse, but the least he could do in return was to be civil!

Seething, she said, "Be forewarned, Tristram. You are soon to have a 'devilish nuisance' foisted off upon you! Mr. Redmond, I believe you are acquainted with my sister?" As she spoke, she flung out a hand to indicate Rachel. Because she was angry, the gesture was exaggerated. It was also unfortunate, because she had completely forgotten that she still held the slipper, which now flew from her grasp and landed squarely in Redmond's face.

Bolster could not restrain a chortle. Leith quickly retrieved the slipper and returned it to Charity. Scarlet with embarrassment, she stammered out incoherent apologies.

Redmond rose to the occasion nobly. It was, he assured her, of no importance whatsoever. Turning to bow over Rachel's hand, he said with an enchanting smile, "Indeed, it fairly gave me back my own. What a block you must think me, ma'am. I trust you will forgive such gauche behaviour. The fact is, you are so slender I'd no least notion you mean to present Leith with *un petit paquet.*"

"Oh, prettily said," Rachel responded, laughter brightening her lovely face. "I am surprised to see you up and about so soon after your injury, Mr. Redmond."

54

Startled, Bolster intervened, "Injury? You hurt, Mitch? Not *another* duel?"

Irked by the awareness that a pair of scornful grey-green eyes were fixed upon him, Redmond shrugged. "Something of the sort."

"Harry won't like that, old fellow. Was saying to me only yesterday that he wishes —"

His brows drawing into a dark line, Redmond interrupted, "My brother is in Dorset?"

"No. Was. Went to see the b-babies, y'know. Told you — twins —"

"Yes, yes! Lord sakes, Jerry! Where *is* Harry?"

"On his way back to the Grange, of course. Likely he'll come here when he don't find you."

"Why the devil should he? Did you tell him I was coming here?" Redmond's dark face flushed with irritation.

Bolster blinked at him and stepped back a pace. "Couldn't. Didn't know, my t-tulip. I only meant Harry might c-come here because I'd said I was coming."

Redmond scowled, and there was a short, uncomfortable pause.

Taking Bolster's arm, Leith led the way into the drawing room, while enquiring heartily after the delightful Amanda, Lady Bolster. Bestowing a disgusted look upon Redmond, Charity swept past beside her sister, leaving the pariah to saunter after them, deep in thought.

Was it only a chance impulse that had brought Bolster into Sussex? Or had he also been summoned? Redmond glanced up and found Bolster watching him from across the big room, his open countenance absurdly concerned. Dear old Jerry. A gudgeon, but the very best of good fellows. Redmond winked, and at once a relieved grin lit his lordship's face.

Redmond wandered over to the window seat and sat there, looking unseeingly upon the fair morning, quite unaware of the indignant glances coming his way from Miss Charity Strand. Bolster and Justin Strand, he reflected, were good friends, so it was natural enough that Jerry should stop here — except that Strand apparently no longer resided here. He and his wife dwelt some twenty miles to the south at an estate called Silverings. It was possible that Jerry had gone there first, and come up here having drawn a blank. Redmond knit his brows in frustration. It would be simple to come at the root of it. He'd only have to ask, "Were you called here by Diccon, Jerry?" But suppose the answer was, "Yes. Were you?" What would he say to that? "Not exactly, old boy. I chanced to open one of my brother's letters and read it." He cringed inwardly, picturing Bolster's horror at such a deed. The ultimate dishonour — to pry into a letter intended for another. And Jeremy could be so dashed high in the instep about some things. "My instincts," he thought defensively, "were purely protective.

Harry has already done battle with the Sanguinets, and he has a wife and little son to be considered." Briefly, he felt not only justified but quite noble, but then conscience began to poke at him. The trouble was that one never really *knew* if one's motives were pure. He might tell himself that he had acted altruistically, but had he? Or was the real truth of the matter that he was driven by a consuming thirst for vengeance? Was his real need to even the score with the despicable Sanguinets? To make them pay for what they had done?

Memory slid backwards. He saw again the woodland clearing . . . Sergeant Anderson sprawled nearby, and Parnell Sanguinet's black-clad figure, those pale, macabre eyes narrowed against the afternoon sunlight. Almost, he could hear the velvety gentleness of that heavily accented, murderous voice. . . .

He was sweating, and a deep trembling weakened his knees. He fought memory away.

Bolster was saying, ". . . so I thought I'd come on here and say hello to old J-Justin, if he was about."

Leith joined with the ladies to renew his plea that Bolster stay until the Strands returned, which should be any day now. Delighted by their eagerness, Bolster agreed to remain. "At least for a few days, and only t-too glad to accept of your hospitality."

Amid much jubilation, Fisher was summoned and required to ask Mrs. Hayward to have a room prepared and to lay an extra cover for luncheon.

Redmond said nothing throughout these proceedings, but when his lordship made his way upstairs to change his riding dress, he did not go alone. If there *was* some reason other than a whim for Bolster having come here, Redmond meant to ferret it out.

"I know you cannot abide children, Mitch," said Lord Bolster, struggling into a pair of dove-grey pantaloons, "but those two new cousins of yours, I must admit, ain't all screwed up and red and screaming like most babies. Shouldn't be surprised b-but what they turned out to be quite tol-tol-tol-bearable."

Comfortably sprawled in a deep wing chair, Redmond stiffened and demanded wrathfully, "Who the devil said I cannot abide children?"

"You did! Said they w-was brats and —"

"Oh. Well — dammit, I wouldn't have, had I known — But that blasted girl was glaring at me as if — Hell and damnation, what are they?"

Bolster stared at him. In less than two years he had watched Redmond change from a shy, likeable, scholarly boy into an abrasive, hot-at-hand rake with a predilection for duelling. But he had never known him to be less than the soul of chivalry where the ladies were concerned, nor to speak of one in as unflattering terms as he had just employed. Sitting down on the bed, his lordship took up a shoe and began to put it on. "Boys. I *said* they was, in the dr-drawing room just n-now," he added in mild reproof.

"My profound apologies," said Redmond acidly. "At the time, I was thinking of something else, which was rude of me." His eyes drifted to the open valise on the bed. "Where's your man?"

"Left him in D-Dor-D-Dorset. Didn't mean to stay here, y'know."

Redmond stared thoughtfully at the valise.

Following his gaze, Bolster bit his lip and amended, "Brought a change of clothes, though. Always the hope I'd be invited to put on the f-feed bag."

"Do you usually wear a night-cap to dinner?"

Bolster gave a hollow laugh, avoiding Redmond's keen eyes as he put on the other shoe. "If you must know, Mitch, it was perfectly d-devilish at the Priory. Place was fairly inundated with ladies c-cooing over the newborns. And — and since we're in a prying mood, what about this alleged duel of yours? Miss Strand told me you took a wound in the b-back."

Ice chilled Redmond's eyes. "She should know. She bound it up."

"By Jupiter!" In the act of selecting a beautifully embroidered waistcoat, Bolster gasped, "Ch-Charity *saw* your back?"

Redmond snarled, "She managed not to vomit at the sight!"

"C-Course not," said Bolster, desperately

retrenching. "Lot of backbone that girl — Oh, egad! What I mean is — true blue, and all, er, that."

"She is a sanctimonious, meddling female," said Redmond deliberately.

"Oh, now really, Mitch! Th-that ain't like you, and — and from what you say, she helped you when —"

"Well, who the devil asked her?" Springing up, Redmond stamped to the window and scowled at the pleasure gardens as though yearning to set a torch to that delightful area. "If you could only have seen the look on her face when —" He checked, the hands loosely clasped behind him tightening into fists.

Watching that rigid figure, Bolster's suddenly austere frown softened. He said gently, "Stupid of me to have said what I did. Apologies." And in a well-meant but disastrous attempt to make amends, "Lord knows, she ain't the first to've seen — Well, what I mean is — you've had enough *affaires de coeur.*"

Redmond growled, "Do you picture me tripping naked around the boudoir? I assure you it is possible to make love to a woman without being stripped to the buff!"

Scarlet, Bolster floundered, "I know! I d-didn't mean — Wh-what I meant was, that Miss Strand —"

"Oh, damn Miss Strand!"

Bolster's eyes opened very wide. Then he

tried again. "Yes, I'm sure you're right, but —"

Over his shoulder Redmond flung a sneering, "What the deuce d'you mean by that?"

"Nothing. Oh, nothing, 'sure you. Only that — er, well she ain't quite in your style, of course."

"Have I one?" Turning to face him, Redmond said, "Do, pray, describe it for me."

Bolster sighed. "I recall your Milanese bird of p-paradise, my tulip. And the fancy piece you found in Fl-Florence. As for the Bruxelloise Belle . . . diamonds of the first water, every one. But I like Charity Strand. She's a lady, and gentle to boot, and she knows —"

Stung, Redmond interpolated, "She's as elegant as a grey fieldmouse!" And he added broodingly, "Yet looks at me as though I were something — unclean."

Bolster's hands, busied with his waistcoat buttons, stilled. He looked up, his grave eyes meeting Redmond's squarely.

Redmond flushed. His own lashes drooped, and he strolled over to lower his tall frame into the chair once more. Drawing a hand across his eyes, he muttered, "I'm a proper clod to speak so of a lady. You're perfectly right to look at me in your Peer-ish way." Bolster smiled faintly but remained silent, and Redmond's head tossed up in a typically impatient fashion. "What are *you* about, my friend? This is a dashed long way to come if you don't mean to stay, I think."

It was the perfect opportunity for Bolster to admit that he was here in response to a note from Diccon, and Redmond waited, his eyes alert under their thick lashes.

"Oh — I don't know." His lordship strolled to the press and extracted a splendid dark grey coat of Bath suiting. "What d'you think of this?" he asked, holding it up for inspection.

"Weston?"

Bolster beamed. "Believe it or not, my lad, it's from a ch-chap I found in Guildford. . . ."

He rambled on, proud of having found so fine a tailor who was also less outrageous in his charges than the mighty Weston. It all sounded very innocuous, but, resting his chin on one hand, Redmond watched him speculatively. If old Jerry *was* here to rendezvous with the elusive Diccon, he was being confoundedly adroit about concealing it, which did not fit the mould. Honest and loyal and full of pluck was Bolster, but not noted for his mental acuity.

His lordship crossed to the dressing table and began to brush his straight yellow hair. "Didn't know you was acquainted with Strand," he remarked casually. "Good old boy, isn't he?"

"I'm not acquainted with him, actually. Ran into a friend of his in Paris and was charged with a message for him."

"Jove! Beastly luck to be waylaid for your tr-trouble."

Redmond agreed and said affably that he

would rest here for another day or two and then head back to Town. Jerry, he decided, was at Strand Hall by pure coincidence. The dear old chap was simply incapable of deception and could never have managed to behave with such *sang-froid* unless he had indeed nothing to hide.

A bright young man, Mitchell Redmond, who in his days at Oxford had been his tutor's delight and widely held to have every chance for a fellowship. That goal, once so assiduously pursued, had been abandoned many months ago. Perhaps, during the dissolute time that had followed, some of his brilliance had dimmed. Certain it was that he did not know Lord Jeremy Bolster quite as well as he supposed.

Chapter 4

Charity's joy at recovering the use of her legs after being confined to an invalid chair for three years manifested itself in her frequent use of them. The weather had to be very inclement indeed to force the abandonment of her morning ride or her afternoon walk. There were many pleasant walks in and around the Strand preserves, and when Rachel was comfortably settled for the daily nap Dr. Bellows insisted upon, Charity slipped out of the house and started off across the park, basket on her arm, in search of bluebells.

The air was quite warm for the time of year; no breeze stirred the trees, and even the birds seemed to pipe drowsily. As she strolled along, Charity's thoughts drifted to their guests. Lord Bolster had come down to luncheon looking very smart in his changed dress. As usual, he was a cheerful companion, and they had all enjoyed his account of the new additions to the family of the Marquis of Damon. Despite his apparently rapid retreat from the Priory, it was obvious that Bolster had been intrigued by the two baby boys. Charity smiled as she turned her steps toward the Home Wood. Dear Jerry. What a wonderful father he would make some day. And Amanda must be the kindest creature any child could have for a mama.

Their other guest had not come down for luncheon; Bolster had said he was resting, which was, thought Charity, very obliging of him. She felt a twinge of guilt. It was unkind to judge so harshly. Mr. Redmond might still be troubled of his wound; a man could not be expected to behave in a courteous manner at such a time. At once, perversely, she could see Devenish lying on the dank cellar floor in Dinan, patiently enduring while the apothecary cut the crossbow bolt from his leg. She had thought he must die from the pain of it, but he had not made a sound, nor uttered a word of complaint through all their desperate flight back to England, with Claude Sanguinet's

64

hounds hunting high and low for them. . . .
She shuddered and, finding that she had stopped
walking, went on quickly.

The shadows were lengthening across the
lush grasses, the mellow light of late afternoon
laying its golden mantle over quiet meadow and
whispering copse. She had wandered through a
corner of the Home Wood, walked much farther
than she'd intended, and had not gathered a
single bluebell. She was, in fact, near the lane
that formed the boundary line between the
Strand preserves and those of their northern
neighbour, Lord Rickaby. She climbed the
gradual slope, beyond which was the lane, and
stood there, gazing about at this green and
pleasant Sussex; so sweetly pure and peaceful . . .

"Damn and blast your miserable little hide!"
Charity gave a jump of fright, for the irate
snarl came from above her. A hand to her
throat, she searched the branches of the
venerable oak that had commandeered this high
ground for itself. A well-shaped leg, clad in
tight beige pantaloons, came into view, groping
downward. Harbouring a suspicion that Mitchell Redmond was, as her brother would have
said, "dicked in the nob," Charity slipped
behind a clump of gorse, and watched.

He came down awkwardly, grumbling and
cursing as he did so. It was a precarious climb
and twice she held her breath, readying herself
to go to his aid once more, and praying she

might know what to do for a broken back. He was not using his left arm at all, naturally enough, though if it was as little botheration as he had insisted, one might think he could do so. But then, as he reached the lowest branch, he appeared to lose his grip on something he had held in that arm. A small shape sailed through the air, landed with a thump, and sprawled at the foot of the tree.

Wide-eyed with astonishment, Charity stood rooted to the spot. It was Little Patches, the smallest, clumsiest, and most intrepid of the house cat's latest brood, and the best beloved of all her contributions.

Peering down at the little creature, Mitchell Redmond called, "Moggy . . . ? Confound your whiskers — do you mean to die now?"

Charity put a hand over her mouth to stifle a bubble of laughter. She was even more hard-pressed a second later, for lifting his deep voice to simulate that high pitch that mankind appears to consider a requisite tone in calling felines, Redmond squeaked, "Kitty . . . kitty . . . ?"

Charity bit her finger. *Redmond?* This sour, sardonic, snarling rudeness would climb all that way to rescue a kitten?

Little Patches blinked, gathered herself together dazedly, then opened a tiny and very pink mouth to emit a shrill mew.

Redmond grinned down at her with proprietory pride. "Take your blasted fleas home," he said. "Wherever that may be. And have a trifle more sense next time!"

As though perfectly understanding this speech, Little Patches proceeded to pick her way with giant kitten strides over the blades of grass that impeded her progress.

"Will wonders never cease?" whispered Charity.

She had erred. However tiny they might be, kittens have exceptional hearing. Little Patches looked with joyous recognition in the direction of the gorse bush and advanced upon it, mewing as she came, her tail, like a small spear, standing straight up behind her.

Mr. Redmond had turned preparatory to descending, but he was clearly experiencing some difficulty and at any second must look around and see that he was being watched. Charity began to back quickly down the slope, Little Patches increasing her own pace to bound in pursuit. Charity was not even comfortably out of view, however, when Redmond glanced her way. She had the presence of mind to shift direction at once, as though just now arriving. "Little Patches," she exclaimed, bending to pick up the garrulous animal. As she straightened, Redmond was in the act of swinging down from the branch. "My heavens!" she cried, honestly dismayed. "Whatever are you about, Mr. Redmond? You will hurt yourself!"

That he had done so was obvious. He said unevenly, "Your perspicacity is — *extraordinaire*, ma'am."

Remembering that high-squeaked enquiry intended only for the kitten's ears, Charity could not be too offended by his sarcasm. Holding Little Patches against her neck, she asked innocently, "Whatever were you doing up there?"

He drawled a bored, "Fiddling, of course."

"And not even in Rome." She smiled and ventured an oblique glance at his profile. It was small wonder his looks had ruined him, for the women must certainly flutter around him. And yet he showed no signs of dissipation, his features, although cynical, also revealing intelligence and sensitivity rather than having the full-lipped sensuality she had noted in some famous rakes, such as Junius Trent, who had been pointed out to her in Town recently and was judged to be exceedingly attractive.

Redmond had said something and was turning to her curiously. She said, "During your solo concert you appear to have scratched your cheek, sir."

Faintly indignant, his eyes slanted to her burden. "On a stray branch."

"Liar!" thought Charity.

"So much for surveying the legendary beauties of Strand's estate," he added.

"Is that what you were doing, then?" Gently, Charity detached Little Patches from her jade beads and set her down. "I trust you found it to your liking, sir?"

"There being only one possible reply to such

a question, I shall say that I found every tree and bush beyond compare."

She flushed. She had been judged insipid, evidently, which being the case she would not further her efforts to make polite conversation.

In silence, therefore, they proceeded across the turf, Redmond setting a rather slow pace. This exactly suited Little Patches, who bounced along more or less with them, but pausing now and then to wage all-out war against the dire menace of some threatening weed or wildflower.

Charity was by nature a friendly person, and after a while the pointlessness of nurturing hostile thoughts against this ill-mannered young man eased her indignation. After all, she reasoned, he would very soon take his boorish way out of her life, and others would be afflicted with him, poor things. She allowed her thoughts to drift to Justin and Lisette, wondering idly what they were doing in Town. Her reverie was broken when Redmond halted and stood looking back the way they had come. Little Patches appeared to have worn herself out, and sat looking after them in a forlorn way.

"Poor little mite," said Charity, stopping also. "I'll carry her in my basket."

"You would be better advised to let her learn a lesson. The stupid animal got out here. Certainly she can find her way home."

"She could have made her way down the tree," thought Charity, but since she was not supposed to know of that event, she did not voice the comment but went to the rescue. Even as she reached for the kitten, a butterfly provided a new diversion, and the contrary Little Patches went bounding off after the colourful insect. "Wretch!" whispered Charity and returned to Redmond, who waited with a decidedly smug expression on his face.

Determined to carry off this minor embarrassment with aplomb, Charity was further mortified when her slipper encountered a shifting pebble and her ankle turned. She staggered. Redmond leapt to support her, but when she looked up gratefully, she surprised a mocking grin. He believed her stumble to have been deliberate! Oh! The insufferable egoist!

"Are you all right, ma'am?" he enquired with questionable sincerity. "You must think me remiss for not lending you my arm long before now."

Charity knew her cheeks were blazing, but refusing to lower her eyes, she tore free from his hold. "To the contrary! I cannot think *such* a sacrifice is necessary, sir," she said, in a frigid tone that very few people had ever heard her employ. She had expected that her response might annoy him, but was unprepared for the fury that turned his eyes to steel. "It is not necessary, in fact," she went on, "for you to accompany me back to the Hall."

He said raspingly, "I hope I am not such a boor as to leave you out here alone, ma'am."

"Oh?" she murmured.

He stamped along beside her. "I must admit to amazement that you are permitted to be forever wandering about the countryside unchaperoned, like any —" He bit off the rest of that remark.

"Wanton . . . ?" prompted Charity. "I know very little of the behaviour of such women. But I am sure you can enlighten me, Mr. Redmond."

What he would like to do, he thought, was to spank her. Hard. They were entering the woods now, and she trod along the farthest edge of the narrow path, preferring to allow her skirts to brush against the undergrowth rather than risk an encounter with his own person. He said haughtily, "I doubt your brother would appreciate my rendering such instruction, Miss Strand. Indeed, I am surprised you would desire so improper a topic of conversation."

The horrid beast had won that round. "Oh, I do not," she assured him. "But you were bored when I attempted to engage you in commonplaces."

Such forthrightness had not often come his way from a lady, and he was so taken aback as to be tardy with a counterattack.

Charity allowed him no extra time. "I expect that was my fault," she went on, "for I've had very little practice at it, since my brothers do not encourage what they consider intellectual trivia. If you insist upon conversation, I must try to find a topic that interests you, for I believe that is *de rigueur* for a polite lady, no? Let me see — ah! I have it! We shall exchange gossip." She beamed upon him kindly.

Redmond blinked. "I think I am being roasted. Unless you have been told I am an unconscionable gabblemonger." He said this, well aware that it would prompt an immediate and flustered denial. Miss Strand, however, did not react according to convention, instead knitting her brows in silence. Irked, but faintly intrigued, he prodded at length, "Ma'am?"

"My apologies, Mr. Redmond. I was casting my mind over some of the things I have been told of you."

"Were you, by gad! It must have been a good deal."

"A deal, at least."

Stunned, his gaze darted to her in time to see the quiver that tugged at her shapely lips. "The devil!" he protested.

"No, no! I assure you, Mr. Redmond, no one has called you that. Not, er, in my hearing, at least."

He was quite unable to hold back a grin at this excellent *riposte* and said promptly, "I am maligned, alas. I pray you will not believe me a monster."

"Oh, of course I do not." And after a thoughtful pause, she went on, fancying she extended an olive branch, "I suppose, for our own secret reasons, we all present a false character to the world, do we not?"

She could scarcely have blundered onto a more unfortunate choice of words. Redmond stiffened. "The ladies certainly do. One way or another."

So much for olive branches, thought Charity, and yearning to push him into the nearest bramble bush, said calmly, "We have little choice. Whatever our private inclinations, we are obliged to conform to expected patterns of insipid accomplishments; to speak inanities lest we be judged blue-stockings; to strive always to meet the male notions of beauty, however far we may be from hoping to achieve such a state."

Scanning her with resentful eyes, Redmond felt no compelling urge to argue the point as she undoubtedly expected him to do. She was not a beauty, nor ever would be. Her face was too gaunt, and her shape more that of a boy than a young woman. The eyes, one had to admit, were quite beautiful, and that red-gold hair not at all bad, especially in the sunshine, but her manners were deplorable. He responded, "I fancy every man has his own unique concept of beauty. As for being a bluestocking, do you perhaps mean that you enjoy to read? Or do you refer to those appalling spinsters who are well informed on everything from politics to philately and delight in proving to any gentleman how inferior is his own knowledge by comparison?"

"Oh, for an axe!" thought Charity, but she

somehow managed a creditable little titter. "Acquit me of that, I beg. Surely you must know that a girl has to do far less to be judged a bluestocking. Let her only discuss anything more intellectual than gossip, fashions, or babies, and she is in real danger of being set down as 'clever.' A state no male can endure in a woman." She parried Redmond's frigid glare with a glittering smile and swept on, knowing she was being outrageous. "It is all based on fear, though few would acknowledge it. The gentlemen *deplore* silly, empty-headed females — and invariably marry them, if only to assure themselves of how superior they are. And also," she appended loftily, "so that they may continue their various indiscretions under the very noses of their wooden-headed wives."

"Which would account, no doubt," he sneered, "for the untold numbers of poor hapless males who are trapped 'neath the cat's foot."

"If a male is poor and hapless, Mr. Redmond, he will sooner or later wind up under *somebody's* foot, whether it be that of his parent, spouse, or superior officer. The point is that a gentleman has so vast a scope compared to a lady. And when one sees what most men make of their lives . . ." She paused, eyeing him with faint reproach.

So now he had been judged a failure in life! Furious, he donned the mantle of polite boredom that had daunted several managing mamas. "I have not the slightest doubt, ma'am, but that you, for example, would have taken the opportunities I have so shamefully squandered and turned them to good account. Had I but a *soupçon* of your ambition I might very well be Prime Minister by now!"

Markedly undaunted, Charity opened her eyes at him and enquired, "Is *that* what you aspire to, Mr. Redmond? My, but I should never have guessed you to have a turn for politics."

"Very astute of you, Miss Strand," he snapped, forgetting to be condescending. "For I find politicians to be a set of pompous bores with whom I mingle as little as possible."

"Really? I expect your vast experience in such matters should influence me to change my own opinion. I cannot help but wonder at Lord Palmerston, you know. Such a charming gentleman, and I have never found him a bore. I must ask him how he came to be so taken in."

Redmond, who admired Palmerston, concentrated upon where he might bury this revolting woman, after suitably strangling her, and how Brutus might be dissuaded from digging her up again.

Charity said with kind encouragement, "Now, surely there must be *something* to which you aspire, sir? Besides being Prime Minister, which might be rather difficult, do you not like to be a politician first?"

He replied with a teeth-bared smile, "Oh,

there was, my dear lady. I like to think I have achieved it."

"A —— *duellist?*" she cried, her eyes becoming so round that his fingers fairly itched for her throat.

For a moment he did not trust himself to speak. Then, a pulse twitching beside his jaw, he ground out, "There are occasions, Miss Strand, when even murder is . . . well justified!"

"Who are you? And what are you doing to Little Patches?"

The clear, girlish voice caused Mitchell Redmond to drop the willow branch he had been trailing to amuse eight ounces of incredible ferocity, and he spun around guiltily.

A scrawny, untidy damsel of some ten or eleven summers stood watching him. Her dark hair was a dishevelled, frizzy mass with an occasional lurking curl that looked surprisingly glossy, perhaps because it was unexpected. There was a streak of mud along one side of her pointed plain little face, and more mud on the white muslin dress, and she clutched a rather wilted bouquet of wildflowers in a slim, muddy hand.

"I am Mr. Redmond," he said. Alert brown eyes scanned him with an eager expectancy, as though he must have something very pleasant to tell her, and his slow smile dawned. "And who are you, Mrs., er . . . ?"

She giggled. "Storm. Josie Storm. And I'm not a missus yet, 'cos I'm only twelve. We think. Here —" She thrust her bouquet at him. "Hold these, if you please."

He accepted the charge, betraying no dismay that his hand thereby became muddied also, and curious because her careful but slightly less than cultured speech did not quite match that expensive, if sullied muslin.

Miss Storm swooped upon Little Patches who had sat down to cleanse one paw, and gathered her up. Returning to stroll along beside the tall man, she cuddled the purring kitten and explained, "Just for now, I'm a ward. 'Course, I might be a missus when I grow up, unless Mr. Dev decides to —" She pursed her lips and peeped up at Redmond, her face all sparkling mischief.

She was, he realized, much prettier than he had at first thought. Her hair was undeniably frizzy, and her chin pointed; her mouth was too generous and her nose, although straight, lacked distinction. Yet there was about her an air of friendliness and trust and an irresistible brightness. He wondered what this "Dev" fellow had in mind for her.

"Who, dare I ask, is Mr. Dev?" he drawled. "And what is it that he's to decide?"

Miss Storm released the now squirming kitten, who at once began to stalk a drifting dandelion seed. "He's Alain Jonas Devenish," she announced, as though the utterance of that name rated a roll of drums. "My guardian. And I'm not 'lowed to say what he might decide. You got very nice eyes, but you're not so handsome as my Dev. 'Specially when you frown."

"Am I doing so? My apologies. Quite terrified, are you?"

The resultant beam illuminated her face. "No," she said with a giggle, and tucked her hand confidingly into his as they walked on again. "But you did look cross. Why? Do you know my Dev?"

He could not tell her of the ugly suspicion her words had awoken in his mind, and so evaded. "The name is familiar. Wasn't he in some kind of trouble a short while ago?"

Her laugh was a merry trill, and she performed a miniature pirouette. "What kind? My Dev's had all sortsa troubles."

"Has he?" said Redmond, smiling with her. "Like — you, for instance, madam?"

"Oh yes. I'm his worstest trouble by far, he says. Do you like cats?"

"But of course."

"Some men don't. Was — were you taking Little Patches for a walk?"

He chuckled. "I fancy it was the other way round. I suppose you are in school? Or have you a governess?"

"Mr. Dev can't send me to the cemetery 'cause I don't always talk just so nice. What you sniggering at?"

Redmond sobered with an effort. "Your pardon. Was I sniggering?"

"I think so. It's what Miss Cassell says I do when she talks jawbreakers at me. Did I say a bad word? Ain't it — I mean, isn't it 'cemetery' where young ladies go?"

"I hope not, Mademoiselle Josephine. I believe the word you seek is 'seminary.' "

Briefly she was silent, then shook her small head as if banishing some half-remembered thought. "When I was little, I was stole by gypsies," she revealed chattily. "My Dev 'dopted me so I wouldn't be sold to a flash house."

"Poor little girl." Touched, he stroked her thick hair in a quick caress.

"Thank you," she said blithely. "Come on, or I'll be late for supper! What's a wretched rake?"

Redmond's jaw set, and the kindness died from his eyes. For a moment he said nothing, then he answered, "A very — unwise gentleman." And having no doubt of the reply, asked, "Whom did you hear say that?"

"Miss Charity. She's the dearest of dears. And so is Mrs. Rachel, even if she *is* so pretty. Miss Charity didn't know I heared her say 'wretched rake.' " She rolled the words around zestfully.

"Were I you, I don't think I'd say it in front of anyone else. Not ladylike. Er, what did Miss Charity have to say about this — er, person?"

79

"She says as the wret — er, the unwise cove —"

"Gentleman."

"Oh. Well, she says as how he's gone and made us lose Little Patches prob'ly, and he wasn't nothing but a iggerant warthog with tall feet."

Redmond stared his astonishment. "She said — *what?*"

"I think that's what it was. Something about warthogs, I know."

Puzzling at it, he asked experimentally, "Could it have been 'boor?'"

"Oh, that's right! A iggerant boar! That means warthog, don't it?"

He grinned, vexation rapidly giving way to amusement. "Not quite. And are you sure it wasn't arrogant instead of ignorant?"

"Yes! *What* a silly I am! Did I get the rest right?"

"Almost . . ." He racked his brain, muttering dubiously, "Tall feet . . ." Then, with a sudden burst of laughter, "I have it! High in the instep!"

Once more her liquid little giggle rang out. "Dev will say I'm a proper goose."

Still laughing, he gasped, "An ignorant warthog with tall feet! Wait till Harry hears that!"

"How lovely it is that Devenish has come," Charity said happily. Already dressed for dinner, she adjusted her taffeta skirts with care and sat on the edge of the bed, watching Agatha thread a gold fillet through Rachel's shining curls. "And little Josie, how happy she is now, bless her."

"She deserves happiness, poor waif." Rachel smiled up at the comely abigail. "That's very nice, Agatha. Now, the emerald pendant I think will look well with this lime gown. Dev still limps, had you noticed, Charity?"

"Yes. And he probably drove today, which he should not do. But you know he never will admit that he is in the slightest troubled by that leg."

"Never," Rachel agreed. "But he looks to be in good spirits and is as saucy as ever."

"Oh, most decidedly. No sooner did he learn that Mr. Redmond is here than he demanded to know whether the gentleman was trying to fix his interest with me."

With the assurance that devoted service and a sharing of peril had given her, Agatha joined in the laughter. "Mr. Redmond is held to be a very good catch, Miss Charity. And," she sighed admirably, "what a lovely gentleman."

"Much chance he would have," Rachel said merrily.

"I cannot guess how he could be judged a 'good catch' with his reputation," Charity argued. "Are the Redmonds very plump in the pockets?"

Rachel dabbed Essence of Dreams behind

her ears and said thoughtfully, "I believe Sir Harry has a charming country seat in Hampshire, besides a comfortable independence. And of course his bride brought him her enormous fortune. But as to his brother . . ."

"Five thousand pounds a year, ma'am," supplied Agatha, draping a zephyr shawl about her lady's shoulders. "But they do say as his gambling has added to that, instead of knocking it all to pieces."

Charity laughed. "I suppose your scamp of a spouse discovered all that for you."

Agatha dimpled and admitted that Raoul did seem to "have a knack" for ferreting out bits and pieces of news. "Besides which," she added, "that man of Mr. Redmond's be such a bragger. When he bean't singing — which is enough to drive a nightingale to crowing! — he's jawing. And most of it about his master, which he shouldn't ought to do if he knowed how to go on. Which he doesn't!"

The sisters exchanged faint smiles. Rachel said gently, "DiLoretto seems very devoted, at least."

"Oh, he is that, surely." Agatha sniffed. "Is this broidered fan suitable, Mrs. Rachel? It has the greens in it." She offered the fan for inspection and went on, "It ain't fair to criticize, I s'pose. 'Specially since he don't know beans about being a valet. How could he? What with being a foreigner and the sort of past he's got."

Rachel approved the fan and, curious, asked,

"What do you mean? Never say Mr. Redmond's man was once a criminal?"

Charity thought, "Why not? His master obviously was!" but she said nothing.

"I won't go as far as to say that, ma'am," said Agatha. "A ostler is what he was. At one o' them dirty little hedge taverns in Belgium, I b'lieve. Mr. Redmond got hisself hurt in one o' them duels and diLoretty looked after him. He's been with Mr. Redmond ever since."

Charity said dryly, "I thought the mighty Mitchell Redmond never was bested at anything."

"Well, he'd likely not have been, miss, 'cept he was ill, and just the same he went up against some Eye-talian count who is famous with a sword."

"How very stupid," exclaimed Charity, disgusted. "And how typical."

"Aye, miss, so I said. But diLoretty gets proper up in the boughs if you dare say anything 'gainst his master. He says as Mr. Redmond is a very brave gent. And very proud."

Charity had a mental picture of Redmond's face, pale and tight with fury after their verbal duel today. "Pride," she said with a twinkle, "goeth before a fall!"

Partly because of Miss Josie Storm's obvious adoration of her guardian, and partly out of interest in the reason behind Devenish's apparently spur-of-the moment decision to visit

Strand Hall, Mitchell Redmond was eager to meet this new arrival. Unfortunately, a small disaster with neckcloths compounded the fact that his encounter with Josie had delayed his changing for dinner. Shooting his cuffs, he ran downstairs just as the gong was being sounded by a stern-faced footman. There was only time for Leith to perform a brief introduction.

Shaking hands, Redmond was more than a little astonished, for this man did not even remotely conform to his mental image of the guardian of a twelve-year-old girl. Alain Devenish was slim and slightly below average height. The cut of his coat was excellent, although his cravat was happily worse than Redmond's. Despite his lack of inches, he was well built and his handshake was firm, but his features were so perfect as to be almost inhuman in their beauty, and the slightly curling blond hair, the dark blue of the wide-set eyes, added to an impression of extreme youth.

With a friendly grin that caused those same eyes to crinkle at the corners, Devenish said an unfortunate, "Jolly glad to meet you, Redmond. Heard you was with the Forty-Third so we're all military men together. No lazy civilians amongst us, eh?"

Charity thought, "Oh, dear!" Bolster looked dismayed, and Tristram Leith groaned inwardly.

A film of ice chilled Redmond's smile, and Devenish knew with a sinking heart that he had erred again.

"I suspect you confuse me with my famous brother," Redmond pointed out dryly. "I was just another 'lazy civilian,' I fear." His quizzing glass was raised, and through it he contemplated Devenish's face. "Do you say you was in the military? How very remarkable."

"Remarkable?" His chin lifting, Devenish said, " 'Fraid I do not follow you, sir."

"Oh, no offence," drawled Redmond, and added, "Only that I had rather fancied you would have been too, er, young."

"Had you indeed? Well, allow me to inform you, Redmond, that our bugle boy was twelve years old!"

Redmond smiled with infuriating condescension. "That, of course, would explain it."

Leith saw the quick flare of Devenish's nostrils. He was very well acquainted with this young firebrand and lost no time in suggesting that they should proceed to the dining room.

Bowing gallantly, Devenish offered his arm to Charity Strand. He knew her laughing eyes were quizzing him, and he muttered *sotto voce*, "Gad! What an icicle!"

Mitchell ignored Bolster's mildly reproachful stare and set Mr. Devenish down as an impertinent, frippery sort of fellow, quite unlikely to have had any association with the elusive, daring, and mysterious individual who occasionally went by the name of Diccon.

Despite their immediate and mutual antipathy, neither gentleman was so ill-bred as to flaunt such a reaction, and dinner went off pleasantly enough, Devenish asking eagerly that he be apprised of any news involving an apparent host of mutual friends and acquaintances, and Bolster, the Leiths, and Miss Strand just as eager that he tell them of developments concerning himself and his ward. Ever the polite host, Leith saw to it that Redmond was not left out of the conversation, and two hours slipped gracefully away. Not until they were ending the meal and Devenish had accepted the Chantilly crème that Fisher offered, did he remark that he planned to go to Town and had hoped the journey could be shared with the Strands.

"Missed 'em," Bolster pointed out sagely.

"Well, I know that, you clunch. What I don't know is what brings *you* into this sylvan solitude."

Selecting a slice of *café gâteau*, Bolster inspected it with minute concentration. "I, ah, just ch-cha- happened to be in the neighborhood."

"— of Dorsetshire," Leith put in with a grin.

"Dorsetshire?" gasped Devenish.

Redmond drawled, "Jeremy has a catholic sense of neighbourhood."

"It ain't so far removed as Gloucestershire," Bolster argued amiably, and watching Devenish, his eyes keen under their heavy lids, he asked,

"Bit of a roundaboutation to travel from Devencourt to Town by way of Sussex, ain't it?"

Redmond also slanted a glance to Devenish, but that young Corinthian appeared totally unaware of the faint tension in the air and directed an apologetic grin towards Tristram Leith's thoughtful countenance. "Wasn't in Gloucestershire. And I know it's devilish bad form to drop in on you unannounced like this, Tris. Tell the truth, I didn't think you and Rachel would be here."

Rachel said teasingly, "Or you would not have come? But how unchivalrous, Dev!"

Devenish's immediate attempt to absolve himself was interrupted by a flurry of barking from the gardens, interspersed by some irate feline yowls, so that it became necessary for Rachel to ask that a lackey be sent to quiet Brutus. "I fear he is chasing the cats again," she explained. "It is all bluster, you know. I don't believe he has any other intention than to prove himself superior."

"I do hope not," said Charity. "It would be dreadful were he to hurt one of the kittens, and Little Patches has a tendency to be slow."

Tristram pointed out soothingly that cats could usually take care of themselves. "Don't worry, Charity. Little Patches will soon show our warrior Brutus that she's a lady to be reckoned with."

"Quite a kitty Cleopatra, in fact," said

Rachel, with a fond glance at her husband.

"I can see that Romans are highly regarded in this house," murmured Redmond, turning his wineglass idly on the tablecloth. "Your sister was speaking of Nero earlier today, ma'am."

Amused, Rachel said, "You do not surprise us, Mr. Redmond. Charity has a deep interest in history."

A spark awoke in Redmond's bored eyes. "Do you indeed, Miss Strand?" He turned to Charity. "Any particular period?"

"I find it all fascinating," she replied, and seeing the immediate sardonic twist of his lips, added hurriedly, "As little of it as I know, that is. But I cannot say I hold Nero in high regard. If the chroniclers are to be believed, the man was a monster. Only look at the hundreds of people he caused to be slain. Even his own mother!"

"But he appears to have been manoeuvred into that, ma'am, by a jealous woman."

"And I suppose he was also manoeuvred into the sack of Colchester and the slaughter of the Ninth Legion!"

Redmond's brows lifted. "You do indeed know your history, Miss Strand. Consider, though, how much easier it is to view the past with objectivity than to apply the lessons it teaches. One shudders to imagine what future generations may think of *our* contribution to the march — or shuffle — of civilization."

"They ought to think jolly well of it, I'd say," Bolster put in heartily. "Rompéd old Boney, didn't we? And a fine state the world would b-be in had he prevailed. Cannot deny that, Mitch!"

"I can deny that our victories were accomplished by reason of any inspired leadership from London. If we won in France and Spain it was because Wellington out-generalled Napoleon. Nothing more, nothing less."

Leith nodded, but said in his calm way, "However brilliant Old Hookey may be, and however deeply the free world stands indebted to him, he had to be appointed before he could fulfil his destiny, and —"

"And do you credit that appointment to the inspiration of the idiots who bungle their way through Whitehall?" sneered Redmond. "Or to the shrewd guidance of our exalted ruler, perhaps? Good God! If our descendants look closely at poor Prinny, they must judge us a fine set of knock-in-the-cradles!"

Deeply patriotic beneath his mild exterior, Lord Bolster sat straighter in his chair and put down his wineglass. "I fancy there are many worse m-men than Prinny, Mitch."

"Then let us pray they do not occupy a throne."

Also annoyed by these caustic remarks, Devenish said, "The man has his faults, certainly, but he has been villified by a particularly vicious Press, who chose to completely overlook his good points."

"Oh, do pray elucidate," said Redmond with his mocking smile.

Devenish flushed. "I have personally known him to be kind, generous, knowledgeable on many subjects, a connoisseur of —"

"Of women?" sneered Redmond. "That certainly! Nor could anyone deny his generosity, especially when applied to his table and his architectural atrocities."

Devenish's eyes smouldered, noting which Leith intervened lazily, "I fear Redmond knows our Prinny's faults too well for us to effectively champion him. Shall we concede the royal gentleman to be sometimes unwise, but — like the rest of us — not all bad?"

"You may concede what you wish," said Redmond. "I shall hold to my belief that the man is a nincompoop! A womanizing, hedonistic spendthrift who is so absurd as to have become a public laughing-stock and thus disgrace his country throughout the world. England would do very much better without the silly fellow!"

Pale with anger, Devenish rasped, "You go too far, sir!"

Alarmed, Charity glanced at her sister.

Rachel smiled serenely and laid down her napkin. "Gentlemen," she said, standing as Bolster sprang to pull back her chair, "I do believe we shall leave you to your" — she smiled mischievously at Redmond — "your patriotic discussions."

90

As his lordship ushered the two ladies to the door, Charity heard Devenish declare hotly, "Mrs. Leith was right, by God! Far from being a patriot, you speak treason, Redmond!"

"Gammon," sneered Mitchell Redmond.

Chapter 5

The morning dawned bright, with a slight breeze ruffling the treetops and an invigorating crispness to the air. Walking downstairs shortly after eleven o'clock, Charity adjusted a crocheted shawl of fine white wool about her thin shoulders, her thoughts turning backwards. The gentlemen had seemed all amiability when they'd come into the drawing room last evening, and if the treasonable debate had continued after she and Rachel had left them, they'd been at pains to give no hint of it. The balance of the evening had been without incident. Tristram had asked her to favour the gathering with some songs, and she had done so, very conscious of Redmond's polite attention and of the inadequacies of her true but small voice. Alain Devenish had made his excuses and retired before the arrival of the tea tray. It was unlike that exuberant individual to go early to bed, and she and Rachel had worried over such atypical behavior. Between them, they'd decided that Alain had spent most of the day travelling and had then been exposed to

Mitchell Redmond's abrasive personality, either of which was sufficient to drive and man to his bed.

Lost in thought, Charity had not realized she was standing at the foot of the stairs until, from behind her, the object of her concern enquired, "Something wrong, m'dear?"

Without turning around, she smiled and reached up, and as Devenish took her hand and stepped down to join her, she answered quietly, "I don't know. Is there?"

The morning sunlight, streaming in through the front windows, gleamed on her curls, and the simple bonnet framing her fine-boned features seemed to emphasize the intrepid tilt to the small head. Devenish thought, "How daintily feminine she is in that pretty blue gown," and suddenly envied the man who would one day call her wife. He answered lightly, "Do you mean — with me? Lord, no. You'd not credit the changes my new steward has wrought at Devencourt. It is really a charming old seat, Charity. You must come down and —" The quick pressure of the fingers he still held stopped him.

Her eyes had always been her best feature, but they also were betraying. The searching anxiety they now revealed touched Devenish's susceptible heart. "Dev, you know very well what I mean," she said, faintly scolding. "Had you a — a special problem to discuss with my brother? I know your visit was not planned, but why would you have expected to find Justin here?"

Contrary to what he had told Leith, Devenish had come to Strand Hall because of a nagging premonition of trouble. If it hadn't been for the fact that his blasted leg had been jabbing at him like fury all day yesterday, he would have snabbled old Tris at some point after dinner, to see what he could learn. Now, however, he opened his blue eyes very wide and said, all innocence, "Oh, gad! Never say I've intruded upon an invitational?"

"Dev!" Charity began, then laughed suddenly. "Oh dear. I did make it sound so, didn't I? It is not, of course. And even if it were, you are always welcome. But I want to know what you are about, if you please."

How like her, he thought, vastly amused, to make so rag-mannered a demand of a guest. But he was pleased that she felt him to be sufficiently one of the family to do so. She was worried, bless her heart; fretting perhaps because her sister looked a trifle out of curl. He'd heard that Rachel was experiencing more than her share of problems with this babe. Heaven forbid he should say anything to cause her more grief, or to add to Charity's concern. He did not want Charity worried. In fact — His earlier thought returned. She would make some lucky man a very nice little wife. . . . With typical impetuosity he answered, "If you must know, miss — to ask for your hand."

Staring at him, her lips a little parted with shock, Charity was both bewildered by this sudden proposal and amused by the faint dismay that now crept into his eyes. She reached out for the hand she had relinquished. It was quite steady and gripped her own with firm assurance. "Why, how very dear," she said softly. "Thank you, Alain. But, you see — I cannot accept."

Devenish was conscious of a deep relief but then, perversely, a rush of disappointment. He was very fond of Charity. He had seen her in suffering and in a nightmare of peril, and she had met both challenges with quiet intrepidity. He thought her a serene and sweet-souled lady who would never serve her mate with selfishness or bad temper. And his own hopes and dreams were dead, after all. . . . His adored Yolande had been wed for almost six months now. To be precise, five months, twelve days, and about an hour. . . .

Charity saw his eyes become remote and, guessing where his thoughts wandered, said with feigned indignation, "Well, you might at least protest a *little*, Dev!"

"Oh! Deuce take me!" he gasped. "What a moment to be wool-gathering! No, Charity" — he moved to possess himself of both her hands — "really, I think it might serve us very well. Only look at it, m'dear. I love and admire you. And you love me." He grinned at her. "How could you help it?"

With a little chuckle she admitted to this

strange failing.

"Well, then," he said, triumphant, "there you are! Your heart is not given, I think? And — and you lead a rather, er, nomadic kind of life, Charity. Oh, I don't say you're not sincerely welcomed wherever you go, but it ain't like having a home of your own, after all. Devencourt's not too dreadful. And you know, of course, that you could make whatever changes you would wish. Josie could have a — a mother, and I would be, er, well, it *is* a trifle lonely. Just now and then, you understand, sort of rattling around the old place. I know that I'm no catch for you. Got this blasted habit of — well, you know how it is with me. Everyone says I'm hot at hand and I think I am. Just a little. Sometimes. Very rarely, nowadays, because I'm getting older. More, er, mature, d'you see, and —"

But the bubble of mirth that Charity had been firmly restraining, burst, and she laughed merrily. Devenish looked taken aback, and repentant, she squeezed the hands she still held, before releasing them. "You are, in fact, entering your dotage," she declared.

He grinned at her. "No, but I'm serious about this, you madcap! I promise I'd, er, cherish and — and protect you. And you must know I'd not be setting up a peculiar a mile or so away and neglecting you, for I've never been much in the petticoat line. And —"

So he really was in earnest. Touched, she

placed her hand over his lips. "You love me, my dear," she interposed gently, "but you are not — *in* love with me."

He turned his head almost at once, but for an instant the look of desolation had been so intense that she cried a dismayed, "Oh, Dev, I am so *sorry!*"

For a taut instant he was silent, then he said in a low and uneven voice, "Pray do not be. I am perfectly resigned, you know. It's only that . . . I suppose I had rather got into the way of — of thinking of Yolande as . . . as . . ." The words shredded into silence.

Longing to take him in her arms and comfort him, Charity said softly, "Yes, of course. But that is another reason, Dev. You have paid me the greatest compliment a man may offer a lady, and I am — oh, so very grateful. Only — my dear, dear friend, do you see? I could not endure such fierce competition."

He did see. And she was quite right, for, as usual, he had been thinking only of Alain Devenish. The yearning ache in his breast was fierce again, which served him right. Smiling brightly, he said, "In that event, m'dear, I appoint myself chairman of the Charity Strand Matrimonial Committee. We must find you some splendid young Duke to husband!"

"Oh no!" she cried, laughing but aghast. "Dev! You wouldn't!" Her eyes slipped past him. "Rachel, you'll not believe the machinations of this rogue."

"I'll own I heard his last remark," said Rachel, pulling on her gloves as she came down the stairs. She was relieved to see that the faint look of strain had left Dev's eyes. He looked cheerful and rested, and if she suspected the former to be a pose, she was pleased by the latter. "Have you been bludgeoned into accompanying us on our walk to the village? Charity sets a relentless pace, and so I warn you."

He smiled. "It would be a joy, lovely one. But to be truthful I've already had my morning exercise in trying to come up with your wandering spouse."

"Oh, what a pity you missed them. Tristram and Jeremy went over to Lord Rickaby's Home Farm. A long-standing invitation for an early breakfast and a look at some new kind of hedge they are hoping to use as boundary markers."

"In that case, I shall beat a path to the kitchens and see if some kindly soul will feed this starving rogue. Fair ladies — adieu." And with a grin, a bow, and a flourish, he strolled kitchenwards.

The sisters crossed the hall, the footman swung open the door, and at once the breeze set their skirts to fluttering.

"Did you mean to take Brutus?" asked Rachel as they trod down the steps and into the brisk freshness of the morning.

"I had thought we might invite him, but you're right, it would not do, poor fellow. My, how the breeze has come up."

The dog, so apparently indomitable, harboured a craven and selective dread of shaking aspen leaves, and although there were few aspens on the Strand preserves, the route to the village was not without such horrors. The sisters therefore set out alone, arms linked, as they walked across the park.

Charity was unusually silent and in a little while Rachel said musingly, "So Alain means to find you a husband. . . ."

"Rachel, I have never been more shocked. The dear boy made me an *offer!* In the foyer!"

"I know. I'm afraid I was somewhat less than truthful when I told you I'd overheard his last sentence. I was at the top of the stairs when he promised to cherish and protect you. I stopped, for fear of embarrassing him, though goodness knows he picked a very public place for it."

They looked at each other, and then burst into laughter.

"Wretched boy," said Charity, wiping tears from her eyes. "I think he spoke in such haste he frightened himself to death! At first, I could not believe he was serious."

"But he was. And you handled it very nicely, I thought." Rachel sighed. "Dear Dev. What a wonderful husband he would make if only —" She asked in sudden dismay, "Charity? You told him that he does not love you, but do *you* love him?"

"Of course I do, you goose. Only not just in that very special way."

Rachel thought with regret that this dear sister had been granted little opportunity to meet eligible gentlemen, when so much of her adult life had been spent in a wheelchair. She said, teasing, "And what, dare I ask, do you know of 'special ways'?"

Charity answered with a faint smile, "I know what I have seen in Justin's eyes when he looks at Lisette. And I have watched you and Tristram and seen how your faces light up if you have been apart a little while and suddenly find one another. And I watched all the joy and hope fade from dear Dev when Yolande married Major Tyndale."

"Yes." Rachel sighed. "That wretched girl has broken his generous heart. However could she serve him so when they had been promised forever? And yet Craig Tyndale is such a very fine young man. What a —" She clutched at her hood, shivering as the rising wind sent her cloak billowing. "How cold it is getting. Charity, are you warm enough with only that thin shawl?"

"It is woollen and quite warm, fortunately. I'd not thought the wind would become so strong. Is it too chilly for you? Perhaps we should turn back. I can send one of the servants for my braid, or go tomorrow."

Rachel hesitated. It really was much more chill than she had anticipated, but — "I must not molly-coddle myself."

"But of course you must. You cannot expect

to feel quite as energetic when you are increasing. Come we'll go home and —"

"We will do no such thing! I will get warm if we walk a little faster."

Charity protested strongly, but Rachel knew how much her sister enjoyed her daily walk, and they went on. When another brisk gust snatched the hood from her head, however, she said, "Well, that settles me, I'm afraid. You keep on, love, and I'll go back. In fact — just the thing! You take my cloak and I'll have your shawl. No, do not argue with me, Charity. It really is getting quite cold. I shall be snug in my parlour in five minutes, and easier in my mind knowing you are cosily wrapped in something warm."

Charity really was beginning to feel goose bumps on her bare arms and so the trade was made. She watched as Rachel hurried back towards the Hall, then proceeded on her way, joying in the buffeting of the wind against her cheeks, and breathing deeply of the clean crisp smells of damp earth, spiced by the fragrance of newly scythed grass.

She had not gone very far, however, before she was again halted, this time by a small but piercing voice. With tiny pointed tail held high, and minute pink mouth vigorously proclaiming joy at encountering a familiar presence, Little Patches approached. The wind deposited a branch directly in her path, but it was evident that for her the shortest distance between two points was a straight line. To turn aside and avoid the obstacle was not even considered. She gathered her plump self into a crouching huddle, waggled minuscule hips and sprang into the air, only to plop down in the middle of the branch. She uttered a wail of frustration and sat down.

Laughing, Charity went and gathered her up. "Foolish creature," she scolded, holding the pleased kitten against her throat. "I suppose Brutus chased you out here. So now I am given the choice of taking you home, or carrying you all the way to the village with me."

Her answer was a grating purr and the busy kneading of little paws at her collar. And so they went on, kitten and bearer together, through the brilliance of the May morning.

Soon, the purrs became softer, but rhythmically even. Charity held out her small burden and surveyed it. Little Patches was asleep. That she was a very sound sleeper Charity knew from experience, and so she deposited the kitten carefully in one of the copious pockets of Rachel's cloak and walked on.

Inevitably, her thoughts turned to Alain Devenish, his handsome, earnest face, and the unconventional offer he had made her. Her first offer. She smiled ruefully. And her last, no doubt, for it was extremely unlikely she would ever receive another. Small chance of marriage for a plain girl who dwelt in the country for most of the year, had never been launched into the *ton*, was not adept in the art of flirtation, and was, besides, a bluestocking. "Rachel," argued a contrary inner voice, "was used to dwell in the country and furthermore had no dowry such as Justin has now settled upon you." But Rachel, said Charity to herself, is so exquisitely beautiful and probably received more offers than she would admit, until Claude Sanguinet monopolized her every moment and spread the silken net that almost dragged us all down to tragedy. She shivered.

"I am not surprised to see that you shake in your boots, madam! All alone again, and far from home! Where is your maid or your footman?"

Charity thought, "Oh, confound the creature!" But, looking up, was just for a moment struck to silence.

Whisper pranced and sidled skittishly, rolling her eyes at Charity as though she resented the presence of another female. Untroubled by her antics, Redmond swayed in the saddle with easy grace. He wore no hat and the mischief of the wind had blown his dark hair into a rumpled untidiness, so that although he scowled fiercely at her, he looked younger somehow and less formidable. The fresh air and exercise had brought a flush to his lean cheeks and a sparkle to his eyes, and the dark red riding coat that fitted his shoulders to perfection so became him that Charity thought a bemused, "My heavens, but he is a fine-looking man!"

The mare capered as the wind tossed a weed, and she reared, snorting with exaggerated panic. Redmond pulled her down, and as she spun, he demanded, "Come, ma'am. I will escort you back to the house."

"I cannot say how you go on in Hampshire, Mr. Redmond," said Charity, recovering her voice. "But here in Sussex a lady need not fear for her safety when she is on her own land."

"Then since you are no longer on your land, perhaps you will agree — like a sensible woman — to go home."

It was true. She had crossed the wilderness area and the meadow and reached the lane at the edge of Justin's preserves. Chagrined, she exclaimed, "Oh, for goodness' sake! I have walked to the village since I was a child, sir. And I scarcely think —"

"Very obviously. Attempt it now, if you please, Miss Strand. Cast your mind back a few days. Have you so soon forgotten the circumstances under which we first met?"

The scorn in his voice was biting. Flushing resentfully, Charity pointed out, "That was some miles to the north of Strand Hall. And —"

"And thus in darkest Africa, I suppose. I should think you would be aware that it is neither — blast you, Whisper! — it is neither safe nor proper for you to jaunter about the countryside in this ill-bred fashion."

Ill-bred! Charity drew herself up to her full

fifty-nine inches and declared with regal disdain, "I cannot feel it incumbent upon me, Mr. Redmond, to be guided by your inhibitions. Do *you* judge it unsafe out here, I recommend that you hurry to Colonel Leith, who will, I am sure, offer you his protection!"

He glared at her, his eyes narrowing unpleasantly. "By Jove, but I've a damned good mind to throw you across my saddle bow."

"Then you will most assuredly answer to my brother-in-law," she retaliated, her face flushed with anger.

"Your brother-in-law, madam, is about to be treated to a piece of my mind! Best!" His voice rose to a shout, and Charity stepped back quickly as the alarmed thoroughbred immediately jumped into the air and whirled about twice.

Redmond made no effort to calm his indignant horse, but waved as the groom cantered from the trees to join them.

"Come along, there's a good man," urged Redmond impatiently. "What in the deuce delayed you? Never mind — get down, if you please, and give me your reins. That's it. Now, I want you to accompany Miss Strand on a, er, vital errand. Her abigail was obliged to return home."

Infuriated by such high-handed tactics, Charity snapped, "I was not with —"

"Without apprehension?" inserted Redmond. "Naturally not, ma'am. Best, see to it that Miss

Strand does not stay out too long in this wind." He added with a meaningful stare at Charity, "Or go too far."

He had as well say she was no better than an infant! Yearning to remind him to give Best her leading strings, Charity restrained herself with considerable effort.

To add to her humiliation, Best's grave expression left little doubt but that he was in full accord with Redmond. Taking back his reins, he tied them to the pommel. "No need for you to bother with this old fool, sir," he said, giving the hack a slap on the rump and watching him trot off. "He knows his way home. I'll take care of Miss Charity. Never you fear, sir."

Turning on her heel, Charity marched off, muttering, "Of all the interfering . . . insufferable . . . opinionated. . . !"

Smothering a grin, the groom asked, "Did you say something, miss?"

"No! And furthermore, Best, I know very well what you are thinking, so you need not address me again!"

Best obeyed this stricture for the next ten minutes, walking slightly behind Charity as she stepped out briskly along the lane, and thinking in amusement that he'd not be too much took aback did Redmond do what he'd said and have a word or two with the Colonel. Better tread careful, had Redmond, however good his intentions. Colonel Leith had not got all his rank without learning how to deal with insolence, and Mr. Redmond had brought insolence to a fine art!

Charity's thoughts followed along similar lines. If that wretched Mitchell Redmond caused Tristram to be so alarmed that her daily walks were curtailed, or she was not allowed to step out-of-doors without being guarded like — Her heart gave a sudden odd little jump. Guarded? Against what? There was little doubt but that she had not made a dazzling impression upon Redmond; the man despised her. Why, then should he care where she walked? Or whether she went alone or with an army of footmen and abigails to escort her? Why did he —

She turned swiftly as she heard horses. Best glanced behind them also, but there was no sign of riders in the peaceful lane.

"I could have sworn," said Charity, "that I heard —"

"Have a care, miss!" Best exclaimed sharply.

She swung around. A coach was coming around the curve of the lane. A large coach, very luxuriously appointed, and gleaming black. Charity's heart seemed to freeze. She saw in a series of cameolike impressions that the four horses were black and perfectly matched; that the coachman and guard wore black and gold livery; that three outriders, clad in the same sombre garb, were coming up quickly, riding in silence on the grassy verge of the lane.

In a croak of a voice, she cried, "B-Best!

Oh, Best! For the love of —"

Best swore under his breath, grabbed Charity by the arm, and jerked her behind him. "Run, miss!" he urged. "Run!"

The wind had sent several branches down, and he snatched up the nearest. It was pitifully inadequate against the three who rode at him brandishing long, serviceable-looking clubs, but it would have to do.

Charity hesitated only a second, then ran, her little feet flying as she sped frantically to the break in the hedge beyond which was the meadow and a chance of being seen or heard. Her heart was beating so madly that it seemed to deafen her, but she heard a sudden choking cry and was anguished by the knowledge that poor Best had fallen.

A man was laughing. Hooves were thudding up behind her. Sobbing with terror, her heart bursting, she could hear heavy running footsteps, harsh breathing. She screamed as a rough hand clutched her cloak and yanked it so hard that she fell. Brutal faces were grinning down at her. "Don't be so scared, Missus Quality," rasped a coarse voice. "We ain't a-goin' ter hurt yer. Not in your condition."

"Do not . . . touch me . . . ." Charity gasped out between numbed lips. "Don't —"

But she was wrenched to her feet, and she screamed again. A large hand smelling of stale beer and dirt clamped across her mouth. Dizzied, half stifled, sick with terror, she felt her bones turn to sand as consciousness faded.

Her last thought was, "Sanguinet. . . ! Oh, my dear God!"

Chapter 6

Riding at a gallop towards Strand Hall, Mitchell Redmond readied Whisper, and with no check in pace, set her at a low wall on the far side of the meadow. The mare soared upwards in a beautiful leap, neighed with fear, and landed in a scramble that would have been disastrous had it not been for the consummate skill of her rider. Even so, she staggered, and leaping from the saddle, Redmond went to his knees. He was up in a second, heedless of his muddied britches as he checked on his mare. Whisper was sweating and trembling violently, but she did not appear to have taken any injury. Relieved, Redmond straightened and saw from the corner of his eye a rapidly departing figure. So that was what had caused the fiasco! Some blasted idiot had been lurking about under the wall! His irritation with Tristram Leith forgotten, he shouted, "Hey!"

The intruder promptly broke into a run.

Redmond turned to Whisper and stroked her. "Sorry, lass," he said, and mounted again. He turned her cautiously, but she gave no evidence of a limp or of reluctance, and he brought her to a canter.

He never carried a riding whip, but there was at all times a Manton in his saddle holster. He slipped it out, levelling it as the mare came up with the fugitive. "Hold, you confounded clod! What in the devil d'you think you're doing?"

The offender cringed, one arm protectively upflung, whining, "I ain't done nuffink, guvnor. Let me be. I didn't mean ter fright yer nag."

He was only a youth; stockily built, with flaming red hair and a pinched-looking countenance that showed the lack of proper food. He had a strong beak of a nose and a pugnacious jaw, and the firm lips, now twisting downwards, parted to reveal regular, if not well-brushed, teeth. The one thing that Redmond found repulsive about his appearance was not so much a feature as the lack of it, for he had no eyebrows, so that his wide-set brown eyes looked naked and abandoned.

"Who are you?" demanded Redmond, conscious of an odd sense of familiarity. "And what in hell were you about? D'you know you damn near caused my mare to break her pretty neck?"

"Wasn't my fault, guv. I works fer Lord Rickaby. Just cutting acrost the field on me day orf. Musta been sleeping, just a bit of a kip, guv, and I didn't hear yer comin'. Don't you shoot, now!"

Glaring at him, Redmond slid the pistol back

into its holster. "I've seen you before some-where. Where?"

The removal of the pistol exerted an imme-diate and beneficial effect upon the youth. Grinning up at his victim, he said with bright insolence, "Me name's Dick. An' I'spect as 'ow yer rolled yer orbs over some lucky cove what happened ter look like me. Ain't likely as I'd ferget a swell like yerself, is it, yer honour?"

Redmond considered him thoughtfully. "You're a brash little bantam," he said, thinking that the boy had a fine pair of shoulders and might develop into a likely fighting man were he decently cared for. "And there's a law against trespassing, whether you work for Rickaby or not."

"Oh, I wouldn't never trespass, sir! I don't set one toe on no land where there's a sign posted. Only thing — I didn't see no such thing round here, milor'."

Redmond's stern lips twitched. "I am not a milord. Now be off with you, and don't hang about Mr. Strand's preserves in the future."

"No, sir. Sorry, sir!" The boy backed away, then ran off, laughing.

Redmond muttered a faintly amused, "Blasted young rapscallion," and turned Whisper for Strand Hall. When he reached the stables, he handed the mare over to a groom who stared in surprise at his muddy knees, and walked across the yard trying to recall where he had seen the redhead before. It had been an

110

association that was not entirely praiseworthy, he was sure of that. But —

A shadow fell athwart his path. He halted, his upwards glance discovering that Alain Devenish stood nearby.

"Been ploughing?" enquired Devenish, his eyes angelic.

"Excellent exercise," returned Redmond blandly. "You should try it some time, Devenish. Might help you."

"I doubt that," said Devenish, smiling with a gleam of very white teeth. "I prefer to stay *on* the horse."

"Good gad," Redmond exclaimed. "Have you been riding, then? In *that?*"

Since Devenish wore primrose pantaloons, a long-tailed powder blue jacket, and an elaborate waistcoat, the question could only be construed as provocation, and he treated it accordingly. "As any fool can plainly see — no. Matter of fact" — he fell into step beside Redmond — "I've been waiting for you. Wanted to tell you that I took a damned dim view of your remarks last evening."

"How difficult for you," purred Redmond. "Tied hand and foot, are you not? Since we both are guests here."

Devenish took his arm and pulled him to a halt. His blue eyes flashing fire, he grated, "We shall not be guests forever, Redmond."

"After which, shall you call me out, I wonder? Oh dear. However shall I endure the suspense?"

"I will shorten it for you," snarled Devenish, his fist clenching.

Fortunately, the hostilities were suspended at this point because Josie ran to join them, the skirts of her demure pink and white gown blowing in the wind. Her animated little face alight, she commandeered a hand of each of the gentlemen, and began to pull them back to the house.

"You must come quick," she urged, "for Mrs. Rachel is going to pour coffee and she said I could have some too if only you will say yes, Mr. Dev. So you will, won't you? And Mrs. Hayward has cooked them scrumptious little cakes, and —"

"*Those* cakes," he corrected, sure that Redmond was amused by his ward's unfortunate grammar. "And I am not in the least hungry." A startled and pleading glance was turned up to him, so that he could not but relent. "You've roses in your cheeks this morning, my elf," he said, smiling reluctantly. "What mischief have you been up to?"

"Not any, sir. Only I was running about a bit trying to find Little Patches. Have you seen her? Have *you*, Mr. Redmond?"

Neither gentleman, it transpired, had seen the kitten.

"I 'spect she's playing, or sleeping somewhere," said Josie philosophically. "She's a good sleeper. She can sleep on a clothesline, Fisher says." And, all healthy young appetite, she tugged at them, begging that they hurry, "else Lord Bolster will have et it all up before we get there!"

The house was cosy and warm, a small fire burning welcomingly in the red saloon, where Leith and Bolster were laughing over a remark that Rachel had made. The newcomers were greeted, and in a moment Mr. Fisher entered followed by a maid carrying a large tray. Soon fragrant cups of coffee were being handed around. Josie, looking very conscious, sat on the edge of a chair, the tip of her tongue just visible as she concentrated upon the desperate business of mastering cup, saucer, spoon, and cake. Bolster lost no time in conferring his approval on the macaroons. With one eye on his lordship and the other on the diminishing cakes, Josie enquired rather anxiously if he had eaten his breakfast as yet.

He replied in the affirmative and, selecting another macaroon, said, "Jolly good, too." Then, becoming aware of the covert amusement on Rachel's face, he glanced around and asked with a touch of uncertainty, "Why? Have I been r-remiss? Was we all to breakfast to-gether?"

"Of course not," said Devenish, with a fulminating look at his ward. "Josie was just concerned, weren't you, child?"

"Yes," she admitted with disastrous honesty, "I was concerned as you were going to pig the lot, my lord."

Redmond threw back his head and laughed heartily. Poor Bolster turned crimson, and Devenish leapt to his feet and thunderously banished the repentant girl from the room. "Devil take the brat," he groaned, clutching his fair locks as Josie fled. "Each time I give an inch, she disgraces me!"

"No, no," said Bolster placatingly. "I'm the one disgraced, Dev. I've a shameful sweet tooth I d-don't make much effort to control." He threw a rueful glance at Rachel's amusement. "From the mouths of babes, eh?"

Sinking down beside him, Devenish mourned, "Babes! Sometimes Josie is as old as time. And sometimes . . ." He gave a despairing gesture.

"She is a darling," said Rachel warmly, wondering why Brutus was going berserk in the garden.

"She is a scamp," sighed Devenish. "I try to teach her, but still she blurts out whatever comes into her head and devil take the consequences. I wonder if she ever will have the faintest notion of how to go on in polite company."

Bored, Redmond drawled, "Whatever did you expect? Surely you did not think to take a gypsy waif of unknown background and turn it into a, ah, silk purse in only —"

Flushed with rage, Devenish fairly exploded to his feet. "Now, by God, it is long past time for someone to attend to that nasty mouth of —"

Slanting a glance at his wife's dismayed face, Leith intervened with a sharp, "Dev! Easy!"

"I see we arrive barely in time to prevent bloodshed."

The rich, laughing voice sliced through that taut instant. Redmond, his face suddenly very pale, sprang up to face the two men who now entered the room. "Harry!" he half whispered. "Oh, my God!"

Beaming, Jeremy Bolster hastened to shake the outstretched hand of the young baronet. With a wink, he said *sotto voce, "Dashed* timely, old fellow."

Sir Harry Redmond was a shade wider in the shoulders and an inch shorter in stature than his younger brother, and lacked Mitchell's good looks, but he was a pleasant-faced young man, blessed with vividly green if rather narrow eyes, the strong Redmond nose and chin, and a usually agreeable disposition. The brief look he turned on Mitchell was grim, but he drew his companion forward and, shaking hands with Leith, said, "Jove, Tris, you've changed a trifle since last we met!"

Leith grinned, while trying desperately to remember just when and where he had met this man. There could be no doubt of his identity, not after that betraying exchange of glances between him and Mitchell; otherwise, he'd have had not the least notion who he was. "Oh, Boney rearranged my face, as you see," he said easily.

"For the better," lied Sir Harry. "You've not met my uncle, I think? The Reverend Mordecai Langridge — Colonel Tristram Leith."

The Reverend, a short, plump, middle-aged cleric of rather colourless aspect and mild brown eyes, acknowledged the introduction bashfully. Neither of the newcomers was known to Rachel or Devenish, and when they had been presented, the little clergyman turned to Mitchell with a look of helpless apology. "Well, here we are, my boy," he said wryly. "You might have guessed we'd find you out."

Mitchell shook hands with him and greeted his brother uneasily. "Now, Harry," he murmured, "do not fly into the boughs. I simply saw no reason why —"

"Did you not? Then you and I have some caps to pull." Anger flared in the green eyes, to be banished by a swift smile. "But not now," said Sir Harry, and clapped his brother heartily on the back.

Mitchell uttered a smothered exclamation and jerked away from the heavy hand.

"Bantling?" Alarmed, Sir Harry reverted to the nickname that had not been used this year and more. "What's wrong?"

"Nothing," gasped Mitchell, but sat down rather abruptly.

Tristram Leith's suspicions, stirred when Bolster arrived, now hardened into cold certainty. He said in his deep drawl, "I'd not call

116

it 'nothing.' Your brother was set upon." His tone was cool; his dark eyes met Sir Harry's frowning ones in a steady warning. "By thieves."

Harry might be temporarily out of his depth here, but not for a second did he imagine that chance had brought these men together. Leith's plea for caution had been unmistakable, however, which meant that someone must be kept in the dark. A shrewd glance at the most logical person confirmed Harry's first impression that she might be in the family way, which explained Leith's concern. To what extent the Colonel was involved with the Sanguinet clan, Harry had no idea. The last time they'd met had been at a ball in Madrid, with the mighty Wellington present, and Leith in his regimentals dazzling all the pretty signorinas. He hadn't been a staff officer then, of course, nor had his handsome face been marred by the scars Waterloo had left him.

With these thoughts racing through his mind, Sir Harry bent over his brother, peered into the strained face and said, "Thieves, is it? Jupiter, but they found poor pickings, I'll wager. Minor damage, old fellow?"

A guarded relief came into Mitchell's eyes. "Very minor, *mon sauvage*."

"Do sit down, gentlemen," said Rachel, who had already summoned a maid to bring more cups. "May I offer you coffee, Reverend?"

Mr. Langridge happily accepted a steaming

cup and needed no urging to further deplete the macaroons. Occupying the chair next to him, Sir Harry stirred sugar into his cup. "My apologies for intruding upon you, Leith. Is — er, Strand about?"

"In Town, I'm afraid," Leith answered.

"Good gad! Listen to that fool Brutus! Better send a footman out to him, m'dear."

Rachel rang her little hand bell, and as the maid hurried in, the Reverend said uneasily, "You dog's a bit of a tartar, eh?"

"Did he annoy you, sir?" asked Leith. "My apologies. I assure you that he is all bark and no bite."

"Oh, really!" protested Langridge. "He was ready to tear us limb from limb! Eh, Harry?"

"That's odd," Leith muttered. "Usually, he's the gentlest creature."

"He must reserve his dislike for Redmonds," said Mitchell. "I rated the same treatment when I first arrived."

"So you did." Leith turned to Bolster. "Well, Jeremy, Brutus was once yours — can you shed some light on this?"

"Far as I know," replied his lordship, looking levelly at Sir Harry, "he only loathes one creature in the whole world. Donkeys."

"Aha!" said Mitchell. "So Mr. Fox is still at Moiré, is he?"

Sir Harry nodded and, seeing Leith's puzzlement, explained, "Mr. Fox is a donkey. A very unusual donkey, I might add."

"I was surprised he was still there," said the Reverend, restoring his cup to its saucer. "I made sure Diccon would have —"

Rachel's spoon clattered ringingly onto the silver tray. Her gasped "Diccon!" was drowned by Devenish's exuberant shout.

"Diccon! I *knew* it!" He sprang up, exclaiming, "I *knew* Sanguinet had come out of his hole at last! *That* is why we are all here! Has each of our lives been touched by that damned villain, then?"

Leith crossed to sit beside his wife and take her cold hand. "My love," he murmured urgently, "never look so afraid. We know very little yet. There may be nothing to it at all."

She clung to him, her face deathly pale. "Tell me truly, *have* you heard from Diccon?"

"I have not. And only look at you working yourself into a spasm. Go and lie down upon your bed, and I will —"

"No! I have always known this day would come, but — Please, dearest, let me stay. I promise not to be a nuisance."

He scanned her face worriedly, lifted her hand to his lips, then returned to the men who by common consent were discussing Devenish's new chaise and appeared to have noticed nothing of the tender little scene. "Very well, gentlemen," said Leith, his voice taking on the subtle ring of authority, "let's have at it. I know, of course, how Claude Sanguinet has affected the lives of my own family, but —"

"Forgive me, Colonel," interjected Sir Harry apologetically, "but *we* do not know of it. Perhaps at this time we should all lay our cards on the table."

Leith was silent, his eyes flickering to his wife. Rachel's hands were tight-gripped but she seemed to have her nerves under control. He said carefully, "I must know first, have any of you gentelmen been in touch with Diccon?"

Jeremy Bolster raised one muscular hand. "I have. Had a letter from the old boy telling me to come here at once, but he didn't say who I was to meet, only not to say anything."

"I had a letter also," said Sir Harry and, looking steadily at his brother added, "I think."

Reddening, Mitchell nodded. "You did." They were all staring at him, especially that clod Devenish. He bit his lip, then added clearly, "You are perfectly correct, gentlemen. I intercepted my brother's letter and came in his stead."

"Jove!" gasped Devenish, appalled.

Redmond turned narrowed, deadly eyes on him, and Sir Harry intervened swiftly, "My brother seems to think that because my wife recently presented me with a very beautiful little son, I must henceforth be wrapped in cotton."

Frowns became smiles. Leith's gaze turned speculatively to the cleric, and Sir Harry explained, "My uncle was up to his revered ears in our little tussle with the Sanguinets,

120

and thus feels entitled to be in on whatever is brewing."

Langridge flushed and mumbled something about likely being of very little use.

"What *is* brewing, Tris?" demanded Devenish eagerly. "*I* had no letter."

"Nor I," said Leith, "though I fancy Diccon knew I was here and means to join us. And in view of the attack on Redmond —"

Sir Harry interrupted intently, "Then they were *not* thieves?"

"They knew me," Mitchell admitted. "It was quite apparent I was to be disposed of before I could get here. Luckily, I'd anticipated something of the sort and so carried my sword."

"The devil!" exclaimed Bolster, indignant. "You might have told *me*, Mitch! I can be tr-trusted, after all!"

Mitchell's cold eyes softened. "Of course you can, Jerry. The thing was that Diccon said to tell no one of it, and —" He was on shaky ground and said hurriedly, "For that matter, you didn't take me into your confidence, either."

"Fooled you," said his lordship with simple pride. "Fooled old Harry, too. At least," he peered at his friend in sudden doubt, "I think I did."

"Oh, you did," Sir Harry acknowledged. "Although Uncle Mordecai and I were both rather curious as to why you suddenly left the Priory and went haring off with some ramshackle excuse about having promised to drop in on Strand."

"All we need now," said Mitchell, "is the omniscient Diccon."

"I hope to God he's alive," muttered Leith. "The man has led a charmed life up to now, but if Claude really is on the move, Diccon may also have been — er, intercepted."

There was a short silence. Mitchell broke it. "Are we to infer, then," he drawled, "that your visit here was a coincidence, Devenish?"

Devenish stared at his boots. "Matter of fact," he said reluctantly, "I came because I — had a, er, feeling." From under his lashes he saw the faint curl of mockery to Mitchell Redmond's lips, and added a defiant, "Yes, I'm aware it sounds stupid, but it's God's truth!"

"Then are we to understand you have also brushed up against our fine Frenchman?" asked Sir Harry.

Devenish grinned. "Might say that."

"You might indeed," said Leith. "Very well, let's pool our information while we await Diccon." Again, his dark eyes sought his wife's beauteous face. "My own initiation into the schemes of the Sanguinets came about rather by accident. I'd taken a bit of a rap on the head at Waterloo, as you can see. Unfortunately, it left me with no memory. My wife, who was Rachel Strand at that time, was in Brussels with her sister, and Rachel was so kind as to help me. Later, I met Diccon, who'd been working for Claude in Brittany, in the guise of a groom."

"He's a damned brave fellow," Sir Harry put in. "We knew him as an itinerant tinker."

"And as a Bow Street Runner," murmured the Reverend Langridge, reminiscently.

"And a Free Trader," said Mitchell, his eyes stern. "Although I've no doubt he in fact is a spy, eh, Leith?"

"At all events," Leith went on, having apparently not heard the question, "Rachel was betrothed to Claude Sanguinet, and she and Charity journeyed to his château in Brittany. Diccon had warned me that Claude plotted the overthrow of the British government, and I suspected, rightly, that Rachel was there to discover something of Claude's plans."

"By Jove!" said Sir Harry, looking at the silent girl admiringly.

"Dev and I decided to follow," Leith went on. "That's about it. We managed to get into the château. We found out that Claude meant to kidnap the Regent, and —"

The Redmonds and Mordecai Langridge were all on their feet, the air ringing with their exclamations of incredulity.

"Kidnap *Prinny?*" cried Sir Harry. "How?"

"Claude had caused a special carriage to be made. It had partitions fitted inside the ceiling that could be rolled down to conceal a central compartment, the outsides of the partitions

123

very cunningly painted to represent an unoc-
cupied interior. Claude, as you may know, had
inveigled himself into Prinny's good graces. He
planned to trick the Regent into entering the
coach. Very soon, our trusting Prince would be
drugged — easy enough of accomplishment —
and the screens would be lowered. To all casual
passers-by, an empty coach would drive through
London Town and away to a secret location."

Lord Bolster, who had been listening in a
rather bewildered fashion, asked, "But why?
Claude Sanguinet already has most of the money
in the world."

"But not the power, my lord," said the
Reverend, nodding solemnly.

"Right you are, sir," Leith agreed. "Claude's
ancestors once ruled Brittany, and the poor
idiot fancies himself royal. With Prinny in his
hands, Lord knows what he could have forced
the government to do."

Sir Harry, his face grim, muttered, "A black
coach. And four black horses."

"And the coachman and outriders wearing
black livery," said Mitchell, broodingly.

"Then you've seen it also?" asked Leith.

"To our sorrow," said Sir Harry. "But ours
was in England. Yours, I take it, was in
Dinan?"

"Yes. Thanks to which we were able to win
free and bring our girls safe home. Later, I was
so fortunate as to persuade Rachel to take me
to husband, and here we are."

"Oh, no, you don't!" exclaimed Mitchell. "I know that damnable château. It's a veritable fortress. If you got out unscathed, it was nothing less than a miracle."

"I got out unscathed. Devenish brought a memento with him. A crossbow bolt."

"Did he, by God!" Sir Harry said. "I'd heard Claude Sanguinet has a passion for medieval weaponry. You are fully recovered, I trust, Mr. Devenish?"

"Perfectly fit, thank you," said Devenish. "However, I had another encounter with our Claude last year. I was visiting a — a cousin of mine who has inherited a castle in Ayrshire. The old place had stood empty for decades and we'd gone up to look it over. Turned out a little clutch of Free Traders had found the castle exactly suited their own nefarious pursuits and took a very dim view of the owner's arrival. At least, that's what we thought at first. Eventually we discovered Sanguinet was behind the whole business and had arranged a neat funeral — for me." His eyes were remote for an instant. He said with a rather forced smile, "He's a busy fella."

Leith said gravely, "He doesn't like you, Dev. After all, you did kick him."

A broad grin spread across Mitchell Redmond's face, and he raised his cup in salute to Devenish.

"Life does have its moments of bliss," sighed Devenish. "Anyway, he had his man put a bolt through my leg, so I cannot see his right to hold a grudge, silly chap."

"He does, however. He has in fact a consuming passion to see you dead, and you know what they say about the third time. It might well behoove you to stay clear of this imbroglio."

"Pooh," said Alain Devenish. "Nonsense."

"What escapes me," said Sir Harry, "is why none of it has been made public. Is it unreasonable to suppose that Claude Sanguinet should have been denounced as a criminal and yourself praised?"

"Praised!" Devenish gave a cynical snort. "Old Tris was politely asked to resign his commission."

"The devil!" said Mitchell. "Is Whitehall run mad?"

Leith said with a wry shrug, "They would not believe us. Whilst we were running for our lives with Sanguinet's pack at our heels, Claude was sending powerful emissaries to London, claiming I had invaded his home for the sole purpose of abducting his fiancée, and had in the process tried to murder him."

The reverend gentleman, who had been following all this with breathless attention, now leaned forward and asked eagerly, "Had you so?"

"Well — not very successfully." Leith's mouth twitched into a faint grin. "I — er, threw him in the pool."

Awed, Mitchell asked, "Never say it was that bottomless one by the Pagoda?"

"You have it," said Devenish, laughing. "Unhappily, Claude survived and is regarded as a much-wronged man, while Tris is disgraced and shunned. Symbolic justice, eh?"

"Enough of me," said Leith briskly. "May we hear your story now, Sir Harry?"

"Since we are all comrades in arms," responded the young baronet, his green eyes twinkling, "we can drop the title, if you please. As to our tale — egad, I scarce know where to begin. I'll try to be brief. We knew Claude to be the motivating force of the clan, but we've not run up against him directly. Our encounter was with Parnell. Did you know him?"

Leith shook his head. "I know they called him Monsieur Diabolique. My wife knew him." He glanced at Rachel, but she was staring at her interlaced fingers and did not look up. "Nasty," he went on quickly, "was he?"

"Very nasty," said Sir Harry.

Mitchell said, "Harry," in a flat, quiet voice.

Harry looked at him sombrely and nodded. "Parnell Sanguinet," he began, "was a savage, gentlemen. I think he was mad, but that didn't help us, of course. My father died soon after I was brought home after Ciudad Rodrigo. I was still very much an invalid, and we were not told until much later that he had been ruined at play and committed suicide. Oh, never look so aghast, it was not the truth — merely what

127

we were led to believe. Needless to say, Mitchell and I and my uncle fought to clear his name."

Devenish's brows went up, and he whistled softly.

In a very small voice Rachel put in, "Parnell Sanguinet came to this house many times. Charity and I were terrified of him although I suppose he was a well enough featured man. I remember that he spoke of a girl who was his ward, and we felt so very sorry for her." She knit her brows. "Nanette — was it?"

Sir Harry hesitated, then said slowly, "Quite right, ma'am. It's too long a story to tell now. Suffice it to say that in trying to help her, we annoyed the Sanguinets and things became a bit, er, frenzied. Towards the end of it, I was fighting my way out of an ambush with my uncle to side me." He saw surprise on their faces, and smiled. "Do not be deceived. This gentle cleric is a fine fighter, you may believe me. Anyway, Mitchell had stayed behind to guard Nanette. We had thought their hiding place quite safe, but they were discovered. Nanette was dragged off, and my brother near killed." He darted a glance to Mitchell, who was gazing with deep concentration into the fire, and there was a small, hushed pause.

Tristram said gently, "You rescued your lady, of course."

"And married her, praise be! But it was a chancy business. For a while, it looked —" He paused, his eyes sombre, then said in a brighter tone, "I believe I have neglected to mention that through all of this I was aided and abetted by a Good Samaritan who called himself Diccon. At the finish he came to Newgate where I was spending an enforced, ah, holiday, and dashed if he wasn't all elegance and the officials bowing and scraping to him. He got me out of a very sticky mess, told me something of his real occupation, swore me to secrecy, and ordered me to stay clear. I rather gather," he ended whimsically, "that I have been recalled."

Devenish said with enthusiasm, "Jove! Between the lot of us, old Claude hasn't had things all his way!"

Leith turned to Bolster. "And you, Jerry? I'd no idea you had tangled with the Sanguinets. Where do you figure in all this?"

With typical modesty, his lordship asserted that he'd had little to do with it, save for trying to "give old Harry a boost, a time or two."

"Stuff," said Sir Harry. "You saved my bacon, Jeremy, as well you know!"

"It would seem to me," said the Reverend, "that — goodness gracious, only listen to your gentle lapdog, Leith."

The terrace doors burst open, and a tall, thin, shabbily dressed man with a mop of curling brown hair that escaped untidily from a disreputable old hat, fairly shot into the room and slammed the door behind him. Turning an irate scowl on Leith, he said with breathless indignation, "Blast it all, Colonel! I had to run like the devil to beat that tiger of yours into the house!"

At the sight of this newcomer, Rachel had whitened and shrunk a little farther back into her chair. The men, however, were all on their feet. Leith said, "My regrets. But you might have let me know you were calling this conference."

"Diccon!" His face one big grin, Sir Harry strode to wring his old friend's hand. "Damme if I didn't think Claude had got you at last!"

"You may believe he gave it a good try!" His own saturnine features breaking into a rare smile, Diccon grabbed Harry's arms for an instant, then turned to run keen eyes of a very light blue over the assembled group, his gaze lingering an extra second or two upon Mitchell's expressionless countenance. He turned to Leith. "As for you, sir, I did send you word. Because of it, my messenger died in one of those clever little 'accidents' at which Claude is so adept. Frankly, I am astonished that so many of you have arrived intact, for I've no doubt our fanatic has my letter and knows what we are about." He went over to grip Leith's outstretched hand and then bowed with courtly grace to Rachel. "How do you go on these days, Mrs. Leith?" he asked gently. "I fancy you must be wishing me at Jericho, rather than here, cutting up your peace."

Her voice quivering a little, Rachel answered, "I have very often thought of you, Major, and wondered how our England might be going on, were it not for devoted patriots such as yourself."

At this, his assured poise deserted him. He all but shrank from her, his lean face flaming. "No, no, ma'am! It is, after all, only a — a job of work. Could I find a l-less taxing one, I'd have backed away long since. Assure you."

"You've properly panicked him, Rachel," said Devenish gleefully. "Lord, but I'd not have thought it possible our famous Diccon would show yellow! Speaking of which, is Diccon really your name?"

With a shaken grin, Diccon said, "One of 'em." He made his way around the group, shaking hands and nodding to each man in a terse way, as though begrudging the time spent in such formalities. His greetings completed, he moved to stand with his back to the fireplace. Leith took him a glass of brandy, and he accepted it gratefully, raised it in a brief salute to them all, and took a healthy swallow. "My thanks," he said. "I needed something to restore me. Claude's run me the deuce of a chase. We started out four. Where the others are, Lord only knows. I can only pray they're alive."

The Reverend asked diffidently, "Had you far to come, Major Diccon?"

"From the Essex coast, sir. Though it was a wild goose chase, as I'd suspected. And time running out, blast it!" He sipped the brandy

131

again and ran his eyes around the intent circle of faces. "You know why you are here, I take it? Dear Claude has been very busy, and I am outwitted and outmanoeuvred, as usual."

"Do you know what he plans?" asked Leith.

"Or when he means to strike?" said Devenish.

Dismayed, Lord Bolster asked, "Have you no backing at all?"

"None, my lord," returned Diccon, answering the last question first.

Leith said, "What of Smollet? He knows the truth, and he told me Wellington knew also and thought we'd done not too badly."

"The General has been packed off to St. Petersburg. As for Wellington. . ." He sighed. "To be brief, Claude baited a trap, as a result of which I convinced Smollet and the Duke that we had pinpointed Claude's headquarters. A great deal of money was spent in staging an immediate military strike at one of the Channel Islands." He leaned forward and said intently, "Gentlemen, I was *on* that island. I *saw* Claude's men drilling. I *saw* vast supplies of weapons. Yet on the night our forces landed they were opposed only by a confused citizenry who'd been told France was invading. They put up a small but gallant resistance."

"Good God!" exclaimed Devenish.

"It didn't take long to get things more or less sorted out," said Diccon. "But when the smoke cleared there was not a sign — not a whisper — of Sanguinet's men or supplies."

"Jove, what a bumblebroth," muttered Sir Harry. "Casualties?"

"Thirty-nine wounded, including two young boys not yet in their teens, and two cows. One damned costly boat lost in the surf, and a small fortune wasted in ammunition. To say nothing of repairing shattered cottages and paying for trampled crops. The miracle is that no one was killed. You can well imagine the reaction in London. Prinny was raging; Whitehall was apoplectic; Smollet was disgraced; Wellington was embarrassed, to say the least. I am decidedly *persona non grata* in Whitehall."

There was a stunned silence. Devenish broke it. "That damned cunning bastard! But surely Wellington must know you were hoodwinked?"

"It was essential we move very fast. We'd been waiting for just such a chance. My word was trusted — and acted upon. It has all been hushed up, of course, but when Wellington finished with me . . . I can only wonder he did not rend me limb from limb." He gave a wry shrug. "Not that I'd have blamed him."

Leith, who had seen the Duke enraged, shuddered.

"Do you say that because of this, er, unfortunate mis-mis-mis- fiasco the entire matter has been relegated to the st-status of fantasy?" asked Bolster.

Diccon shook his head. "Smollet still believes me. Wellington . . . I don't know. He requested that in future before I invite a disaster I at least produce proof of my findings. Proof!" He swore softly. "Small chance of that!" With an impatient movement he straightened his shoulders, the sense of restrained urgency that so often characterized him radiating from him as he went on briskly, "Of one thing I am very sure. Sanguinet is mustering a ragtag army of dissidents, traitors, soldiers of fortune, malcontents. And he has top military men from all over Europe whipping them into a well-armed, well-trained force that will all too soon be capable of rolling over any resistance our ill-equipped depleted garrisons might drum up to meet them."

"Capital," muttered Sir Harry, cynically. "Is that all?"

"I'm afraid not." Diccon paused. "As a prelude to his little venture, Claude means to do away with the Regent!"

Chapter Seven

Through the following stunned silence, the Reverend Langridge gasped, *"Do . . . away with — ?* Good heavens, man! You cannot be serious! Do you tell us that — that miserable conniver means to murder Prince George? But — but he's the heir-apparent!"

Mitchell said scornfully, "Why go to the trouble? Prinny's an ineffectual, bungling fool. What threat could he be to Sanguinet?"

The remark provoked several frowns, and Diccon turned a gaze of ice onto the younger man. "Your personal, and unfortunately expressed views, sir," he said in a tone as cold as his look, "do not alter the fact that our Prince could become King at any moment. Were he to die just now —"

"There would be widespread rejoicing," drawled Mitchell acidly.

"By God!" Devenish sprang to his feet, eyes ablaze. "I'll be *damned* if I will stand here and listen to —"

"Enough!" Angry, Leith also stood. "Mr. Redmond, I take leave to remind you that you are a guest in my home and that both your words and manner are offensive to the rest of us! Also, that my wife is present."

Mitchell had the grace to redden. With his brother's glare transfixing him, he said, "I apologize, Mrs. Leith. Not for my views, but for having voiced them in your presence. I shall hold my tongue." He moved to a chair at the rear of the room and sat down, having apparently lost interest in the proceedings.

"As I was saying, gentlemen," Diccon resumed, "for the Regent to be slain would be disastrous. The Princess is beloved, but she is in the family way and it would be some time before she could be expected to function capably. Prince Leopold is foreign and with little power. More than this, the aftermath of our long war has resulted in widespread public unrest and dissatisfaction with the status quo. Only look at the uproar in January when the Regent drove to open Parliament. A near riot. Hostile crowds, rocks thrown, the possibility even of a shot having been fired at his coach. Our national debt is staggering and cripples our economic policies. The death of the Regent would be the final straw to throw the nation into anarchy. What a perfect time for Sanguinet to strike! Our army has been largely disbanded and it would take more time than we would have to conscript sufficient men or weld them into efficient regiments." He bent forward slightly and, looking at them in turn from under his bushy eyebrows, said with slow emphasis, "This nation, gentlemen, would be at the mercy of a soulless fanatic and a well-equipped army of murderous rabble!"

They eyed one another, appalled, while the midday sun slanted in pleasant golden gleams through the tall windows, and distantly, Brutus could be heard barking in a desultory way.

"But you must have *some* idea of where Sanguinet is headquartered," said Leith. "Certainly so large an operation cannot have gone unnoticed."

"One would think not. But" — Diccon spread his long bony hands expressively — "I had my first hint of Claude's new plan a year since and am little the wiser today. Six weeks ago I had what seemed a second glimmer of hope, and I went into Essex to sniff around.

But it was another red herring. I dare risk no more precious time. The men loyal to me are being whittled down, either by violence or by their need for regular meals. Thus, gentlemen, I now call upon you who have good cause to loathe the Sanguinets. For the sake of our England, I ask your —"

Imperceptibly, the bulldog's barking had drawn nearer, and it became increasingly difficult to distinguish Diccon's grim words as a disturbance in the hall grew to a small uproar. Abruptly, the doors were flung open. The butler and a footman came in, supporting between them Best's sagging form. The groom's head and face were streaked with blood, one coat sleeve hung in shreds, and the visible areas of his face were deathly white.

Leaping to his feet, Leith cried, "Best! What on earth — Over here, Fisher. Lay him on the sofa."

Pushing through the men who crowded around the stricken groom, Mitchell exclaimed harshly, "I *knew* it! Best, where is Miss Strand?"

A faint, horrified cry broke from Rachel, and Leith turned to throw an arm about her. Turning a taut face to Redmond, he demanded, "What the devil do you mean?"

Mitchell ignored him. "Best? Try to tell us, man. Has Miss Strand come to any harm?"

The groom tried valiantly to answer, but his words were inaudible. Diccon came up with a glass of brandy and handed it to Fisher.

Rachel quickly came between them, took the glass, and dropped to her knees beside the sofa. "Hold his head up," she urged and, as Fisher obliged, held the glass to Best's lips. He took a few sips, coughed, and waved the brandy away. "Colonel," he gasped out, "I tried! As — as God be my judge . . . I *tried!*"

Leith dropped one hand on his wife's shoulder. "Of course you did, poor fellow. Just try to tell us what happened. Where is Miss Charity?"

"Gawd knows, sir. Mr. Redmond is right. He made me go with her. She didn't . . . want me, but . . . then this great big black coach come and . . . and they was just too many on 'em, sir. I told her to run quick . . . and I tried . . . to hold 'em, but . . . Oh, I *do* be that sorry, Colonel! They got her! They took Miss Charity . . . they *took* her . . ."

Uproar followed his words. Leith, terrified for his ashen-faced wife, picked her up bodily and deposited her in a deep chair. Mrs. Hayward hurried into the room, followed by two of her maids bearing medical supplies and a bowl of hot water. Even as they ministered to the injured man, Diccon continued to question him relentlessly.

Devenish meanwhile caught Mitchell by the arm and spun him around. "What the devil do you know of all this?" he demanded angrily.

"It was the very thing I was hastening to take up with Leith when you saw fit to delay me in the stables," Mitchell answered, a miserable sense of guilt gnawing at him.

Leith, who had sent the footman running to make hot tea for his wife, now left her and came up, his face pale and taut. "Explain, if you please."

Mitchell said, "I was appalled to find that Miss Strand was in the habit of wandering about the countryside unescorted. From the moment we first met I made every effort to convince her not to do so."

His handsome features contorted with fury, Devenish snarled, "You *thought* this might happen? And you said nothing to Leith here? Or to me? Why, you —"

Leith threw up a restraining arm. "Dev, not now. Had you previously seen that coach in this neighbourhood, Redmond?"

"No, dammit! Of course I had not! And how could I say anything about Sanguinet when I had no way of knowing who else knew what was —"

"It was Claude's doing," Diccon intervened briskly, turning from the sofa. "No doubt of it. Black coach, livery, horses, the whole ugly article. Your groom thinks they headed west. You shall have to get your men after them, Leith. Fast. Before that swine gets your sister to Dinan. I doubt you could broach his fortress château a second time."

Leith thought, "God forbid!" He looked to the men who watched him. "Gentlemen, are you with me?"

Diccon's voice cut through the immediate chorus of affirmation. "No, by God! They are not!"

Stunned, they turned to him.

"Heaven forbid that I should not sympathize with Miss Strand's predicament," he said. "But *England* has first claim on you."

His dark brows drawing together, Leith argued, "You want Sanguinet, no? Our ways then take the same path."

"Not if you mean to follow your sister to the coast. You would play right into Claude's hands. I now believe his fortress must lie northward."

Devenish said keenly, "Scotland? Then you *did* pay some heed to what I told Smollet last year!"

"Of course. We have had your cousin's castle watched ever since your confrontation with the smugglers, but there has been no sign of free trading, nor any apparent link to Sanguinet. Even so, there are parts of Scotland that would provide more than enough privacy for Claude's activities, and 'tis there I mean to search next. My apologies, Leith. Get your men away at once, but I must ask that you and these other gentlemen go with me."

Leith looked at his wife's imploring face. Tears crept slowly down her cheeks, and her hands were gripped so tightly that the knuckles gleamed white. But she said nothing, leaving

140

the decision to him, trusting in him. When he turned back to Diccon, his eyes were implacable. "My regrets, Major. My first duty must be to my sister."

"Aye! And we're with you to a man," declared Devenish stoutly.

Mitchell contradicted, "Not quite. My regrets, Leith, but I'm with Diccon."

Devenish's lip curled. Impatient, he said, "Come *on*, Tris! They gain on us every second that we stand about jawing!"

Leith took his wife's hand and hurried with her into the hall, Devenish, Bolster, Sir Harry, and the Reverend following. At the door Harry turned back. "Mitch," he said quietly, "have a care."

His brother smiled in that warm, transforming smile so seldom seen of late. "You also, *mon sauvage*."

Diccon's face, however, was thunderous. "I'd not expected this of you, Harry," he said bitterly. "You owe me."

"I do." Sir Harry looked troubled. "But Nanette was in just such a situation two years ago, Diccon. Knowing what terrors she endured, I simply cannot stand by and see another lady so abused. I swear we shall ride like fury to come up with you, once we have Miss Strand safely away. Only tell me where to go."

"Do not tempt me," said Diccon sourly. Then, "I'll go bail you ride on a fool's errand. But when you've done, head for Castle Tyndale.

141

I'll leave word there."

Sir Harry nodded and turned away.

Diccon called after him, "I hope you *do* rescue the lady." And as Harry disappeared into the hall, he muttered, "But I doubt it."

A sharp pain in her thigh jolted Charity back to a befuddled awareness. She was in a strange place; dim, very warm, and stuffy. In addition to these peculiarities, the room was rocking. Puzzled, she wondered if they were at sea; perhaps Justin had taken them out on the *Silvering Sails* and she had dropped off to sleep in the cabin. . . . But Justin did not much care for the sea, certainly not sufficiently to have taken them across the Channel at night. It was all very odd. . . . With what seemed a great effort she reached for the lamp beside her bed. Her groping fingers encountered a yielding yet scratchy surface, rather like starched linen. And there was a sound to accompany the jolt and sway of her room: a continuous pounding and rattling.

The stabbing pain in her thigh came again, and with it a faint, high-pitched cry. As in the gradual recollection of a dream she saw herself walking . . . Mitchell Redmond's haughty, arrogant face . . . Best. She reached downwards and felt the soft irregularities of a woolen garment. A pocket. Groping inside, her hand was at once thrust against by an impatient, indignant, and very small furry head.

142

Charity drew forth a small, dimly seen shape. And she knew, and dropping the kitten, shrank against the squabs of the carriage, so terrified that she could not seem to catch her breath or do anything but huddle there, shaking, gasping, frantically sobbing.

The dark partition was drawn aside. Charity was dazzled by the afternoon's brightness, but she saw a man who peered in at her. He was youngish, clean-shaven, and neatly dressed as would befit the occupant of so luxurious a vehicle.

"So madame is awake," he said, with the hint of a French accent. "You should not weep, for we treat you most kindly, you must agree. We have not bound your hands, nor a gag placed in your pretty mouth. Although —" he added thoughtfully, raising his voice, "the lady I find not so *extreme* pretty as we were told, eh, my Clem?"

The screen to Charity's left was drawn aside, and another man, a dark silhouette against the glare, said in a coarse London voice, "They never is when they're breeding." The screen was drawn shut again. "Fair turns me stummick to see a mort all swole up like that."

"My Lord!" thought Charity, fighting back tears. "They wanted Rachel! They think *I* am Rachel!"

The Frenchman was speaking again. "But this lady is not yet very much — ah, swole, as you say. Nonetheless, madame, it is for the

143

sake of your condition that you are coddled thus. I must desire that you be sensible and conduct yourself quietly." He smiled faintly. "For your own sake, I ask it."

"Wh-where are you taking me?" gulped Charity.

He chuckled. "But you first should ask, 'Where am I?'"

"I know p-perfectly well where I am. I have been in this horrid vehicle before. I know it is Claude Sanguinet's wicked coach that he uses for his — his murderous plots. And that you are keeping me hidden in this concealed space." This brought hilarious laughter from both men and, because whatever happened they must not go back and try to take Rachel, she went on in desperation. "Oh, you may laugh. But when my husband comes, it will be very different."

The Frenchman called, "Shall we tell her, my good Clem?"

"No, we won't me good Jean-Paul," rasped the Englishman. "We're comin' inter Godalming. Shut 'er up. Else I will."

The man called Jean-Paul leaned nearer, a gentle smile on his sallow but pleasant countenance. "Only keep it in your head, lady," he urged, "that we have a long journey. Your babe will not like it if you are tied for many leagues. And you will not like for my crude friend to, er, shut you up. Soon, you will have the food and drink. Now —" He put a finger to his smiling lips and closed the screen.

Trembling, Charity leaned back against the squabs, closing her eyes. While she had been speaking, one hand had automatically caressed the kitten who had snuggled contentedly on the seat beside her. Now, as though sensing her terror, Little Patches scrambled up the cloak and began to butt her head against Charity's chin. Grateful for this small comfort, Charity held the little shape close. "Poor creature," she whispered. "They did not see you, I think. But whatever is to become of us?" She restored the kitten to her lap, fondling it while her mind strove desperately with this terrible predicament.

How Sanguinet's agents could have confused her with her sister was imcomprehensible. Nonetheless, she breathed a grateful prayer that the mistake had occurred. To have been subjected to such an ordeal as this would have completely overset Rachel's precarious health, and if she lost the babe she and Tristram wanted so badly . . . There was no point in thinking of such awful things. She must escape these brutes. But that they were armed, she did not doubt. And there were the outriders. Well, there was no chance at this moment, perhaps, but it would come. It *would* . . . it must. . . . She blinked away fresh tears. Besides, Tristram would follow. And dear Dev. She must have been missed by now. Only . . . what on earth were they doing in Godalming? If she was being taken to Château Sanguinet they should be heading south to the coast. If they were bound for Sanguinet Towers, the great estate near Chatham that Parnell had once ruled, they would be driving northeast. Godalming lay north and west of Strand Hall, which made no sense. Unless perhaps it was an attempt to confuse their pursuers and they meant to eventually turn about.

She could hear other traffic now, and soon they were bumping over cobblestones.

"Keep yer mouth in yer pocket, missus," said the Englishman roughly. "If I was ter break yer jaw, it'd keep yer quiet, and I don't 'spect it would hurt yer babe neither."

Charity shrank, trembling.

Jean-Paul called, his voice sharp with indignation, "I see no reason for such words. The lady she has ample grief to come."

Charity closed her eyes and prayed. "Dear God, help me. Please, please, help me."

The carriage slowed and gave a lurch. The shouts of ostlers rang out, and there was much jolting and the trampling of many hooves. Jean-Paul was conversing cheerfully with a man who said in a slow country voice that it was "a fine, fair day. Be ye goin' far, sir?" To which the Frenchman replied, "Very far, and very fast, *mon cher campagnard.*" The ostler, for Charity supposed he must be such, laughed, and she wondered miserably if he had any idea how Jean-Paul had mocked him. She sat up straighter, and at once Clem growled, "Behave,

146

woman! Or ye'll be sorry for't!"

Behave . . . If only she dared behave like the heroines in the novels she had read. If she screamed at the top of her lungs, help would come, surely? Or would they even hear her, with all the uproar and prancing and snorting of the horses, the jingling of harness, the shouts of the ostlers. Certainly, before they could reach her, Clem would strike her down. And even as she hesitated, trying to nerve herself, the coach lurched again. She felt the seat bounce to Jean-Paul's weight, the door was slammed, and with a jerk and the pounding of sixteen hooves, they were away again.

Charity's heart sank. She had failed. She was no heroine, but a shivering, miserable coward. . . .

Jean-Paul called, "Clem? You have opened your curtains again, yes?"

"No, I ain't. No reason to. No one can stick their long nose in here."

"The reason is because monseigneur does not wish a coach that shows closed curtains and might *en effet* have very many persons within. Monseigneur wishes a coach that carries one gentleman. You comprehend?"

"No," jeered Clem. "I'm too stupid, Frenchy!"

But Charity heard him moving about and the faint increase of brightness in her stuffy prison told her he had done as Jean-Paul commanded.

On they went, bounce and rattle and sway

and jolt, while the air in the central enclosure became ever hotter and stuffier and Charity's head began to ache. Little Patches had gone back to sleep, which was as well, for Charity was very sure they would not treat the little animal kindly once she was discovered. If she was permitted to alight at the next stage, she would try to smuggle the kitten out and let her run off. "You are so pretty, tiny one," she whispered. "Someone will take pity on you and give you a home." She pulled her cloak gently over the kitten, closed her eyes, and tried to sleep.

She awoke with a start. The faint glow at the edges of the screens was tinged with red. It must be sunset, and still the carriage steadily ate up the miles. If they had turned back to the south coast while she slept, they would come to the end of this part of their journey very soon.

Clem was grumbling about the advanced hour and his need for sustenance. "Ain't had a perishin' crumb since morning," he declared. "Abaht time we stopped fer a bite o' supper."

"You know where we are told to stop," Jean-Paul pointed out. "You would not wish to vex monseigneur."

Clem's response was a growl of profanity that left little doubt as to his opinion of monseigneur.

Wondering wretchedly whether poor Best had survived; whether Rachel was making herself ill with grief and worry; whether

Tristram and Dev had already set out in search of her, Charity's eyes fell. She gave a gasp. Little Patches was very obviously feeling the effects of this long confinement. She had jumped to the floor and was scratching with one minute paw at the screen, trying to thrust her nose around the edge. Charity bent cautiously and took her up. The pink mouth opened protestingly, but they were crossing a bridge at that moment and the sounds of the wheels on old cobblestones drowned out the kitten's cry. Trying to soothe her, Charity murmured, "I have the same need as you, little one, but whether we will be permitted to attend to it is another matter."

"Monsieur Jean-Paul," she said, timidly.

"The lady's awake," jeered Clem. "What a pity!"

Ignoring him, Charity said, "I, er, have a problem, I fear. Of — of a personal nature."

"Cor blimey!" said Clem in an affected voice. " 'Ere we is, miles from the nearest water closet!"

Charity's cheeks burned and she longed to toss her slipper into his nasty face, even as she had done to Mr. Redmond. Redmond . . . a clear picture of his haughty elegance rose in her mind's eye, bringing with it a pang of longing for family and friends, and all the dear and gentle security of Strand Hall.

Jean-Paul said reasonably, "The lady has been quite good, Clem. She is, after all, only human, and carries the babe besides."

"A sight better orf she'd be if she didn't," grunted Clem.

"Not insofar as our kindly employer is concerned. He wants this babe very much, and I for myself should not wish to bring our guest to him in a poor state. No, no. We must stop for the new mama, I think."

Charity felt chilled. Claude wanted Rachel, but more, he wanted her child! So this was the vengeance he planned for Tristram. That gallant man's heart would break were his wife to fall again into Sanguinet's hands, but to know his helpless child was in those same hands, to guess at the horrors the Frenchman meant to inflict . . . Shivering, she thought, "But Claude does not have his intended victim!" And if the worst should happen, if she herself were murdered, Tristram and Devenish would know — surely they would know, and they would be prepared. Rachel would be guarded night and day.

Her nobility faded away. She was shaking like a leaf, for however hard she tried to be brave, she could not stop thinking of the moment when she would face Claude. Of the look that would come into those hot brown eyes when he saw her. . . . Of the violence he might visit upon her in his rage and frustration. Her blood ran cold, and her knees turned to blancmange.

The carriage began to slow, and she recovered her wits, snatched up the kitten, and thrust her back into her pocket.

Jean-Paul pulled the screen aside. The scarlet glow of a magnificent sunset flooded in, and Charity blinked, dazzled by that warm light after the gloom of her little prison.

"Come, madame." Jean-Paul opened the door and let down the steps, then sprang down and reached out to her. Charity took his hand and moved stiffly to stand beside him.

They had stopped on a lonely country lane. There was no sign of habitations, woods stretched out to either side, and distantly hills rose, dark against the crimson sky. The outriders walked their horses up and watched, grinning.

Clem had left the carriage also, and came around to grumble at Jean-Paul because of the delay. "Take her in them trees. It ain't Carlton House, yer royalty, but you gotta take what's here, as they say." His beady eyes flickered down Charity, and she drew her cloak around her, trying to create the illusion of breadth around her flat middle.

"This way, madame." Jean-Paul led her to the trees, Clem following.

The two men stopped and turned to face her. Shrinking with mortification, Charity pleaded, "You will allow me some privacy?"

"Privacy!" Clem spat at a passing butterfly. "Cor! Go on, missus! Or it's up in the coach again!"

Jean-Paul said curtly, "Do you try to run from us, I shall not be responsible for you. But we will turn our backs, madame."

"Ho, no, we won't!" argued Clem. "You got maggots in yer head, Frenchy? When she hoists up them dainty skirts, it'll be ter run like a rabbit!"

They glared at each other. Charity fled quickly into the trees, released the indignant kitten, and looked about her in desperation. Nothing. No lane, no cottage, no sound of voices. It was hopeless. If she ran or tried to hide they would catch her and then Clem would have his way. At the very least, they would beat her. . . . Despairing, she attended to the wants of nature, then glanced around for the kitten. There was no sign of her. It was as well. The poor little creature would be safer out here than —

Some way off, a woman laughed.

Charity's heart gave a great leap, and she began to run wildly in the direction of the sound. A frantic mewing arose. She had looked too far afield for Little Patches. The kitten had evidently been playing about her skirts and now was being bounced about as she strove to climb up. Charity retrieved her and returned her to the much used pocket. The woods became denser as she ran, and she could hear no more laughter, no sound except, terrifyingly, the thump of heavy feet behind her. "Help!" she screamed at the top of her lungs, and tried to run faster. There was no response to her scream, no friendly call or sudden appearance of country people to come to her rescue. Only those remorseless boots coming even closer. They were closing the gap, but she must get away . . . she must! She could hear heavy breathing now, a savage panting mutter of rage. She gave a panicked sob as a sudden jerk at her cloak wrenched her backwards and she fell.

Cursing, his face distorted with fury, Clem loomed over her.

Charity knelt, drawing the cloak around her and huddling lower, one hand upthrown to protect her face. "Please don't . . . don't" she implored.

"I have . . . warn you, madame," panted Jean-Paul, coming up with them.

Clem drew back his brawny hand.

"My — my baby!" sobbed Charity in desperation.

The Frenchman's eyes drifted down her crouched figure. "*Mon . . . Dieu . . .*" he breathed.

"You want a lesson, you do," snarled Clem.

Jean-Paul caught his arm. Following the Frenchman's gaze, Clem's jaw dropped. "By grab!" he gasped. "It's — *moving!*"

Charity glanced down. Little Patches was settling herself again. The cloak bulged and shifted.

"I'll be gormed!" Clem muttered, awed. He lowered his fist and took Charity gingerly by the elbow. "You got spunk, ma'am. I'll give yer that."

Charity fought an almost overpowering need to laugh. She clambered to her feet and at once Jean-Paul was supporting her. She said with a plaintive sigh, "I am . . . so very tired. . . ."

"Soon, madame," said Jean-Paul soothingly, "you shall have good food and a comfortable bed. Very soon, now."

The sky was a glory of crimson and turquoise when they emerged from the trees, and the carriage waiting on the dusty lane, the outriders standing chatting beside their horses, the verdant landscape, presented an idyllic pastoral scene well worth setting upon canvas. Usually so aware of beauty, Charity viewed it without one jot of appreciation, until — Her eyes opened wider. The sun was going down, but it was going down on the wrong side of the carriage! If they had turned southwards, the right side should be presented to that descending orb, instead of which the sun was setting beyond the *left* side! So they were still heading north! If they continued thus, they would eventually come to Scotland. Surely Dev and Tristram were already close behind, and Dev would follow for only a short while before he would guess their destination!

With this first faint glimmering of hope to sustain her, Charity climbed bravely up into the great black coach.

Chapter Eight

Diccon set a pace that was as brisk as his tongue was still. Hour after hour they rode steadily northwards, crossing beautiful Sussex and entering Surrey above Horsham, but avoiding that old town, as Diccon had avoided all main thoroughfares and populated areas. Three times they stopped to rest the horses and refresh themselves, always at secluded taverns or farmhouses, and always for the briefest possible period. On each of these occasions, Mitchell attempted to learn more of Diccon's plans, but his questions were turned aside. The intelligence officer was morose and uncommunicative and would only repeat that since the last authenticated encounter with Claude Sanguinet had been in Ayrshire, it was the most likely place to start. He had earlier said that the castle had been under observation for a year with no sign of further activity. It therefore seemed obvious to Mitchell that more recent information must have been received, but that Diccon chose not to share it with him.

The miles slipped past, the afternoon deepened, and Diccon's taciturnity began to gall. Instead of being welcomed as an ally, Mitchell was evidently mistrusted. He refused to acknowledge that his caustic references to the Regent might have inspired such an attitude, and began to think resentfully that he might better have stayed with Leith's intrepid little band. At least, when they came up with Sanguinet's coach — and he had no doubt but that they *would* do so — they would not only be able to rescue Miss Strand, but might even be able to pry some information from the men who held her.

Charity's image haunted him. A most contrary girl, but she was gently born and had known more than her share of grief. Besides, the thought of any female being a helpless pawn in the hands of so soulless a villain as Claude Sanguinet sent a tide of rage seething through him. He consoled himself with the conviction that her captivity would be temporary. Soon, perhaps even at this moment, Tristram and Harry and the rest would gallop to her rescue. He could picture the depth of her relief and gratitude. And as soon as she was safely restored to her home, Leith would be coming after them hell for leather. They might even join forces before they reached Ayrshire.

The sun was low in the sky when they neared Woking, the tired horses clattering wearily over a bridge across the River Wey. Diccon turned off the road and led the way into an isolated stretch of woods. Quite suddenly, gypsies were all around them. For an instant, Mitchell suspected an ambush and his hand streaked down for his pistol, but Diccon was welcomed respectfully, and the travellers were guided to a wide clearing close to the bank of the river, where stood a ring of about ten caravans.

Mitchell was given into the care of an aged little man wearing a brilliant red scarf about his head and having very bright black eyes and a great, upcurving chin. His caravan was neat; Mitchell was invited to take off his coat; a bowl of hot water was provided, and while he washed, the old man brushed the dust from his coat. Thanking him, Mitchell went back outside. He found Diccon already seated by the camp fire, eating stew and conversing in the Romany tongue with three grim-looking men. A bowl of stew was brought to Mitchell, together with a thick slice of crusty bread. Simple fare, but he found it beyond words delicious, partly because it was eaten in the crisp fresh air, and partly because he'd been working up a hearty appetite since leaving Sussex.

He no sooner finished the stew than fresh horses were brought up. Indignant, he declared that he had no intention of leaving Whisper here. At once a dozen heads turned his way, and a dozen pairs of hard black eyes bored at him.

Diccon said, "She'll be safer here than going on at the pace we must travel. I'll grant he's no Arabian, but this hack is used to long hauls and hard knocks." Lowering his voice, he murmured, "And were I you, friend, I'd not be questioning the integrity of these folks. Unless you want another knife 'twixt your ribs."

Mitchell mounted up and reached into his pocket for his purse.

Diccon caught his eye, and Mitchell checked, then bent to shake the hand of the man who held the hack. "Thank you for your hospitality, friend," he said. "Shall you be camped here when we return?"

"Who can say, Gorgio Rye? Your beautiful mare will be at Moiré Grange when you reach there."

Astonished, Mitchell said, "How the devil do you —"

"If you are quite ready, Mr. Redmond," Diccon interrupted, "I've to be in Abingdon tonight."

Jerking his head around, Mitchell gasped, *"Abingdon?"*

"Too far for you?" Diccon shrugged. "I fancy your brother could teach you a thing or two about forced marches!"

Through a rather set smile, Mitchell said, "I am very sure he could," and rode on.

For three long hours scarcely a word was spoken. They were slowed when the dusk deepened into evening, for there was no moon and it was difficult to see their way. It was quite dark when Diccon at last rode into the yard of an isolated and inexpensive little hedge tavern.

Mitchell dismounted warily, followed the eager host into a low-ceilinged foyer, and up a winding stair. His room was tiny but clean, and he sprawled with a sigh of relief onto the soft feather bed. He forced himself to stand after only a moment, however, knowing he would be asleep in no time and having not the slightest intention of granting Diccon the opportunity to remark that Harry would not have been so easily tired. He took his toilet articles from his saddlebags and spent a short time in restoring himself to some semblance of tidiness before going downstairs.

The coffee room the host showed him into was long and low, with whitewashed walls and dark settles and benches. A fire burned on the wide hearth, but the room was deserted. The host brought a bottle of wine, and Mitchell ordered a light supper, and still Diccon had not appeared. He was grinning to himself, thinking that *he* might be the one to scoff in the morning, when another gentleman entered.

The newcomer was clad in a peerless riding coat and breeches, his neckcloth unostentatiously but impeccably tied, his topboots gleaming. A slender gentleman, with short curling hair arranged in a simple but attractive style, the aristocrat written in every proud inch of his tall figure.

"Your thoughts must be exceedingly pleasant

to bring such a smile to your face, sir," he said.

Mitchell gasped, "Diccon! By Jove — I didn't know you!"

Crossing to occupy the opposite chair, Diccon said coolly, "Good. Let us hope Sanguinet's spies don't."

"I cannot believe it! Who cut your hair?"

"I did. Have you ordered? Ah, I see you have."

The host and his plump lady carried in a juicy ham and a plate of cold beef. Pickled beets, sliced cheeses, hot bread, and a steaming gooseberry pie completed the repast, and the two men applied themselves to it with enthusiasm.

Not until the host had removed the covers and left them to their wine did Diccon say, "Too tired to talk for a minute?"

"It will be a novel experience," said Mitchell dryly.

Diccon stared at him in puzzled questioning.

"No one," said Mitchell, "could accuse you of being garrulous, Major."

"Oh." The suspicion of a smile twitched at the thin lips. "Nor you of being a lover of the quiet life. You've built quite a reputation since last we met, Mr. Redmond. I was surprised to learn that you are now reckoned a fine shot and a master swordsman."

Mitchell took a walnut from the bowl. "They seemed desirable skills to cultivate — under the circumstances."

"Did they?" Watching the younger man's inscrutable face and cold eyes, Diccon thought with a faint regret that the Sanguinets had much to answer for. "And what of the skills you once hungered after? What of your passion for musty old books and ancient history? Your dream of a fellowship at Oxford?"

"Dreams change."

"To become vendettas?"

Mitchell cracked the nut between his strong fingers and said nothing.

"I had thought your quarrel was with Parnell Sanguinet," Diccon went on blandly, "and he is dead."

"Claude manipulated Parnell, as he manipulates everyone. And Claude is very much alive. And as for vendettas — Claude's rogues attacked *me*, if you remember."

"Ah, yes. Your, er, duel. They likely mistook you for a patriot."

In the act of selecting another nut, Mitchell paused and looked up. "Mistook . . . ?" he echoed softly.

"You said yourself you care not what happens to the Regent, which being the case I can only suppose that you accompany me in pursuit of personal vengeance."

Mitchell frowned, then said deliberately, "It would give me the greatest satisfaction to assist the Sanguinets towards the hell they richly deserve."

Up went Diccon's bushy brows. "Plural, is it? I'd have thought you would feel an obligation to Guy. After all, you shot him, and yet he was decent enough to stop —"

"If he is in this with Claude, then of a surety Guy too!" The sly amusement in Diccon's eyes caused Mitchell's to become bleak. "Furthermore, Major, I do not recall remarking that I did not care what became of Prinny. If I happen to consider him to be a liability rather than an asset to England, it does not imply a lack of patriotism."

"I doubt the royal gentleman would agree. In point of fact, you could be clapped up for such a remark. And, speaking of liabilities, I am rapidly coming to the conclusion that is exactly what *you* are to me."

"So I gather." Irked, Mitchell said, "Considering how you begged my brother to come, I would think —"

"Ah," murmured Diccon, "but that, you see, was your brother."

"Who has just as much reason to detest the Sanguinets as have I!"

Diccon smiled infuriatingly and began to push a walnut around his wineglass.

"Sanguinet, I will remind you," gritted Mitchell, leaning forward, "murdered my father."

"But we were never able to prove that, you know. Parnell contrived to Sir Colin's ruin, certainly, and persecuted the lovely lady of whom you were so fond, but —"

Mitchell had raised his wineglass, but at these words his hand jerked so that the rich port splashed onto the gleaming oak. His eyes lifted to meet Diccon's, and that intrepid gentleman was put in mind of the glare he had once beheld in the eyes of a cornered panther. "Perhaps," said Mitchell with silken softness, "you will be so good as to explain what you mean by that . . . insinuation."

"Insinuation? But, my dear fellow, I had always understood you to be, ah, very fond of Miss Carlson."

"She is not Miss Carlson," said Mitchell, still with his head slightly downbent while he glared up at Diccon from under his black brows. "She is the lady Harry Redmond. And if you dare to imply —"

"That you were in love with her? Of course you were. *She* knew it — Harry knew it — Parnell knew it! And when he found you alone together in the woods —"

Mitchell's chair went over with a crash. Standing with fists clenched, he raged, "I never laid a hand on her, damn you! She loved Harry. I respected that, and I respected *her!*"

Diccon leaned back, very much at his ease, his eyes as cool as Mitchell's were blazing. "You loved her," he repeated. "Parnell persecuted and terrorized her and victimized you and your brother. And Claude pulled the strings for all of it, and engineered your father's death.

Wherefore, you want him dead at your feet — no?"

"Yes!" snarled Mitchell. "I'll beat him at his own game, and call him out or strangle him with my bare hands if I have to! Is *that* what you want? Is that what you've been sneering and hinting and prying after? Then hear this, Mr. Tinker or Spy, or whatever you are, I may not be the man my brother is, and I may be no more than a liability to you, but with or without you, I'll find Claude Sanguinet, and —"

Diccon laughed jeeringly. "And you'll die in that moment! Oh yes, that's what I wanted, Redmond. To know just how you will behave in a crisis. And it is as I suspected. You don't give a groat for England. Your only interest in this is personal vengeance!"

"You lie, blast you! I love my country!"

Leaning forward then, Diccon slammed one clenched fist on the table and demanded tensely, "And do you love it enough to be ruled by my decisions? Will you agree to do exactly as I say? Will you swear that if Sanguinet's throat is within your grasp and I give you a no, you will obey me?"

Mitchell stared down at him. His taut body relaxed. He laughed. "Like hell!"

Diccon leaned back again. "Goodbye. And good luck." But as Mitchell strolled to the door, he called slyly, "Pray tell me before you depart, sir. Where do you mean to search? La Mancha?"

Gritting his teeth, Mutchell flung around. And the mockery on the lean face of this strange man banished his own scowl abruptly. "Why, you slippery devil," he said in belated comprehension. "You *know* where he is!" He stalked back to stand facing Diccon once more. *"That's* why you called together the few men you trusted, all victims of the Sanguinets, all intent on their destruction no matter what the cost! You did not come asking us to search them out, but to go in there and fight! Only you are too damned devious to say it straight out!"

"Nonsense. A handful against hundreds? I cannot afford such heroics, Redmond. Mine is the meaner task. To spy and creep and learn, so that England may be forewarned — if only she will listen! — and gallant heroes such as yourself can later charge in to glory."

There was bitterness in his voice. Watching him, Mitchell remembered some of the things Harry had told him of this man. And of Leith's story of the months Diccon had spent in Brittany inside Claude Sanguinet's fortress château, risking death every instant and knowing that few in England would care if he paid the ultimate penalty for his devotion.

"Small thanks you get for your trouble," he acknowledged slowly.

"Thanks?" Diccon's lip curled. "I want no thanks. What I need is support! But to most of the powers in Whitehall I am a fanatical gloom merchant. A glory-seeking opportunist whose fearsome dragons have been created purely for my own aggrandizement! While Claude Sanguinet — ah! What a gentle philanthropist; a confirmed Anglophile; a God-fearing, loyal, and fond friend of the Regent. A gentleman *sans reproche!* And I, a bungling idiot, so that Smollet has been forced to retreat, and even Wellington looks at me askance!" He stood and paced to glare broodingly down into the fire.

Mitchell watched him for a moment, then sat on the edge of the table and said in a subdued voice, "So you have tested me all day, have you? Well, I fear your judgement was well-founded." Diccon swung around, surprised. Mitchell admitted wryly, "You want more of me than I've the courage to give. God knows I'm willing to side you in a scrap, but if you mean to venture into Claude's camp, to masquerade as one of 'em — Lord, no! That kind of heroism is beyond my —"

"What a blasted awful thing to say," interrupted Diccon with considerable indignation. "Heroism, indeed! And if it did come down to that, I'd not be astonished to find you've more of your brother in you than I had at first —" He broke off, his head tilting, listening intently. "Ah! Here comes my word, at last!"

"So *that's* why we had to reach here tonight! I was —" And in turn Mitchell paused, his eyes widening. From the hall came a familiar voice upraised in song. A tenor voice growing louder until the door was flung open and the song died away.

Antonio diLoretto bowed with a flourish and straightened, his dark eyes full of mischief as they flashed from Mitchell's astonishment to Diccon's scowl.

"Tonio!" exclaimed Mitchell.

"It's past time," grunted Diccon.

"I am here," proclaimed diLoretto, redundantly.

"You're a blasted spy!" cried Mitchell with justifiable wrath. "For nigh two years I've paid you to be loyal to me, while all the time you worked for" — he gestured towards Diccon — "*him!*"

"Ah, but, signor, have I not-a serve-a you well? Am I not-a loving you like the brother? Did I not —"

"You're late," Diccon interpolated sharply.

DiLoretto came into the room and closed the door, then removed his cloak. "I was detained," he said with a shrug.

The left sleeve of his shirt was ripped and darkly stained, the tear revealing a crude bandage around his forearm.

"Is it bad?" asked Mitchell, stepping forward quickly.

"Were you followed?" Diccon rasped, his eyes darting to the door.

"Me?" protested diLoretto. "I am the eel, the shadow! They do not-a see even what is the way I go!"

Pulling up a chair for his valet, Mitchell

167

observed, "Someone saw the eel long enough to inflict that."

"A chance shot at the night. This, she is-a nothing! Less-a than nothing!"

Impatient, Diccon demanded, "Then give me *something*. Was I right?"

"Major de-Conn, I bow! I am all of admiration. You are —"

"For God's sake," roared Diccon. *"Was I right?"*

"Yes," said diLoretto gravely.

Diccon breathed a gratified sigh.

"And-a yet again," diLoretto went on with a flourish, "no!"

Sir Harry Redmond was blessed with remarkably keen eyesight, but peering into the moonless night, he failed to discern the hole in the rutted lane and swore as he stumbled and went to his knees. Following close behind, Bolster almost cannoned into him and exclaimed with a breathless laugh, "I s-say, old tulip, if you're that t-tired, you'd best mount up again."

From out of the gloom, Devenish called cheerily, "Poor advice, your lording; farther to fall. Tris? Are you still amongst us? Do you know where we are?"

"I'm here, Dev. And unless I mistake it, we're a shade west of Folkestone. There's a fine old posting house ahead we shall have to have a look at. It would never do for us to pass our quarry in the dark."

"Small chance of that," muttered the Reverend, surreptitiously clinging to the tail of his nephew's mount. "I'd never fancied one rode to the rescue at this dashing crawl!"

"We're moving," Leith pointed out. "Which is likely more than Sanguinet's people are doing. You know the legend of the tortoise and the hare, sir."

"Quiet!" cried Sir Harry sharply, and, still kneeling, bowed forward.

"What the devil's he doing?" hissed Devenish, peering down at the baronet.

"P-praying, I think," Bolster whispered.

Redmond sprang up. "Don't be an ass, Jerry! Leith, there's a heavy vehicle coming up behind us. A dray, perhaps. Though I'd not have thought they'd move produce at this hour of a moonless night."

"Nor I." Low-voiced, Leith called, "Gentlemen, I suspect we've dawdled faster than we knew. Let's give a look at this nocturnal traveller."

They separated, Redmond and his uncle moving to the left side of the road, Devenish and Bolster to the right, and Leith sitting his horse squarely in the middle.

Soon, they could hear the slow beat of many hooves, the snorting of nervous horses and the grind and creak of wheels. A dark, moving mass loomed against the night sky.

"Halt!" commanded Leith ringingly, adding a fallacious, "In the King's name!"

"Mon Dieu!" a man screamed. *"En avant! En avant!"*

A whip cracked. Neighing in panic, the coach horses plunged forward.

Sir Harry raised his pistol and a stab of flame sliced the darkness, the explosion deafening. All then was confusion. The Frenchman on the box was shouting; the terrified horses screamed and plunged; the right wheeler got one leg over the trace; the left leader collided with his partner; the carriage rocked crazily. A shotgun blast added to the din.

Devenish flung himself recklessly at the side of the coach, clambered up, and grappled with a shadowy individual who ripped out ferocious Gallic oaths even as he beat madly at his attacker. On the other side of the vehicle, Bolster wrenched open the door and plunged inside. Leith dismounted and grasped the ribbons, attempting to quiet the terrified team. Coming up beside the box, the Reverend Langridge levelled an enormous and quite inoperable blunderbuss. "Do you surrender?" he howled.

"Mais oui! Mais oui! Do not fire, monsieur, *s'il vous plaît* — do not!"

Devenish, whose flying fist had connected to good effect, panted, "This one will give us no trouble, sir. Tris, throw me your tinderbox and we'll have a little light here."

Leith went over and handed up his box, and Devenish lit one of the lamps.

A chaotic scene was revealed. The coach horses were in a hopeless tangle; the guard sagged, unconscious, over the side of the box; the driver cringed, whimpering before the menace of Langridge's blunderbuss.

"Jeremy," Leith called, "is Charity all right?"

Bolster stuck his golden head out of the wide-flung door. "Fraid we've made a, er, slight error," he said in a decidedly hollow voice. "Charity ain't here. *This* coach really *is* empty!"

"Oh, God!" Leith groaned. "We've been duped, then. That damned rogue has had us following a decoy coach!"

Sir Harry muttered sombrely, "God help poor little Miss Strand. We've lost her!"

Far beyond the dark depths of sleep, someone was calling, "Miss! Miss! Wake up!" Charity was warm and snug, and the effort to respond was great, but respond she must, and somehow she forced her eyes open and blinked stupidly around the dim and unfamilar room.

A plump woman, her features indistinguishable, was bending over the bed, tugging at her shoulder. "Your brother and your French cousin be waiting," imparted this shadowy individual. "They axed me to wake ye. Be ye 'wake now, miss?" The heavy hand commenced the tugging again, and Charity pulled away, saying drowsily that she was indeed awake and where in the world was Agatha?

The tugging ceased. The woman deposited a

candle on a rickety chest of drawers. "Fit for Bedlam, poor lass," she muttered under her breath. "Just like the genelmens said." She turned back to the bed. "Now you please to wake up, miss. I'll fetch a pitcher of hot water directly."

She was gone when Charity fought her way out of the morass of the feather bed and tried dully to recall the events of the previous day. They had reached this lonely inn at nightfall when she was so exhausted by the long hours of rattling about in the great coach that she had barely been able to totter into the old building. She had a dim memory of Jean-Paul engaging in a murmurous conversation with a little round-eyed fat man who had peered at her in obvious unease and remonstrated until the Frenchman brought out his purse. This civilized act had apparently lulled the host's fears, and she had been ushered upstairs by all three men and shown into a tiny, low-roofed chamber under the eaves. It was the oddest thing that she had been unable to talk to the innkeeper. Every time she tried to speak, her voice was suspended and the words would not come. The door had been slammed shut, and a key turned in the lock. Rushing over to the window, she at once discovered why this particular room had been chosen. The window frames had been painted with a too generous hand so that there was no way to force the windows open. Wearily, Charity had unfastened her cloak, released a yawning kitten and, staying only to remove her gown and hang it on a convenient hook, had crawled into bed.

She had a vague recollection of a woman appearing beside the bed, with a glass of warm milk and a sandwich of cold roast beef. And there had been something do with Little Patches. She sat up, holding her head which ached dully and seemed vexingly wooden. . . .

A touch aroused her. The buxom woman was again beside her, a kind smile upon her broad, rosy-cheeked face. "Come along, poor creature," she said in that soft country accent. "Sad it is to see ye still so sick and wan. Your genelmens has paid me handsome to care for ye, and so I will. Only look, ma'am, I do have bringed your little friend." She held up Little Patches, and the kitten struggled free and leapt onto the bed to butt and purr and generally greet a familiar human.

Charity stroked her and fought to speak. It was a tremendous task. She said indistinctly, "You must . . . help. I — I am pris'ner. Please — help —"

"There, there, poor soul." The woman stroked her hair gently. "Such a sweet face. What a pity. What a pity. Come, me dearie, and let Polly just wash you a little bit."

So Charity was washed and dressed. She lowered her head obediently when asked to do so, and a hairbrush was applied to her thick

173

hair with brisk strokes. She was sitting at a table beside the window, drinking tea and eating some toast and strawberry jam. The woman was talking about Little Patches and how the kitten had gobbled up the leftover fish last night. "Oh, but she's a saucy little sprat of a cat. Polly would like to keep her, yes, she would, surely."

And there was something she must say. Something very important. . . . "Polly . . . brother will — come. Justin . . . tell him . . . tell him . . . ."

"Yes, for sure I will, my dearie dear. Only he do be downstairs, this very minute. Waiting for ye. And so grieving and sad he scarce can speak, poor soul. And no wonder." A cloak was draped about Charity. Someone was holding her arm. It was Clem — not Justin. And Jean-Paul was arguing with the kind-hearted Polly.

"No, but it *do* be her cat, sir. I beg ye will not take it from the poor lass, so fond of it as she is. I'll have the boy put a box and earth in your carriage . . . no trouble. . . ."

They were in a cold, fresh dawn. The great black coach waited like the chariot of death.

Throwing off her strange lethargy, Charity tore from Clem's grasp and ran back to Polly, who watched, wringing her apron in distress.

"Help — help!" she cried frantically. "Do not let them . . . take . . . ."

Jean-Paul said in a soothing voice, "No, no, dear Mary. We shall not take your little friend.

You shall keep the cat." His arm slipped about Charity's shoulders, his fingers gripping cruelly even as he said a loving, "Dear lady, your poor brother waits to care for you." He turned her, shaking his head helplessly at Polly as Charity screamed shrilly. And under his breath, he grated, "Into the coach you go, madame. And — *vite!*"

She was inside the coach again, her shoulder feeling bruised and sore and her head spinning so. She leaned back against the squabs. Far, far off, she heard Clem grumbling, ". . . should have thrown the dratted creature at the fat mort! A rare sauce she's got, saddling us with one of her unwanted mogs!"

"Situation is," explained Jean-Paul patiently, "that the fat one has now a kind heart for us. Not a suspicious heart. This rough ground we travel must be got over as light as may be. Besides, this is a cat of many colours. I find it pleasing."

"You would," grunted Clem, disgusted.

Charity fell asleep.

It seemed that she dwelt in a strange void, midway between sleep and waking, in which she was aware of what took place around her, but only in a remote fashion. A portion of her mind told her that she was drugged, but she supposed they must not have dared give her too strong a dose, so that instead of being completely unconscious, she drifted in this trancelike state. The journey went on interminably, but the carriage was no longer stuffy, because the screens had been rolled up. She knew when, at some time in the later afternoon, the outriders left them, and she realized this would confuse the men who followed, for no longer was the coach escorted, nor did it appear to contain only one passenger. The men who guarded her were less antagonistic. Jean-Paul amused himself in playing with Little Patches, and even Clem chuckled occasionally and joined in entertaining the little animal.

Quite suddenly, Charity was in a bedchamber, a chambermaid caring for her. A tray was brought to her, but she was not hungry and could only eat a few mouthfuls despite the maid's urging. She tried to talk to the girl, but was unable to form the words, and when she tried to write, her eyes refused to focus and the pen wavered erratically over the page.

She was back in the coach again, and the wheels went on and on until they spun her into sleep. This time, for what seemed an eternity. . . .

She awoke to find the carriage rocking so violently that it seemed they must overturn. Her head ached, and her mouth was dry as dust, but she could see clearly, and her mind seemed less clouded. She was bathed in a scarlet glow, which was peculiar because it could not be sunset again — unless she had slept all night and throughout the following day. They must have made a bed for her on one of the seats, for she lay full-length. The blanket thrown over her was warm, but it smelled musty, and the wool was rough, scratching against her chin. There was a familiar scent in her nostrils; a frightening scent. She threw back the blanket, sat up, and yelped as she struck her head on the roof. Only it was not the roof. And she was no longer in the carriage.

Fear spurring her, she stood and ran to the window. A round window. And her bed was a bunk, with another over it, from which a tiny arm stretched out while a pink mouth voiced a scratchy greeting.

Charity stood on tiptoe and looked out the porthole. A grey tumbling sea stretched away to the dim horizon. Even as she watched, the vessel rolled into a deep trough and the waves loomed up until they blotted out the crimson sky.

Despair overcame her. She sank down the wooden side until she knelt huddled on the floor. The carriage must have turned about while she slept. She was on her way to Brittany after all. And once she was in that terrible château she was doomed. If Tristram or Justin or Dev should come, it would be to their deaths, for Claude would be ready and waiting.

There was no hope now. No hope at all. She bowed her head into her hands and wept.

Chapter Nine

"I'm getting old, Redmond," said Diccon gloomily, watching diLoretto, who stood in the rainy yard, haggling with the ostler of the Jolly Tar tavern. "Why did I not think of Ireland? God knows it's logical enough. It should have been one of the first places I'd guess, yet it never so much as occurred to me."

Mitchell rested his shoulders against the wall of the inn and finished the ale in his tankard. They had been in the saddle since dawn, most of that time spent in a misting drizzle. They'd traversed Oxfordshire, progressing damply through the beauties of the Cotswolds, and now faced a chill and rainy afternoon with many miles still before them. Diccon had hoped to be in the Black Country by now, but for reasons best known to himself, he had twice detoured, first far to the east, and then doubling back southwards again, before continuing to this quiet inn near Stratford-on-Avon.

"You still don't know it's Ireland," Mitchell pointed out. "All Tonio discovered was that Sanguinet's people have been spotted on the docks at Birkenhead. Which could mean anything." He glanced at the intelligence officer curiously. "How was he able to find out that much, by the by?"

He half expected a polite evasion. Diccon surprised him. "One of my most promising men is a young gypsy. Lucian St. Clair sent him to me, and he's proved to be invaluable. His people know more of what transpires on moonlit nights on unfrequented byways and secluded coves than our fellows at Bow Street will ever know. And as you've already seen, they provide me with an efficient network of eyes, ears, and sometimes help. I'd seen Daniel, my gypsy, on my interrupted search in Essex. Dan was on the trail of one of Claude's lieutenants. A man whose very presence in England indicates that Claude is almost ready. Daniel was sure he would have news for me very soon, so before you and I left Sussex, I sent Tonio to seek him out and report to me at Abingdon. You, ah, may have noticed he was missing."

"Damned rogue! I had to pack my own saddlebags. But how did he know where to find this Daniel?"

"There's an ancient church in Little Snoring at the edge of the Ashdown Forest. It has a leper's window that was, I believe, put to much use during the Jacobite Rebellion. It has been used by the Folk for many years, and a note left in that window reaches Daniel in jig time."

"I see. You've lots of tricks up your sleeve. And Tonio?"

"Has been indebted to me for some time. I arranged for your meeting with him, knowing you harboured a grudge against the Sanguinets and that sooner or later you'd come to grips with them. Had you stirred up anything interesting, Tonio would have reported it to me at once."

After a pause, Mitchell asked, "And you believe Claude will make his move this year?"

"This *year?* Good God, Redmond! Mine has not been a life free from hazard. I've several old wounds that make riding unpleasant in rainy weather, and I haul a lead ball in my back that can be deuced annoying in the face of sustained travel. Do you think I'd essay this mad dash had we a half-year to spare?"

"Considering I number one-third of your army," said Mitchell with dry sarcasm, "I've not been kept well informed, to put it mildly!"

Diccon glanced at him, a sudden twinkle in his eyes. "Very well, General. I think our Claude means to strike within the month."

"My God!" Mitchell pushed his shoulders from the wall and regarded his companion in horror.

Diccon nodded. "You carry identification papers, I presume? Letters, calling cards, that sort of thing?"

"Yes. Of course. Why?"

"Get rid of 'em. Anything that might identify you."

Staring at him, Mitchell said slowly, "You think they're after us?"

"Sanguinet has eyes everywhere. I changed my appearnace, but . . ." Diccon paused and went on with obvious reluctance, "If anything should chance to go awry, I carry a small notebook in a special inner pocket under my left arm. It contains much of what I already know, and a good deal that I suspect. If I should be downed, that book *must* reach Smollet, or failing him — Wellington." He looked up, met two steady grey eyes, and said, "It is quite vital, or I would not ask you."

"I'm very sure of *that,*" said Mitchell, rather ruefully.

Almost, Diccon smiled. "I may rely on you, then?"

"I'll do my damnedest," said Mitchell Redmond.

The rain continued. In late afternoon they caught a blurred glimpse of the seven-hundred-year-old might of Kenilworth Castle, then swung west, keeping to the wooded country and avoiding the plateau where perched old Birmingham, once so famous for its fine swordsmiths and cutlers and now wreathed in smoke and grime and frenetic with the hurry and bustle that machines had brought. Heading north again through the Black Country, Mitchell was so tight-lipped and silent that diLoretto enquired anxiously if his back was troubling him again. But it was the desecration of these once lovely heaths and moors that troubled him, and he answered rather savagely that there were worse things in life than a clean knife cut.

Soon, drifting mists combined with gathering darkness to make further travel impossible. They stopped at a cosy wayside inn and bespoke two rooms. An excellent supper, topped off by a board of Cheshire's famous cheeses sent Mitchell up to bed so drowsy that he fell asleep on top of the eiderdown. DiLoretto pulled off his boots and threw a blanket over him, and he did not stir until Diccon shook him awake in a gloomy dawn, and they were off again.

Wolverhampton was smoky and depressing, and although Mitchell was impressed by Abraham Darby's magnificent iron bridge across the River Severn that had dazzled England almost four decades ago, he was very glad when they left the Black Country and came again to clean streams and pure green fields.

In late afternoon the sun came out to illumine Shropshire's emerald hills and they rode past farms nestling gently in their rich valleys; past chuckling rivers and quiet pools, making good progress until the mists came up again, impeding both the view and their speed. They had to pick their way through the shrouded beauties of Cheshire, past heaths and desolate moorlands where hills loomed unexpectedly, and they would come without warning upon ancient towns and hamlets enriched by their wealth of black and white half-timbered houses.

They left the mist behind and at sunset were approaching the fine old walled city of Chester, nestled in the bend of the River Dee. Here they encountered happy crowds and chaos, for it was time for the annual race meeting down on the Roodee, a level tract of land along the river, where all Cheshire, Staffordshire, and Shropshire seemed bound to come together to attend the races. The roads were clogged by a merry, jostling throng, who had bespoken the last bed and bench at every inn, tavern, and posting house for miles around. Even diLoretto could find no heart to sing after a long search confirmed there was not a room to be had. They were able to get some food and to find fresh mounts, and then reluctantly pressed on.

It was past ten o'clock when the horses slowed. Mitchell, bowed forward half asleep over the pommel, straightened, yawned, and glanced at Diccon. The tall man was turning back to peer along the lane they travelled, and there was that in his attitude that instantly brought Mitchell to full awareness. "What's to do?" he asked.

"Half a dozen horses following. I hoped we'd lost 'em, but they're coming up fast."

Mitchell gave the cuffs of his gauntlets a tug. "Forewarned," he said.

Diccon knew with an uneasy assessment of

the odds that they were all very tired, and it would be an uneven fight, for diLoretto, however willing, was no swordsman. The smell of the sea tinged the air, and the new moon, a faint sliver of palest gold in the sky, lit the heavens just sufficiently to reveal a strange distant forest lifting bare thin arms against the night. Masts. He said grimly, "They mean to stop us before we take ship. Hasten!"

They drove home their spurs and were away in a burst of speed. And, at once, from behind came an answering thunder of hooves in hot pursuit.

The winding lane they followed was shut in on both sides by hedgerows and was lonely and deserted at this hour, but two or three miles ahead was the Mersey, and shipping knew no light or dark. There would be loadings and offloadings, and too many men about for Sanguinet's bullies to dare attack. It soon became evident, however, that they would be overtaken long before they reached the estuary. The hacks they'd found had been far from prime, but the best available; their pursuers had evidently fared better. They were gaining steadily so that soon the creak and jingle of harness could be heard in addition to those relentlessly beating hooves. A shot rang out, then another, the balls whistling unpleasantly close. To add to their woes, the moon seemed to be brightening and there was water everywhere now, the light reflecting from river, mere, and marshland. The lane straightened ahead. Soon they would be in open country with not even the occasional hedgerows to hinder the aim of their pursuers. "We'll be picked off like clay pigeons," Mitchell thought grimly.

The river saved them, offering deep banks and a bridge that spanned the hurrying waters. It was a narrow, humpbacked structure with low sandstone walls; a place where three determined men might stand a chance against many. Mitchell pointed urgently, and Diccon nodded. "Right. It's there or a spot of their choosing. God forbid!"

They galloped hard until they reached the bridge, then drew up sharply. The hacks reared and plunged. Mitchell dismounted in a smooth leap. Diccon staggered but, recovering his balance, slapped his hat under the noses of their scared horses so that the animals panicked and ran back the way they had come.

The onrush of the men following was halted, confusion reigning as the riderless hacks careened in amongst them. Mitchell raced up the bridge a short way, drew his pistol and dropped to one knee in the deeper shadow of the wall. Taking the opposite side, Diccon muttered, "Damn! There are more than I'd thought! Make your shot count, friend. With luck we'll get a couple of the bastards! Then it will be fists — or knives."

Mitchell said belatedly, "Tonio! Where in the devil —"

There was no time for more. In a thundering charge, the assassins came at them. Mitchell took careful aim. His ears rang to the roar of Diccon's pistol, followed by a faint cry. A brilliant glare dazzled him as another shot rang out. He held his own fire until five dark figures were almost upon them. Even as he pulled the trigger someone else fired. Mitchell heard an odd little grunt from Diccon. Then they were engaged in hand-to-hand combat and it was too close for any more shots, even if any of their assailants still had loaded pistols.

The big man confronting Mitchell sent steel flashing at his throat. He gripped the barrel of his pistol and flailed out with it, sending the dagger spinning, but the attacker swung up his other fist and Mitchell was staggered by a blow he was only partially able to deflect. He struck out again with his impromptu club, felt it crunch home, and the big man disappeared. The bridge became an eddying maelstrom of desperate conflict; of thudding blows, hard-drawn breaths, hoarse curses, and the shift and sway of dim-seen forms battling in the elemental need to kill or be killed. Driving home a solid right to the jaw of one bully, Mitchell was barely in time to duck from a cudgel that would have brained him had it landed. He slammed his pistol butt under someone's ribs, and a cry was torn from an unseen throat. Again, steel darted at him. He saw the gleam of it and leapt madly to the side. A dark shape rushed him, a heavy blow dazed him, but he managed to retain sufficient of his wits to kick out as someone blundered past. His boot struck hard, and a diminishing wail was followed by a splash and much noisy thrashing about. Dizzied and gasping for breath, he clutched the wall. A bubbling scream rang out behind him, and someone else went down. Peering about, wondering why no more attacks came, he realized in dazed disbelief that, so quickly, it was all over.

"Diccon . . . ?" he panted, gingerly investigating a throbbing contusion on the side of his head.

"H-here," wheezed Diccon.

"Signor . . . Mish-hell . . ."

Responding at once to that woeful cry, Mitchell ran down the bridge, vaulting over the sprawled forms of downed men, until he saw the little Italian crumpled in the shadow of the wall.

"Tonio! Are you badly hurt?"

"I fall from . . . my stupid horse," wailed the valet. "Mama mia! My dear little . . . head!"

"Rest for a minute." Some instinct warning him, Mitchell turned back.

Diccon was sagging to his knees. Even as Mitchell raced to him, he sank onto his face.

"Oh, gad!" Kneeling beside that lax form,

Mitchell turned him gently. He could see the wetness of blood on the jacket and groped for his handkerchief. "Let me —" Diccon's hand was staying him. From the direction of the Mersey he could hear horses, coming fast.

Diccon whispered, "Notebook. You . . . promised. Smollet. Go! Before —" The next word faded into a long sigh, and the tall man who had devoted so many thankless years to his country lay very still.

Stunned, Mitchell stared down at him, then started to search for a heartbeat, just in case. But the sharp ring of an ironshod hoof against cobblestones was very close, and he dared wait no longer. Groping frantically, he found at last the concealed pocket and retrieved a small, battered, leather-bound book. He thrust it into his boot and sprang to his feet.

Someone was behind him. The sharp edge of a dagger bit into his throat just below his right ear. "Don't move," a man growled, "or —" Mitchell sprang away, only to check as something rammed hard into his back. A low, jeering voice urged, "Go on, me bucko. Hop abaht again, why don'tcha? Up wi' yer mauleys."

Fuming, Mitchell raised both hands slightly, and stood motionless.

There were three of them; the two who had caught him and who were now very interested in Diccon's limp form, and another rider coming up at a less rapid pace.

"By gorm! It's that there damned cove from

188

Bow Street!" exclaimed the larger of them, bending low. "So Slope got him!"

"Devil he did!" said Mitchell, his mind racing. "*I* got him."

"Liar!" The gun was jabbed savagely into his back again. "You wasn't with Slope! You're a flash cull if ever I heard one."

"And sent from London," said Mitchell. "Slope was with *me*, fellow! Not I with him. Had I not told him where Diccon would go, the slowtop would have made mice feet of the whole."

The big man, kneeling beside Diccon, looked up. "Search him," he said. "If he don't like it, brain him first."

Mitchell submitted, thankful that he'd obeyed Diccon's edict and discarded anything that might have identified him.

"Nothing," said the man who'd rifled his pockets. "Whatever he is, he's a downy cove."

The big man clambered to his feet and came over to stand facing Mitchell. "Where's his book?" he demanded aggressively. "If the Frenchy sent you, you know what I mean."

"I know. And I'm to give it to Claude. Not to you." He flung himself aside as the ruffian came at him. The man behind him fired in the same instant that Mitchell struck the pistol upward.

"Perce, you stupid damned dog's arse!" howled the big man. "You near blowed *my* head orf!"

Perce began to stammer frantic excuses.

The last rider was walking his horse up the bridge. Mitchell, praying his desperate ruse would succeed, said coldly, "Monseigneur needs all the good men he can find." He turned to the unhappy Perce and, cutting through his babbling, commanded, "You there, go down and see if Slope is alive. And be quick about it unless you've a fancy for the nubbing cheat!"

His brief acquaintanceship with a pickpocket paid dividends. That a "flash cull" knew cant seemed to reassure these men. Grumbling, but grateful for a chance to escape his companion's justifiable wrath, Perce stuck the pistol in his belt and went off to inspect the casualties.

The third man reined up. He was a thickset individual with a deep growl of a voice. "That you, Billy?"

The big man acknowledge it was, and when the mounted man asked, "Is it done?" he gestured towards Diccon. "The runner's done fer, Beach."

"Is he! His royalty'll be pleased for once! You get his book?"

Billy jerked his shaggy head to Mitchell. "He did. He was with Slope. Says he's from London."

Beach stared at Mitchell, and snapped his fingers. "Give it here."

"Not likely," said Mitchell. Beach swore and started his horse forward. "I've orders to hand it to Monseigneur and no one else," said

190

Mitchell. "Of course, if you mean to counter-mand my orders, Beach . . ."

The newcomer hesitated. "Damned Quality," he muttered. "Wouldn't trust one so far as I could throw him."

"Sanguinet would be pleased to hear that," Mitchell observed jeeringly.

"I 'spect you *love* the Frenchy, eh?" said Billy. "I 'spect —"

"Shut yer jaw," contributed Beach. "He's likely from the Admiral. Just his stamp, he is." He spat contemptuously.

"Slope's done fer," called the small Perce.

"And so will we be if we stand here jawing much longer," said Mitchell boldly, wondering which admiral was involved in this ugly plot.

There was a brief pause.

Billy said dubiously, "Wotcha think, Beach? This 'ere cove wouldn't want to go if he wasn't in on it."

"Might," Beach argued, glowering at Mitchell. "If he was a government spy. And Monseigneur wouldn't like *that*."

Billy chuckled. "I dunno. The Frenchy'd give him to Gerard. *He'd* have a jolly time getting the truth outta him."

"What's your name, Mr. Flash Cove?" asked Beach roughly.

"Rivers," said Mitchell, grasping at the first thought that offered.

"All right," Beach said. "Come on, then. It's your funeral if you're lying."

"What about Fritch?" called Perce. "He's alive, I think. And these others might —"

Beach turned his horse impatiently. "Leave 'em be. They knew the risks when they hired on. Bring up a couple of them nags. And quick. There's a wagon coming."

In the cold light of dawn, Mitchell stepped onto the gangplank of a sleek schooner tied up at the Birkenhead docks. Glancing inland, he wondered if Tonio had been able to get help for Diccon, or if he would send word to the gypsy, Daniel. At least in that way someone would know what had happened. His attention turned to the men who watched from the rail. A hard-faced lot. Rogues, by the look of them; soldiers of fortune with not a *soupçon* of patriotism, who would give him short shrift if he was unmasked, but fortunately, containing among them not one familiar countenance. If he survived this journey, his prospects were very slim. He had not met Claude Sanguinet, but he had been to the great château in Dinan; he had fought a duel with Guy Sanguinet — purely by accident, because he'd mistaken the silly fellow for Claude — and Claude's lieutenant, Gerard, had good cause to remember him.

He had started out with the simple, straightforward goal of facing Claude Sanguinet across twenty yards of turf and doing his level best to rid the world of the obscenity. And now look at the complicated bumblebroth he'd got himself into. "I'm ripe for Bedlam, that's what it is," he thought, his heart sinking. But Diccon's words echoed in his ears, "I may rely on you?" and he went on up the gangplank.

Despite her apparent frailty, Charity was a good sailor, and even when they encountered bad weather on the third day out, she did not become unwell. To a degree she had been treated with consideration. A woman was allotted to attend to her needs; her food was excellently cooked and served, and for the most part she was spoken to with civility. The servant, however, was a surly creature named Ella, and Charity summoned her as seldom as was possible, fearing that with too easy familiarity her true identity might soon be betrayed. A trunkful of clothes had been placed in her cabin, and she lost no time in selecting a long shawl and binding it daily about her middle. Since the garments, having been obviously purchased for Rachel's more bountiful figure, were slightly large on herself, the resultant extra fullness of the skirts was a godsend, and all in all, she judged the effect believable.

Her initial debilitating despair had eased somewhat. At least during the hours of daylight she was able to stay relatively calm, knowing that Claude was not on board and that so long as she was on this voyage she was safe from him. Each night she knelt beside her bunk and whispered fervent prayers for rescue, but when she lay staring wide-eyed into the darkness she felt alone and small and afraid, and the demons of imagination conjured up images so horrible that her trust in a merciful providence would waver, and she would tremble and weep until Little Patches ran up the bed and tried in her small way to be of comfort.

The kitten was Charity's one link with her happy life in Sussex. More than that, she became the means of providing an unexpected champion. Charity was permitted to take a stroll around the decks, morning and afternoon. It was evident that her captors were afraid she might try to kill herself by jumping overboard, and always a guard accompanied her on these excursions. On the first morning after their sailing, the guard was the surly Clem, who spoke not a word, but looked as though he had rather be eating ground glass than spending his time in such fashion. That afternoon she had a new companion; a sturdily built youth of rather unprepossessing appearance in that he had no eyebrows and his hair was a flaming red that did not seem to match his rather sallow skin and hard dark eyes. Charity was struck by the notion that she had seen him somewhere before and under different circumstances. He seemed a little less hostile than Clem, but when she questioned him, he shrugged and refused to answer. She was mildly surprised that when they returned he had the courtesy to help her over the step of her cabin door, but when she thanked him he only muttered a gruff, "Ain't no need," and stamped away.

Little Patches had been provided with a box of earth for her personal use and seemed to adapt quite easily to her new surroundings. Next morning, Charity tied a ribbon around the kitten's neck and took her along when she was allowed to walk out. Once again, the red-haired youth was her escort. His eyes lit up when he saw the kitten, and he begged, rather gruffly, to be allowed to hold her. Charity withdrew that privilege, and the youth sulked and said, "Much I care, lady." But she knew that he watched the kitten constantly, and when Little Patches took exception to her leash and went into a mighty acrobatic feat, trying to climb up it, the boy laughed hilariously.

On her next excursion, Charity allowed herself to be persuaded into letting him take charge of her pet. The boy was overjoyed, and Charity's walk was considerably extended so that he could play with the kitten. By cautious questioning, Charity learned that his name was Lion, and that he haled from London, where he had been employed by a "gentry cove." They began to exchange comments on the kitten's antics, and soon a tenuous friendship had sprung up between them. Charity made not the slightest attempt to enlist his aid, however. The time for that was not yet. But when he showed her into her cabin late in the afternoon, she said with a wistful smile, "Thank you, Lion."

"Here's your tiger, ma'am," he said, grinning as he thrust Little Patches at her.

The kitten decided his strong hand was a mortal foe, and pedalled furiously at his arm with her tiny back legs.

"Oh no!" exclaimed Charity. "Do not let her hurt you!"

He ruffled Little Patches' head playfully. "Never you mind, Mrs. Leith. She wouldn't hurt me, would you, fleabait?"

Charity murmured, "Lion — if . . . if anything happens to me, I want you to have her."

Stark horror came into his face. Without a word, he backed away, then hurried off. But after that, she caught him watching her from time to time, a troubled expression on his face, and once, when a member of the crew uttered a crude remark as they passed, Lion turned on the man in a fury, snarling that he'd best mind his mouth. A tiny flicker of hope lightened Charity's heavy heart.

It was from Lion that she eventually learned their destination. Two days after they sailed, her straining eyes had glimpsed another coastline, but the following morning it was out of sight. They were becalmed and progress was minimal, but even so France's coast should have been visible and Charity murmured a puzzled, "Why ever is it taking so long? Surely we should have been off Brittany long ago?"

"Brittany?" scoffed the boy with the lofty authority of youth. "Cor, ma'am, we ain't heading south. I'd a' thought even a landlubber'd know we was heading nor'west."

"Oh dear," she said innocently, "I know so little of such things. Can you read the stars and navigate, Lion?"

He declared that he was not so bad at such stuff, and regarding him with patent admiration, she sighed, "So we are bound for Ireland. You see, I *do* know something of what lies to the northwest."

He laughed and fell into her small trap. "Not no more it don't, Mrs. Leith. We left Ireland off our stern yesterday, so we did."

"Oh, Lion, never say we are to sail all the way to the Americas?"

His eyes kindling, he exclaimed, "Cor, but I'd like that I would! But we'd need a sight more food an' stuff than we got on this old tub!" He glanced around the deck and leaned a little closer. "I dunno as I'm s'posed to tell."

"I won't breath a word — I swear it."

Lion made a show of playing with Little Patches and murmured, "The Hebrew-didies, ma'am. That's where we're bound fer. And you know what? That there Frenchy's put a lot of lettuce in them four ugly old islands. But if *I* was rich as Golden Ball and could go anywhere what I'd like, I'd stick them Hebrew-didies right up at the top o' my list of places what I never want to see again!"

At this point they were approaching a little knot of sailors busily engaged with ropes and tackle, and the boy said no more. The information he had imparted, however, appalled Charity. Returning to her cabin she sat on her bunk, plunged into despair. The Hebrides? What on earth had possessed Claude to choose so remote and inaccessible a location? But of course that was precisely why he *had* chosen it. She thought achingly of her loved ones, so far away. Even dear Tristram could have no possibly inkling that Sanguinet was ensconced in such an unlikely spot. "I shall never see you again, my darlings," she whispered, in an agony of grief. "I shall not see you, or my dear England, ever again. . . ." And she wept until she was exhausted and fell into a deep sleep.

The following night, she was disturbed several times by the violent plunges of the vessel. Lion had told her that afternoon that the glass was falling, and at dark the sky had been gloomy and overcast. At dawn she awoke to the sound of a crash, and starting up in fright, she saw that the cabin was tilting at an impossible angle. From outside came shouts, the howling of a mighty wind, the creaking of protesting timbers, and the snapping of sail. Staggering to the porthole, she peered out. The morning sky was a boil of dark, angry clouds that, even as she watched, began to be blotted out by sheeting rain, and the sea that had been so deceptively quiet yesterday had become rank upon rank of mountainous waves. It took all her strength to return to her bunk. She huddled there, alone and terrified as the storm raged on, wondering if this was to be the final chapter of her uneven life, and if Claude was to be cheated of his revenge after all.

Hour after hour crept past, and still the stately ship climbed the soaring waves, hung breathlessly at the peak, then dropped sickeningly into the next deep trough. The rending crash of a snapping mast sent Charity to her knees beside the bunk, fearing that this was the end indeed, but despite the chaos that raged beyond her small cabin, they contrived to remain afloat.

She was sitting braced in a corner of the heaving floor, a blanket wrapped around her and Little Patches trembling in her lap, when the door flew open and Lion swayed in the aperture, then came in with a rush, fighting to keep a tray of crockery from tumbling.

"Hey, here's a proper turn-up, eh, missus?" he cried cherrily. "So you ain't sick! Good fer you. Most of the other passengers is so green as grass, and a lot o' the crew as well. I brung some tea and cakes, but you'll have to go careful or you'll get it over you, 'stead of in. And here's some fish fer you, fleabait!"

He plunked the tray on the floor, then stayed to help Charity enjoy the small meal. His efforts to tempt Little Patches with the fish failed; the kitten refused to eat, although she did lap at a little dish of milk.

"Shall we be blown miles off our course, do you think?" Charity asked hopefully.

"Should've landed hours back," Lion said rather indistinctly, his mouth full of currant cake. "Captain says we can't put in to the Channel in this weather. Have to stand off, he says, and from the look of the glass," he added importantly, "it'll be several days."

He was right. Although the fury of the storm abated somewhat, the seas ran too high for the Captain to dare take his ship into harbour. And the rain was so heavy and so constant that, peer as she would, Charity could catch no glimpse of the island whereon Claude Sanguinet was no doubt waiting impatiently.

For three days they rode out the weather, while the Captain raged, the crew grumbled, the cook swore, and even Charity, dreading the next phase of her captivity, began to long for this waiting to end. Her friendship with Lion deepened during this time. Despite his lack of education, the boy had a quick intelligence and a mind hungry for knowledge. He had taught himself to read and write, and when Charity exclaimed over these accomplishments he was rather pathetically grateful and told her shyly that it was his dream to become a physician. "Much chance I got," he added, reddening in anticipation of ridicule. Inwardly astounded, she would not dream of belittling his hopes and said all she might to encourage him, writing down the titles of several books for him to read and urging that he work hard at improving his vocabulary. Instead of thanking her, he stared in silence at the list she handed him. When he did look up, his eyes held abject misery, and he left her without another word.

That night, Charity awoke to a sense of strangeness. It was quiet. The room was no longer heaving erratically. She lay in her bunk listening to the officers shouting orders, to the creaking of winches and the flapping of sail, and very soon the motion of the ship changed. They were under way again. She slipped from her blankets and ran to the port, but it was too dark to see anything, anad she went back to bed, falling at last into a troubled sleep.

Ella brought her breakfast next morning. The woman looked drawn and wan, but vindictiveness glistened in her dark eyes as she demanded that Mrs. Leith get up at once. The motion of the great ship had gentled to a lazy rocking and Charity's apprehensive enquiries were met by the grim confirmation that they were tied up to the dock, that Monseigneur was waiting, and that Mrs. Leith better look sharp.

The moment of truth had come. Involuntarily, Charity shrank. The immediate satisfaction in Ella's eyes stiffened her spine. Whatever else, she was an English lady. Her bones might be jelly and her heart thumping a tattoo, but no one must see those weaknesses. She told Ella her services were not required, waited until the sour-faced woman went grumbling off, and then ran to the port.

Had she not known this was an island, she would have thought them docked along the Thames, or the Clyde, or some such great inland waterway. Certainly not at a small island, for peer as she would, she could see only land. Directly before her eyes was a scene of frenzied activity. Cranes were swinging loads of bales and barrels onto the dock, and brawny labourers swarmed like industrious ants around the small mountains of supplies thus created, swiftly transferring the goods into waiting wagons and wains. Sailors, their meagre belongings carried in rolls over their shoulders, struggled down the gangplank, vying for space with the passengers Charity had glimpsed from time to time on the lower deck. A motley lot she had thought them, but she noticed now that they were uniformly tall, sturdily built, and aggressive, shoving the sailors aside as they disembarked, quick to raise voice or fist against any who impeded their progress. Once on land they milled about uncertainly, but a tall individual, soberly clad in black, relayed orders through an aide and soon the new arrivals were lined up neatly enough. Charity watched the dark figure of authority with sombre dread. He turned and glanced up at the ship, and she spun away from the porthole and pressed against the side, a cold perspiration bathing her whitening features.

So *Gerard* was here! Gerard, Claude's icily remorseless lieutenant who had lusted after Rachel when she arrived at Dinan as Claude's affianced bride, and who had never forgiven her for the rebuff she'd handed him. Gerard who had suffered a broken jaw when Tristram and Devenish had battled with such invincible courage to get them all safely away from that nightmarish château. . . . She closed her eyes, sick and shaking with fear for what was to come.

Because she was so terribly afraid, she took great care with her toilette, for Claude must not fancy her so disheartened she had given up all hope. She was sitting on the bunk when the knock came, and she nerved herself to meet Gerard's soulless black eyes. She had seldom been more relieved than when Lion's bright head came around the door, and she could not restrain an involuntary cry of relief.

The boy came quickly inside and closed the door behind him. To her surprise, he ignored Little Patches, who frisked about his boots, marched straight to her side, took her hands and drew her to her feet.

"I 'spect you know what I am," he said in a low, hurried fashion. "I ain't never been nothin' but gallows bait. Never had no mum or dad. I was a foundling — a love child." His lip curled. He muttered bitterly, "Some kind of love! I was sold to a sweep when I was five — a sight of love I got from him, I can tell yer! So I hopped the twig — runned orf, and got slammed in a flash house. More love — cor! They put me on the padding lay — and the dubbing lay! Thieving, ma'am. Pickpocket. And I was flogged if I did and whipped if I didn't. No one never give me nothing but a stripe or a box aside the ears. Then I tried ter prig orf a gentry cove, and he caught me. Broke me arm, but then he see I was just a nipper. He took me to a 'pothecary, and when I was better, he let me work fer him."

Her kind heart touched, Charity whispered, "Oh, poor little boy."

"A ugly customer he is," Lion went on grimly. "Got hisself all mixed up with this Frenchy. And made me —" He broke off, eyeing her uneasily. "You don't want to hear all that. Thing is, he don't beat me much and I gets fed reg'lar. So I puts up with the rest. Only . . ." He took up the kitten and stroked her soft fur absently. "I thought as they were going to keep yer to stop the Colonel from sticking his nose in. I thought they didn't mean you no harm, account o' you being in the family way. But that Frenchy on the dock" — he glanced broodingly at the porthole — "he talked to me like I was a slug. I told him I been looking arter you. And he said . . ." He put the kitten down and grabbed Charity's arms. "Don't you be scared, now. Lion ain't good fer much, but I'll see they don't hurt you. I promise. I ain't sunk so low I'd let no lady be hurt. 'Specially you." He was scarlet, and his eyes fell away bashfully. But he looked up and reiterated, "Don't be scared, mind."

The door latch was lifting. Lion snatched up Charity's bandbox. "I'll take this, ma'am," he said as Jean-Paul stuck his head inside. "You bring fleabait."

Blinking away tears, her knees shaking, Charity followed him through the door, prepared to meet her fate.

Chapter Ten

Outside, the air was bitterly cold, and Charity drew her cloak tighter about her shoulders. Clem and Jean-Paul walked along the deck on each side of her, Lion following. She saw now that the ship was tied up in a landlocked harbour, a place teeming with activity, a large yawl moored next to them, and two other vessels standing off in the channel, waiting a chance to dock. The island was quite large, as she had gathered, and looked a harsh, bleak place. Far off to the east a long range of hills lifted bare and jagged teeth against the cold sky. Northwards rose another hill, solitary and surmounted by a frowning old castle that appeared to Charity to crouch there as though gloatingly awaiting her arrival.

Jean-Paul assisted her down the gangplank, from which all other passengers had been cleared. When they reached the ground, it seemed to Charity to sway as though she were still aboard ship. A closed chaise was waiting, a groom holding the door. To her relief, it was empty. Jean-Paul handed her up, and he and Clem occupied the seat opposite. The coachman cracked his whip, and they began to edge through the noisy, bustling confusion of the dock area, coming at last to a well-kept road that wound inland.

Despite her terrible apprehensions, Charity tried to notice as much as she could of this strange place. The area they had left appeared to contain most of the major buildings, and there were many of them; large sheds and warehouses, crude houses and huts and long low buildings that, as they climbed higher, she could see were erected around a parade ground where men were drilling and where she fancied to glimpse Gerard's dark figure.

The road curved around the hill, and rows of dense, high-growing trees shut out the view of the docks. The ocean was visible now, slate-grey and frigid-looking with lines of whitecaps stretching to the misty horizon. A schooner was approaching the island, her sails being reefed in as she neared the channel. The sight of the vessel, so much smaller and sleeker than the ship that had transported her, put Charity in mind of the *Silvering Sails*. Only last year,

Justin had worked so hard to refurbish the yacht. . . . Her brother's kind, loved face drifted before her mind's eye, and tears blurred her vision.

Clem said, "Well, 'ere's your new 'ome. Ain't it a fine cottage? Proper cosy like, eh?" He laughed. Jean-Paul chuckled. Charity's gaze shot to the right.

From this elevation the castle was even larger than it had appeared earlier; a great threatening bulk against the gloomy sky. Even had she not known who dwelt there, Charity must have thought it a brooding pile, its massive walls spreading out over the brow of the hill in a low sprawl, rather than soaring up in lofty splendour like the castles she had known.

She asked in a shaking voice, "What . . . is it called?"

"It's Tordarroch Island, yer ladyship," Clem said. "And the little hovel up yonder" — he jerked his bullet head to the castle — "that there's Tor Keep. And that's what they're a-going ter do, lady, keep *you* there. At least till yer brat's born."

Jean-Paul gave him a contemptuous look, but was silent. Charity stared at Clem and wondered in a remote fashion how a tiny, innocent babe could grow up to become so bestial, so without feeling as this coarse, ignorant man. And she remembered what Lion had said of his own early years. "He could be the same," she thought sadly. "If no one rescues him from his hopeless servitude he might eventually become like this creature, lacking all compassion and humanity." She sighed and asked, "Where is my kitten, please?"

"Lion has her," said Jean-Paul. "He is upon the box, madame."

They were rattling across cobblestones. A dark shadow slid over them and with it a chill that seemed to pierce Charity's heart. They jerked to a stop. The door was swung open and the steps let down. A liveried footman bowed and handed Charity down. The bitter wind blew her skirts about. The great dark walls loomed over her. Wide steps, worn by the elements and the tread of countless feet, led up to an enormous door embellished with bands of black iron and great iron studs. To Charity it seemed the door of doom, beyond which could lie only horror, and she faltered, her wide eyes fixed upon that fateful entry.

A familiar voice grunted impatiently, "Hurry up, do, ma'am. This worthless mog's clawing me!"

Her terrified gaze flashed to meet Lion's. He was scowling ferociously, but the eye that was farthest from Clem twitched into a faint wink. Immeasurably heartened, Charity tried to stop trembling. The door opened slowly, and somehow she managed to walk across the chill yard and into the ancient frowning keep that was Claude Sanguinet's stronghold.

She entered a great hall. A fire blazed on an enormous hearth to her right, and lofty walls were beautified by fine tapestries. Several gleaming suits of armour were placed here and there, and the furnishings were antique and massive.

The footman who had admitted them passed them on to the butler, a dapper gentleman who ushered them to a broad stone staircase and thence to an upper floor and a wide hall hung with weapons and banners, the shining floors strewn with thick rugs. Tall lackeys stood about, their eyes following the little procession curiously. The butler paused outside a carven door. "You will wait, *s'il vous plaît*," he murmured, and slipped inside, closing the door behind him.

Clem muttered a profane imitation of the Frenchman, and Jean-Paul grinned. "I hear as his royalty's generous when he's pleased," Clem hissed. "We'll likely rate a fat bonus fer this job of work, mate."

Knowing Claude, Charity thought they would be far more likely to rate a thrashing, at the very least.

The butler reappeared. "Madame Leith and you" — he gestured to Jean-Paul — "are to be received. You two may go."

Clem growled resentfully, but shambled off. Still carrying the kitten, Lion followed, backing away, his gaze fixed on Charity in undisguised apprehension.

Jean-Paul took Charity's elbow. *"En avant,* madame."

He led her into a magnificent apartment, all red and gold and for the most part appointed in the same semifeudal fashion as the lower areas. Rich red velvet hung at the window embrasures; deep chairs were set about before the fire; fine tapestries and paintings softened the mighty walls. All this, Charity saw only dimly. Her attention was fixed upon the two occupants of the room. Claude Sanguinet, slender and very dark, was seated at a large, ornately carven desk near the fire, looking up at his brother. Guy, a man at least ten years his junior, with brown hair, a sturdier frame and a lighter complexion, stood beside Claude's chair, leaning back against the desk and speaking in a low, intent manner. Neither man glanced up as the newcomers entered, but the very sight of them caused Charity to feel as though the blood had frozen in her veins, and she leaned giddily upon Jean-Paul's arm.

Guy glanced at them idly. With an expression of horrified astonishment replacing his gravity, he sprang up. *"Sacré nom de Dieu!"* he gasped.

Delighted by such a violent reaction, Claude chuckled and swung his chair around. His eyes fell on Charity. He checked, as though turned to stone.

Pale with shock, Guy stammered, "Ch-Charity . . . ?" He spun to face his brother.

"For the love of God! *Now* what have you done?"

Claude came to his feet and stalked around the desk. For a man of such enormous wealth and power, he presented a disappointing appearance. He was elegantly clad, but, despite the care with which his nearly black hair had been brushed into youthful curls, it was obvious that he would not see forty again. His figure was slender, but he was neither tall nor muscular; his features were regular but lacked distinction; his complexion was inclined to be sallow; and only his eyes were noteworthy, being wide and of an unusual brilliance, although the colour, somewhere between brown and hazel, was not admired, some maintaining that Claude Sanguinet's eyes glowed red when he was angered. He was angered now, and those hot eyes deepened the terror in Charity's heart.

"*You!*" The word was a hissing whisper. His hands crooked into claws as he advanced on her. "*You!*" It was a howl this time, his face contorting with frustrated rage as he sprang forward.

Guy leapt between them. "Are you gone entirely mad?" he cried in French. "Why in heaven's name have you brought her here?"

Claude gave vent to a muffled sound somewhere between a snarl and a sob. His arm flailed out, and Guy was sent staggering. Crouching, looking up from under his brows,

Claude turned on Jean-Paul. *"Peasant!"* he cried shrilly. "How could you mistake this insipid girl for a glorious creature like Rachel Strand? Idiot! *Animal!"* He advanced on Jean-Paul, his expression so twisted, so maniacal, that Charity retreated, trembling.

Backing away also, one hand flung out protectively, Jean-Paul whimpered, "We do as we are told, monseigneur. Your spy tell us to take the lady wearing the cloak. We take the lady wearing the cloak. Monseigneur! Name of a name! The lady say nothing. I beseech you — how are we to know?"

"You . . . were . . . *paid* . . . to know!" screeched Claude, his tight clenched fists raised and quivering with passion. "Moronic dolt of a *canaille!* You were *paid* to know!"

He flung around to face Charity, but Guy again came between them.

Very softly, Claude said, "Stand aside . . . little bastard."

His fists lifting, Guy replied grimly, "Not this time."

On a marble platform in one corner of the room stood a tall marble clock; a cunningly wrought mechanical device that now shattered the tense quiet to begin its preordained salute to the hour. Doors opened on each side of its wide base, and a parade of porcelain figures began to emerge and make their jerky way from left to right to the accompaniment of a peal of merry bells.

212

Claude's narrowed, glinting eyes turned to the source of that sound. He ran to seize the massive timepiece. With astonishing strength, he raised it high above his head and turned to his brother.

Guy uttered a gasp, jerked Charity behind him, and threw up both hands prepared to defend himself against that great weight.

Face purpling, teeth bared, Claude hesitated, his enraged glare shifting to Jean-Paul. *"Mais non!"* gasped Jean-Paul, retreating.

Claude turned and hurled the still chiming clock straight into the large and lovely Chippendale mirror that hung over the fireplace.

The crash was deafening. For an instant the room was alive with hurtling shards of glass and marble. Guy whirled around, pulling Charity closer and bending above her. Jean-Paul essayed a frantic leap for the shelter of a bookcase. Only Claude did not attempt to shield himself, but stood there, his shoulders a little hunched, his arms slowly lowering as the porcelain parade was ended for all time and the pealing little bells gibbered discordantly into silence.

Peeping at Claude, Charity saw the slim shoulders rise and fall again, as though he had sighed deeply. She saw also that Guy's hand was cut and that Jean-Paul had suffered a graze across his cheek.

Claude turned to them. His face shone with perspiration, but the madness had faded, and a mild smile curved his mouth. Astonishingly, he was completely untouched, although he had been closest to the exploding mirror.

Guy wrapped a handkerchief about his small injury while watching his brother steadily.

"So," said Claude, strolling forward to eye Charity with amused contempt, "you said nothing. Why, I wonder? Did you fancy you were protecting your sister? Your fine sister who broke her promise to me as soon as my surgeon had restored your health?"

Charity thought, incredulous, "He behaves as though nothing had happened!" Somehow she managed to answer, "Your doctor kept me chained to an invalid chair long after I should have been well. You used my illness and prolonged it, so as to force Rachel to agree to marry you."

"And now I shall use you once more, I believe." Claude stepped closer, saying gently, "Were I to have one of your fingers removed and sent to your so-gallant brother-in-law every three of four days, say, I wonder how long it would be before he agreed to exchange his life for yours. . . ."

Charity felt sick.

Guy said in a low growl, "She will not be harmed, Claude."

Claude threw back his head and laughed merrily. "Whilst you live to prevent it? Ah, do not tempt me, Guy." He sauntered to a crimson and black bell-pull and tugged it.

The door opened at once, and a scared-looking footman entered, his eyes becoming round and more scared when he saw the condition of the room.

Claude said, "This lady is Mademoiselle Strand. Take her to the room we prepared for Mrs. Leith." He nodded to Charity. "Go with him, foolish girl. And do exactly as you are told else, despite my noble brother, I shall be quite happy to arrange that your stay with us is very uncomfortable indeed."

The bedchamber to which Charity was conducted was not uncomfortable in the least, however, except for the iron bars outside each window, and the large, hard-eyed woman, incongruous in the uniform of an abigail, who waited there. Stamping about the room, hanging up gowns and flinging undergarments into the chest of drawers, she informed Charity that her name was Meg and that she wasn't nobody's fool. "Gulled poor Ella proper, didn't you, Miss Strand? Well, you won't gull Meg, so don't never try it."

Charity did not deign to reply, quietly putting off her cloak and bonnet and dropping them on the bed.

Two footmen arrived, bearing a hip bath and followed by a line of servants carrying buckets of hot water. Charity's attempt to dismiss her truculent abigail was not successful. Folding massive arms, Meg revealed that "the Frenchman gent" had ordered her not to leave her charge for an instant. "Me bed's in there," she added, nodding her untidy, greying head towards the adjoining dressing room. "So you needn't think as you can get up to mischief after dark, neither."

Charity ignored her and began to disrobe. Meg snatched the garments as they were shed, but beyond tossing a sponge and towel onto a chair and pulling it within reaching distance, she made no further attempt to help. Charity was painfully conscious of the woman's scornful gaze and of her own small breasts and boyish slenderness. She fought against betraying an awareness of Meg's insolence, and only later, when she was seated before the dressing table and the woman drew a hairbrush so roughly through her curls that it brought involuntary tears to her eyes, did Charity say sharply that there was not the need for such force.

"You'll want to look your best, I thought, my lady," smirked Meg.

"I have no title," said Charity, her chin high. "You are as aware of that as you are aware I am not here of my own free will. You are insolent, and also I have to assume you are a criminal."

"Hey!" protested the big woman angrily. "Who you calling a criminal?"

Charity lifted one hand in an unknowingly regal gesture. "I know Monsieur Sanguinet well enough to believe that he does not wish me to be served with impertinence. If you address me in so rude a fashion again, I shall ask that you be replaced."

The woman glared at her, but after a moment she said grudgingly that there was no need to fly into a pucker. She was more tractable after that, but her pale blue eyes glittered with malice and Charity could not be at ease with her.

Whatever her shortcomings, Meg knew her trade. She arranged Charity's hair in a most becoming style, completing that task when a knock came at the door, and Guy asked to be admitted. Charity slipped into a wrapper and went to sit beside the fire.

Impeccable in a dark brown velvet coat and beige pantaloons, Guy said, "*Merci*. That will be all."

Meg, standing militantly behind Charity, said, "Monseigneur said I was to stay by her. Day *and* night," she added with a sneer.

Guy smiled. "Would you wish your feet to direct you through that door," he enquired, "or should you prefer that I bodily convey you?"

"Monseigneur says —" Meg began, folding her arms.

Purposefully, Guy walked towards her.

"Like to see you try it, I would," she shrilled.

"By all means." He reached for her and she squealed and ran. Closing the door behind her, he turned to Charity, both hands held out, his comely face a study in regret. "Oh, *ma chérie, mon petit chou,* how very much I am sorry for this."

To be in the company of this man who had been such a good friend after her father's death, to see the sorrowful apology in his hazel eyes, to hear the fondness in his voice, overwhelmed Charity's tattered nerves. She was in his arms in a rush and sobbing gustily into his cravat. "Oh, Guy! Oh, Guy . . . he will murder me, I know it! Or . . . worse . . . ."

"Now you know that I will not allow such a thing to happen, little one." He hugged her tight for a moment, then drew back, smiling into her tearful eyes. "Claude has, alas, very many faults but you need not have the fear he means to violate you." He patted Charity's blushing cheek gently. "He has, you see, a most willing lady residing here. And besides, whatever else he may be, I never have known him to force a woman. He has too much of the pride for that. Now come, compose yourself, for we have only a little moment of the time." He led her to the small sofa and sat beside her. "Tell me this quickly, does anyone know you are here? Is there any hope for help to come to you?"

She shook her head. "A red-haired boy named Lion was kind," she whispered. "He said he would help me if he could."

"So there are two of us . . . ." He looked grave, then said bracingly, "And two it is better than not one, eh? Now, you must be brave,

218

chérie, and have some faith in this Guy Sanguinet who is not such a bad fellow, despite his bad blood."

Charity wiped impatiently at her eyes. "If you did but know how grateful I am. But, Guy, forgive me, but . . . so often Rachel and I wondered why . . ."

"Why I remain with my infamous brother?" He said with a twisted smile, "It is a debt of love. One I have been tempted very many times to cancel. But cannot. Some day, perhaps, I will tell you of it. But for now, I am sent on the errand. Claude's yacht is to be readied for departure. Some men have come with letters from England and news of importance. I do not know what this is. But you are summoned to dine with him. I shall contrive to have this boy, Lion, assigned to guard you if I can. You are sure you can trust him?"

"Quite sure. Oh, Guy, when is the yacht to sail? And where?"

"This, I do not know. Now, listen to me, *chérie*, you must not show my brother a tearful face. Claude, it shames me to say it, is a very bad man, but he have admiration for courage."

"Yes, I'll try, but . . . I am very afraid, you see."

He took up her hand and kissed it, but said nothing.

Charity asked hesitantly, "Does he — can he possibly still want Rachel?"

He frowned. "He want her. Not with love,

assurement. But because she dared to — how do you say it? — to spurn all he offered. His hand, his wealth, his power — so much power, *chérie.* This, for the first time in his life, a lady rejects. He does not quite, I think, comprehend. For with love, you see, he has not the acquaintance. He wants control of Britain. He wants Rachel. And, you must know this, little one, he wants your fine brother-in-law, Leith and his good friend Monsieur Devenish — he wants them very dead."

"I know," she whispered, wringing her hands. "Oh, I know!"

"He will use you in any way he can to win these things. So you must be brave and clever. And you must be patient, Charity, for I can help you only at just the right time, or —" He paused, raising one hand for quiet.

From outside came the sound of hurried footsteps. Guy stood and walked toward the door. "If things are very bad, send your Lion to me. Courage, *mon pauvre.*"

He opened the door. Meg, accompanied by two tall footmen, stood beside a shrunken-looking woman. It was obviously the housekeeper, clad all in black, her grey hair pulled tightly back from angular features. She had eyes as cold as the ocean beyond the windows. She said in French, "This servant has displeased monsieur?"

"She has. She is an uncouth, ill-mannered, insolent peasant. And no fit companion for

Miss Strand. How came you to hire such?"

A thin smile did little to warm the housekeeper's face. "She was engaged by Monsieur Gerard, sir. No doubt" — a sly light crept into her eyes — "you would wish to discuss the matter with him."

"I think not. I shall discuss it instead with my brother. Good day, Miss Strand." And he strode off, to return before the door closed and push it wide again. "You," he said to the startled Meg, "keep a civil tongue in your head, or I shall tell Monseigneur to move you to one of the other islands."

Meg turned to the housekeeper as the door closed. "You wouldn't let him, would you, madame?" she asked agitatedly. " 'Course, that one and Monseigneur ain't whatcha might call bosom bows."

"If you refer to Monsieur Guy," said the housekeeper in flawless English, "he and his brother are not devoted. What they are is Sanguinets. It would be most unwise to forget that!"

How Charity contrived to set one foot beneath the other as she walked down the stairs, she did not know. Every inch of her fought to draw back, and she was shaking, only the knowledge that Meg watched from the landing forcing her to continue. Guy's threat of banishment to another island had evidently been a major one, for the formidable abigail had since been almost desperate in her eagerness to please. The housekeeper's parting remark had troubled Charity, however. She had known Guy for years and had always found him a perfect gentleman and a most delightful companion. That he was an honourable man also, she had no doubt, but he *was* a Sanguinet. Even though he did not admire his brother and was deeply fond of her, Claude's wrath could be a terrible thing. Guy might be willing to risk that wrath, but to assist her to escape must also spell his brother's doom and the end of the grandiose plans for which Claude had plotted and schemed through so many years. It scarcely seemed realistic to expect Guy to hazard so much for her sake. "But it is not for me alone," she thought. "It is for England!" A foolish thought, as she at once realized, because Guy was French — not English.

At the foot of the stairs, the housekeeper waited. She led the way to a large room, ushered Charity inside, and withdrew. Charity glanced around apprehensively. She stood in a warm and graceful salon furnished in the French style; all white and gold daintiness. At first, she fancied she was alone, but the smell of tobacco smoke hung on the air and served to warn her, so that she was able to school herelf to react with outward calm when Claude Sanguinet arose from a high-backed chair beside the fire.

He wore evening dress, as did she, and he

looked, she decided, trying to quiet her leaping nerves, gentle and benign as he threw a cheroot into the fire. "How charming that I may have the pleasure of your presence at dinner," he said suavely.

Usually, he preferred to speak French, but now he used English and Charity noticed that his command of the language had improved since last they met. "He has been preparing himself for his ascension to the throne," she thought cynically. She also thought his sentiment the epitome of mockery, but because she knew his reputation with women, could scarcely force her reluctant legs to carry her closer to him. "Am I to be the only female, then?" she asked. "I had thought to find you surrounded with the type of, er, lady you admire."

"Like a harem?" His brows rose. "Oh, very good. So our insipid little invalid has some spirit after all." He bowed her to a chair, snapped his fingers, and a footman, who must have silently followed Charity into the room, brought ratafia served in an exquisite crystal wineglass, offered on a gold tray. Claude waved, and the man bowed and withdrew, closing the doors softly.

"Unfortunately, my dear Miss Strand," said Claude, returning to his chair, "the women who come here must remain. At least, until my plans are brought to fruition. For you will apprehend that no one having seen my fortress can be permitted to leave."

A sharp pang pierced her heart, but glancing at him over the rim of her glass, she saw the sly amusement in his eyes. He was deliberately frightening her. Anger brought a defiant recklessness. "How could anyone desire to do so?" she said sweetly. "If nothing else, the climate is so salubrious."

He stared at her. "Have I misjudged you, I wonder? Stand up."

She had never been commanded so contemptuously. Further irked, she set aside her glass and stood, looking down at him with her head held high.

Claude leaned back in his chair, wineglass held lazily in the air as he scanned her with insolent deliberation. "Turn around."

She murmured, "How nice it would be did you only say 'please.'" But she obeyed. Facing him again, she saw the speculative light in his eyes, and her heart almost failing her, enquired, "Are you deciding how much I will bring on the slave market?"

"*Tiens!*" he exclaimed admiringly. "So you have guessed your fate."

Then it was truth. She was to be sold to some loathsome Eastern harem. Or worse. The room seemed to sway, and her knees began to buckle. Dimly, she knew that Claude would be delighted if she fainted, and as from a distance she heard Guy's words echoing, ". . . he have admiration for courage . . ." She dug her nails

224

hard into her palms and fought away the dizziness.

Claude was speaking again, his voice amused. ". . . are not beautiful, as is your sister, but you have improved a good deal in looks since last I saw you. You have spirit, which I admire. You have the family background that is essential. Have you ambition also, I wonder? Some women do, you know."

Astounded, she said unevenly, "The ambition to — to rule as your consort?"

"Bravo!" He sprang to his feet. "Most women in your present position would be fainting at my feet, or in screaming hysterics. Not only do you succumb to neither revolting condition, but you stand here proudly and bandy words with me. You are times ten the woman I had supposed you to be. Ah — you are startled. Naturally so. Never mind. You will learn that part of my success derives from my ability to reach decisions with great rapidity. I have a clear mind, you see. Think on it, and upon all I offer you, and —"

Daring to interrupt this ridiculous speech, she said, "How may you offer what you do not possess?"

He laughed. "Must you see England at my feet before you agree? You do not know me very well. The prize is as good as mine, I assure you. And, in ten days or less . . ." He paused, eyeing her reflectively. "You had as well know.

225

Either way, you are powerless to interfere. Come."

He walked to the door and held it open. Not averse to seeing some of the rest of this mighty old castle, and consoling herself with the fact that she had carried off the interview quite well, Charity followed.

Claude bowed her from the room, then led the way along a high vaulted hall paved with gleaming stone, strewn with rich furs and rugs, lit by fine old ships lamps hung from the massy walls, and peopled by innumerable elegant footmen and lackeys who stiffened to attention at their approach. Around a corner and along another hall, to a recessed door that a lackey sprang to open.

Three men waited inside a luxuriously equipped book room. Jean-Paul and Clem were unpleasantnesses that Charity was able to ignore, but with them was an individual she knew to be almost as dangerous as his master. It was all she could do not to shrink when his glittering black eyes turned to her. He smiled with thin mockery and bowed. "Gerard," Charity half whispered.

Claude looked with benevolence from one to the other. "How pleasant it is," he purred, "when old friends are reunited. You two" — he snapped his fingers at Jean-Paul and Clem — "wait outside."

Jean-Paul's face did not change, but Clem scowled as they went out.

A sturdy little brass-bound wooden chest, dark with years, lay on the reference table, and Claude walked across to rest his hand on it for a moment almost caressingly. Glancing up at Gerard, he asked, "This not once has left your sight?"

"Not for one instant, monseigneur."

Claude nodded. He drew a small key ring from his pocket, fitted one of the keys into the lock, and opened the lid. It seemed to Charity that his face softened as he surveyed the contents. Certainly, when he looked up at her, his eyes were kinder than they had been since her arrival.

"You have an interest in history, as I recall," he murmured. "You will find this to be intriguing."

Curious, she trod across to him and peered into the box. Somehow, she had expected something ugly or evil; instead, she saw the interior of the little chest to be lined with purple velvet, and on a thickly cushioned base a thing of beauty: an exquisitely fashioned crown, clearly of great antiquity and richly bejewelled, the gleams of great sapphires, emeralds, rubies, and diamonds flashing even in the dimness of the chest.

Watching her rapt face with delight, Claude took a pair of cotton gloves from the table. He put them on and lifted the crown very carefully. "See," he said softly, holding it up to the light.

It resembled a small helmet, the top portion

supplanted by two intricately carven golden hoops, and the sides consisting of eight plates, variously encrusted with jewels or adorned with enamelled paintings, the colours still clear and true despite the passage of the centuries.

"Oh," whispered Charity, overawed. "How *very* beautiful."

"Can you date it, do you think?"

Her brow wrinkled. She said hesitantly, "I would say it is Frankish. Tenth century, perhaps . . . or even earlier. It could, in fact, very well be —" Breath held in check, she looked up. "My heavens! Never say — It cannot be —"

Claude chucked his triumph. "But it is, my clever little creature."

"*Charlemagne . . . ?*" gasped Charity. "But — but it must be priceless!"

"Just so. I hate to part with it. I really do. Although I shall get it back, of course. But to know this spendid work of art actually rested on the head of the mighty Charles . . . Such a fall from grace that it soon must adorn — however briefly — your poor foolish George."

Charity met his innocent smile with a sharpening gaze. "You mean to present this to the Regent?"

"Oh yes." He sighed. "Such a pity that it was necessary to tamper with the pretty thing. But clever, very clever, I must admit. Here — let me show you." Very cautiously, he placed the crown on its side in the chest, then turned it until the great ruby in the centre front was face down on the velvet.

Gerard murmured. "Sir, Miss Strand can scarce be in sympathy with your plans. Do you think it wise to demonstrate —"

"Miss Strand is our guest," said Claude. "She will not leave us until our coup is *fait accompli*. If then. See, my dear . . ." He pointed to one of the round small discs that linked the main plates of the band, this disc alone being slightly out of alignment with its fellows. "A small substitution we have made. Watch. . . ." He pressed his index fingers on the right side of the little golden disc, pushing it gently into line. And as it straightened, Charity thought to detect a faint flicker in the centre; nothing more, but gooseflesh started on her skin, and Claude, drawing back, looked up at her like a schoolboy who has just performed a brilliant feat.

"What — what is it?" she whispered.

"A little needle. So long as there is no pressure on the band, it is withdrawn, but I learnt the size of the so dear Prince's hats. When the crown is in place on his empty head it will fit very snug. The right side of the disc it will of necessity be pressed into its proper position. That small straightening is all that is required to cause the needle to spring forward. Scarcely a threat, eh? So tiny a thing. Ah, but you see, dear mademoiselle, it is death. The needle is coated with a poison many times more venomous than than of a cobra. The merest

229

scratch will bring about all the symptoms of a seizure of the heart. Within a few minutes of donning the crown your fair Florizel will expire. And do you see the delicious touch of it? He will appear to have died from natural causes!" He beamed at her, eyes bright and triumphant.

"How *horrible!*" Charity groped for the nearest chair and sank into it, her fascinated gaze fixed on his pleased face. "And for what earthly purpose?"

"What else but to be of aid to my fellow man," he answered piously. "To relieve the conditions so intolerable that now exist among Britain's poor. Consider the riots, the unrest among the masses. And who shall blame them? They fought an endless war. Their reward for all the death and suffering and privation is taxation of the most crushing. They are cursed with mounting unemployment and working conditions that are very bad."

"And do you say that *you* mean to correct all these injustices?"

"Let us say," he qualified with a grin, "that they must be brought to *believe* I shall. The time it is right for change. And so I help matters. My men are everywhere about, guiding and, ah, consoling your unfortunates."

"You mean stirring them up for trouble!"

Claude winked at Gerard like a crafty schoolboy. "The lady thinks me very naughty, eh *mon ami?* No, no, Miss Strand. My people merely educate your peasants. To a point. But you must not — what is it you say? — put the whole in my dish. I may be the natural leader, but you would be very surprised to know how many of your Prinny's most trusted advisers are loyal to me. To say nothing of certain high-ranking army and navy officers who will do whatsoever I tell them. Now — allow me to continue."

He righted the Charlemagne crown, locked the little chest, and, removing his gloves, restored them to the table. "Within twenty-four hours of the Regent's death," he went on, "Liverpool, your admirable Prime Minister, Lord Palmerston, and Lord Castlereagh will have been assassinated, apparently by angry mobs." Smiling at Charity's horrified gasp, he picked up the chest and handed it to Gerard. "Be careful of it," he said. "*Extreme* careful, my dear friend."

Gerard took the box. "Be assured, monseigneur," he murmured and went out. The appalled Charity caught a glimpse of Clem and Jean-Paul and of several other men still waiting there, and then the door closed.

Claude settled himself on an adjacent sofa. "What," he enquired smugly, "do you know of such institutions as Child's and Hoare's, and Coutts', dear lady?"

Watching him with fascinated disbelief, Charity managed, "I — I know they are fine banks. My brother deals with Child's."

"And you know, of course, of this rising

leviathan, the Bank of England?"

"Yes. A little."

"I wonder if this is possible — that you comprehend such intricacies as gold reserves? Ah, I know the minds of you gentle ladies are fashioned for simpler matters, so I shall be very brief. Your bank of England holds in its vaults sufficient gold to enable it to supply smaller banks, in the event they may suffer a setback." He drew a fine enamelled watch from his waistcoat pocket, glanced at it, wound it absently a few times, then restored it to his pocket. "On the day following the assassinations," he said, "there will be just such a setback. Throughout the world, large businesses in which I either hold a controlling interest, or with which I have, ah, connections, are heavy depositors with the establishments I have mentioned. On the day designated, every one of those concerns will demand immediate withdrawal of all their funds. Even so formidable an institution as your noble Bank of England will be forced to refuse aid." He smiled happily at Charity. "Simultaneously, into the major banks of every large city in your island, my dear, will come prominent men of business also demanding their funds. They will speak of a Panic — and alarm will become consternation, and consternation, in the event, a Panic. One after another, the banks will fall. Oh yes, I do assure you they will. The greatest banking houses, the mighty financiers will be helpless — this, it has been contrived. One man — at last — will intervene. *One man* will rescue the toppling economy of dear, damp England."

Her wide eyes fixed on his bland smile, Charity whispered, "You."

He bestowed a slight bow upon her. "Not alone, of course, although ostensibly so. I have my backers in Vienna, Paris, Berlin, in Switzerland, and Rome. But to all intents and purposes *I* will be the saviour. And I will be proclaimed as such. Did you know that our Prinny has arranged for me to become a legal citizen of Britain? So accommodating. My eager supporters who even now await the start of this train of events, will soon demand that I be named to some public office. Such as . . . Prime Minister." He gestured gracefully. "Do you see? It is just beginning, but — do you see?"

"Then . . . you do not mean to invade England with an army?"

Claude put back his head and laughed merrily. "How jolly that would be. And with myself astride a white charger twice as mighty, and one hopes better behaved, than Copenhagen. Alas, no, my dear. However, there *will* be an invasion of a sort. You have seen my men — very few, but you have seen some, yes?"

She nodded.

"The reason there are so few now here, is that most are already in place. I have, shall we say, shock troops, strategically placed throughout England. They have gathered near military barracks, armouries, naval installations, even around my so dear friends, the Runners of Bow Street. They poise — ready. Awaiting the word only, not to strike necessarily, but to, ah, dissuade any attempt at interference with my manoeuvrings."

"I cannot believe it," Charity said breathlessly. "I cannot credit that you really could expect to succeed! You — you say it is only the beginning. What, dare I ask, is the ending? King Claude the First?"

He pushed back a perfect cuticle. "Who shall say?"

"I shall say!" Leaning forward in her chair, bold with rage, Charity cried hotly, "And I say — *stuff!* I know little about banking, as you said, but even I have heard of the Rothschilds. What of them?"

He smiled. "How you do impress me, dear and quite uninsipid creature. Did I not say I have contrived?"

"I don't believe you! My brother told me that Nathan Rothschild kept Wellington supplied with bullion all through the war; that he managed somehow to transport it right across France. I cannot believe he would fail now!"

Claude spread his hands. "Then you must doubt me, poor child. Until I prove you mistaken."

He sighed, but his smile was full of mischief,

and she was shaken.

"And — and what of Princess Charlotte? Or the royal Dukes? Do you mean to assassinate them also?"

"There is not the need. So many in this land have never admired the House of Hanover. So many of your oppressed citizenry are eager to embrace a truly democratic state. To be done with all the pomp and nonsense of royalty. You will not deny that many of your aristocrats live in dread lest the yokels follow France's lead and launch a revolution?" He saw her whiten, and murmured slyly, "Thousands of malcontents; the victimized, the starving; the once-proud weavers now herded like animals into stifling factories; the country families no longer allowed their small holdings. All waiting. All ready to burst into flame. Needing only the spark I shall provide." He chuckled. *"Liberté . . . ? Egalité . . . ? Fraternité . . . ?"*

"Never!" Charity denied stoutly, her voice rather hoarse despite her efforts. "England's pomp and nonsense, as you call it, is dear to the hearts of us all, because it is an inherent and vital part of the history that binds us together. Our people may grumble at times, and heaven knows there are social reforms that are decades overdue, but we *try!* Our leaders *try* to improve matters. And our people have only to leave these isles to see how much better we are served than are the citizenry of most other nations. Not for one moment would the average Briton stand for a Frenchman on our throne! Do you not know what happened only seventy or so years ago when a Scot — a gentleman with a thousand times more right than you — attempted to seize power? No, I tell you! No Frenchman will rule my country!"

Gently laughing, he applauded. "Well said, my valiant one. *Mon Dieu,* but I admire you more with each moment that passes. But be reasonable, I beg. A Frenchman ruled you after the Battle of Hastings — no? Your people have endured a stupid, extravagant, Germanic hand for many years. Why not a brilliant one of royal birth from Brittany? Have I not pointed out that I do not seek the throne? Not until the time is right. . . . By then, with an English lady at my side, with the admiration and gratitude of all, I shall be quite acceptable to the populace. And I assure you I know how to deal with dissent. Thus, sooner or later, shall I assume my rightful place in the history of the world."

Had any other man uttered so grandiose a statement, Charity would have laughed outright. But here, in this great fortress, surrounded by the evidence of his wealth and power, she did not laugh. Staring at his poised confidence, she thought, "He believes it all! How utterly ridiculous that he really *believes* he will succeed!"

And on the heels of that thought, came another: "It *is* ridiculous . . . isn't it?"

Chapter Eleven

Charity slept poorly that night. Guy had not returned to join them, and she had dined alone with Claude, managing somehow to maintain a calm demeanour, constantly astounded that this egomaniac could address with affability a lady he had wrenched away from home and family; that he could profess concern for her welfare despite the ghastly fate he planned for her; that he could seem so relaxed even as he plotted a disaster that would shake the world, and evince no trace of regret for the callous murders his plans necessitated.

Tossing restlessly on her bed, her fears for her own welfare became secondary to the nightmare that might all too soon engulf her country. Any thought that Claude would realize his ambitions, she dismissed as nonsensical. Her greatest dread was that his scheming might bring about a public revolt. England had known the bitter tragedy that is civil war; she was still recovering from a long and horribly costly conflict with Bonaparte. That she should be plunged into another bloodbath was too terrible to contemplate. That wretched, smiling little savage must be stopped. But how? *How?*

There must, she thought, be *someone* in Whitehall who had not dismissed Diccon's warnings as valueless. When they had escaped from Dinan and Tristram had reported to General Smollet, he had been ridiculed and only reprieved from a court-martial by resigning his commission. Yet surely the General would believe this time? *If* the word could reach him! It was terribly evident that there was very little time. That deadly crown might — She sat up, appalled. Had Claude given the wooden chest to Gerard not for safe-keeping, but to be conveyed at once to the Regent? "Oh . . . my God!" she moaned.

A very small companion, who had watched drowsily, roused at these sounds of distress and made her little pilgrimage with high-held tail and grating purrs to render what solace she might. Charity gathered the kitten close, lay down again, and resumed her worrying until, quite exhausted, she dropped off to sleep.

She did not awaken until Meg brought in her breakfast tray at eleven o'clock. An investigation of her wardrobe revealed many charming gowns, cloaks, and shoes. She regarded them without enthusiasm, but her long rest had restored her fighting spirit. However bleak the prospect, she would die sooner than allow Claude to know how deep was her despair. She selected a morning dress of white muslin with pale pink buttons fastening to a high squared neckline. Meg threaded a pink velvet ribbon through her curls and brought forth a lacy white shawl embroidered with tiny pink flowerets. Charity pinched some colour into her pale cheeks and went into the hall.

Lion was lounging on a bench, engaged in desultory conversation with a lackey. He looked at her with cold dislike, his eyes warning her not to betray their friendship. She was so intent upon him that she did not close the door fast enough, and Little Patches dashed out.

Guy came along the hall. "Pray, what is this great brute of a creature?" he said, amused, and bent to appropriate the kitten and hold her up for inspection.

Charity had prayed to see him. She explained Little Patches' presence hurriedly. Lion stood and began to saunter off. Glancing back over his shoulder, his lips formed one word. It seemed to Charity that the word was "Careful." He must be warning her against Guy. Certainly, he could not know that this particular Sanguinet was her very good friend.

Guy was captivated with the kitten, and he carried her as he conducted Charity through the vast halls to a quiet central garden, shielded from the bitter northeast wind. The air was cold enough to cause Charity to pull her shawl closer about her shoulders, but the sunlight and fresh air were invigorating. Glad to be out of doors at last, Little Patches raced madly about, attacking waving blooms and, much to Guy's amusement, throwing up both front paws at a gardener who toiled inoffensively at a nearby flowerbed.

Wandering to a safe distance from the kneeling man, Charity murmured urgently, "Guy, have you seen the Charlemagne crown? Do you know what Claude intends?"

His hazel eyes slanted to her. "To my sorrow. He has told you of his foolish ambitions, then?"

She nodded and, placing one hand on his arm, murmured beseechingly, "He *must* be stopped! I know it is dreadful to ask your help, but —"

"And useless, *chérie*. If such a one as Colonel Leith could not convince the wooden-heads in Whitehall, what chance has a Sanguinet? Ah, do not look so despairing. My brother has large dreams, but they cannot succeed, you know."

"They could succeed in the murder of the Regent and the setting off of an uprising. We British are fighting people, Guy. And when Claude told me of all his meddling with the banks, at a time when England is —"

"Banks?" he intervened sharply. "How is this? I know nothing of banks."

"He means to cause a —"

"Pardon, monsieur. Mademoiselle Strand, Monseigneur desires your immediate presence in the book room. You will please to follow . . . ?"

The lackey's quiet voice had sounded almost

in Charity's ear. Her heart jumping into her throat, she reached for the kitten.

"May I keep her for a little time? She is a pretty creature." Guy spoke calmly, but his eyes and his smile said, "Be brave."

Following the lackey, however, Charity did not feel brave. When she had been trapped at Claude's château in Dinan, she had been with Rachel and Agatha, and very soon had come Tristram and Dev, with Raoul adding his dauntless support. Now she was all alone. She forced her drooping chin higher. No, she was *not* alone. She had Guy and the boy Lion! She walked into the book room proudly, only to stop, stunned.

Two men stood laughing softly at some private joke. Claude was one, his hand resting in a friendly way on the shoulder of the other. A tall, dark, and much disliked Englishman . . .

Claude looked up and saw Charity. "Ah, so here you are, dear lady," he said, all joviality. "Come and meet a countryman."

Mitchell Redmond turned, still smiling. Abruptly the amusement was wiped from his face. His lips parted, and for an instant he looked dumbfounded.

With scathing contempt, Charity said, "That any Englishman could be so *low*, so treacherous, is beyond belief!"

Recovering his wits, Redmond groaned, "Oh, egad! I am judged and found wanting." And as

Charity's small head tossed higher, he went on with a bored smile, "Do pray present me, Monsieur Sanguinet. Who is this, ah, patriotic lady?"

Who *was* she? The conniving traitor knew perfectly well who she was! Her mouth opening to scourge him, Charity saw the swift gleam of warning in the grey eyes, and she was again shocked. What on earth . . . ?

Glancing curiously from one to the other, Claude murmured, "You were about to say, my dear. . . . ?"

Her mind reeling, Charity managed a chill, "That I have no wish to meet this turncoat."

"Ah, but I must insist. Mr. Rivers has rendered me so great a service, the least I may do is reward him with an introduction to so charming a lady. Rivers, this fiery creature is Miss Charity Strand."

Redmond bowed, but made no move to take Charity's hand, nor she to extend it. Claude was saying something about her relationship to Tristram, and she was vaguely aware of Redmond making a sneering response, but she scarcely heard, her every effort bent upon concealing her emotions. It was obvious that Redmond played a part, in which case he had either come here to attempt a rescue or to spy upon Sanguinet. Numbly, she thought, *"Redmond!"* The last man in the world she would have expected to take up the challenge. But he certainly had not come alone. Tristram must be close by, and Dev — and perhaps her brother. A rush of joy and weakness threatened her with tears. As from a distance, Claude's voice penetrated her introspection.

"Miss Strand? Are you still amongst us?"

She forced her eyes to meet his. "Unwillingly, sir."

He chuckled. "Is she not a delight? So sharp a tongue, in despite her unhappy situation."

"Do you admire such in a lady, monsieur?" drawled Redmond, very obviously bored.

Claude turned his head slowly. There was no amusement in his eyes now. "I admire courage," he said, "especially in a female. I do not permit impertinence. Especially in an Englishman of whom I know but little."

Frowning, Redmond pointed out, "You know that I come from Admiral Deal."

"So you tell me."

"Jupiter! You are hard to convince, monsieur! I put Diccon to rest for you. I brought you his journal. If that does not win your confidence —"

Claude made an impatient gesture. "Oh, enough! Enough! Have I not admitted that I stand indebted to you?" He stepped closer to Charity and led her to a chair. "You are upset, my dear. Is it because this turncoat has murdered your old friend?"

Redmond had not killed Diccon, that was certain, but he had evidently managed to convince Claude he'd done so. Lord, but he trod a dangerous path, this man she had judged so contemptuously! She answered, "I had not thought one so brave as Diccon would be slain by such as your friend."

"But he is not my friend, you know." Claude darted an amused smile at Redmond. "A valuable tool, merely."

"Alas," mourned Redmond. "I lose on every suit. However, ma'am, console yourself. I was not alone in ridding the world of the pest that called itself Diccon. Merely the lucky one."

Charity raised a hand to her eyes and had no need to feign a trembling. "Monseigneur," she whispered, "*must* I remain in the same room with this creature?"

Claude bent over her and with a hand on each arm of her chair, asked, "Do you truly find him so repulsive? He is very fair to look upon — no?"

Redmond looked smug, and Charity had to struggle to conceal her admiration. "He is an abomination," she exclaimed, her lip curling. "Pray excuse me from breathing the same air!"

"Oho!" Laughing, Claude stepped back. "Run along then. Now do you see how well I am mastering your strange English sayings? But friend Diccon's writing I cannot unravel, so Rivers must stay to help me. I shall send for Gerard, to —"

Two hearts missed a beat. With his hand on the bellpull, Claude paused. "No, he is gone, of course — what am I thinking of? Ah, I have it! My so dear kinsman shall be pressed into service." He eyed Charity mockingly. "You will not object to that, I fancy?"

When Charity was shown into the central courtyard, however, Guy was nowhere to be seen. She could have wept with chagrin. She *must* discover what Claude meant when he said that Gerard was gone. Was the infamous crown really on its southward journey? Her desperate anxieties were eased slightly when Lion came to take her for a drive around the island. As he escorted her upstairs in order that she might put on a warm cloak and hood, she said, low-voiced, "I must speak with Monsieur Guy. Can you get word to him?"

He stared at her, and she was obliged to caution him lest his surprise attract attention. "What fer?" he hissed, striding along the corridor beside her. "He's dog's meat. The same rotten breed as the other."

"No. He is a good friend, but you must not let any other person know of this. Oh, Lion, I am trusting you. I *beg* you will be true to me."

"Don't need to," he muttered, then, opening the door, added a surly, "Hurry up, miss. I got more important things to do." And he gave Meg a disgusted look which pleased and amused that sour handmaiden.

How Lion managed it, Charity could not tell, but when they drove out, Guy Sanguinet rode escort. The closed carriage proceeded around the island in bright, pale sunshine and bitter

245

cold. Charity saw several ships in the landlocked harbour: a fine schooner, probably the vessel that had brought Mr. Redmond here; three ocean-going barges, and a yacht that she recognized at once as Claude's luxurious *La Hautemant*. She breathed a sigh of relief. If Gerard had sailed for England, he almost certainly would have travelled on that vessel. Her optimism was soon shattered, however. When Guy ordered the coachman to pull up and invited her to walk along the cliffs, he pointed out *La Hautemant,* and asked if she remembered the yacht. "Claude bought a new and more modern vessel last spring. He calls her *Se Rallumer*. She's very fast."

"To . . . rekindle . . ." whispered Charity.

"*Oui,* to rekindle the flame," he said sardonically, and as Charity lifted scared eyes to his, he shrugged. "We are from an old and royal house, you know. Our ancestors once ruled Brittany. Claude thinks that he will relight the fire of our destiny." He shook his head and muttered in disgust, *"La folie plus profonde!"*

Very frightened now, she cried, "He has gone, hasn't he? Gerard has taken the Charlemagne crown to England?"

Guy stared at her, then looked fixedly out to sea.

"He's scared to open his budget, 'count of me being here," Lion said scornfully. "I won't blab, guvnor."

Guy looked at the boy steadily, then turned

to Charity and said in French, "My dear lady, I do *swear* to ensure that no harm will befall you."

"Never mind about me! Help me get word to England. Guy, I *implore* you! My God, what we have all suffered in these endless years of war! Do you want it to start again? Oh, Guy, it must not! It *must* not!"

He walked away and with his back to her muttered, "If it was you and your own Justin, would you betray *him* to his death?"

"Justin is an honourable gentleman," she cried. "And always he has been kind and good to me. Claude is cruel and vicious — a murderer many times over, and he treats you —" She bit her lip and was silent.

"Yes. As if I were beneath contempt." His fists clenched. With his eyes on the horizon, he said, "Perhaps I am."

Not understanding their words but alarmed by their intensity, Lion asked, "What's up missus? Is that there Frenchy —"

Charity reverted to English. "He plans to kill Prince George."

The boy gave a yelp of shock. "Whaffor? He might have maggots in his head, but that ain't no reason to scrag the poor perisher! And we don't need no Frenchy a-doing it!"

"A philosopher," murmured Guy dryly.

Charity said, "Lion, this is very, very important. A friend of my brother has come to try and help. He was at my home when I was kidnapped and must have discovered I was brought here. You may have had him pointed out to you in London, for he is quite a noted duellist. If you recognize him, you must be careful not to show it. Will you promise me this?"

His voice squeaking with excitement, Lion exclaimed, "Love a duck! I *did* see a gent like that at Strand Hall. Is it Mr. Redmond? He's a right game 'un to —"

"Redmond?" Guy interpolated sharply. "Sir Harry Redmond?"

"His brother," said Charity. "Lion, do you say you were at Strand —"

Astounded, Guy again interrupted, *"Mon Dieu!* Is he mad? Claude will kill him without the one instant of hesitating! Gerard knows him well and there are others here who would recognize him at once!"

"Does he know *you*, Guy? Have you met?"

He said a clipped, *"Oui,"* then added with a faint smile, "Once, we fight a strange duel. He mistake me, do you see, for my brother."

"My heavens! Still, I beg you will help him get away from here."

Guy's smile faded, and he said nothing.

Tugging at his sleeve, Charity said desperately, "It has *started*, don't you see? It has *begun!* And we stand here — doing *nothing!*"

Guy remained silent, avoiding her eyes.

Lion said staunchly, "Don't you never worry, missus. I'll help yer get orf this perishing island. We'll save ol' windy wallets Georgie!"

"We will go back now." Guy's voice was cold and final, and when Charity attempted to plead with him, he walked to the coach and held the door open, his face inscrutable.

Helplessly, she climbed inside.

The castle was quiet when they returned. A brooding quiet, Charity thought as she walked with Guy across the echoing vastness of the Great Hall. At the foot of the main stairs, Guy bowed and prepared to leave her. Several footmen and lackeys were watching, but made reckless by anxiety, Charity caught at his arm and said a low-voiced, "Guy, *please*. Will you not —"

"It is too late, ma'am," he reiterated quietly. "Your people had every chance and did nothing. Now they are doomed by their own folly."

Angered, she said, "You are just as bad as he! By your very refusal to oppose him, you condone what he does!"

He gazed at her for a moment, his face unreadable. Then he bowed again and walked off towards the book room.

The housekeeper rustled over. "Monseigneur is delayed on a matter of business. He asks that you join him at luncheon, and later he will conduct you around the castle."

Charity went upstairs to change her gown. Claude had evidently decided there was no real need to guard her, for when she went into her room Meg was nowhere to be seen. It was some small relief, at least, not to have to deal with the surly woman. Wandering over to the window, Charity looked yearningly towards England. If Gerard had sailed last evening, he must already be far down the Scottish coast. Perhaps he meant to go ashore somewhere and travel overland to the south country. Sighing heavily, she turned to see Meg coming in from the parlour, a scowl on her face.

"Ain't no manner o' use to blame me if she's lost," she grumbled. "The fireboy didn't move hisself quick enough, and the dratted cat was through the door quicker'n a bee's knees. Not my fault. I tried."

Dismayed, Charity knew there was no point in asking the household staff for help. Most of the lackeys and footmen were types whom she would not be surprised to see in Newgate Prison and who would be glad enough to help Little Patches along her way with a well-placed boot. With this unhappy conviction to spur her, she hurried through her toilette, noting vaguely that the lime green crepe looked quite well on her. She selected a crocheted shawl that promised some warmth, allowed Meg to drape it around her shoulders, and hurried from the room. Luncheon was to be served at two o'clock, and it was now a little past one.

She prowled up and down the corridor with no success, ignoring the smirks of the servants as she called the kitten and hoping Little Patches had not wandered outside. Her efforts not succeeding, Charity went downstairs and again searched to no avail. She was about to go outside when a shy maid bobbed a curtsey and imparted the information that she had seen *la chatte très petite* run down the basement stairs. Charity thanked her and hastened in the direction indicated.

She came to a flight of deeply hewn stone steps that wound around the massy wall, and she trod down with care. The lower regions followed the slope of the hill, and thus, although there were no windows at her end of the hall, far at the other end were narrow slotted apertures through which gleamed daylight. At this end, one lamp was lighted, revealing luxurious carpets and wall hangings with occasional chests or tables as elegant as those above stairs.

Charity had thought the upper floor quiet and brooding, but down here it was as if the busy activity all about her had ceased to exist, so heavy was the silence. She wandered along, her "Here kitty, kitty, kitty" echoing off to be swallowed up. None of the heavy doors was open, save for a double door at the far end. She started towards it, thinking that the most logical place to search. It occurred to her, however, that if a servant had come down for something and Little Patches had followed, she might accidentally have been shut in. With this in mind, Charity reached out to try the latch of the next door she approached, only to recoil with a little gasp of terror. The latch was lifting. Suppose Claude was inside? Suppose he thought she was prying? The door began to open. Charity backed away.

"Meeooooww . . . ?"

Limp with relief, Charity paused. Her heart gave a leap of excitement as Mitchell Redmond appeared, candle in hand and Little Patches squirming under his arm. In that first instant, Charity thought she saw alarm in his wide grey eyes. Then a twinkle came into them. He closed the door, let the kitten jump to the floor, and murmured, "No chaperone again, I see."

The light words, the quirkish grin, brought such a surge of emotion that Charity flew to give him her hand, murmuring incoherent thanks, and stammering out questions until he put his fingers across her lips.

"No time for all that. Besides, you've small need to thank me, Miss Strand. I didn't come galloping to your rescue."

It was like a dash of cold water in her face, and she drew back.

He added, "Didn't even know you was here. Duece of a shock when I saw you, I don't mind admitting. Thank God you had your wits about you!"

It was foolish to be hurt. The important thing was that he had come. "It doesn't matter about me," she said staunchly. "How on earth did you reach here?"

"Diccon learnt that some of Claude's rogues

had taken ship from Birkenhead, so we went up there to sniff around. We were set upon just before we reached the Mersey. We fought off the first lot, but unfortunately Diccon was wounded. He begged that I take charge of a notebook for him, and I was going through his pockets in search of it when some more of Claude's fellows arrived."

Charity intervened anxiously, "Poor Diccon is not dead, is he?"

"I don't know." He looked sombre and went on, "I managed to convince 'em I'd killed him and here I am."

Eyeing him with horrified disbelief she whispered, "You mean, you *cannot* mean that you came here — all *alone?*"

He said cynically, "A disappointment as a relief force, am I?"

"No! Oh *no!* I was so *very* glad to see you!"

He looked down into her upturned, earnest little face. "Poor chit," he thought, "she's had a frightful time." But the glitter of tears lurked in those great eyes, and appalled, he took her arm and began to lead the way back along the corridor while saying at his most sardonic, "*What* a rasper! The instant you laid eyes on me you were at your judgements again, deducing I was hand in glove with the Emperor of the Darrochs!"

She blinked. "Well, what could you expect me to think? He had his hand on your shoulder as though you were veritable bosom bows."

"But of course. I had just presented him with Diccon's notebook."

"You — Oh, you *never* did?"

In her dismay she halted, and halting also, he said with a grin, "It so happens, my doubting friend, that I also carry a little notebook. Luckily, I was able to copy most of what Diccon's had contained and to, ah, revise his a trifle, before I handed it over."

"Oh!" Exuberant, she flung her arms about and gave him a strong hug. "How simply *splendid!*"

Redmond laughed softly, and looking down at her curls, caught in the light of the candle he'd hurriedly swung aside, he noted again that they were quite pretty. Like spun gold, in fact.

Recollecting herself, Charity flushed scarlet and stepped back, but she presevered. "What did you do with your own notebook? If Claude should find it —"

"Never mind about that. Tell me this, ma'am. Those carrion who stole you. Did they, er, I mean, were you . . . mistreated?"

He looked very grim now. Grateful, she said, "How kind of you to ask. Actually, I was fortunate in a way. They thought I was Rachel, you see, and Claude did not want anything to harm her before the babe was born."

One dark eyebrow lifted. "Did he not, by God! So it was Leith's child he was after!" He whistled softly. "A good hater is our Claude!"

Charity nodded, and they walked on in

silence. Suddenly, to his his surprise, Charity gave a little ripple of laughter. In response to his curious glance, she said, "I just realized what you said — the Emperor of the Darrochs — such a good name for him."

Redmond stared at her, then said gravely, "You are a remarkable girl, Miss Strand. Between us, I pray we may contrive so that these miserable islands become the sum total of Claude's kingdom." Little Patches suddenly shot between them and raced ahead towards the stone stairs. "I came down here on the chance of discovering something," Redmond went on. "But to no purpose. Have you learnt anything of Claude's plans?"

"Yes. I expect you already know most of it. For instance, that he means to murder the Regent."

"So Diccon was right! Please go on, I've not been a great success as a spy, I fear. Claude's been a touch close-mouthed with me." He grinned. "Don't think he trusts me yet."

"And will trust you less if Guy tells him who you really are."

"Aha, Guy's here, is he? I was afraid he was the kinsman Claude referred to."

"Thanks to me, he knows you're here now." Distressed, Charity met his startled glance. "Guy is an old and dear friend. I know he would help me if he could, and he swears he will allow no harm to come to me. He was with me when I warned the boy not to recognize you. I should have thought — But I feel so *safe* with Guy. Only, something he said later . . .'' She bit her lip. "Oh, I *do* so wish I hadn't identified you. I should've had more sense!"

"It wouldn't have made much difference. He's sure to see me, sooner or later. Unhappily, I'm known to him — to many of Claude's people, in fact."

"And yet you came. How mad of you! But thank God you did. Now, let me tell you as much as I know." As quickly and concisely as possible, she put Redmond in possession of what she had learnt. At the finish, he was very quiet, his face set in stern lines. Abruptly, he swept her a low bow. "Miss Strand, I salute you. You are a spy *par excellence!* Now I think we must reappear before we're missed. You go first — take your ravening beast, and if you're questioned, explain that you were searching for her. One thing, you are perfectly *sure* of this Lion? He sounds suspiciously similar to a lad named Dick whom I caught lurking about your home in Sussex."

"I'd not be surprised. But there is much of good in him. As there is in Guy . . ." She broke off, then said distractedly, "How terrifying it all is! I scarce dare think of what will happen if Guy feels bound to tell Claude —"

"Then don't think of it," he said bracingly. "Guy is of a different mould to Claude, thank God! Perhaps he will not betray us. Go! Off with you, now."

Hesitating, her anxious gaze upon him, she asked, "But, what do you mean to do?"

A wry smile touched his mouth. "Jove, do you fancy I'm ready with a plan of campaign like our superb Wellington? I must disappoint you again, for I am a mere mortal man!"

"But — but you must have *some* plan?"

"Only to leave this island paradise. Today, if possible, since we cannot go yesterday."

"Oh. How?"

"Madam, *begone!*"

But as she turned and reluctantly started away, he added in a penetrating whisper, "I don't know how. We shall just have to play the cards as they are dealt. And — pray!"

Chapter Twelve

Charity returned Little Patches to her suite without incident, went back downstairs, and followed the sounds of conversation and laughter into a lavishly decorated salon, rich with crimson velvet, crystal chandeliers, thick rugs, and gold draperies. Quite a crowd was gathered, but the moment she entered Claude was at her elbow and she was introduced to a succession of cold-eyed men, most of whom, in some capacity or other, were his employees. Amazed by his effrontery, she looked up to find him regarding her in amused expectation. He bent to her ear. "Aren't you going to cry out for help? It would be so diverting."

She clenched her hands and tossed her chin a little higher, but said nothing.

"Admirable," he said with a chuckle. "Such poise, such dignity. I vow, Monsieur Rivers, the women of your land may look sweetly soft, but they have the core of steel."

Charity darted a glance at Redmond as he sauntered up, impressive in shades of grey. He sneered at Claude's remark, but she did not hear his answer. That he should be present in such a gathering horrified her, and the ensuing two hours became an interminable nightmare. The food was served buffet-style, and people seemed to drift in and out unannounced, so that she was in constant dread lest someone arrive who knew him. If Redmond shared her apprehensions, he gave no sign of it, apparently thoroughly enjoying himself, and so relaxed and at ease that she began to seethe with irritation because he did not have the sense to take himself out of so perilous a situation and retreat to a quiet corner where he could be unobserved.

Meanwhile, Charity did not lack for company. Many of these mercenaries sought her out since she was one of very few ladies present. When they discoverd that she ignored them, however, they soon gave up, and moved on to more congenial company. As she had expected, the food was superb, but she had no appetite, contenting herself with a small puff pasty and a glass of lemonade. She had to fight to conceal her anxieties and to avoid seeking out Redmond's dark head, easily discernible above the crowd. She thought she was succeeding until a suave voice murmured, "Your countryman fascinates you notwithstanding, mademoiselle?"

She stiffened. "If one could be said to be fascinated by evil, monsieur."

Sanguinet offered a glass of ratafia and handed her plate to a hovering lackey. "You eat like the little bird," he scolded. "I shall instruct my chef to prepare a very British dinner expecially to tempt your appetite."

She reminded him that she was a notoriously small eater, and then came near to fainting.

Guy Sanguinet strolled into the room. His eyes flickered over the gathering and stopped abruptly when they came to Redmond. As though he sensed that he was being watched, Redmond glanced around. Charity's blood seemed to congeal; she found it difficult to breathe as the seconds stretched into an eternity. Still the two men looked at each other in a silence that became excruciating. Surely, she thought, everyone else in the room must be aware of this tense confrontation. Guy would denounce Redmond. He must, or betray his brother by remaining silent, which he had said he would not do. And then Redmond turned away, Guy wandered over to a group of sea captains at the buffet table, and Charity could breathe again. Astonishingly, no one seemed to have noticed anything out of the way. Claude was chatting with a distinguished older gentleman at a side table. Charity breathed a silent prayer of thanks and took a healthy gulp at her wine.

Trying to recover her equanimity and watching the occupants of this luxurious room, she thought how extraordinary was this gathering. Most of these men must be aware of the terrible events that were even now being set in motion; certainly, they knew she was a prisoner here. Perhaps that was why so many avoided her eyes. Perhaps, as ruthless as they might be, to see a lady so blatantly held captive was too much for them to face without shame. Some of those whom Claude had presented had murmured acknowledgements in French, and for them she did not feel such scorn. They might truly believe Claude could prevail and bring their ancient enemy crashing down into defeat at last. However base their actions, they were not treasonable. But the Britons she could not excuse. Even if they despised the Hanoverian succession, they must know Claude for the murdering madman that he was; they must suspect his ultimate ambitions, yet they followed him, lured, she supposed, by his gold rather than by his cause.

Claude was talking to Redmond again. Poor Redmond, she thought. He must be seething with frustration. He had made his way here against tremendous odds, learnt everything he had come to learn, only to be trapped and powerless to get away.

They came over to her, Guy, looking sombre, bringing up the rear. She had hoped that Claude would be unable to conduct his promised tour of the castle. He had once taken Rachel through his superb château in Dinan; Charity had been spared the experience because she'd been confined to an invalid chair at that time, but Rachel's description of Claude's pride in his possessions had been sufficient to convince her she never desired such a doubtful pleasure. It had, it developed, been a pleasure deferred. Claude offered his arm as he commenced the tour. Reluctantly, Charity stood, but she did not take his arm. He apologized with a crafty smile for "Mr. Rivers" presence, explaining that the Englishman had expressed a desire to be allowed to accompany them. They set out.

An hour later, Claude had ushered them through a wearying succession of elaborately restored salons, lounges, bedchambers, and suites; the kitchens and stillroom; the various dining rooms, galleries, ante-rooms, game room, and an enormous music room. Charity's fascination with antiquity was dulled by her other preoccupations, but she could not fail to be amazed by the amount of time and money that had been expended on a structure that Claude admitted he had no wish to see again once his coup was accomplished. To brag of his possessions and his achievements delighted him, and

261

he discoursed at length upon the history of the castle which had, he said, been constructed in the twelfth century by a deposed Scots clan chieftain.

They went downstairs again at last, and he rested one well-manicured hand upon the ten-foot-thick outer wall. "They built well," he observed, "else this great fortress she would not have so long survive the atrocious climate. But you, dear mademoiselle" — he turned suddenly to Charity — "do not view my castle with pleasure, I think."

She had been pondering on how unfortunate it was that two burly footmen were bringing up the rear, but she responded without hesitation that she preferred gentler structures, gentler climes, gentler people.

With an amused smile he said, "And how unfortunate that I am about to show you my war room, which is not so gentle as the chambers we have seen thus far. Still, Mr. Rivers will find it interesting, perhaps."

He led them to the basement, the corridor now brightly lit, and along the length of it to the room at the end with the double doors Charity had seen earlier. It was a vast and chilly apartment, hung with every imaginable type of weapon, from a slingshot to a very modern rifle that brought a brief consternation to Redmond.

"By Jove!" he exclaimed, walking over to inspect it. "I'd heard about these. Didn't know

262

they'd been perfected."

"Not perfected, exactly," purred Claude, "but —"

"Monsewer." A beefy man with a coarse English accent slouched into the room, and Charity's heart gave a frenzied jump. "Cap'n Elkins wants as —" He halted, his craggy features reflecting shocked recognition. Crouching, he snarled, *"Redmond!"*

Mitchell was already leaping forward. A derringer flashed into his hand, and gripping Claude by the hair, he jammed the little pistol under his ear.

Eyes round with shock, Claude shrieked, "Kill him! Dolts! Mindless clods! *Kill him!*"

The newcomer started forward. " 'E can only shoot once with that there toy!"

"Stay where you are, Shotten!" Guy waved him to a halt. "That 'once' will kill my brother."

"Tell 'em to drop their pistols," ordered Redmond curtly. He twisted his hand in the black hair when Claude was silent, and added in a voice of steel, "They may kill me, friend, but if I go, you go with me, *sans doute.*"

His face twisting with pain and rage, Claude gasped, "Do as he says."

Reluctantly, three pistols were dropped.

"You cannot get away!" Claude shrilled. "Fool! Imbecile! Do you not know you are a dead man?"

Redmond jerked his head at the pistols.

"Pick them up, please, ma'am, and keep them for me. We may have need of 'em."

She ran to obey, but with one of those unlikely and inexplicable mischances that so often occur to disrupt man's schemes, fate intervened. One of the pistols that had been flung down was old and not as well cared for as it should have been. The hammer, which had been thumbed back, had remained so, and chose this of all moments to snap down. The shot rang out deafeningly, just as Charity reached for the weapon. Her nerves, already ragged, betrayed her into a squeal of fright. Redmond thought she had been hit, and his horrified gaze darted to her, the derringer wavering for just a split second.

It was the opening Sanguinet needed. With all his strength, he drove his elbow under Redmond's ribs and wrenched free. Redmond staggered, fighting nausea as he tried to restore his aim. Shotten leapt forward, uttering a howl of triumph. His fist struck down hard, and the derringer was smashed from Redmond's hand. Shotten's hamlike left whipped savagely for Redmond's jaw, but the slighter man dodged nimbly aside. His right hand was useless, but his left came up in an immediate reprisal.

The two footmen, however, were upon him. They seized him from behind, wrenching his arms back, one of them swinging his fist high.

Claude shouted a frantic, "Don't hurt him!"

Then, seeing Redmond helpless, he added softly, "Yet."

Guy, who had rushed to Charity, slipped an arm about her. "You are all right, little one?" he asked anxiously.

She felt sick with shock and fear, and, clinging to him, whispered, "My . . . fault. My fault. Oh, Guy, they'll kill him!"

"Not until they discover how much he knows. How much Diccon knows. Who is in this with him." A small moan escaped Charity. Tightening his arm, Guy muttered, "He *had* to come. What folly!"

Claude had been carefully tidying his hair. He now stepped closer to Redmond, peering up into the high-held proud countenance. "So you are brother to dear Sir Harry," he murmured. "If you knew . . . if you but *knew* how I have yearned for this moment."

Redmond said a cool, "I also, monsieur."

"The word is monseigneur." Claude spoke the correction in a low voice that rang oddly. "Say it."

Redmond sighed. "Alas, my French is as poor as your English. I had thought monseigneur applied to a prince or a cardinal. Not to a lunatic."

Claude's eyes began to glow with the red light that Charity dreaded to see. He nodded, his smile striking terror into her heart. "Oh, but I shall teach you," he promised softly.

"Claude," said Guy, "I am going to take

Miss Strand out."

"*Au contraire,* dear brother. You are going to remain. Miss Strand is going to remain. She knew who this vermin was, did you not, my sly little English actress?"

With an odd detachment, Charity thought, "It doesn't matter now. Whatever we do or say, he will kill us both. That's why Mr. Redmond was defiant just now. He knows it makes no difference. And if he can be so brave, I must try." She heard her own voice reply, "Yes, I knew."

"This was quite logical," Claude said, surprisingly. "I forgive you it. My brother knew also, however. Did you not, Guy? Of course you did. You were there — a witness — when Parnell left his task half finished. This I shall not forgive, but we will deal with it later." His sparkling eyes turned back to Redmond. "Why, how pale you are become, my dear friend. Is it because I mentioned my late brother?" He stepped a pace closer, the footmen gripping Redmond's arms brutally. "Parnell," said Claude, "was the only creature in this world for whom I had a fondness. And your brother, your miserable worm of a brother, killed him! I swore I would be revenged. Did you know *that* when you crept in here, you sneaking spy?"

"Parnell was an unmitigated, murdering rogue," said Redmond. "Harry was trying to protect the girl Parnell was terrorizing, but he did not —"

Claude drew back his hand and smashed it hard into Redmond's face. Charity smothered a sob as Redmond sagged against the men who held him.

Claude smiled. "I waste no more time. You brought me a book. You said it was Diccon's book. Was it?"

Redmond heard the words dimly. His head rang, and he could taste blood. He said thickly, "Yes."

"Do you know," purred Claude, "I think I do not quite believe this. Why would you give me a notebook you knew to be of such great value?"

Shaking his head in an effort to clear it, Redmond answered, "It got me in here."

"And you gave it me in exactly the same condition as when you received it?"

Redmond lifted his head and looked this maniac squarely in the eye. He said with a faint grin, "Why, Claude, are you accusing me of forgery?"

Guy swore under his breath. Charity bit her lip and shrank, waiting for Claude to strike again. Instead, the hot glare in the brown eyes faded. He murmured, "Such admirable courage. Such staunch devotion I find difficult to comprehend. Why, Redmond? Why should an intelligent, educated man such as yourself be willing to risk all for that — that fat little German fool? Do you so revere him?"

"Yes. Because he is not an individual. To all

intents and purposes, he is England."

It was said quietly and without bravado, but Charity's heart swelled with pride. She said clearly, "Bravo!"

Claude smiled at her. "Guy," he called, "be so kind as to bring Miss Strand over here."

Charity's knees turned to water. She saw Redmond's tense face turn to her. The side of his mouth was bleeding a little. She thought, "I must not make him ashamed for me."

Frowning, Guy said, "I shall not see her harmed, Claude."

"But, my dear, how can you think such wickedness of me? Of course I shall not hurt her. It is quite unnecessary that I do so. Mr. Redmond is going to tell me every detail I want to know — I promise you."

Guy murmured, "Be brave, little one," and led her forward.

"There," said Claude, rubbing his hands together and beaming from one to the other of them. "Now we can all be comfortable and not have to lift up the voices. Dear little Miss Strand, you have the fortitude most admirable. But you have also too much trust, you know. Let me explain this. We have here" — he waved a graceful white hand toward Redmond — "a fine example of British manhood. He has looks, birth, breeding, and you see him as a manly, brave fellow, *oui?*"

"I think him very brave indeed," she said, her heart fluttering frantically against her ribs.

"Would you believe me," said Claude, all benevolence, "if I say that within ten minutes — less perhaps — this so-called brave man will kneel before me? Will grovel? Will tell me each detail I ask? Will betray his king, his country, his family? Will even plead that I question *you* instead of himself?"

Charity slanted a quick glance at Redmond. He stood very still, watching Claude levelly. "No, sir," she said. "That I would not believe."

"Ah. So — I must prove what I say." He beckoned to Shotten, who had stood with his head slightly tilted, watching the quiet drama as one somewhat perplexed by it all. Claude turned aside a little, murmuring something into Shotten's ear. The big man began to grin, laughed, looked at Redmond, and walked to a corner of the room.

Charity was trembling. She felt Guy's hand tighten on her elbow. She saw Shotten take something from the wall and come back. At first she thought the object he carried was a long-tined broom of some kind, but as he came closer she saw it to be a multithonged whip, and for an instant the room blurred before her eyes.

His grin exultant, his eyes very bright, Claude said, "Do you know, Redmond, you do not look well. I wonder if perhaps you are . . . remembering?"

Redmond said nothing, but his gaze was fixed unblinkingly on that murderous whip, and suddenly his face was drawn and white as chalk.

"You may let him go," said Claude. "He will do nothing. You see, he is too frightened." He took the whip from Shotten, and the footmen stepped back.

"I wonder," Claude said, "if you really came here to save Miss Strand. If so, I expect you labour under that strange delusion that men of your stamp call *l'amour*."

Redmond shook his head.

"You must not lie to me any more," chided Claude. "Do you know, Miss Strand, this poor fellow is acquainted with one of these. See —" He reached out and shook the whip in Redmond's face.

Flinging one arm before his eyes, Redmond fairly leapt back.

Claude laughed delightedly. "You see? He is terrified. I shall tell you why. It happened — oh, one year ago, or thereabouts. My beloved brother, Parnell, had a ward he admired deeply. An annoying chit, but he planned to make her his bride. Harry Redmond had the gall, the unmitigated insolence, to persuade her that Parnell was a bad man, and so frightened her that she ran away with him. Parnell followed, *naturellement*. When he came up with their camp, Harry was gone and had left this fine fellow to guard Annabelle. She knew that she had been very naughty, and she was afraid she might be spanked, so she hid. Now, my Parnell had a little — just a trace you understand —

270

of the temper. And he did not propose to spend a great time searching the woods for his capricious lady. So he tied Sir Harry's brave brother to a cart, and he whipped him until Annabelle heard how this hero screamed, and came back. To save him.''

Her eyes enormous in her pale face, Charity stared at him. So that was how Redmond's back had been so brutally scarred! Appalled, she kept her eyes from Redmond, but she knew that he was standing with his head downbent.

Guy said in a strained voice, "He did not make one sound, Claude. You know this.''

"I saw Mr. Redmond's back, Monsieur Sanguinet,'' said Charity. "I wonder he did not die.''

"It *is* a pity,'' sighed Claude. "But we shall take up where my dear Parnell left off. Or would you prefer to tell me now, my dauntless Briton?'' Again, he shook the whip and, again, Redmond shrank, one hand lifting protectively. "Look at the pride of it,'' said Claude, laughing. "Will you not observe the valour? Do you not find it pathetic, mademoiselle?''

Redmond's dark head sank lower. His fists were tight-clenched, but he neither moved nor spoke.

Hilarious, Claude said, "Do you — do you know what he has been doing this year and more? He has been roving Europe, fighting, womanizing, getting himself such a wicked reputation as a rake and a duellist — no? No!

He has been trying to prove he is still a man! And now — here we are again, brave one. Another lady to watch you whine and crawl. Another whip. Is it worth it, eh?"

Redmond's head came up. He leapt for Claude, but was pulled back, his arms twisted so savagely that he gasped with the pain. "Damn you . . ." he said brokenly. *"Damn you! Face me man to man* — with swords or pistols, or bare hands, if you've the —"

"Nonsense! I do not play silly heroics. You will tell me now. You *did* tamper with my book, did you not? You changed some of the entries."

Redmond watched, haggard-eyed, as Claude swung the whip lazily, the thongs swishing in a faintly metallic whisper. Hypnotized, he muttered, "I — did."

Charity winced and had to turn away.

"And the matter of Admiral Deal's treachery. This was your invention?"

Redmond was silent. One of the footmen shoved him and said contemptuously, "You should have a care, monseigneur. I think he will very soon faint."

They all enjoyed this witticism, while Charity blinked away tears, Redmond's eyes closed and his head bowed low, and Guy stood very still, face grim.

Without warning, Claude cracked the whip so that just the tips of the steel-laced thongs touched his victim's chest. Redmond jerked

272

back against the footmen's restraining arms. His voice a harsh croak he admitted, "Yes. I altered it."

"Now that," said Claude, sobering, "was very bad in you. You see, a brave man you are not, but an actor you are. I believed you when first you came here. And thus, Gerard carries with him the Admiral's death warrant. I fear I cannot at all hope to countermand that order, and the Admiral was useful. I am vexed with you, Redmond. But, we must proceed. Now — there was very much in Diccon's little book that was quite the — what is it you say? — the eye-opener. It would be only sensible for you to make a copy for yourself, no? So that when you go back in triumph to London, having slain this wicked dragon that is Claude Sanguinet, you may lay your so dangerous proofs at the feet of your foolish Prince. So you see, I must ask, did you make a copy, my friend? Did you?"

Redmond shook his head, perspiration streaking down his agonized face.

Smiling, Claude trod closer yet, the whip lifting.

"Don't . . ." Mitchell whispered, shrinking back. "Please . . . please don't."

Claude swept the whip high. And frenziedly, Redmond cried, "I copied it!"

Gripping her hands together and pressing them against her trembling lips, Charity prayed.

Amused, Claude said, "Do you see now of

273

what stuff heroes are made, my dear? This whimpering apology for a man would cut your heart out if I asked it." And turning back to his victim, he demanded, "Where is the book you copied? Speak up, Sir Gallantry. Where is it?"

Redmond's head was low again, but he did not answer. Charity could guess the shame he must be feeling, and she felt an aching pity for him.

"Do you know," Claude murmured, enjoying himself hugely, "I believe that now I shall prove a point." Swinging the whip, he strolled towards Charity. "Watch, Redmond, and give me my answer when you tire of hearing this innocent girl scream. . . ."

"Like *hell* I will!"

Two startled footmen found that the shaking craven they so contemptuously held had become a wild man. With a primeval growl Redmond tore free from their careless clasp, caught an arm of each man, and swung with a strength born of fury. Two rogues came suddenly and violently eye to eye and, groaning, clutched their battered faces.

Whirling about, Claude swung the whip and sent it hissing at Redmond's back. Charity heard the crack as those wicked thongs landed. She saw Redmond's slim body arch, his head jerking back. Claude laughed shrilly and swung up the whip again.

Guy leapt to catch one of the whirling thongs

and tugged with all his strength. The whip was wrenched from Claude's hand and sent spinning into a far corner. With an incoherent snarl of fury, Claude turned on his brother.

Through his teeth, Guy said, "You have threatened those I love, kept me in subjugation, shamed me all my life. But, by God, I'll not stand for this!"

Claude's hand darted to an inner pocket.

Propelled by the accumulated misery of long wretched years, Guy's fist came up. It landed hard and true. Claude did a little backward leap into the air and lay down before he touched the floor.

The two footmen, meanwhile, recovering and enraged, had plunged at Redmond. He met them eagerly, dealt out a whizzing left and sent one staggering, but was himself half stunned by a mighty uppercut that reduced the room to a shimmer and brought a deafening roar into his ears. He reeled blindly.

Grinning, the second footman snatched a heavy fourteenth-century mace from the wall and advanced, lifting the spiked iron weapon with both hands.

Guy was engaged in a desperate battle with Shotten. Frantic, Charity also purloined a weapon from Claude's prized collection, and the footman gave a shriek as she drove the spear home. Dropping his mace, he clutched his wounded dignity and spun to confront Charity. His face contorted with rage and pain, he ran at her. Frightened, but still holding her spear level, she retreated.

Redmond shook the mists from his brain, came up behind the footman, and tapped him on the shoulder. "Pardon," he said politely.

The footman whirled into a right that came at his chin like a sledgehammer, and he sank from the fray.

"Look out!" screamed Charity.

Not lacking courage, the first footman was doggedly returning to the attack. Redmond laughed and dispensed a left jab which sent the man to join his friend on the floor.

In the other contest Shotten's hamlike fist had sent Guy reeling back. Shotten followed with a sizzling right jab. It was blocked. From some unsuspected reserve of strength, Guy summoned an uppercut that caught Shotten squarely under the chin, and the big man went down with a crash.

Redmond had started for Claude, and Guy staggered to catch his arm. "Hurry!" he panted. "My . . . carriage, it waits for me. We can —"

"In just . . . one minute," grated Redmond.

"No!" Guy struggled to hold him.

Redmond ripped out a string of profanities and wrenched away. "He may be your brother, but he's a stinking bastard and not fit to live! I've —"

"There is no time for your vengeance! We must get Charity away. The whole staff will be after us in a second only!"

Dazed by this swift chain of events, Charity experienced a jolting sense of excitement. It had sounded — it had *really* sounded as though Guy could help them escape! Certainly, he himself would have to leave now, for Claude would never forgive him. She ran to tug desperately at Redmond's other arm. "Please, *please*, Mr. Redmond! If Guy will help us, we may still have a chance! Please, for England, we *must* try!"

Diccon's voice echoed in Mitchell's ears: "You don't give a *groat* for England. . . ."

The blaze of madness died from his eyes. For a moment, he still stared down at her. Then, drawing quickly away from her touch, he muttered, "Yes. Of course." He strode to open the rear door and peer outside.

Guy meanwhile had hurried to drop to one knee beside his brother's motionless form. He touched Claude's wrist and, reassured, stood, then bent again to slip a large ruby ring from the lax hand.

Redmond called, "The coast is clear now. . . ."

"My regrets," said Guy, taking Charity's hand, "but we have not the time to pause for wraps."

She smiled, undaunted. Watching her, a twinkle came into his eyes. He asked gravely, "Do you really mean to keep the spear?"

Charity had quite forgotten she clutched the

weapon and, with a rather shaken laugh, dropped it.

They went outside. This level of the castle was encircled by a drivepath that curved up to join the main approach road. A brisk breeze was blowing, ice on its breath, but Charity was too nervous to notice such a trifle. Hope was reborn in her breast as she followed Guy along the drive, but she trembled with the fear that, just as this miraculous chance was offered, it might be snatched away.

A closed barouche was before them, the coachman having providentially walked his horses a little way while waiting. A groom jumped down and opened the door, then let down the steps.

Guy handed Charity into the luxurious vehicle and she sank into a corner, praying, "Please God, let them not come. . . ."

Redmond climbed in, sat in the other corner, and looked out the window. Guy entered and pulled the rug over Charity's knees before sitting beside her.

The barouche lurched; the horses' hooves clattered on the cobblestones.

They were moving!

A great tide of thankfulness welled up in Charity's heart. To her horror, she burst into tears.

PART II

The Race

Chapter Thirteen

The Captain came into the luxurious saloon as the yacht began to make its way along the channel towards the open sea. "One might think," he grumbled, "one might think, I say, that Monseigneur would have allowed us the small time of preparation!"

Charity turned from the porthole and Guy ushered her to a chair. "When my brother says 'at once,' I do not argue, *mon capitaine*. But if you tell me this cannot be done, I shall be happy to convey your message to him."

"I do not say it *cannot* be done," answered the Captain, turning his very round and very red face from its preoccupation with the channel and directing a hard stare from Guy to Charity to Mitchell. "I only say it is odd."

"Odd?" Guy's brows lifted. "I brought you a message yesterday, sir, that you were to provision and prepare *La Hautemant* for Monseigneur's imminent departure. You have, I presume, done this?"

"I have, of course," replied the Captain, his snowy whiskers bristling. "But it was my understanding that Monseigneur was to board us. Not" — his gaze turned pointedly from Charity's unlikely garments to Redmond's bruised face — "others."

"My brother appears to feel he has the right to change his plans," Guy said cuttingly. "He desires that his betrothed be conveyed to England with the utmost speed, so as to await him there."

Captain Godoy was relatively new to the service of Claude Sanguinet, a fortunate happenstance, since the former captain of *La Hautemant* had known Charity well and been aware of the circumstances of her flight from Brittany. Nonetheless, Guy's nonchalant announcement of a betrothal he had never heard of caused the fat little Belgian to direct another hard stare at this girl he judged to be somewhat less than a diamond of the first water. Guy took up Charity's left hand, on the third finger of which glittered the great ruby he had appropriated from his brother. "You are not, I am assured, doubting my word?"

The Captain knew that ring. He was fond of rubies and had in fact admired the peerless stone. "I must return to the bridge, monsieur," he said with an immediate and considerable lessening of his annoyed demeanour. "It shall be as you say. Once we are clear of the channel, we — Yes, Monsieur Esmon?"

A thin young man, resplendent in his officer's uniform, came in and said in a high-pitched falsetto, "A boat is putting out from the shore, sir. We are signalled to wait."

Godoy strode to the porthold again.

Charity gave a gasp. Redmond stood, his mouth becoming a thin, hard line. Guy rasped angrily, "No! My brother distinctly ordered that —"

"These are Monseigneur's men, monsieur," the Captain interpolated, peering shoreward. "We shall wait."

And so they waited, nerves stretched tight and eyes straining to the small craft that came rapidly over the choppy grey water, her six oarsmen rowing hard and the one passenger hunched over in the stern. A man of small stature.

Frozen with despair, Charity thought, "It is Claude. He has won, after all."

Redmond, his keen eyes fastened to the distant figure, his body tensed for desperate action, let out his pent-up breath in a faint hiss and said, "Your fiancé is all consideration, ma'am. He sends your little pet along."

With a leap of the heart, Charity cried, "What? You mean it is not —"

"Alas, I fear Monseigneur could not himself come," Guy interjected swiftly. "You will see him very soon, Miss Strand. I think you know the messenger. . . ?"

Watching the boat come alongside, Charity said, "Oh, it is Lion! With Little Patches. How very kind of Monseigneur!"

Captain Godoy grunted and gave it as his opinion that he did not like cats on board *La Hautemant*. "They bring bad luck!"

"Nonsense," said Charity, her heartbeat subsiding to a gallop. "You should be glad to have one on board, to keep down the rats."

"So you are to keep down the rats, are you, *petite chatte?*" Guy stroked the kitten who purred ecstatically on his lap. Laughing, he added, "A very small rat would make short work of this one, I think."

They were gathered in the comfortable parlour of the private suite to which they had repaired as soon as the yacht was well out to sea. Guy was occupying a deep chair, Charity sat beside Lion on a small sofa, and Redmond leaned against the bulkhead, arms folded, his eyes turning often to the porthole beside him, searching the dusk for any sign of a pursuing vessel.

"How glad I am that you brought her, Lion," said Charity. "But however did you manage it?"

His eyes alight with excitement, the boy said, "It was pure luck, missus. That there old fusty-faced maid of yours done it. I went up to see if you might like to go for a ride, and that maid was so busy jaw-me-deading that Little Patches went hopping off. Straight for the basement steps she goes like a flash, and I runs arter her."

"I wonder why she kept going down there?" murmured Charity.

"Rats, probably," offered Redmond, without turning from his vigil.

Charity laughed.

Lion went on, "Lucky I follered her. She ran to the first open door, which was the war room. Strike me silly if ever I see anything like that! People lying about all over the floor, moaning and groaning something terrible."

"You must have been very close behind us if they were not up and about," observed Guy.

"Well, I think I was, sir. But that Shotten cove was trying to get up, so I thought I'd best slow him down." He grinned broadly and said with relish, "I tore up his neckcloth and tied him up with it, and I gagged him with his own stocking, and if that don't stifle him, nothing will!"

Charity clapped her hands. Guy said, "Excellent rascal!" and Redmond slanted an amused smile at the boy.

"Oh, I served them up very fine," boasted Lion. "Did you see that big net hanging on the wall? Monsieur Gerard told me Parnell Sanguinet fetched it back from India, and that he'd used it once to catch a tiger. Well, I trussed Monseigneur and his men up very tight, and then rolled them one by one into the net, and I tied it to the handle of the inside door."

"And the door opens into the corridor," said Charity, watching Lion in awe.

"That will make it something difficult to open," Guy said. "I salute you, my young friend. But — how if my brother's people simply go around to the outer door?"

"I locked it on me way out," said Lion, "and dropped the key in the channel. I rode as fast as I could go, with the kitten in me pocket, and when I see the yacht coming, I told some sailors Monseigneur had sent me with a urgent writing for the Captain. They didn't believe me at first, but then they see the yacht and they didn't dare take no chance but what I was telling the truth. So they rowed us out. Me and Little Patches."

"How clever you have been!" Charity clasped his hand impulsively.

Lion blushed scarlet and looked down in embarrassment.

"And now," said Guy, "we must decide what we do. How you say, Redmond? It is to Birkenhead for us? Or do you think Gerard will sail around Land's End to Portsmouth or Brighton?"

Redmond went to sit on a chest apart from the group. "Has Claude another ship that could come up with us before we reached Birkenhead?"

Guy frowned. "Had he *Se Rallumer* . . . even so, is not impossible."

"I cannot feature his failing to give chase, and at sea we will be very visible, and powerless if he signals Godoy. I think our best chance is to make straight for the Scottish coast. Devenish, I believe, has a cousin dwelling there who has already encountered Claude and who will certainly help us."

"Major Tyndale!" exclaimed Charity. "Of course! And his wife's grandfather is a general who must have great influence with the authorities!" Elated, she turned to Guy, and surprised a look of sadness. With her usual warmheartedness, she crossed to sink to her knees beside his chair. "Guy, *mon pauvre ami*. How difficult this must be for you. We owe you our lives, but when we reach England you must do no more. We shall ask no more of you, shall we, Mr. Redmond?"

Redmond evaded, "Do you mean to return to France, Sanguinet?"

"Who shall say? As for tomorrow, Scotland it shall be." He stood and with a forced smile asked, "For where must I tell our captain to steer?"

Redmond hesitated. "The castle is in Ayrshire, but do you know whereabouts, ma'am?"

"Good heavens!" exclaimed Charity, dismayed. "I've not the least notion."

Lion said, "I knows. It's Castle Tyndale, near a village called Drumdownie. Sticks up like a bloomin' great lighthouse it does, on the very edge of the cliffs. Can't miss it."

The following morning, however, it seemed that they would very easily miss the castle. Charity had retired to her stateroom soon after dinner and gone to bed after offering up some very grateful prayers. She awoke to grey skies and pouring rain, conditions that prevailed all that day. *La Hautemant* sailed on steadfastly, her bow slicing waves that grew even higher. By nightfall they were running before the wind with shortened sail, but in the wee hours the seas became less violent, and at dawn the winds died. They prowled the Scottish coast at a snail's pace, bedevilled by mists that drifted fitfully, threatening to thicken into fog.

Charity went on deck wrapped in one of the greatcoats that had been hung in the wardrobe of Guy's cabin. The air was clammy, and visibility had shrunk to less than a mile. Shivering, she peered at the dark line of hills that was the coast of Scotland.

"You are up early, little one," said Guy, joining her at the rail.

She turned to him with a smile. "Shall we land today, do you think?"

"If our gallant captain can find your friend's castle."

For a little while they both watched the coast, then Charity observed, "It looks very mountainous in places, Guy. Do we sail northward?"

"I think the mists deceive us, and yes, we have had to go south around Kintyre and the Island of Arran, but now we are off Ayrshire. When the sun she come up, you shall see better."

Charity laughed. "The sun! What an optimist!

Is Lion awake?"

"*Oui*. And on the bridge, advising the *Capitaine* how to sail his ship. Redmond is there also."

They glanced at each other.

"He was not really afraid, you know," Guy said quietly. "It was just the clever pose to make my brother's men relax their guard the little piece."

"Yes. And it worked!"

A pause, and now although both stared at the coastline, neither saw it.

"Charity," Guy said hesitantly, "has he spoken to you since we came aboard?"

"A few words only. But I don't believe he has once looked directly at me."

He sighed. "He avoids my eyes also."

"My sister once told me —" Charity began.

"Look!" Lion was shouting from the bridge and pointing eastwards in great excitement. "There it is! There's Castle Tyndale!"

Wreathed with tendrils of mist, the great castle rose at the brink of the cliffs. It presented a very different picture to that of Tor Keep, for although massive, it soared high and gracefully. Constructed of grey stone with large Gothic windows, three tall conical towers and crenellated battlements, it looked majestic, and Charity murmured, "Oh, how very beautiful it is. Like a castle from a fairy tale."

Lion, who had run down to join them, said with a derisive snort, "That ain't what Mr.

Devenish thought of it, Miss Charity. Monsieur Claude pulled all manner of tricks on him and Major Tyndale, 'cause Monsieur was using the castle for hisself and tried to drive 'em out. Mr. Garvey said Devenish was so scared he like to died o' fright!''

Appalled by the awareness that Redmond had also joined them and was standing close by, she said, "We all have an Achilles' heel, Lion. Something that may cause the very bravest person to weaken, even if only briefly.''

"Oh yus,'' the boy scoffed. "But a *real* man wouldn't never let it beat him. He'd be brave and stand buff, no matter what, he would!''

"That would depend on how deep was his fear. Or how sensitive his nature. We are all so different, you know. And surely, the important thing is not that a man never be afraid, for such a one must be a fool, but that, however afraid, he goes on and does his best. That, I think, is true heroism, Lion.''

Unconvinced, Lion grunted.

Guy glanced around, saw Redmond standing there, his face expressionless, and was dismayed.

"Your Captain says there's a cove below the castle, Guy,'' said Redmond. "He will drop anchor there, and have us taken ashore. Then he means to return to Tordarroch. He asks that we prepare to land.''

Dogs began to bay frantically as Charity, holding

Guy's arm, followed Lion and Redmond along the winding path that led up the cliffs to Castle Tyndale. She heard a door slam and thought with relief that someone was here, even if the Tyndales were from home. Panting, she paused at the top of the path, looking back to the cove far below, but *La Hautemant* was already disappearing into the southern mists.

A howl of excitement rang out. *"Mitch!* By God! It's my brother! And he's got *Miss Strand!"*

Charity's heart leapt with joy. "They're *here!"* she cried wildly. "Oh, thank God!"

She began to run, and heard whoops and shouts, distant at first, but coming closer as they rounded the side of the great structure. She had a brief impression of broad lawns and fine old trees and flowerbeds, but then the wide steps at the front of the castle were suddenly full of men.

Redmond drawled, "Our reinforcements have arrived, certainly."

Guy drew back, but Charity saw her brother leap down the steps and she gave a shriek and ran joyously to meet him. With an answering shout, Justin Strand galloped to grab and hug her so hard she thought her ribs would crack. "You're safe!" he cried emotionally, swinging her around. "Now — thank God! Thank God!"

She kissed him wholeheartedly, saw the glint of thankful tears in his blue eyes, and then was torn from his arms, swung higher and soundly kissed by her brother-in-law, Leith's deep voice ringing with gladness. Again, she was wrenched away, and Alain Devenish was adding his own salutes to her radiant face.

Everyone was shouting at once. An exuberant Sir Harry Redmond pounded his quiet brother on the back, and the little clerical gentleman, Reverend Langridge, wrung and wrung at Mitchell's hand, while beaming upon them all.

Charity was grateful to see Tristram go and grip Guy Sanguinet's hand and say something to him that brought a smile to Guy's face. Devenish turned to Lion, who looked scared and ill-at-ease.

"Look!" shouted Devenish, laughingly, holding Little Patches aloft. "Another prisoner rescued!"

There was a sudden silence. "Jupiter!" gasped Leith, staring at the kitten. "She was with *you*, Charity? But —"

"H-hey!" shouted Jeremy Bolster, running from the castle, pulling on his jacket and minus one boot. He came up with the happy crowd, halted, and threw out his arms. Charity ran into them gladly, was hugged once more, and a shy kiss planted on her cheek.

The air rang with questions, laughter, and badinage. And Charity stood there, weeping happy tears, her heart too full for words while these dear friends and loved ones she had feared never to see again closed in around her.

A tall, fair-haired man she had never met

came out onto the steps and stood watching. Over the uproar, Leith shouted, "It's my sister, Tyndale. Mitchell Redmond found her for us!"

Strand asked anxiously, "My dearest girl, you *are* all right? They didn't harm you?"

"They frightened me very badly, Justin. And made me horribly drugged. But, oh, I am *home!* Thanks to Mr. Redmond, and Guy — and Lion!"

Strand's rumpled fair head jerked around to stare at the youth. *"Lion. . . ?* By Jove — it *is!* But, you're Garvey's tiger!"

Afraid, and his conscience extremely uneasy, Lion stammered, "I — I ain't not — no more, I ain't."

"Oh," said Strand. "Well, I shouldn't wonder! What the deuce have you done to your hair?"

And suddenly it seemed so hilarious that Charity began to laugh and couldn't stop, her peals of mirth so infectious that they all were drawn in until the castle rang with the sound of it. "Oh," gasped Charity, wiping her eyes. "If that isn't just like you, Justin! Here — here we are . . . just this minute escaped from that wretched man . . . and you must worry because Lion was made to dye his hair!"

"Well, it looks awful." Strand grinned. "Come along now, and meet our host!"

They proceeded to the steps, where Major Craig Tyndale was presented. His hair was a few shades darker than that of his cousin Alain

Devenish, and his pleasant features showed small trace of that ebullient young man's famed good looks. He bowed over Charity's hand and begged that she come inside. "My wife is away, ma'am, but I know she would wish you to borrow whatsoever you might need. I'll send a maid upstairs with you do you wish to refresh yourself and change your dress."

Charity thanked him as he led the way into the lofty Great Hall and thence to a large and comfortable drawing room, since she told him she could not bear to be parted just yet from her loved ones. She had been determined to dislike this man who had stolen away the girl Devenish loved so devotedly, but she found that despite herself she warmed to him for his quiet manner, his grave smile, and his pleasant Canadian accent. His grey eyes were not perhaps as fine, but much more friendly than those of Mr. Redmond, she decided.

Devenish said brightly, "Welcome to the haunted castle."

Tyndale glanced at him, but said nothing.

"If you could only know how glad I am to be here," Charity said fervently. "I have so much to ask you — and so much to tell."

Tyndale led her to a comfortable chair and went over to tug on the embroidered bell-pull. Strand and Leith seated themselves on a sofa, Devenish perched on the arm, Bolster, Sir Harry, and the Reverend Langridge pulled chairs closer, and Lion sat on the jut of the hearth, watching Little Patches creep about, making a dramatic stalk of this new place.

"My poor girl," said Leith kindly, "you have had a dreadful time. You know, of course, that we failed you miserably."

"Followed the wr-wrong coach," Bolster said with a wry nod. "Lot of silly g-g-gudgeons!"

"Just so soon as we realized what had happened," put in Sir Harry, "we rushed up here, because —"

"Because I'd told them what transpired here with good old Claude last year," Devenish interposed. "We was expecting to find Diccon here. . . ." He glanced curiously at Mitchell.

"It looks," said the Reverend in his mild voice, "as though my nephew was luckier than us all."

Mitchell, who had drifted away to stand quiet and aloof beside a side window, met his brother's curious stare. "Diccon's dead, I think," he said flatly.

Sir Harry's face twisted. "Oh, never say so!"

"Are you perfectly sure?" Leith asked, his own face paling.

"Then you've not heard from diLoretto?" Mitchell countered.

"Your man?" Puzzled, Sir Harry shook his head. "What has he to do with Diccon, bantling?"

Mitchell's lips tightened. "It's a long story. I'm not sure we've the time." He turned to Leith. "I don't mean to be melodramatic, but could you send a man up to the battlements to keep watch?"

"By Jove!" Devenish exclaimed, his handsome face brightening. "Old Claude?"

Mitchell nodded. "Very likely, I'm afraid."

A rather rumpled butler hurried in and crossed to receive Tyndale's orders. He looked astonished and left quickly.

Mitchell glanced at the clock as it chimed the quarter-hour. "I'll be as brief as possible," he said, and embarked on a very abbreviated version of his journey to Birkenhead and the fight at the bridge. "If Diccon was not killed," he added, "he showed no sign of life. I knew diLoretto had apparently escaped detection. I fancied he'd have contacted you by this time."

The butler and a maid came in at this point with trays of coffee and cakes. Mitchell drew up a chair and continued his tale, pausing only to ascertain that a footman had been sent to the roof to warn of any approaching vessel. He spoke tersely until he reached the point of their final confrontation with Claude. Hesitating, he finished abruptly, "There was a bit of a tussle in the war room, but thanks to Guy we were able to get away and —"

Indignant protests interrupted him. Devenish said, "Come on now, Redmond. You can't fob us off like that. What *kind* of tussle? And *how* did you escape?"

His face as expressionless as his voice, Mitchell said, "I escaped because Miss Strand wields a fearsome spear. And because Guy rescued me." When the shouts of excitement died down, he added, "Excuse me, gentlemen. I shall let someone else finish the story." He stood amid a flat silence and sauntered from the room.

Bolster and Harry exchanged mystified glances.

Guy said quickly, "Perhaps I may tell you. . . ?" Urged to do so, he described the battle with typical modesty, so that Charity often felt called upon to interrupt. No mention was made of Mitchell's ordeal, but between them they painted so graphic a picture of that struggle that cheers rang out when they finished.

As soon as he could make himself heard, Leith asked, "Do you know when the crown is to be delivered? Is there a definite time?"

Leaning in the doorway, Mitchell said, "It is to be taken to the Pavilion at Brighton. There will be a dinner party before the ball to commemorate the Battle of Waterloo, and Claude has sent Prinny a note saying that the crown is presented to him in honour of the occasion."

His news was greeted with dismay.

"*Wednesday?*"

"And today's Saturday! Egad!"

"Can we reach London in less than five days?" the Reverend wailed.

"Not London, sir, Brighton," corrected Leith. "And we *must!*"

"If we ride like hell," said Devenish, ever the optimist, "we could do it in half the time. Certainly by the eighteenth!"

Leith said thoughtfully, "If we could just get some backing."

Tyndale nodded. "Someone will have to go to the authorities."

"Authorities!" Devenish regarded him with scorn. "Just like you, Craig, to want to bring in a lot of pompous officials."

"Doubt they'd listen, old f-fellow," said Bolster.

"They wouldn't listen to me," Leith agreed. "Or even to poor Diccon. The only other man who could help us is in Russia. We're on our own, gentlemen. Dev's right. If we appeal for help, we not only invite endless delays and the prolific red tape of officialdom, but we're more than likely to be clapped up as dangerous lunatics."

Charity intervened hopefully, "But Mr. Redmond said your wife has a relation living nearby, Major. Her grandpapa?"

"Very true, ma'am. General Drummond. And the old fellow is a fighter — he'll move heaven and earth to help."

Automatically assuming command, Leith said, "Then you must go to him at once, Tyndale."

"I'd sooner go with you, Colonel. At all events, I doubt the General could find us help in time."

"Perhaps not. But if we fail, somebody in

authority must attempt to make the truth known."

Tyndale looked downcast, but he strode over to tug on the bell-rope once more, and when the butler ran in with an immediacy that betrayed the fact he'd been close by, he said, "Send word to the stables, if you please. We shall need six" — he scanned the tense group — "no, forgot Mr. Redmond — *seven* fast horses, and a coach and four. Quickly, man!"

The butler flew.

Also taking inventory, Guy said, "Major Tyndale, you have also forget me, I think?"

Tyndale glanced questioningly to Leith.

Tristram said, "Guy, under the circumstances, I think it best you stay clear. You can help us most by going with the Major and providing any needed details."

"And what about me?" demanded Charity, as they all stood. "I'll not be left, Tris!"

He smiled at her fondly. "My dear girl, you have done splendidly, but you surely do not intend to gallop down Scotland and the length of England with a bunch of wild men who —"

"Of course she don't," Strand interjected. "My sister will ride with you, Tyndale."

"Precisely why I ordered up the coach and four," said the Major.

Her eyes blazing with indignation, Charity declared, "Well, I'll not! I have been kidnapped and bullied and petrified these two weeks and more! I'll not now be abandoned miles from home. Besides, I want to see how Rachel goes on."

"For heaven's sake, do not talk such rubbish, child," said Strand in his impatient fashion. "A fine sight you'd present in your muslin gown, riding at the gallop!"

Mitchell drawled, "Do you mean to argue about it much longer, we'd as well start preparing our blacks."

Tyndale said briskly, "We'd best arm ourselves, gentlemen. The gun room is this way."

As they hurried into the hall, Strand seized Charity's elbow. "Find yourself a cloak, love. The wind's coming up."

Overhearing, Tyndale said, "You will find whatever you need in my wife's room, ma'am." He walked beside her and gestured to a hovering lackey.

The brothers were alone. Michell regarded Harry without expression. A faint smile curving his lips, Harry went over and tilted his brother's chin up. "Caught one here, I see," he murmured, lightly touching the bruised mouth. He dropped his hand onto Mitchell's shoulder. "Well done, halfling! Gad, but I'm proud of you."

Mitchell met his eyes squarely. "Only because Guy and Miss Strand did not tell you the whole. I was listening outside." He saw Harry's smile fade into a look of consternation but nerving himself, ploughed on. "Do you know what Claude said? He said I'd spent these last thirteen months trying to prove my manhood."

Harry had thought the same. Shocked, he managed to say with relative calm, "Is that so? Well, if it was truth, you've certainly proved it."

"No." Mitchell turned away, picked up a dainty Sèvres compote dish and inspected it unseeingly.

Angered, Harry exclaimed, "Good God, Mitch! If this coup does not convince you, I do not know what will! You longed to face Claude. You did, and —"

"And learnt to the full what cowardice — real, *panicked* cowardice — feels like."

Harry caught his breath. With his tense gaze fixed on that stern averted profile, he waited.

"When Claude discovered my true identity, he —" Mitchell set the compote dish down with care and turned to face him. "He questioned me."

"Bastard! With his fists, I take it?"

"No. With a whip."

Harry stiffened and his dark brows drew together over slitted eyes.

"I showed yellow as a dog," said Mitchell flatly, his head well up, but his thin hands clenching and unclenching nervously.

"Well, er, well, dammit, of course you did! What more natural, considering that only a year ago you were near killed by that flogging you —" Mitchell jerked his head away. And longing to throw an arm about those rigid shoulders, Harry said stoutly, "You recovered yourself. That's the important thing. In spite of your very natural reaction, you got them out of there."

"Guy got us out. I recovered myself, I suppose you could say; to a point, that is all."

Indignant, Harry argued, "Miss Strand said you fought like a tiger. That don't sound like 'to a point.'"

Mitchell could no longer meet those fiercely loyal eyes, but Harry must know the bitter truth. His voice began to falter, as he said, "When Claude threatened me with that whip, I couldn't describe how I felt. And — when it struck me . . . oh, it wasn't the pain that I mean, exactly. It was as if I was — petrified. I simply couldn't move. If — if Guy hadn't torn the whip from Claude —" He took a deep, trembling breath. "I doubt you'd be proud of me today, *Sauvage*."

Damning Claude Sanguinet from the depths of his soul, Harry growled, "I am not proud of you now. You blasted idealistic young idiot! What you experienced was shock. And perfectly understandable. Good God, Mitch, *must* you set yourself on a pedestal so impossibly high you're not allowed to be human?"

"Set myself on a —" gasped Mitchell. "Well, of all the —"

"Be still! Now you just listen for a minute! I've seen better men than you, or me, or even Leith, panic in battle: seasoned fighting men who suddenly faced something they could not deal with, so that they ran, screaming, from the field. And I've seen the best of them come back and fight again — more gallantly than before." Harry paced to grip Mitchell's arm strongly. "Give yourself a chance, you blasted high-in-the-instep young chawbacon!"

Mitchell shook his head miserably. "You say that now. But if I'd behaved in so cowardly a way on a battlefield, you'd have likely had me shot out of hand." Before Harry could comment, he pulled a small, battered notebook from his pocket. "I carried this in my boot until today. You take charge of it, Sir Captain. Diccon thought it vital that it should be delivered with the greatest despatch to someone in authority. Wellington, I'd think would be —"

"The devil I will!" Harry waved the book away. "I don't want the blasted thing! *You* got it. *You* deliver it."

"For the love of God! Have you understood *nothing* I've told you? If Claude should get his hands on me again, and I have this, I might —"

"Turn yellow, as you did this time?" finished Harry brutally.

Stunned, Mitchell stared at him.

"Panic for an instant?" went on Harry. "Then fight on, as you did this time? Well, what in hell's wrong with that? Oh no, my lad! You'll not shove the responsibility off onto me. I've the utmost faith in you. Besides —" he slanted an oblique glance at Mitchell's pale face, and added, "I've done my share. I fought on the Peninsula. *You* didn't, you young rapscallion." His own heart twisted as he saw his brother flinch. "I'm getting old," he said blandly.

"Old!" exclaimed Mitchell. "You're not *thirty!*"

"Ah, but I've lived hard. . . ." He paused, the twinkle fading from his eyes. He said awkwardly, "And you forget, I've watched you grow up. I *know* that you could not possibly be a coward, Mitch."

Through a long silent moment their eyes met and held, the affection they usually disguised now very apparent. Then Harry said with an embarrassed laugh, "You'd *better* not be — else I shall have to break your stupid neck!"

Mitchell turned away. His voice rather muffled, he said, "Damned . . . cawker . . ."

Yolande Drummond Leith was only a little taller than Charity, and if her figure was more rounded, the difference in dress size was not so marked as to be impossible. Torn by guilt lest her determination cause the gentlemen to be delayed, Charity changed into a dashing dark blue riding habit, with trembling haste jammed a jaunty little blue hat on the curls the abigail had hurriedly brushed into a semblance of neatness, and all but ran along the hall once more.

She had been quicker than she knew; the men were gathered on the drive, watching grooms lead fine saddled horses from the stables, a closed carriage following.

Lion, holding Little Patches, came over. "You'll let me go along wi' you, Miss Charity?" he pleaded.

"Of course," she answered with a reassuring smile. "However could we —" She checked to a faint sound like a distant shout that seemed to be coming from — She jerked her head back. A small figure, high atop the battlements, waved madly. Spinning around she saw many men racing up the side path from the beach. Men armed with pistols, muskets, clubs, or the gleaming steel of sword and dagger. And to one side stood Claude Sanguinet, bruised and hatless, aiming a pistol at Tristam Leith's back.

"Tris!" screamed Charity.

Leith whipped around.

Without a second's hesitation, Guy sprang in front of him.

A bright flame blossomed from the pistol. Horrified, Charity heard the following blast of the shot. Guy jerked backwards and fell.

The men grouped about Leith exploded into action. A volley of shots sent the attackers scattering for cover.

Leith shouted, "Mitch! *Go!* We'll hold 'em as long as we can!"

Mitchell, now clad in a riding coat and boots borrowed from Tyndale, at once swung into the saddle of a fine grey horse. Crouching low over the animal's mane, he drove home his spurs and was away like the wind, a flurry of shots following.

Devenish sprinted to throw an arm around Charity and drag her around to the far side of the castle. Far below she caught a glimpse of a large ship riding at anchor, a longboat making towards the shore, crowded with more men.

"That triple damned idiot," fumed Devenish, glancing at the battlements. "Was he asleep up there?"

"Look! Look!" cried Charity. "Another boat, Dev!"

"The devil! Our Claude has brought a whole blasted battalion of his rogues with him! You must get out of this!"

Another outburst of shots, and Strand ran up leading a frightened bay horse. "Here you go, love," he cried, beckoning Charity to him. "Hurry!"

She ran to his side. He kissed her and threw her into the saddle. It was not a sidesaddle, but she threw one knee over the pommel and took the reins, bending to call a frantic, "But what about you and —"

"Follow Redmond!" said Strand. "We'll come."

The shots became louder and closer. Devenish slapped the horse's rump sharply. The mare needed no more urging and bolted madly down the drive.

Chapter Fourteen

Half an hour later, having caught sight of Mitchell Redmond only three times, Charity surmounted a steep hill and scanned the road ahead in desperation. Her anxious gaze swept across dimpling emerald valleys and gentle hills framed by the dark blue of distant mountains. Here and there the chimneys of some isolated farmhouse rose above the trees. A corner of her mind scolded that the Scots called them crofts, not farms. . . . Black-faced sheep grazed contentedly on the slope to her left. The sun came out from behind racing clouds, sending shadows scudding across the land. At any other time she would have joyed in the beauty of it all, but now she knew only dismay because as far as she could see there was no sign of horse and rider.

She turned in the saddle, looking fearfully back the way she had come. There was no sign of Claude's relentless followers, but neither did any loved and familiar figures gallop to accompany her. She urged her mount on, wondering miserably if Justin was unhurt . . . if Guy had been killed, or —

She gave a squeak of fright as she rounded a sharp curve and a horseman charged from a stand of birches beside the road.

Lowering his levelled pistol, Redmond gasped, "You! Good God! I thought —"

"Thank heaven," Charity babbled. "I was afraid I had quite lost you!"

He restored the pistol to his saddle holster, glanced northwards and asked, "Where are the others? Is my brother all right, do you know?"

"I don't! I dare not think —" She broke off, biting her lip and trying not to cry. "Justin threw me onto this horse and sent me after you. Another longboat was coming ashore and many men. I am so afraid. . . ." Her voice shredded into silence.

Redmond said harshly, "Nonsense. They'll do their possible. They're a damned fine bunch. Just now, ma'am, I am going to have to ride like fury. Keep up if you can, but when we come into Dumfries I must leave you and head south very fast, if I'm to have any chance of reaching the Pavilion by Wednesday evening."

So he doubted her ability to keep up. It was true that she was not used to lengthy rides, but her health was vastly improved these days. She just might surprise the gentleman! And so, when he spurred, she spurred also. Redmond rode a big grey gelding; her own mount had an untiring stride that ate up the miles steadily. But their way led through country that became increasingly hilly, and often Redmond had to slow to rest the horses.

Five hours later, Charity was aching with fatigue and parched with thirst. But she knew that Redmond often glanced back the way they had come, and she resolved to fall dead from the saddle before she would beg him to stop.

The wind was colder and the clouds darkening when he turned into the yard of a croft nestled in a small valley. He dismounted with easy grace and no sign of weariness, but when he reached to lift Charity down, she stared at him blankly for a moment, doubting her ability to move.

One dark brow lifted, the side of his mouth twisting into a faint sneer that inflamed her. She slipped from the saddle. He caught her waist, which was fortuitous, for her legs were numbed, and she tottered for an instant.

He murmured, "I'm sorry, Miss Strand. This must be very taxing for you."

"I shall . . . manage," she gasped defiantly, but Mitchell's steady gaze caused her to be oddly flustered. She stepped back and remembering, took out her handkerchief, unwrapped Claude's ruby ring and thrust it at him. "Here, take this horrid thing."

He stared down at the great ruby, then put it into his waistcoat pocket as the door of the small house opened.

The crofter came out to them. "Is it food or fresh horses ye'll be after, sir?" he asked in a thick Scots accent. "I can gie ye the vittles. But ye'll need tae ride tae McDougall's fer hacks."

A scrawny woman, wiping red, work-roughened hands on an immaculate apron, came to the door. " 'Tis only a wee way, sir," she said with a friendly smile. "If ye'd prefair it, ma mon can gae fer ye, while ye set and eat. I've some pork pie ye're welcome tae."

"Splendid." Redmond handed the reins to the crofter. "Will you be so very good as to take care of these animals until they're sent for? And get me the best mounts you can hire from your neighbour. My sister and I are summoned to Carlisle. Our father lies dangerously ill there." He discussed the arrangements briefly, pressed a guinea into the man's hand and was rewarded by a delighted grin. "Now, ma'am," he said, turning to the farm wife, "if we may impose on you?"

She bobbed a curtsey and ushered them through a tiny overfurnished parlour and into a wide kitchen, fragrant and cosy, with a fine fire leaping on the hearth, and a small table before it.

Twenty minutes later, washed, fed, and refreshed, they went outside to find two likely-looking mounts already waiting. Redmond paid the costs from the fat purse Harry had thrust into his hand only seconds before Sanguinet's appearance. He turned to boost Charity into the saddle, only to hesitate and remark frowningly that she could not continue without a proper sidesaddle. "You had best stay here until —"

Charity was already very unpleasantly aware of the long and awkward ride this morning, but she said a dauntless, "No! Help me up, if you please. I'll ride astride."

"Astride!" His gaze flickered over her habit. "In that?"

"It will serve," she said confidently, while praying the skirt would not split when she mounted.

He scowled. "Of all the ridiculous —"

"We waste time, brother dear," she reminded sweetly.

Redmond gave her a level look and bent to receive her boot, which he thought absurdly small, and tossed her up into the saddle.

Before her accident, Charity had been something of a tomboy, and this was not her first experience at riding astride, so that her mount was not as gruesome as Redmond had anticipated. However, although Yolande's habit was sturdily made, it had not been intended for such a reach and it slid above Charity's ankles revealingly as she settled into the saddle.

The crofter and his wife stared, patently astonished. Redmond slanted an embarrassed glance at them. "Women!" he muttered, and strode to his own mount.

Watching them ride out, the crofter said

dubiously, "I'll allow 'tis warranted. Under the caircumstances. Their pa dyin', ye ken."

"Aye." His wife nudged him in the ribs. "If 'tis Carlisle they're bound fer in sic a tearing rush. They didna look much like kinfolk tae me. Him sae bonny and dark, and her sae fair."

"Whist! They didna act like lovers, neither. Scarce a worrud 'twixt 'em the entire time."

"Much ye know o' lovers!" she scoffed, then squealed as he chased her into the house.

Redmond set a steady pace that afternoon, so that Charity soon began to chafe at their rate of progress and wonder if it was out of concern for her that they travelled so slowly. She glanced at him, preparing to broach the subject, but he had not spoken for the past hour and his face was set in such grim lines that she decided to say nothing. After another hour, their route followed what was little more than an uphill footpath, becoming ever more steep. When they reached the summit, Redmond looked back, and Charity turned also. Green hills and gently sloping valleys spread as far as she could see, but still there was no sign of riders, and her heart sank. Surely, if all had gone well, Justin and Tris and Devenish would have come after her. Surely, at least *they* would have come . . . unless . . . She thrust such dark conjecture away and turned back. Redmond's eyes were shifting away from her. He said quietly, "They may have led Claude's lot in another direction, you know."

She brightened. "Yes! Or perhaps they decided to go to Steep Drummond and ask the General for help after all."

"Very likely. Do you have any notion how many men were in the boats you saw?"

"About twenty in each, I should think."

He was silent, frowning slightly.

"Oh!" exclaimed Charity. "You are thinking that even if my brother and the rest of them did ride to Steep Drummond, Claude could afford to split his men!"

He said dryly, "No one could accuse you of being dullwitted, Miss Strand."

"Then why do we go so slowly? It will be dark soon, and this is *Saturday*, Mr. Redmond."

He pointed ahead. "That is why," he said simply.

Looking where he indicated, Charity gave a gasp. Gone were the gentle hills. Before them lay an increasingly rugged landscape with jutting crags and boulder-strewn ravines. The white plume of a waterfall shot out from a steep bluff a mile or so distant, the sunlight awakening a small rainbow about the descending spray. Below them, a hurrying stream sparkled, and the lesser slopes were rich with trees and shrubs and the royal carpet of the heather.

Watching her thin face, Redmond saw her lower lip sag a little and the great greenish eyes take on an awed glow. "Oh, how magnificent," she breathed.

"I doubt the horses would agree," he said with brusque impatience, and started his chestnut forward again. "If we're to reach Dumfries before dark, ma'am, we must go along as steadily as we can without overtaxing these poor hacks."

"Before *dark?*" she echoed anxiously. "Good heavens! I'd fancied we were almost there. How far have we to go?"

"About twenty miles." He added, "As the crow flies."

But they were not crows. The terrain became ever more difficult. There were no paths now, and he could only be on the lookout for the few landmarks the crofter had told him of. They had to dismount often and lead their horses, clambering over rocky and uneven ground. Charity, her balance not good at best, followed Redmond's mare, stumbling often and glad he did not see her clumsiness. As the miles slowly slipped past, she began to tire again, but she persevered doggedly, refusing to look ahead, struggling to keep pace, and determined not to allow exhaustion to overpower her.

She soon discovered that going up was dreadful, but that going down was worse. They were leading the horses, another waterfall booming to their left, when her boot turned on the slipper surface and she could not restrain a shriek as she fell. An arm of iron whipped

around her. She was slammed against Redmond's chest, her nose buried in his cravat.
Shuddering, she clung to him for an instant,
then pulled away, panting out her thanks.

This time when she looked up at him, he did
not evade her glance but scanned her face
narrowly. "Are you all right? I'm a clod for
not remembering that you were ill for a long
time."

"No, really. I'm perfectly . . . fine, now."
She fought to regain her breath and — ignoring
the catch in her side, her stiff aching muscles
and sore feet — summoned a smile. It faded
when it was returned by a scowl. Her heart
sinking again, she faltered, "I am slowing you
dreadfully . . . am I?"

A reluctant smile dawned. "You are doing
splendidly. All this clambering about and no
word of complaint. How fortunate I am that
you are no pampered beauty, else I do not
doubt I'd have been dealing with the vapours
long since."

He was surprised that these kind remarks
should have produced such a stormy look.
Guessing (wrongly) at the reason, he admitted,
"I should have kept to the main road, I suppose. But it seemed safer not to do so. And
the crofter told me we could lop ten miles from
the journey by following this route. Cheer
up, ma'am. We will rest for a moment. The
horses —"

"Are doing very well," she put in with a

determined little nod. "Mr. Redmond, you must not think of me as a woman. I am simply a — a comrade in arms!"

It was fortunate that at that moment of nobility she should stumble again. Steadying her, Redmond's eyes began to twinkle. "So that's what is meant by that term," he said, his arm about her waist.

Mortified, she pushed him away. "You mistake it! I had not the least intention — I mean, pray do not suppose I want, er, I mean —"

He released her as though her touch burnt him. "But of course. I am not to think of you as a woman. Very understandable." And with his faintly sneering smile he said, *"En avant,* Monsieur Mulot."

"Fieldmouse?" expostulated Charity, indignantly.

"I am told not to think of you as a woman. I must think of you as you requested — a comrade. A male comrade. And fieldmice are small as is my comrade. Also, they have very bright eyes." He shrugged. "Now, if you are done with this frivolity, miss — monsieur, perhaps we might continue?"

He took up his reins and walked on.

Following, Charity muttered, "Fieldmouse, indeed!"

Soon, they left the rugged passes and came out into more open country. Redmond seemed relieved and, suspecting he had been lost,

Charity asked if he knew where they were.

"Still in Scotland," he replied noncommittally.

She sniffed. "How very illuminating."

The corners of his lips quivered. He slanted an amused glance at her. "Wildcat!"

"Do not confuse your creatures, sir. I am the fieldmouse, remember?"

"True. Very well, monsieur. Prepare yourself. We must travel faster now, else we'll be caught out all night."

"How fortunate that I am not a 'pampered beauty,' " she retorted dryly.

So that was what had irked her. With a furtive grin he said, "Yes, indeed," thereby further infuriating her, and spurred to a gallop.

Unaccountably, tears stung Charity's eyes. She had pushed back the hair from her perspiring forehead so many times that she was very sure she had a dirty face. And if her coiffure had suffered as badly as she suspected, she must look a fright. But she *had* managed to keep up, and all he could do was speak scarcely a word for hours and then be horrid. Spurring so as to come up with him, she thought, "I wonder if Claude is near?" Shivering, she glanced back. The hills rose green and peaceful and majestic, with no sign of pursuing riders.

"Monsieur Mulot, wake up!"

The voice was far away but there was an

urgency about it that demanded a response. Opening heavy eyes, Charity saw something dark and hairy within an inch of her nose, and she sprang up with a small shriek.

It was dusk and cold, and she was still mounted on the poor hack. Mitchell Redmond stood at her left stirrup, looking up at her. Reality burst in upon her, and her mouth drooped.

"Bad dream?" Redmond enquired mildly.

"I thought it was a great spider," she said foolishly. And then, overcome by guilt, "Oh, I am so sorry! What a widgeon I am."

He stared up at her, his smile fading.

Stung, she thought, "He might at least have denied it!"

"Where are we now?" she asked, and added a pithy, "Or do you know, Mr. Redmond?"

"We are coming into Dumfries. See the lights yonder? But your horse has thrown a shoe, I think, and you cannot ride through the town with your skirts hoisted up over your knees. Although they're pretty knees, I grant you."

"How dare —" Her gaze flashed downward. Aghast, she saw that he was perfectly correct, but when she instinctively made to tug at her skirts, her hands refused to move.

Redmond said, "If you will dismount now. Monsieur Mulot. . . ?" His voice hardened. "I assure you I mean only to lift you down."

"Yes. I heard you. But I — I cannot seem to move."

Frowning, he reached up and began gently to unpry her fingers. They were icy cold and white from the sustained effort of holding to the reins. "Poor fieldmouse," he said in a very kind voice. "At least tonight should see the end of this for you. There — lean to me, now."

She obeyed, but when he set her down, she could not walk and would have fallen if he'd not continued to hold her. She thought no more of it than that she was stiff from the unaccustomed exercise, but Mitchell, recalling that she'd been without the use of her legs for three years, was terrified. Having not the least notion of that fact, she wailed faintly, "How stupid!"

"Nonsense," he said gruffly. "But you shall have to endure my touch, I'm afraid."

She glanced at him sharply, but he was looking around the rough moorland rise whereon they had halted. He carried her to a small boulder nearby and sat her on it.

"Here we go," he said, and whipped up the skirts of her habit.

With an outraged shriek, Charity sprang up. Redmond straightened also and made a lunge for her.

With all her strength, she slapped his face and tottered back. "Beast!" she screamed. "Horrid, womanizing, cowardly beast!"

Even in the dusk she saw his face whiten. Then he was upon her. Ignoring the little fists that clawed and beat at him, he swung her into his arms, carried her back to the rock and slammed her onto it once more. He flinched as her nails raked his cheek, and he seized her flying fists, holding them so tightly that she was powerless and crouched in helpless fury, glaring up at him.

"Had you an ounce of common sense, madam," he snarled between his teeth, "you would know my *only* thought was to restore the use of your limbs as quickly as possible. Certainly not to roll you around in the grass for a jolly interlude!"

Her cheeks flamed, and her eyes fell before the fierce blaze of his own. He muttered something furiously, but she made no further demur as he pulled up her skirts again. He began to massage her legs, his hands firm and strong and efficient, until she began to fear the frail stuff of her lacy chemise would rip under his ministrations. Soon, the blood was coursing through her legs so painfully that she could scarcely keep from weeping. Somehow, she kept silent, sitting there feeling beyond words ridiculous with her legs stuck out and her flaming face averted, until he sighed and drew back.

He said with cold but meticulous politeness, "There, ma'am. See if you can stand now."

Without a word, Charity took his hand and stood. She gasped as she began to totter about, but she did not fall.

Redmond said judicially, "That's better. We'll walk a little way, and then you can ride my horse. We shall have to get yours shod, but with luck we can ride these hacks again after we find some food for all of us."

Charity's attempt to answer was foiled by the refusal of her voice to obey her wishes. She felt sunk with shame that she had behaved in such a way, but also horribly embarrassed that Mr. Redmond had seen her undergarments and had touched her legs. Yet she knew also that he did indeed regard her as an object, not as a woman. And that his intentions had been so far from what she'd imagined that he must think her a total henwit.

Looking at her averted face, he said scornfully, "Lord, are you still trembling, then? I do assure you, Monsieur Mulot, that you've no least cause for such maidenly fears. This — coward — will never lay hands upon your, er, limbs again."

She heard the brief pause before he said "coward" and the harsh bitterness with which it was ground out, and her heart thudded into her shoes. Why *ever* had she called him so? How could she have used that word after what had transpired in Claude's war room? How *could* she have been so thoughtless and so cruel? Wretchedly, she stammered, "No, I did not mean — That is, I — I know you were trying to —"

"Here," he said impatiently, "mount up, and we'll be on our way. You can ride sidesaddle for this last leg — er, I mean, for this last part of the journey — if you can manage."

Meekly, she allowed him to boost her into the saddle. She could have wept when her blistered bottom struck the leather, but she clenched her teeth, clung to the pommel, and endured.

Redmond stalked ahead, leading her hack. Charity watched his ramrod-stiff back. He had behaved disgracefully with Claude, at first. But he was no coward, for a coward would never have walked alone into Tor Keep; besides, once freed of the menace of the whip, he had fought bravely and well.

Glancing up miserably, she saw the lights drawing nearer. Puzzled, she called, "Mr. Redmond, I had thought it a larger town."

He hesitated, then said, "I believe it is built on hills. We likely only see a portion of it, but I fancy there will be an ordinary where we can get some supper after we find a smithy."

Charity hadn't known how hungry she was until he said "supper," but the suggestion of an ordinary was confusing. "Could we not eat in the inn, or wherever you mean to pass the night?" she asked.

Again, he did not at once reply. Then, "It should be fairly bright later," he said. "The skies are clear now, as you see, and the moon should be nearing the half."

Charity, whose thoughts had dwelt with unutterable yearning on a bed — if only a blanket on the floor where she might stretch out and sleep — said bravely, "We will go on then, after we eat?"

In the darkness, Redmond's lips quirked to the sound of that wistful little voice. He said, "*I* shall go on, monsieur. You will —"

"Oh no!" She spurred the tired hack until she was level with him. "You would not leave me?" She reached down to tug at his sleeve. Please, *please!* I know I am a — a nuisance, but —"

"Not at all. I merely think you will be safer here with the stalwart Scots than you would be in the wilderness with a nefarious individual such as —"

"But I did not *mean* it! You *know* I did not! You are a brave gentleman, and I was tired and did not think before I —"

"Foolish mouse." He patted her hand gently. "You are so weary you're all but asleep at this very minute. How could I ask you to go on? Be sensible."

"If you leave me, Claude will find me! I know it! I *beg* you, do not!"

He frowned up at her. "You have little faith in your brother, ma'am. What if *he* finds you first?"

"How I pray he will. How I *pray* they all are safe! But what chance is there that they should come to this town and stop in the very same locale as we? Mr. Redmond, you *cannot* desert me."

He turned away, and because he was troubled

and shared her fears, he said jeeringly, "Here is very much concern for 'I,' my staunch patriot."

Charity stiffened. "Oh, but you are horrid! Were the truth told, I doubt I have delayed you by one instant!"

"And even had you not, how do you feel, ma'am? How does that soft little *derrière* of yours —"

"Oh! How *dare* you!"

"I'd dare more than that to convince your stubbornness. Good God, woman! Don't you realize that if you're stiff and sore now, you will be scarce able to move tomorrow? A sheltered gentlewoman such as yourself could no more ride at the gallop for three days and nights than —"

"Juanita Smith was a sheltered gentlewoman," she flung at him, "and she not only rode at the gallop, but forded rivers and froze in the snow and —"

"And climbed the Pyrenees beside her husband," he interjected. "Aye — and she is as brave as she's lovely, but —"

Forgetting her resentment, she asked eagerly, "Were you in the Peninsula then? How splendid! Have you met her?"

"Her husband was a Brigade Major with the Ninety-fifth Rifles. My brother was with the Forty-third Regiment. Both Light Division. They served together, so that it was my honour to meet Juana after her husband sailed for

America. And, no, ma'am. Another of my many failings. I was not with the army."

She frowned at his back. His head was very high against the night sky. "Lord," she thought, "but he is eaten up with pride! Foolish creature!" Still, part of what he said was truth. She was so weary it was all she could do not to sleep where she sat, and there seemed not an inch of her that was not cold and aching. She would be better after she had eaten and rested, though. And tightening her lips, she vowed fiercely, "He *shall not* leave me!"

They were coming to the first straggling dwellings of the town now. Lamplight gleamed from cottage windows; the delicious smells of woodsmoke and cooking hung on the air. A dog barked at them and then trotted alongside companionably, and somewhere two cats traded shrill feline insults. At once, Charity was reminded of Little Patches, and her shoulders sagged forlornly.

"Wake up!" called Redmond impatiently. "Look, a smithy!"

A bright glow lit the night ahead; a sturdy barn, the doors wide, the brazier pulsing with brilliant coals and leaping flame. Despite the chill of the night air, several men were gathered by the doors, chatting amiably, and the smith, his broad features lighted by the fire, stood with sooty hands on hips, watching Redmond lead up the limping horse.

"Well, now," he said in a deep North

Country voice. "Be ye and yer lady coom fer me services?"

Staring at Charity, one of the men chuckled and dug his neighbour in the ribs. Redmond scowled at him. "I amuse you, sir?" he asked, well aware that Charity's dishevelled state had inspired this insolence.

"Och, but the feisty cockerel will spit me wi' his claymore, belike," said the offender, then flung up a hand as Redmond tossed the reins to Charity and started towards him. "No offense, y'r lordship. 'Tis aw in guid clean fun, y'ken?"

There was certainly no ill will in the broad grins turned upon him. "They're all bosky," thought Redmond, pausing. "That damnable Scotch whisky, I'll warrant!" And with a sigh for some of that damnable stuff, he turned about and reached up to lift Charity from the saddle.

Again, her knees betrayed her and she sagged against him. Stifled giggles arose from the onlookers as Redmond was obliged to hold her for a minute, and he cursed under his breath.

"I'd not interrupt ye, sir and ma'am, but y'r nag'll need a new shoe," the smith pointed out redundantly. "And ye'll likely want the pair fed and watered, eh?"

Looking at him over Charity's pert little hat, Redmond demanded, "How long is all this going to take?"

"A wee bit, er, pressed, are ye?" asked the

smith, reducing his friends to convulsions. "Where might you and the lady hale from, sir?"

"We *might* hale from Timbuctoo, but —"

"Mr. Redmond is from Hampshire and London," Charity intervened wearily, stepping back from his supporting arms. "And I am from Sussex."

"Thought so," the smith said, nodding smugly. "I bin to Lon'on. Recernized yer way o' talking. Now didn't I tell ye so, Bert?"

"I am in a hurry," imparted Redmond.

"Ar. Well, we all is, ain't we, sir?"

The smith grinned at his friends who, ready to laugh at anything apparently, guffawed loudly, one uptilting a flask which confirmed Redmond's suspicions. Aggravated, he whirled on them sharply and they scattered, still whooping, into the night.

"Ye'll likely find our ways a mite different up here," said the smith. "But I reckon ye won't be much upset, eh?" His beaming grin faded when it met a cold glare. "Ar," he said, with a sniff. "All right, then. Redmond be the name, eh? Ye get that, Jamie?"

A shock-headed lad, writing laboriously in a ledger, nodded. "Fust name?" he asked, yawning.

"You certainly do things differently," grumbled Redmond, trying to contain his building wrath.

"I've heard the Scots are very thrifty,"

whispered Charity, tugging at his sleeve. "Please, could we hurry? I am so very tired."

She looked wan and exhausted. Redmond snapped, "My name is Mitchell Redmond. M-i-t-c-h-e-l-l." He added sardonically, "You get that down, Jamie?"

"Ar. And the lady?"

"The deuce! If ever I —"

Charity intervened hurriedly, "I am Charity Strand. But we are only *renting* the horses, you know. Is that all you need?"

"Cripes, missus!" The smith scratched his grizzled head. "Folks ain't usually in *this* much of a hurry. Was ye meaning to leave the nags here, then?"

"Good God!" gritted Redmond. "Do you want the bill of sale, I've not got it!" The smith stared at him open-mouthed. Relegating him to the status of an escaped Bedlamite, Redmond tried another tack. "My apologies if we, ah, violate your regular ways of conducting business. We are, as I'd thought to have made clear, in a great hurry. I'll make it worth your trouble to expedite matters."

He had spoken the magic words. "Ar," said the smith, grinning broadly. "In that case, we'll make do wi' what we got. And don't ye never worrit, everything'll be done right and proper and yer nags took good care of."

"Thank you. Now, the lady is tired. If you'll direct us to a tavern we will return when you've finished." The smith blinked and, anticipating some further cause for complaint, Redmond added a sarcastic, "Unless you disapprove."

"They'd oughta sign first," said the boy with an offended frown.

"Great stamping snails!" Redmond marched to the dim corner where the boy hovered. "Sign — where?"

Jamie jabbed a grubby finger at a well-worn ledger. " 'Ere, sir. The lady, too." And alarmed by the glare sparking from those deadly grey eyes, he cried hastily, "It do be the law, sir!"

"Then you've some damned stupid laws up here," raged Mitchell. "My apologies, ma'am, but to satisfy these dolts . . . ."

She tottered over and scrawled her name, the page blurring before her eyes.

Slipping a steadying arm about her, Redmond said, "Now, kindly direct me to an inn where we may be comfortable."

A dead silence followed this reasonable request.

Breathing rather hard, Redmond enquired grittily, "You *do* speak English, I think?"

"I'll . . . be gormed," whispered Jamie.

"You'll be damned well sat on your brazier in a minute!" roared Redmond, his right fist clenching.

"Down the lane, yonder," said the smith hurriedly. "The New World. Sits back, it do. Quiet and reasonable like. Will ye be paying me in the marning then, sir?"

"The morning! Devil I will! Have the horses

fed and watered and the mare shod in an hour, if you please."

Still supporting Charity's wilting form, Redmond strode into the lane, muttering maledictions upon all bacon-brained Scots blacksmiths.

They left behind a stunned silence.

Looking at the boy, the smith whistled. "The bare-faced gall of some o' they Lun'on folks! Lor', but it's a wicked city and no mistake!"

"If ever I see a pair on the run," the boy said, nodding owlishly.

"Didn't want to give his *name*. . . ?"

Jamie grinned. " 'Where we may be comfortable,' " he said, mimicking Redmond's cultured accents.

The smith gave a rumble of laughter. The boy joined in, and they laughed until the night rang with the sound of it.

Chapter Fifteen

Charity awoke slowly, resenting the heavy hand that tugged at her shoulder. Blinking heavy eyes, she saw a round white blob that gradually materialized into the wavering flame of a candle with beyond it a comely, rosey-cheeked face framed by a frilly mob cap.

"Och, but it be a wicked shame tae wake ye afore dawn, missus," said this vision repentantly. "But last nicht, ye ken, ye was sae fashed lest I promise tae rrrrouse ye afore y'r mon was abrrroad."

Charity regarded her drowsily. Her man. . . ? What on earth was the girl — "Good heavens!" she gasped, sitting up as memory returned. And, "Ahhh!" she cried to the protest of muscles seemingly nailed to her bones.

"Puir wee lassie," commiserated the maid, but with a dimple of mischief appearing in her cheek.

"He — he's not . . . gone?" Charity managed to enquire.

"Gone? What — and leave ye sae soon? Losh! He wouldna be sae hearrrtless, surely?"

"Much you know of it," grumbled Charity, but seeing consternation come into the guileless face, she smiled and went on, "He worries that I cannot ride again today. Ride we must, and I've no wish to be left alone, you see."

"Ah," said the girl, smiling and nodding as though much relieved. "Is't stiff ye are, then? I'll run fer me liniment. Nae, do ye not stirrr, missus. We'll hae ye up and aboot 'fore the rat can wink his eye!" And she was gone, leaving Charity to the amused reflection that there were more differences than accent in the way English was spoken in Scotland.

The maid was as good as her word; Charity was anointed, massaged, and bathed, and all with firm expert hands, so that by the time she was ready to dress she felt much restored. Her garments had been laundered while she slept, and her habit brushed and pressed. The maid

331

told her that Mr. Redmond had arranged this, and Charity felt a warm gratitude as she donned the fresh, clean clothes.

Thus it was that when Mitchell Redmond emerged from his room, it was to see the door opposite opening and Charity stepping into the hall. She looked neat as a pin, he thought. The touch of yesterday's sun and wind glowed from her cheeks and the end of her little nose, and her hair seemed to have been lightened a shade or two so that it shone like guinea gold against her skin.

Charity greeted him with a shy and rather anxious smile. "It was very kind in you to let me rest here, when I know you had planned to leave at once. And I do so thank you for having my clothes laundered. I only hope we've not lost a great deal of time because of it."

"We'd not have got very far at all events," he said, politely offering his arm as they walked to the stairs. "A mist came up which must have stopped any traveller. I was tired myself, to say truth. But we created quite some consternation when I carried you up the stairs. Do you remember?" He chuckled. "I think the host's good lady was shattered when I left you and went to my own chamber."

Blushing, Charity said, "It's very clear they do not believe we are brother and sister." The words at once brought thought of Justin and Rachel, and the swift thrust of worry.

Redmond was beginning to recognize the

emotions that flashed so swiftly across her small face. He murmured, "If they had come up with us I'd have asked Dev or your brother to stay here with you. As it is . . ." His lips tightened and he left the sentence unfinished.

She looked up at him as they came to the downstairs hall. It was the first time she'd seen his face clearly since the previous afternoon, for everything after dusk was a vague blur. Guilt seized her when she saw the scratches she'd put on his cheek. He looked stern, and she said, "You must be just as anxious as I. Your uncle seems such a warm-hearted man, and Rachel told me that you and your brother are very attached."

His expression softened. "Yes. I've seen little of Harry this past year, but he's a dashed good fellow."

At this point the tavern keeper bustled up to them, all smiles, to usher them into the coffee room where a fire was already roaring up the chimney, and a branch of candles brightening the table he led them to.

Pulling out Charity's chair, Redmond said, "I'm afraid we can't wait, host. We'll have whatever's ready. When does the smithy open?"

"Which one, sir?" His dark little eyes beaming merrily, the rotund man answered, "There be an ample sufficiency of 'em hereabouts."

"Natural enough in a town this size." Redmond took the opposite chair. "It was a short way down the lane."

"Ah, ye'll be meaning Samuel's, I expect. He's likely at work this hour and more. Now, sir, we've some rare cold ham, and me old woman's already got eggs a-sizzling in the pan. With some fresh bannocks and coffee — would that suit?"

It suited very well, and when they had done justice to it and the host had poured two steaming mugs of excellent coffee and departed, Charity asked, "Should we not delay long enough to look about the town a little before we leave? Our people may have come up with us in the night."

"So might Sanguinet. And we'd waste a good hour until full light."

Charity trembled and raised no more demurrals. Redmond paid their tariff, and they went into the cold misty dawn and started down the lane. Despite the abigail's ministrations, Charity was aghast to find she could scarcely put one foot before the other, and her knees seemed during the night to have become markedly farther apart than they'd been hitherto. She had the unhappy impression that she was waddling like a duck and was grateful for the darkness as she struggled along.

The smithy door was wide, the bellows busily at work, the brazier glowing. The horses were ready, and Charity noted with delight that a sidesaddle had been put on the mare. Redmond ignored her thanks, being himself exasperated by the charges, which he grumbled were excessive. The smith gave him a hard look, and for a moment Charity thought he was going to refuse to divulge the direction to Carlisle, but he barked out a few instructions, then turned and went off, to come back with a folded sheet of paper that he thrust at Redmond. "Here," he grunted. "Ye might find this of use."

Somewhat mollified, Redmond put the paper in his pocket. He paid the man off, threw Charity up into the saddle, and they rode into the lane.

"Odd old duck," Redmond muttered.

Trying not to whimper as she adjusted painfully to the movements of the horse, Charity pointed out that it was nice of the smith to write down the direction for them.

"Nice, but scarcely necessary. His instructions were not so complex I can't remember 'em."

Despite this assertion, it was still too dark to see very far, and Redmond had to strain his eyes to find the narrow lane the smith had suggested they follow. Charity tried to ignore her many discomforts and sent up a belated prayer of thanks for their having journeyed this far without being caught by Sanguinet's men. She followed this with a plea that today she might do better and not become so exhausted as she had done yesterday.

They left the lane when they came to a wider thoroughfare, and soon were clattering over a bridge. By the time the sky in the east was lightening, they had turned south and the intervening hills blocked any view they might have had of Dumfries. They held to a steady lope for several miles, and it seemed to Charity that she ached less, perhaps because she was so much more at home in the familiar sidesaddle.

The sun came up; a few clouds drifted lazily about, and the azure sky promised a lovely day to come. Redmond was quiet and withdrawn. His shirt looked freshly laundered, and his cravat was as neatly tied as though his faithful little valet had dressed him. His lean face was slightly bronzed, which made him, thought Charity, better looking than ever, but he seemed troubled and she wondered if he'd lost his way again. She said nothing, fearing to ruffle his famous pride.

Meeting her gaze, he said, "D'ye see the water to the west of us? That'll be the Solway."

The sparkling blue Firth looked cool and inviting against the deep green of the meadows. "How very pretty it is," she murmured.

Redmond scowled. "We can't dawdle like this, ma'am." She looked at him, and he added grimly, "It is Sunday."

She thought, "Heaven help up! It is!" and urged her willing mare to a canter.

It was very early, and for a time they encountered little traffic. An occasional cart rattled northwards, and once a stagecoach bowled past at a great rate of speed, the outside passengers hanging on for dear life and looking tired and rumpled.

Soon Redmond slowed to the lope again. The miles and hours slipped away, and the sun became warmer. Up hill and down they went, through dappled drowsing woods and beside serene lakes, until gradually the trees gave way to rolling heathland, mile upon mile of it, stretching away to the horizon. Charity was beginning to long for a rest when Redmond reined in and sat motionless, staring ahead so fixedly that her heart gave a leap of apprehension. Looking where he looked, she saw what appeared to be an elevated path, long and narrow, winding away to east and west as far as the eye could see, the stone sides that supported it covered with mosses and small plants, the narrow surface grassed over.

Awed, she whispered, "Hadrian's Wall! Oh, I had never realized it stuck up so high!"

"Twelve feet or thereabouts," he murmured. "Higher in the east."

It was quite a different voice. Charity glanced at him sharply. The stern expression had given way to a dreaming look; a younger look. She thought, "So this is the scholar." And wanting for some obscure reason to prolong this new mood, she said, "Only think, it has been standing here on guard like this, for seventeen hundred years."

He smiled in proprietary fashion at that

mighty wall. "There were one thousand cavalry at Carlisle."

"Yes. Romans, with their tunics and swords and helms . . . Oh, Mr. Redmond, can you not picture them riding proudly along the top? Dare we . . ."

He turned to her, a boyish eagerness lighting his eyes. "The horses should have a rest . . ."

They grinned conspiratorially at each other, galloped down the slope, and turned off the road at the foot of the wall.

Redmond leapt from the saddle and lifted Charity down. They tethered the horses to some nearby shrubs. Redmond put out his hand, Charity put hers into it, and they ran along until they came to some rough steps leading upwards. Redmond helped Charity over the more difficult spots, and at the top they stepped gingerly onto the ancient surface, their feet treading where the sandals of Rome's Centurions had trod so many long centuries ago. They walked only a short way and by mutual consent stopped, looking north to the rugged grandeur that was Scotland and south to the blue mountains of England.

There was no sign of another human being. The sweet warm air whispered against their faces; a solitary puffy white cloud meandered across the heavens; a little clump of wildflowers danced to the tune of the breeze, lifting pink and violet faces to the sun. Charity closed her eyes for a moment. Only the faint call of a cuckoo disturbed the silence — a silence that might have been that of almost two thousand years past. . . . Almost she could hear the tramp of feet, the clank of sidearms; almost she could see the glint of the sun on armour. . . . Opening her eyes, she saw Redmond watching her, faintly smiling.

" 'The inaudible and noiseless foot of time,' " he quoted.

"Yes. I wonder what they talked of, or hoped for. One pictures them as having been so strong and merciless. But I suppose they were only ordinary human beings, marching along this wall in a strange, barbaric land. Dreaming of sweethearts, perhaps, or wives and children left behind. . . ."

"Or of dinner, waiting up ahead. But only see how it goes on and on. Is it not marvelous? Yet how many wretched lives were spent in laying these stones one upon the other, day after day, year after year."

Charity stumbled, and his arm went out instinctively to steady her. Unthinkingly, she allowed her arm to slip in a reciprocal fashion around his waist. "I wonder," she said, "if they had any notion it would last this long?"

Her words jogged him back to harsh reality. "We have been here too long," he said. And only then did they both notice exactly how they stood.

They each stepped back hurriedly. Redmond glanced to the north, trod on a crumbling edge that disintegrated beneath his boot, and toppled. One instant he was beside Charity. The next, with a shocked cry, he had fallen from sight.

She gave a little shriek, picked up the skirts of her habit and fairly flew to the steps. Backing down, she slid the last three, skinning her knees, but she scrambled up at once to race, panicked, to where he lay.

He lifted his head and peered up at her. "*What* a gudgeon you must think . . . me," he panted laughingly.

She sank down beside him. "Are you all right? My heavens! You might have broken your back!"

He felt his side and one hip, and said with a rueful grin, "I think my, er, dignity is bruised."

Relieved, she said, "Another affliction we share."

He lay there for a minute, catching his breath, watching her. Touched by the sun, her hair formed a bright halo around her fragile features, and he saw that now, in this light, her eyes were more green than grey. "She's really quite a taking little thing," he thought. "And pluck to the backbone. . . ." "What," he asked, "is the other?"

"Why, our love of history, of course."

"Yes." He sat up. "And if we're to see England's history prosper, Monsieur Mulot, we must be on our way."

Charity picked up the paper that had fallen from his jacket during his rapid descent. "Your directions . . . comrade."

He accepted the paper, stood, and assisted Charity to her feet. Starting off, he gripped his side. "Jove," he said, as her anxious eyes flew to his face, "the ground's harder than I'd thought. Never mind" — he flourished the paper — "on to Carlisle! Now how do you suppose that slowtop thought I could read his directions in the dark?" He unfolded the sheet, glancing at it idly.

Holding up her habit, Charity walked along a few steps, realized he was not beside her and turned back.

He was staring down at the directions, the paper shaking in his hand, his face white as a sheet, and his expression one of stark horror.

Frightened, she cried, "Oh! Whatever is it?" and ran back to him.

He whipped the paper behind him and retreated a step, his eyes very wide as he stared at her. "My God. . . !" he gasped. "Oh, my *God!*"

"What? *What?*"

"Of all the *damnable* things!" He withdrew another step, still staring at her as though she had suddenly changed into a griffin. "I *thought* it took us too long to get to Dumfries! But that stupid crofter said if I didn't know the country 'twould likely seem a *three* day's journey rather than one, so I never suspected —"

Wringing her hands, terrified by his distraught manner, she demanded, "What are you talking about? I do not understand. Why should it be so bad if we are a little out of our way? We've still time, have we not?"

"A *lifetime!*" he groaned, throwing up one clenched fist to his forehead. And then, recovering a little, he took a deep breath, drew himself up, and his face still very pale, his mouth twitching, said hoarsely, "Madam . . . I — I scarce know how to tell you." He bit his lip and went on as steadily as he could manage, "That *damnable* smithy last night was — was not in Dumfries! It was —" Words failed him, but he squared his shoulders, gripped his hands tighter, and ploughed on. "It was in — Gretna Green."

"Oh, was it?" Charity said. "How I should like to have seen the marriage chapels. It was so dark when we got there, that I saw very little . . . of . . ." Her words trailed off, a dread suspicion striking her. How desperately he watched her, and a little pulse was beating and beating beside his mouth.

"Most of the marriages performed in Gretna Green," Redmond croaked, "are not performed in churches, ma'am, but over the . . . the anvil of a . . . smithy."

A faint, squawking shriek escaped Charity. Her attempt to speak was foiled because her throat seemed to have closed entirely.

"We," Redmond confirmed in anguish, "are . . . *married!*"

"*No!*" She snatched the paper from his

palsied hand, spread it, and read her doom. "It *cannot* be!" she wailed. "We took no vows! We made no promises!"

"We — I told them we were in a — a hurry, and — and to expedite matters."

"Oh! *Oh!* How *could* you? I do not *want* to be married to you, Mr. Redmond!"

"By God! Do you think that I —" He bit back the rest of that unchivalrous rejoinder and ground his teeth in a passion of rageful frustration.

"You *must* have known," she accused, her eyes flashing with panic, "when those beastly men all giggled and behaved in such a way. Oh, *how* could you have been so lost you thought we were in *Dumfries,* when all the time —"

"I have never been in Scotland before," he defended irately. "I thought they were laughing because y — we looked so tired and rumpled. And besides, *you* were no more aware than was I!"

"I was too tired to know where I was," she whimpered, close to tears. "You are a *man.* I thought you *knew* what you were doing!"

Furious with her and more furious with himself, he snarled, "Do you seriously think I'd have signed that blasted ledger of his, had I suspected?"

"Oh. *Oh!* And you made *me* sign it!"

"For Lord's sake, ma'am, never accuse me of forcing you into wedlock!"

"Well, you *did!* I relied on you and — and you said for the sake of satisfying that dirty man . . . Oh!" Her voice shredded. "What a disgrace! What*ever* am I to tell my family? I shall *never* be able to hold up my head again!"

Redmond regarded her smoulderingly. "Dash it all, there's nothing to cry about. We'll — make it right somehow."

She had turned away to dab a tiny handkerchief at her nose, but now she whirled on him like a tigress. *"How?* Tell me that! *You* signed that miserable book and so did *I!* Oh . . . I am *married*. . . . Married. . . !"

Smarting, he said, "There are worse fates, you know! Matter of fact, I know one or two ladies who might not swoon at the thought of wedding me."

"Horrid . . . braggart . . ." she sobbed.

He glared at her. Then, glancing northwards, he said stiffly, "Madam, you've my humblest apologies. I'll own I've made mice feet of the business. But might your preoccupation with yourself perhaps be set aside until we reach Brighton?"

He was right of course. Charity dashed her tears away and tried to control her quivering lips as her husband tossed her into the saddle.

His brow black as thunder, Redmond mounted with considerably less grace than usual.

The newly married pair came swiftly to a canter and rode all the way to Carlisle in grim silence.

The round little ostler standing with hands clasped behind him rocked gently back and forth, his bright dark eyes turning appraisingly from the Corinthian gent to the quiet, fair-haired young woman who watched them from the coffee room, and back to the Corinthian. His round bald head shone in the light of the morning sun, and his permanently arched bushy eyebrows seemed to ask a silent question, "Are they — or aren't they? . . . Are they — or aren't they. . . ?"

Scowling at him, Mitchell demanded an irked, "Why the devil not? There's a road through there I know, for some friends rode this way only last year. I believe they said they passed through Keswick and went down through Windermere."

"Ar," the ostler agreed, his eyes rounder than ever. "And very beauti*fool* it be too, sir. But did these friends of yourn have a lady among of 'em, might I ask that?"

"Oh," said Mitchell glumly.

The ostler's hands parted and he lifted one. "Straight up, and straight down, sir," he said with corresponding gestures. "Not so dif*fee*cult for gents at this time of year. But the ladies, Gord bless 'em . . ." He shook his head, clasped his hands as before and added blandly, "Less'n your, er, the lady *ain't* going along, sir?"

"The lady *will* be accompanying me. I

suppose — a coach, or a curricle?"

The ostler regarded him pityingly.

"Well, blast it all," fumed Redmond, "which way *do* we go? Dammit, man, I've to be in, er, in London by Wednesday!"

The ostler stopped rocking and stared at him. "If so be you had wings, sir," he said with a faintly incredulous smirk. "Or if so be the, er, lady wasn't to ac*com*pany you."

"I already told you, she is to accompany me." Redmond thought a bitter, "More's the pity!" "Must we take ship, then?"

"Could," said the ostler, recommencing his rocking. "Could be be*calm*ed, 'course. Or could be stuck in the fog, which would likely have you lying off Black*pool* come Wednesday. . . ." He grinned at this jolly jest, but his amusement faded before Redmond's glare. "Or," he added hastily, "you could ride to the far west, follow along the coast, and then take the Morecambe Bay sands to Lan*cas*ter. From there you could make for Preston and Liver-*pool*."

Redmond thanked him, arranged for fresh horses, and stamped out of the yard grumbling about the lack of decent roads in England.

Watching that tall straight figure, the ostler's bright eyes were thoughtful. His entire person seemed to ponder the question, "Are they — or aren't they? Are they — or aren't they?"

"Is he never going to rest again?" thought

Charity, and wondered for how much longer she could keep upright in the saddle. She ached all over, she was parched with thirst, and her stomach cramped with hunger. She knew that her curls were tangled, and she'd given up pushing flyaway wisps from her dusty face. Her husband had not spoken for an eternity and looked ready to do bloody murder. "Still in shock, poor fellow," she thought cynically. "Only fancy, he has married a poor little dab of a girl, instead of one of his famous beauties." But despite this venture into bitterness, her initial rage and resentment had faded somewhat. Initially, she had considered only her own predicament, but his must be as miserable. And although it was very well to blame him for their unorthodox wedding, he had likely been as tired as she in that wretched smithy, and perhaps more concerned for her weariness than he had betrayed. Certainly, she could not blame him now for riding as hard as they'd done since leaving Carlisle. . . .

She was slumping again. She straightened up wearily. The weak sun was beginning to dip over the grey waters of the sea. It must be midafternoon, she judged. Only midafternoon? So many endless hours since they'd left Carlisle. The beauties of the coastline had impressed her at first, with the broad stretches of golden sand, the lush green of its meadows, the soaring might of the mountains that rose to the east. But for this past hour and more she had scarcely noticed her surroundings, her full concentration bent upon keeping up, on not causing Redmond one more moment of delay by begging him to stop and find her some water. And still, on and on they went, the pound of hooves, the sway and jolt of this interminable ride sapping her strength.

"We must rest the horses now, Madame Mulot."

Charity was startled to find them halted and Redmond standing at her stirrup. She slid into his arms and tottered where he led her, to sink gratefully against a tree. For a moment she just sagged there, eyes closed, enjoying the blissful freedom from effort. When she looked up, he was glaring at her ferociously, but he said nothing, bending to thrust a flask into her uncertain hand. He had left her in the coffee room at Carlisle for a short time, and when he'd come back she had seen him stuffing some purchases into his saddlebags, but had not suspected he had bought strong spirits. "What is it?" she asked, eyeing the flask dubiously.

"Oil of belladonna," he said grittily. "I positively yearn to be a widower!"

She gave him a withering glance and raised the flask. To her dismay, her hand shook and she could not stop it. Redmond muttered something under his breath and stamped off, leading the horses towards a river that joined the sea a short distance ahead. He went down a gradual slope and disappeared from sight under a narrow, rock bridge.

Charity took a swallow from the flask, spluttered and choked, her eyes watering. She supposed he must have given her some very strong wine, for it burnt down her throat. She was horrified upon looking up to see an open landau passing by, the two middle-aged couples seated inside viewing her with patent horror. Scarlet, she thrust the flask behind her, but the two quizzing glasses that were levelled at her positively shone censure, and she heard one of the ladies say a shocked, "Poor creature! A victim of Demon Rum at her age!"

The carriage slowed. For a terrible moment she fancied she was about to be saved — then, to her intense relief, they abandoned her and drove on. Shattered, she took another sip of the Demon Rum, and within a minute or two she felt warmer and restored to a surprising degree. She stoppered the flask, settled back against the tree and closed her eyes for a moment.

She awoke to a heavenly smell, and blinking, saw a sandwich hovering an inch from her nose. A king among sandwiches, with two great slabs of freshly baked bread enclosing thick slices of Cheddar cheese bright with mustard. "Oh," she gasped, accepting this incomparable gift joyfully. She sank her teeth into it, chewed, and uttered a faint moan of pleasure.

Redmond tossed a bulky parcel to the turf between them and sat down rather stiffly. He ignored her indistinct thanks as he unfolded another sandwich and grunted, "Why could you not have said you were so tired and hungry? I often forget to eat, but I'm not a monster."

"I have slowed you too much already," she said, restraining her appetite so as to look at him over a protruding wedge of cheese. She thought she saw approval come into his eyes and said hopefully, "I am going on much better than yesterday, do you not think?"

"You are a positive Amazon," he sneered, but his eyes fell before her level stare and he bit rather savagely into his own little feast.

After a moment, she asked, "Where did you get this?"

"Village. Half a mile inland."

"Good heavens! You *left* me here? All alone?"

"I checked the road in both directions and saw only one landau that looked much too respectable to cause me concern. Besides, you were snoring like —"

"I do *not* snore!"

His eyes glinted at her. He said nothing, but that one dark brow lifted provocatively. However, she wondered, did he do that? She turned away and struggled singlemindedly to master the trick.

"Ma'am?" Redmond was peering at her. He looked frightened and, perversely, likeable. "Not having a seizure, are you?" he asked uneasily.

She gave a chuckle, a reckless indulgence

because it enabled a piece of cheese to go down the wrong way. Her chuckle turned into a whoop and then a frenzied choking. A strong hand whacked between her shoulder blades, dislodging the obstruction. Gasping, she reached out blindly, but with no result. Opening watery eyes, she found herself alone again. "Confound the wretch," she gasped, and wheezing, wiped at involuntary tears.

Redmond reappeared. He was moving very fast as he climbed the rise from under the bridge, holding a beaver hat that dripped water, and obviously concentrating upon holding it as level as possible.

It seemed a shame, thought Charity, to let such selfless dedication be wasted. . . . She arranged herself as gracefully as possible against the tree and closed her eyes.

He moaned an agonized, "Oh, my dear God!" And water was dabbed gently at her face. She'd not meant to recover rapidly, but the water was so icy cold it made her jump. She gave an artistic sigh, fluttered her lashes, and opened her eyes. "Am I . . . dead. . . ?" she murmured faintly.

"No! No! Oh, Lord! Forgive me, ma'am. I never dreamt I had —"

The frantic utterance faded away. She was afraid she'd not be able to keep her lips quite as firm as they should have been, and peered up at him. He was staring at her throat.

"Poor girl's got spiders all over her," he muttered.

With a shriek, she sat up.

"You little wretch!" snarled Mitchell. "I but now bought this hat!"

"Where are the spiders?" she shrilled.

His eyes narrowed. "Down your bosom."

Gasping with horror, she pulled out her bodice and peered inside.

"How *very* gauche," he drawled at his most cynical. "Is everything, ah, intact, ma'am?"

"Why — you vulgar brute!" She pressed one hand chastely to her bodice. "There was nothing there at all, was there?"

Incalculably suggestive, his eyes roved her bosom. "Not much, I'll own."

"Vicious rake!" she hissed.

He said with a reluctant grin, "Serves you right. Of all the Cheltenham tragedies! First, that ghastly seizure, and then —"

"I was *not* having a seizure! If you must know, I was trying if I could not —" She stopped.

"Could not — what? Frighten the spiders away?"

Glaring at him, she said, "Make one eyebrow go up, the way yours does."

He burst into a laugh, then clutched at his side, wincing. "My cousin was used to do the same thing by the hour," he said breathlessly. "My father told him one day he would be struck like that. . . ." A wistful nostalgia came into his eyes. "He never could do it. Very few people can, you know."

"How extremely fortunate," she said with regal disdain.

He chuckled, threw up one hand to acknowledge the hit, and bowed slightly.

Charity struggled to restrain an answering smile. "Have you hurt your side, Mr. Redmond?"

"I've a few bruises, I do believe. Mrs. Redmond."

She gave a gasp and jerked her face away. Astonishment eased her misery as a warm strong hand closed over her trembling fingers.

His deep voice very contrite, he said, "Ma'am, pray believe I am truly sorry. It was all my fault — no use denying it. I swear, when we're done with this unholy mess I shall purchase you a Bill of Divorcement."

Her face turned from him, she quavered, "It is . . . kind in you, sir. But, I would be just as surely ruined. It is one thing for a gentleman to be divorced. But a lady merely becomes . . . notorious."

There was a brief silence. Then he said, "In that event, I guarantee to find some unexceptionable gentleman to husband you. Someone of impeccable birth and background, who is gentle, kind and" — a pause — "gallant. Unless . . . perhaps there is already such a gentleman who admires you?"

She thought wistfully, "I wish there were

. . ." and shook her head.

His grip on her hand tightened. "Then I shall shop for one," he declared bracingly. "I've a host of friends sadly in need of good wives. Hey! What about Leith's bosom bow, Devenish? Now, you could not find a more handsome fellow and he seems likeable enough, though a trifle hot at hand. Do you think —"

"He already offered," she replied, turning to throw him a rather shy smile. "I refused."

He muttered a distinctly surprised, "Did you, by God!"

Bristling, she said, "Yes. And he has also announced his intention to find me a husband!"

"Ah, then I must succeed before him. Let me have your requirements, ma'am, so I can be making lists."

"Requirements? Oh, well, firstly, a sense of humour."

"Good idea," he nodded. "Requirement one," he held one finger, "humour. Next, ma'am? Looks?"

"Oh no. Nor would I expect him to be, er, *aux anges* about — about me. I would like to be married to a gentleman who did not find me altogether repellent, but —"

"The devil! Why should any man find you repellent?"

He looked quite fierce. Charity's lingering resentment vanished at once. She said meekly, "Well, for one thing, I am not pretty."

"You have countenance," he declared. And,

his eyes narrowing, added, "And good bones. You'll likely keep your looks long after some plump and pretty widgeon is a fat matron with a dumpling for a face."

She blushed with pleasure, but with unyielding honesty pointed out, "And I am held to be a bluestocking."

"You are?" His eyes twinkled at her. "I did not notice they were blue."

"Oh!" Her blush deepened. "How naughty in you to — to speak of that!"

He laughed. "No, really, ma'am, we've travelled alone together for two days already, and it will likely be close to a week before we're done. You'd certainly be ruined were we *not* married!"

Her eyes wide and aghast, she gulped, "Oh my! I'd not thought of that!"

"So I gathered. Perhaps my blunder was just as well, eh?"

"But" — her eyes lowered, and she said hesitantly, "but you wouldn't expect . . . I mean we are not *really* wed, so . . ."

"A fine rogue you think me! I'll not so much as steal a kiss from my bride. And so soon as this is over with, we'll to our divorce proceedings and our shopping spree. A bargain, Madame Mulot. . . ?"

Her eyes searched his face. She smiled wanly and took the hand he held out. "A bargain — Mr. Redmond."

"That being the case . . ." He fumbled in

his waistcoat pocket, then reached for her left hand. "With this ring," he murmured, and slipped an intricately carven and obviously old golden band onto her finger.

Charity stared down at it until it blurred, and she had to turn quickly away. She really was married! How different her wedding from Rachel's beautiful ceremony, how foreign to the holy joining of Justin and Lisette before the altar in St. George's. She managed a stifled, "Thank you."

"Cheer up," he said kindly. "Your next marriage will likely be as grand as this one is grim."

For some odd reason, his well-meant words only made it worse.

Chapter Sixteen

Wherever they were now, the sun was going down, and so was she. The spirited animal Mr. Redmond had rented in Black Combe sidled about, eager to go, but Charity was just as eager to stop. She looked about for her husband and discovered him riding down the hill towards her, closing a telescoping glass. Mildly puzzled, she remarked that she'd not known he had a glass, and then shivered to the increasingly chill breath of the wind off the sea.

"I thought it might come in handy," he said, shoving it into his pocket. "Here . . ." He jerked something from the bulky parcel tied to his pommel and handed it to her. "Put this on."

The dark cloth bundle unfolded into a thick woollen cloak. Had he given her the crown jewels they could not have been more gratefully received. "How good of you to buy it for me," she said, managing, with his assistance, to shrug into the warm garment. "But —" She reached up to investigate the folds of his cravat.

Apparently much shocked, he drew back. "Madam! Restrain your ardour, I do entreat. We may be wed, but —"

"Odious man! Where is your sapphire pin?"

"No matter." He shrugged. "Only think of the vast reward we shall win by saving your so admired Regent."

She knew him well enough by this time to be aware that he was trying to turn her attention. "Never mind all that. You pawned it. And that is how you were able to buy our lunch. And my ring, and —"

"It is quite old," he interposed hurriedly. And in a suddenly shy voice, "I had thought that although ours is such an, er, unplanned match, with your love of history you might like a ring that was happily worn, many years ago."

Touched, she thought, "Oh, and I paid so little heed!" Aloud, she said, "And you also bought a glass."

"Scafell is so very lovely. Would you care to come up the hill and see, ma'am? We can allow the horses a few moments more."

She fell into his trap and climbed with him up the gentle hillside. The sun was starting to sink now, but because they were so far north it would be a long sunset. The air was very cold and clear. Redmond adjusted the glass and handed it to Charity. She gazed out over the crimson-tinted sea. A sailing ship was bearing southwards, her sails pink against the darkening waves. Turning the glass to the east, Charity saw the upthrusting might of a great mass, majestic, but rather disappointing. "Oh," she said. "Is that it, then?"

Redmond reached around her to readjust the position of the glass. "I think you saw Scafell. It is a great sight, certainly, but look now and you should find Scafell Pike."

Leaning in his arm, she looked obediently and gave an exclamation of delight. The mountain rose, high and proud, its snowcapped shoulders warmed by the sun's radiance and backed by the turquoise skies.

"How superb!" She turned against him, her glowing eyes uplifted.

He smiled. "Now you see why it fascinates me."

"I do. May I look again?"

"Be quick, then."

She was very quick. She swung the glass to the northwest and the way they had come. "This is really why you bought it, to see if anyone follows!"

He reached around and took back the glass, saying nothing.

She put her hand on his arm and, scrutinizing his face, accused, "You *have* seen someone! Tell me!"

"If I had, you would have seen. The road is clear of any but an occasional carriage for as far —"

"I don't mean now. What did you see?"

"I always heard that wives were vexatious at times —"

"I am not your wife! I am your *comrade!* I face the dangers *with* you, Mr. Redmond."

He was silent, his head bowed. When he looked up, his eyes were very grave. "You are the best comrade any man could ask," he said quietly. "Very well, then, Madame Mulot. I saw a group of riders when we were on Hadrian's Wall. That was why I fell. I was looking at them, not where I was walking. And that is why I turned to the west. I had intended to strike eastward to Newcastle-upon-Tyne, and then head south through Yorkshire, instead of taking this interminable loop. But I thought, if we turned back, they might not expect that. Either I was right, or they were simply a group of friends bound somewhere together."

"Or else," she murmured, "we have made such good time we have eluded them." Watching him, she said, "You believe they still follow. What do you want to do?"

He said hesitantly, "I know how tired you

must be, poor girl. But if we could just get across the sands before full dark, we could rest in Morecambe."

Across the sands! Oh, she could not ride so far! She *could not!* *"You are the best comrade any man could ask. . . ."* She drew a deep breath. "Mr. Redmond, I'd not have you think you married a drunkard, but . . ."

Grinning broadly, Mitchell led the way back to the horses, threw her into the saddle, then handed his flask up to her. "Not too much, wife."

She took two swallows, coughed, and returned the flask. "Now," she said bravely, "Lead on, MacFudd!"

"That's Macduff," he said, peering up at her. "And I don't think the word was 'lead.' "

She thought, blushed, and said, "Never mind!"

Chuckling, Redmond swung into the saddle and led on.

They crossed Morecambe Bay sands under a bright moon, the horses making heavy going of it and Redmond glancing back frequently to be sure his exhausted bride had not toppled from the saddle. He was just in time to catch her on his final check, and rode the rest of the way with her in his arms.

Charity opened her eyes as she was being carried up some stairs. She blinked and ascertained that it was Mitchell who carried her, which seemed a satisfactory arrangement. Her mumbled enquiry elicited the information that they were at a farmhouse, and she slept again.

She awoke to a room bright with moonlight. What had jolted her from sleep she did not know, but she was completely awake. She lay in a soft feather bed in a strange room. Bulky furniture loomed darkly here and there. The casement windows stood open, admitting the smells of hay and horses and the sounds of voices raised in dispute. Her muscles were stiff and sore, but not so painful as yesterday, and slipping from the cosy bed, she pulled the eiderdown about her and crept to the window.

Two men, holding the reins of weary-looking horses, were arguing with a stalwart figure, the farmer probably, who wore a coat over his nightshirt, his nightcap still on his head. "In the normal course o' events, I *could*, genelmen," he was saying doggedly, "but I've me best room taken, as I said, so it'll be the back parlour or nought, and no amount o' money to change me mind."

One of the new arrivals said something in a grumbling way. The farmer gave a hail and a youth staggered sleepily from the barn, holding up a lantern. By that light Charity saw the faces of the riders, and her heart seemed to stop. Their names were unknown to her, but those hard, lean features were impressed on her memory. They were Claude Sanguinet's men; one of them in fact had been at that last dreadful luncheon, so he must be of some importance. She shrank away, watching, trembling, as the boy led their mounts into the barn and the farmer brought his new guests into the house.

Charity spun from the window. She must find Mr. Redmond! Running for the door, she stumbled over him, outstretched on the floor, a blanket wrapped about him.

"What . . . the. . . ?" He yawned, sitting up.

Charity knelt beside him and put her hand over his lips. At once, his drowsy eyes were alert. He removed her hand and, watching her intent face, whispered, "What now?"

"Outside. Two of Claude's men. The landlord, I mean the farmer, brought them into the house."

Mitchell threw off the blanket. He was fully dressed except for his coat and boots, and he paced swiftly and silently to the window. Following, Charity saw another man walking with a weary stride towards the house, but the youth was leading three more horses into the barn. She thought, *"Five!"* and her heart sank. "The farmer said they could have the back parlour," she whispered.

Mitchell sat on the edge of the bed and began to pull his boots on, his eyes fixed on Charity's face. "I allowed us two hours here. I'm sorry, but —"

"Of course." She discarded her eiderdown

and realized belatedly that she was in her chemise. Her eyes dilating with shock, she snatched up the eiderdown again.

"Too late," said Redmond with a grin. "I'm the villain who removed your habit."

"Oh!"

"My apologies. Our worthy farm wife was very willing to help, but she has a frightful cold, and I decided we could not ride all the way to Brighton sneezing!"

"Hmmnnn," said Charity rather feebly. She kept the eiderdown more or less about her as she ran to take her habit from a hanger behind the door.

"Hurry." He trod softly to the window and swung one long leg over the sill.

Checking, she gasped, "Good God! You're never going out *that* way?"

"*We* are going out that way. But not just yet. I'll have a look around, first. Do you get our things together. We have to depart in a hurry, monsieur."

She smiled faintly, but held her breath as he quite suddenly disappeared from sight. Running to the window, she saw him staying in the shadow of the buildings as he ran swiftly towards the barn.

Watching, breathless, until he was inside, Charity waited for shouts and the uproar that must waken the house, but none came. He had told her to gather their things. She forced herself to leave the window, finish dressing, then collect their belongings. Mr. Redmond's parcel rustled loudly. She removed the contents and was appalled by the sight of three long-barrelled pistols, a smaller pistol, two boxes of shells, and a bag of powder. She next unearthed a lady's hair comb, two toothbrushes, and a box of tooth powder. The latter items brought a smile to her lips. She placed everything in a pillowcase and carried it over to the window. Outside, all was still. An angry dispute some-where close by sent her heart leaping, but then she realized the voices were inside the house, not in the barn, and she breathed a sigh of relief.

The moments dragged past, and at length she saw a movement in the yard and Redmond's slim figure reappeared. He was carrying a large wooden crate which he upended beneath the window. Climbing onto it, he looked up at her. She saw the quick gleam of white teeth and he said, "Time to elope, ma'am!"

She lowered the pillowcase to him. He eased it to the ground, caught the coat and cloak she tossed down, then commanded, "You next, Madame Mulot."

She bit her lip. It looked so far down. She sat on the windowsill as he had done and swung her legs over the side.

Redmond hissed, "Turn around and hang onto the ledge. I'll catch you."

She did as he instructed, lowering herself, her heart pounding with dread, and horribly aware that he must be getting another splendid view of her undergarments. Strong hands caught her ankles and slid up to her hips. Even in the darkness she felt her cheeks blaze.

"All right," he whispered. "I've got you. Let go."

"No! I dare not! I shall fall!"

"Mrs. Redmond," he growled angrily, "let *go!*"

Clinging to the sill with all her might, she wailed, "Oh, I *cannot!*"

"Good God!" he groaned. "My first elopement and we're to hang about all night!"

Perhaps because she was so terrified, she found this excruciatingly funny. Laughter bubbled up, weakening her. Redmond gave a sudden tug, Charity fell with a little yelp of fright and was caught in a steely grip. He staggered, and she heard a whispered oath as they jolted downwards. Then her feet were on the ground.

"You're heavy . . . as any pound of feathers," he muttered, retrieving the cloak and throwing it around her shoulders. He shrugged into his coat, took up the pillowcase, and together they ran to the barn.

Inside, two fine horses were saddled, and eight others were haltered together. The farmhand, a big loutish boy, was tied to a post, a gag in his mouth and his eyes terrified. Startled, Charity glanced at Redmond.

He shrugged wryly. "Nuisance. He wouldn't

let me just pay him for our hacks and leave, and started yelling he was going for his master, so I'd no choice." He tied the pillowcase to his saddle, then bent to stick two flimsies into the youth's pocket. "My apologies for your discomfort, lad. I'll leave the horses in Warton." He helped Charity mount, and waved her ahead. Swinging into his own saddle, he took up the lead rein and followed her through the open back door of the barn, the eight appropriated horses clattering after him.

They skirted the environs of Lancaster as the sun rose on a damp, cloudy Monday. Redmond turned his string of horses loose on the south side of the town, and he and Charity rode steadily southwards until at half-past nine o'clock they came to the outskirts of Preston. To her delight, he stopped at a reputable appearing hostelry and made arrangements for a post chaise and four to convey them to Warrington.

Settling back in the vehicle she would, a month ago, have apostrophized as shabby, but that now seemed the height of luxury, Charity ventured a mild remonstrance. "Can we afford such magnificence, Mr. Redmond?"

He climbed in beside her. "Certainly not. But these hacks look to be good goers. I've promised the postboys a guinea apiece if we reach Warrington by noon. And also, this may be a less conspicuous mode of travel."

The horses leaned into their collars, the chaise lurched, and they were off.

"If you wished to be inconspicuous, Mr. Redmond, why did you tell that farmhand where you meant to leave his master's horses?"

"I told him I'd leave 'em in Warton. Warton's north, ma'am. I chanced to hear the farmer speaking of it when we first arrived. Did you think I was so daft as to leave 'em where I'd said I would?"

"I didn't know the name of the place where you did abandon the poor things."

"Don't worry yourself into a state over the beasts. I fancy they'll be rounded up, soon or late. And now, Madame Mulot, if you could see your way clear to cease criticizing my poor efforts and instead compose yourself to sleep —" His eyes were quizzing her. "You had precious little before our elopement."

She laughed. "No, but I feel quite comfortable, thank you, kind sir. Indeed I do believe I am becoming hardened to our hectic journey, and I should like to see the countryside."

Leaning his head back against the squabs, he scanned her animated little face. "You have managed remarkably well. Are you sure you were not hoaxing me with your tales of illness and invalid chairs?"

"I wish I had been. The thing is that so soon as I was able to stand, well, it was such a joy, you know. I could not bear to let a day pass without walking or riding, however inclement the weather. Perhaps all that exercise helped prepare me, to some small extent, for — for this.''

"I would judge it to have prepared you very well indeed. Nevertheless, I wish you would sleep, m'dear. I'll not be able to afford another such luxury as this chaise. After we pay off the postboys it will be bridle and spur the rest of the way.''

His praise had delighted her; his concern was heartwarming, but his final words brought a tremor of fear, and she asked anxiously, "Are we going to be in time, do you think? *Can* we hope to stop Claude's murderous plot?''

"We'd *best* have a hope of doing so, after all this! And if we are able to keep on steadily until dark today, with luck we should reach Brighton by Wednesday afternoon.''

"How I pray we shall. And surely we will be able to stop along the way and ask for help? There must be *someone* in London who'd believe us?''

He frowned. "I'd not care to hazard a wager on it. Frankly, ma'am, I doubt it. Claude did his work well and is everywhere regarded as a close friend and admirer of our sterling Prince. If we could get to Wellington himself, perhaps. But he's likely to be already en route to, or in, Brighton, by the time we could reach London. At all events, with Claude's bullies so close on our heels, I think we dare not take the time to apply for assistance that would more than likely be denied us." He glanced at the window. "Blast! I think it means to rain. Your view will be spoiled, my mouse."

A light drizzle was falling, the misty air quite effectively shortening the view. "Oh, well," said Charity, "I saw Hadrian's Wall. I had hoped to see the cathedral in Carlisle. Did you know that Sir Walter Scott was —" She broke off, biting her lip.

"Married there?" finished Redmond. "I wonder was his bride such a prattlebox as mine."

Charity turned to him indignantly, but with a lazy grin he closed his eyes and settled into his corner. Charity opened her mouth for a rejoinder.

"Go to sleep, you little wretch," he murmured.

She told him with some vehemence that it would likely be quite impossible for her to do so since *he* snored like three Minotaurs.

"Minotaurs," he pointed out, yawning, "do not snore any more than I do."

"Wherever did you read such a thing? I believe you are making it up. You do tell the most awful whiskers, Mr. Redmond."

"And have some, eh?" He opened his eyes again and felt his stubbly chin. "I shall have to take the time to shave when we reach Warrington, else I'll be arrested for my unkempt appearance. As for my snoreless minotaurs, ma'am, I did not read about that trait. Rather,

I observed it firsthand."

"First . . . *hand?* Oh, come now! They are purely mythological creatures!"

"No such thing! I have two perfectly healthy specimens at Moiré Grange. In point of fact, before I left I promised to return with some dainty morsel for them to consume. My jaw-me-dead wife is the" — he yawned again — "the prime candidate."

She laughed, but he really did look very tired. In fact, she had not noticed until now that there were dark smudges under his eyes and deep lines beside his nostrils. With a twinge of unease, she wondered if he had been able to sleep at all when she herself had done so, and she said no more, settling back and closing her eyes. At once, her thoughts turned to her brother and Leith and Devenish, and she prayed fervently that they might have escaped and that poor Guy might not be desperately hurt. Her fingers were turning the ring on her finger. She looked down at it, then took it off so as to inspect it more closely. The wide band was intricately carven into a design of inter-twined roses and hearts, with a solid section at the back. Turning it this way and that, she thought to see something engraved inside. The letters were so faint as to be almost undeci-pherable, but she made out the words at last. *Amor vincit omnia.* She stared at the beautiful sentiment that had been engraved there so long ago.

" 'Love conquers all things,' " Redmond murmured.

"You are supposed to be asleep, sir."

"How can a mere man sleep when your brain spins so noisily?" He stretched and eyed her with faint amusement. "At what was it puzzling this time?"

"I was wondering," she said slowly, "if love did conquer all things for them, whoever they were."

"Does it ever?"

"Cynic! Have you never seen two people so attached that they seemed not complete if fate parted them? Have you never seen a devotion so deep that you longed for just such a happy state?" Her voice dropped to a murmur. "My grandparents on my mama's side had that kind of marriage. They were wed forty years and knew much sorrow, but sometimes when they looked at one another, even when they were old, they would smile as if . . . as if they shared a lovely secret."

She was silent, dreaming, but becoming aware at last that Redmond had not responded, she looked his way, expecting to find him fast asleep. Instead, he was watching her. He wore the strangest expression. A look almost of regret.

Charity slept at last and awoke to the feel of a gentle but persistent tugging at her hair. Redmond was bending over her. She could smell rain, but she was warm and dry and, darting a quick glance around, saw that they were in a stable and that she lay on a pile of hay, her cloak wrapped around her and Redmond's coat spread over her. "Good gracious!" she exclaimed, starting up. "I do seem to have become a prodigious heavy sleeper."

He smiled. "It's all the fresh air." He helped her to her feet and in response to her question told her they were in Warrington. "Are you hungry? I've sent the ostler up to the tavern to bring us some food."

It seemed to her that it would have been simpler for them to go to the tavern themselves. The chaise and the postboys were gone. "I didn't even hear them leave," she said in astonishment. "Did they lift me from the carriage, sir?"

"Of course not. That is my privilege, for the time at least. Besides, you deserved your sleep."

"And what of you?" She looked at him searchingly. He looked as though he'd not slept at all, but when she asked if he had, he teased her, saying he wondered he was not scolded again for his snoring. The troubled look refused to leave Charity's eyes, and he went on, "Jove, but I can see there's something to this marriage game, after all. It's rather nice to be fussed over."

"Was I fussing? I'd not meant to. It is only that — that it disturbs me to think you feel obliged to stand watch over me."

Embarrassment made her colour rise, and she looked down, making quite a business of brushing haystalks from her habit.

Redmond took her by the shoulders. Startled, she lifted her face. He was gazing down at her, a tender smile curving his lips and his eyes very soft. "Of all my wives," he said caressingly, "you are the one I most enjoy watching over."

A terrible thing was happening to Charity's lungs. She could scarcely breathe, and her heart was hammering madly. It was very odd, because when her dashing brother-in-law put his arm about her or gave her a hug of greeting, it did not cause her such a spasm. Nor had Devenish's embrace created havoc in her breast. Redmond was bending closer. She wondered vaguely what it would be like to be kissed by such a famous rake and, quite sure she was about to find out, could think of no reason to object.

Redmond could, apparently. He jerked back his head, his face suddenly bleak. "My apologies," he muttered. "I forget that I am a gentleman and you a lady who is not really my wife. Now where in the devil has that ostler —"

A shadow crossed the rainy doorway. Glancing past Redmond as he stepped back, Charity saw a brutish grin and coarse, familiar features. "*Shotten!*" she screamed.

Redmond hurled her aside and spun about, dropping into an instinctive crouch, one hand flashing for the pocket of his coat where he had carried a pistol. But he had spread his coat over Charity and even as he faced Shotten the big man leapt forward, heavy club upraised. Redmond sprang to one side and aimed a lightning left at that heavy jaw. Shotten grunted and collapsed like a sack of oats, but another came running, and another behind him; big men, their faces alight with a savage eagerness that spoke of the price that had been placed on his life.

Charity saw him whip off his jacket and wrap it around one arm, and wondering, saw the glitter of a knife. A terrible fear plunged through her. They were both rushing him. He fought with skill and practised timing, but he was outnumbered and Shotten was already stirring. Charity made a dart for the fallen club and swung it upward. Shotten's bullet head raised. He saw Redmond and began to clamber to his feet. Charity brought the club down as hard as she could bring herself to strike, felt the shock, and Mr. Shotten slept once more.

Redmond had felled one brute, but as she turned to him he reeled and went down and his remaining opponent swung back a large boot and sent it smashing into his ribs. A red haze obscured Charity's vision. She was vaguely aware of such a fury as she had never known. her club swung light as a feather in her grasp. She saw a triumphantly grinning, dirty face lift to her, and then Mr. Shotten's club hit home and the man was hurled backwards.

Without an instant of regret, she ran to bend over Redmond, who lay doubled up, his arms clasped about his middle, his face contorted with pain. With a sob of terror, Charity ran to the door. Just outside, a rainbarrel was almost full, the raindrops plopping in busily. She plunged her handkerchief into it and flew back to kneel beside Redmond.

He was gasping, his face livid. "Oh, Mitchell! *Mon pauvre! Mon pauvre!*" she whispered, and began to bathe his face gently. The long grey eyes opened narrowly. *"Go!* For the love . . . of God!" he gasped out. *"Go!* One of us must . . . get there!"

Imperceptibly, the light dimmed. Two men peered in at the wide-open door.

" 'Ere!" gasped the plumper of them. "Wot you gone and done, missus?"

"Horses," cried Charity, still holding the wet handkerchief to Redmond's brow. "Quickly! Please — *please* hurry!"

"Not till I knows what's to do." The plump little man walked inside, surveying the carnage. "I'm Joseph Miller, the proprietor of this establishment. Your man been and killed they three?"

Charity bent over Redmond. "Are you stabbed, sir?" she asked urgently.

He shook his head weakly. "Boot — merely. Be . . . all right. Go. May be — may be more."

"There ain't no more," said Mr. Miller.

"You done for the lot. Jem, you run for the constable."

"No!" Constables meant talk and notes and more talk. Charity cried desperately, "Help us, I beg of you. These men are from my uncle. My husband's father has died, you see. The news was kept from us, but we just learned that if he does not appear at the funeral on Wednesday, my uncle inherits the fortune, and we will be left penniless! They tried to murder him just now. Please! *Please* help us!"

Mr. Miller's jaw dropped at this dramatic tale. "Why, them dirty villins!" he exclaimed indignantly. "Here, Jem, let's put 'em where they can't cause no more trouble. Bring the wheelbarrer."

And so Jem and the obliging host disposed three limp and groaning rogues into the muddy wheelbarrow and trundled them ignominiously into the rain.

Charity returned her attention to Redmond. He was breathing hard still, his pale lips tight-gripped, but he eyed her with awed astonishment and whispered, "Jove! *What* a splendid tale!"

She tried to move aside the arm that was clamped across his ribs. "Never mind that. Let me see." She began to unbutton his shirt.

"Good heavens, woman! *Must* you always be . . . striving to undress me? Not content with cutting my breeches off —"

"*Mit-chell!*" She tugged at his wrist. "Will

you be sensible and let me —"

"No, little mouse."

She glanced up, surprised by the gentle voice. He was smiling at her in a way that reduced her knees to blancmange.

"If you will just be so good as . . . to bring me the brandy."

She thought numbly that it was no wonder he was so successful as a rake, but after a stunned second she recovered her sensibilities and sped to take up his coat. Removing the flask, she cried, "Oh, Mitchell! The pistols were here all the time and I never had the sense to . . ."

"You were marvellous," he said, gritting his teeth as he struggled to sit up.

She hurried back to kneel beside him and hold the flask to his lips. He took a mouthful, coughed, and gasped. For a moment his head sank onto her shoulder. She held him close, her cheek against his rumpled hair, her heart aching for him. "Oh," she whispered, "if *only* I could help you!"

He did not answer, but reached for her hand. She thought it was the wrong hand and that he wanted more brandy, but instead, he pressed her fingers to his lips.

Something about that gentle, civilized gesture proved her undoing. All the terrors and dangers, the constant anxiety for her brother and her friends, the endless effort, and now this terrible fight overwhelmed her. Reaction caused her to tremble violently, and tears filled her eyes. "Oh, Mitch . . . They — they almost —"

His arm was about her. He said in a steadier voice, "Almost killed me. And would have done but for you, my so intrepid fieldmouse. Now, listen, Madame Mulot, if I *should* be downed, you must take Diccon's notebook. I carry it in a clumsy sort of pocket I've fashioned inside my coat lining. You must —"

"No, no! Do not even think such a dreadful thing! You will *not* be downed!"

He smiled. "Very likely not with you to aid me. Gad! When I think of how well you wield spears and clubs, I wonder —"

"I see as the lady was properly done up when you driv in, sir," said the host, returning to peer anxiously at Charity. "And no wonder! Be blowed if *ever* I heard of such wickedness. How far you got to go, might I henquire?"

"Brighton," Mitchell answered succinctly.

"What? By *Wednesday?*" The round face was dubious. "Best report it to the law, sir. Two days ain't much time. Not with your lady alongside —"

Redmond reached out. "Help me up, there's a good fellow."

The host obliged. Charity scrambled to her feet, clinging anxiously to Redmond's other hand. His eyes closed briefly, but then he recovered himself.

"Oh, you are so tired! You *must* rest!" she cried.

"Rest . . . and lose my fortune?" Incredibly a whimsical grin was slanted at her. "I've not much reliance on your law, host," he went on. "Rather, saddle us your two best horses and we'll be off."

The man shrugged. "Like as not, you're right. Precious little law we got." His voice rose in a sudden raucous howl that made Charity jump. "*Wal-ter!*"

Redmond said fondly, "Can you gather our things m'dear?"

Her heart leaping, Charity hastened to do his bidding as an ostler hurried in and was instructed to saddle up Mr. Pitt and Short-and-Sweet.

"We named the bay arter Mr. Pitt, 'cause he's all fire and brimstone," explained Mr. Miller, helping Redmond to where he might lean against a feed bin. "Short-and-Sweet will do nicely for your lady. Was you intending to rent 'em sir? I've a friend down to Stoke-on-Trent as will return 'em do you wish to pay the fees. Then you could rent another pair from him."

Redmond completed the negotiations, then asked, "Where did you put our rogues?"

"In the smokehouse, sir. Quite safe they'll be there till morning, never you fear. Here, let me help you, though I'm thinking 'twould go kinder on you was you to take my best room 'stead of riding in your condition."

He boosted Redmond into the saddle, then

helped Charity mount the black mare. Patting the animal, he said, "Be gentle with her mouth, if you will, ma'am. A rare little creature she be."

Charity nodded, promised to take care of his horse, added her fervent thanks to Redmond's, and followed her husband into the rainy afternoon.

For a little while Redmond walked the horses along the wet lane. Then he drew closer to Charity. She asked anxiously how he felt. "Oh, I shall do nicely, thank you. The thing is" — he hesitated, regarding her with grim intensity — "we've to make a dash for it now. There will be others, you see. And they know where we are. Charity . . . I wish you will stay here. I could find you a —"

"No. I must keep with you."

He smiled faintly. "My faithful wife. I shall manage, I swear. I'll not fail this time."

She knew he was thinking of Sanguinet and that hideous interrogation in the war room at Tor Keep. She said calmly, "I am quite sure you will not. But I must stay with you for as long as I can without being a hindrance."

"Hindrance!" He reached over to clasp the hand she at once stretched out to him. "Lord! The way you swung that club! What a fighter you are, my mouse!"

Her eyes glowed with joy. "And you," she said warmly. "How you managed to fight off all three, I shall never know. I am very sure no other man could have done it."

Incredulity touched him. After a wondering moment, he said, "Come then, Madame Mulot. We'll do our damnedest." He paused, then added, "Together."

Charity nodded, smiling resolutely into his grave eyes.

Already they were out of the village. Redmond urged his big bay to a canter. The black mare at once kept pace. They rode on along muddy lanes, the rain becoming heavier, driving into their faces, the horses sending up sprays of cold water as they splashed through puddles. A grey mist hung over the fields, and the afternoon settled into a sullen wetness. Charity began to be very cold. She scarcely noticed it. Had she been given the choice, she would have been nowhere else in the world.

Chapter Seventeen

"Take it off!" Redmond's voice was a snarl.

Her teeth chattering, Charity said, "Very w-well. B-but turn your naughty back, sir!"

Water trickling down the sodden locks of hair that plastered against his forehead, Redmond scowled, but did as he was asked, fixing his gaze sternly on the deplorable green chickens of the wallpaper in the grubby bedchamber of this deplorable hedge tavern. After a moment, a wet habit was thrust at him. He took the garments and eyed them, his heart contracting. So small. So cold and soaked. A hand was on his arm. He looked up. Her great eyes were scanning him worriedly. His gaze flickered down the chemise that clung revealingly to her thin shape, and a great ache of longing surged through him.

He strode to whip a blanket from the bed and wrap it about her, then carried her to a chair by the fire. "Sit there!" he said raspingly.

Charity watched as he draped her habit over two wooden chairs to dry. Steam curled up almost at once. She began to feel a little less freezing, but, oh, how she ached. And she had blisters, dreadful raw blisters, where no one should have such fiendish annoyances. Starting to nod, she forced her eyes open. Redmond had taken off his coat and set it on a third chair beside her garments. His jacket was just as sodden.

As gruffly as possible, she said, "Take it off!"

His tired eyes flashed to her, and at once a grin lit them. "Hot-blooded wench," he said. But he took off his jacket revealing a shirt that clung wetly against his lean body.

Charity said a sympathetic, "Oh, my poor dear. You are soaked through!"

His smile died. A look of yearning tenderness crept into his eyes. He came to her as if irresistibly drawn. And the weariness, the ache, the hopelessness of striving against impossible odds, were as nothing. Charity saw only his ardent gaze, the sensitive face, the tall lean manliness of him. She tore the blanket away and stood as he advanced on her, and her arms went out.

She was clasped in a strong but contained hold. His head bowed, his mouth seeking hers. And she lifted her face, yielding her lips with a willingness, an eagerness, that some distant part of her mind marvelled at. After a dizzying eternity of heaven, Mitchell left her mouth and began to plant a trail of kisses down her cheek, down her throat, lower yet, until she gasped to the thrill of his lips upon the curve of her slight breast.

"Mitchell . . ." she whispered. "Oh — Mitchell. . . !"

He picked her up and carried her, still kissing her, to the rickety bed. "We have . . . so little time," he said softly, as he laid her there.

She smiled and reached up to him.

Mitchell moved cautiously onto the bed and took her in his arms. "My precious . . . Madame Mulot . . ." he said huskily. And he gathered her closer, kissing her again and again, his hands caressing every part of her frail body. But when he raised his head to bend over her, she was asleep.

Mitchell Redmond, notorious rake and duellist, smiled faintly, sighed, and kissed her white brow. He eased himself from the bed, and gazing down at her, muttered wryly, "Just as well, beloved. . . ." He pulled the musty blankets over her, carried the lamp to where it would not trouble her eyes, and returned to the fire. He checked the pistols one at a time, then laid them close by. Crossing to the window, he peered out, but could discern only the gleam of lamplight upon the wet surface of the lane, the tossing branches of trees, and, distantly, a great red glow in the sky that brought an angry scowl to his face. For a while he occupied himself with the business of shaving. Finishing, he went back to the fire and took out his timepiece. One hour more and they must be gone. Even now, he flirted with disaster by stopping here. His eyes slanted to the bed. She must have rest. God bless her valiant soul, she must sleep — just for a little while.

That blessing being denied him, Redmond sat straighter, keeping his vigil over the girl he once had judged as elegant as a grey fieldmouse.

The sky was ablaze, the heavy clouds pulsing a sullen crimson, the rainy night lit by the lurid red glow.

"Whatever is it?" asked Charity breathlessly as they halted the horses for a moment at the top of a rise.

Redmond said savagely, "It is what they have done to our England. The money grubbers with their tools and wheels and the steam for their Satanic machines. These black fields were once green and lush. These gentle people each owned

384

a little trade and plied it with honour and dignity. And then came the machines that could do as much in a day as a man could do in a week. Now, the countryside is dying, the streams are polluted with vat dyes and soot so that even the fish are gone. From here to Birmingham and beyond, the machines spread starvation and disillusion."

Appalled, and yet impressed by the depth of his anger, she asked, "And — the people?"

He shrugged. "The craftsman who took pride in the cloth he wove on his own loom is the slave of today, who works at a grinding pace for a man he may never even meet and who can no longer have any sense of dignity or personal accomplishment. Because he makes so little, his wife has to work beside him; their children toil for fifteen, sometimes sixteen, hours a day at the shuttles, their little hands —" He broke off. "I should not rant so, but — God, how I hate them! These soulless money grubbers and their stinking machines!"

"But can nothing be done? Do not the officials, the people in Whitehall know what is happening?"

"Much they care! They live safely in their London mansions and on their lush south country estates. What do they know of these once beautiful moors and heaths? Do you think they care if the valleys are blasted by smoke-stacks; if the trees wither and die; if factory towns spring up that are an abomination to

God's green earth?"

Fascinated by his grim face, Charity cried, "Then they must be *made* to know! Somebody must —"

A sharp, staccato explosion sounded. Something whistled past Charity's ear. Redmond jerked around in the saddle. A small knot of horsemen was coming up fast. Even as he looked, he saw the flash of another shot. They had not resorted to pistols in Warrington. Even that wretched Shotten had carried a club, not a gun. Sanguinet must be getting desperate. He reached over and slapped Charity's mare hard across the rump. The animal leapt forward and was away at the gallop. Redmond adjusted his own pace and reached down for the pistol in his saddle holster, but glancing back again, he decided the distance was too great for accuracy. He urged his horse to a faster gait, keeping ever between Charity and the merciless hunters who followed.

It scarcely seemed possible that Shotten and his crew had come up so soon. The innkeeper in Warrington had vowed to keep them locked up until morning. True, he had risked that stop in Stoke-on-Trent, but they'd only rested for two hours, surely not sufficient to — And the answer came with a jolt "Liverpool! Claude must have sent another lot by ship!" But how they could have been seen, how they could have been tracked down so swiftly, baffled him. They had ridden hard all through the evening and into the night, their way lit by that devilish red glare from the foundries. He had pushed Charity so hard, so mercilessly, even when she sagged with fatigue. And bless her brave heart, she had responded, her own care seeming to be for him. He pressed one hand to the unending throb in his side and wondered how much longer they had. If they were run down, if he was killed, what would become of Charity? He gritted his teeth. Harry would come. Harry never failed. If he himself should fall, Harry would take up the torch and take care of Charity. . . .

Another shot rang out, and he felt his sleeve plucked by invisible fingers. Someone back there was a fine marksman. Charity's face, frightened, turned to him, and he waved reassurance at her, but glancing back, he saw that they were close. Much too close.

He snatched up a pistol. Then, reining his horse to a sudden rearing halt, he turned about, drew the second pistol, took quick aim, and fired once and twice. He was quite prepared for death and was mildly surprised when a ball whistled past without touching him. The first rider had pitched from the saddle at once. The second man aimed a long-barrelled pistol and fired, but the lead horse reared in fright as its master fell and then caromed into its neighbour, and the shot went wide. The second man was thrown, and a wild melee ensued as the following riders were unable to swerve in time. Grinning with delight, Redmond drove home his spurs and tore after Charity.

Soon, the rain began again. The clouds seemed ever lower and ever more lurid. Charity cringed as thunder rolled distantly and the red heavens were split by a blue glare. Southwards, a hilltop loomed, studded with the angular shapes of buildings and chimneys. They were coming into a town — a large one by the look of it. Perhaps they would have a chance there. Perhaps they could hide from Claude's hunters.

Lightning flashed again as they raced side by side across a bridge, the flash reflected briefly from a boil of fast water far below.

"Coventry!" Redmond shouted. "Stay close beside me, my mouse!"

They galloped through the almost deserted streets of the suburbs. A man leaned from the window of a chaise, shouting unintelligible wrath because they had rounded a corner so suddenly they almost collided with him. A heavy dray was ahead, but they were past like the wind, one to each side, thunder growling as though pushing them ever faster. They overtook a rumbling stagecoach, and Charity saw the pale blur of a face at the window, a young boy, awake and staring out at them.

Mitchell shouted a warning and turned sharply onto a very narrow, cobblestoned street lined with tall, half-timbered houses that seemed striving to kiss the opposite gables as they leaned across the narrow thoroughfare. Lightning flashed vividly, and the thunder was almost instantaneous, shattering the night with a deafening clap of sound. Charity's mare screamed with fright and reared madly. Taken by surprise, she was hurled from the saddle. She landed very hard. . . .

She was riding across the Downs, laughing as Justin demonstrated that he could stand on his saddle. And then, suddenly she was falling. Justin was running to her, shouting, "Charity . . . my precious! My beloved! Dear God, not *her* — please, not her. . . ."

Only the voice was not that of her brother. And it was so agonized, so broken. She must help him. . . . She managed to open her eyes and tried to smile. It all came back, then. Her legs felt not so bad. It was her head that ached so fiercely. And Mitchell Redmond's was the dark, grief-stricken countenance that bent above her. "I'm . . . all right," she managed.

He gave a great shuddering sob and raised her very gently. But when she did not cry out or seem hurt, he crushed her against him for a brief, but exquisite, few seconds.

"Can you stand?" he asked unsteadily. "I'm afraid your horse bolted, back towards them. If they saw where she came from . . ."

She stood, his arm tight about her.

"We'll take my hack," he said, guiding her wavering steps, "until —"

A thunder of hooves. A triumphant shout. Redmond groaned a curse, grabbed for his holster, and cursed again as the hack panicked and cantered away. He swept Charity into the looming darkness of a recessed door and swung about, fists clenched, knowing helplessly that he had a minute or two at most.

Charity said, "Mitch! Here!"

And something was thrust into his hand. Sanguinet's bullies were galloping straight at him, but there was no shooting now, as there had been none in the stable. He thought, "They've no need to fire. They can ride me down and get the book. . . ."

He swung up the walking cane Charity had passed him, only to discover that he held not a cane, but a long, wet gentleman's umbrella that had apparently been left out to drain. He grinned suddenly, jumped into the centre of the street and, as the five horses thundered at him, whipped open the umbrella with a snap, right under their highbred noses.

Chaos. A turmoil of rearing, neighing, kicking horseflesh and cursing, howling men. To top it off, Charity was screaming at the top of her lungs. Windows were flung up. Lamps began to shine from upper floors.

A burly ruffian, wielding a serviceable-looking cudgel, raced at Mitchell. He dodged at the last second, but this man was skilled in his murderous calling, and he struck out, the blow grazing Mitchell's temple and sending him staggering. The burly man whirled and came in, grinning.

"En garde . . ." gasped Mitchell breath-lessly, flourishing the umbrella as if it had been a sword.

His adversary's reply was crudely profane, but as he came on full tilt, his cudgel whipping for the head, Mitchell's right foot stamped forward and he thrust in a superb return from the wrist driving by a hairsbreadth under the whizzing cudgel. The point of the umbrella rammed into the burly man's middle. He sat down abruptly, opening and shutting his mouth, his eyes round and staring like a landed trout. His friends had sorted themselves out and they came at a run. Mitchell stepped back a pace, his umbrella circling warily. From above, someone shouted, "Hey! Four to one! That ain't fair! Play the game square, you coves!" And a bottle ricochetted from the arm of one of the ruffians, drawing a howl of rage and pain.

The last man had halted and drawn a pistol. The shot was deafening in the narrow confines of the street.

A white-hot pain lanced across Mitchell's scalp. Dimly, he heard windows slamming shut. Lamps were extinguished. He must not go down . . . he must not. He shook his head desperately, wiped blood from his eyes, gripped his umbrella and stepped forward. "Come on . . . you bastards . . ." he croaked.

They came on in a hurly-burly of swinging fists, flailing clubs, and jeering profanity.

Mitchell jabbed the umbrella into the stomach of one, swiped it across the face of another, and was staggered by a blow that sent him to his knees. Dazed, he saw a boot flying at his eyes and managed to sway aside. A knife way plunging down at him. He thought, "Charity . . ."

A shot rang out. The knife coming straight for his chest fell ringingly onto the cobbles. A wild hussar yell echoed along the street. Mitchell stiffened, a gleam of hope lighting his blurred eyes. Horses — coming fast. The little knot of men around him was scattering as a flying body launched into their midst. Flattened under a brawling mass of humanity, Mitchell saw a familiar dark head and the gleam of narrow green eyes. "Harry. . . !" he gasped.

Somebody howled and thudded to the cobbles. Jeremy Bolster blinked up at him. "Well, don't just sit there, old f-fellow. Missing a jolly good scr-scrap!"

"What I do not understand," said Mitchell, holding a foaming tankard and submitting while Charity gently bathed the gash in his head, "is how in blazes you found us."

They had ridden to this quiet inn as soon as Sanguinet's troop had been, as Alain Devenish blithely put it, "dealt with." Charity had been pulled into her brother's arms for a crushing hug, then thrown up into the saddle of her hack which had apparently followed the other

392

horses and was found to be standing placidly nearby. Mitchell had mounted the best of the Sanguinet animals, and they'd quickly departed a neighbourhood that resounded with shouts for the Watch and a belated blowing of shrill whistles. They had spoken little on the way here, but now, gathered in a cosy parlour Leith had bespoken, the friends were exuberant, and everyone started to talk at once until Leith said laughingly that Mitchell deserved the first hearing.

Now, in response to that initial question, Bolster beamed despite a split lip and said, "Didn't find you, old boy. Followed *them*. Been following 'em since Liverpool. They n-never once looked behind, silly bacon brains."

Watching his brother anxiously, Sir Harry said, "Sorry we were so long coming up with you, Mitch. But we lost them after they crossed the bridge. Had it not been for the gunfire, we might not have found you at all."

Mitchell grinned up at him, then lowered his head again as Charity pulled at his ear. He said fervently, "I've never been so glad in my life as to see your old phiz. When I rode away from the castle, there were so damned many of 'em, I was afraid, er —"

"So were we," Leith supplied gravely. "We delayed them as long as we could, but some of them stole Tyndale's horses and were off after you."

Devenish said, "We'd have been dog's meat

for sure, save that General Drummond and his friends were out hunting. They heard the uproar and came at the gallop."

Strand set down his tankard and added, "Sanguinet's men ran back to their boats when they saw our reinforcements, and Drummond was good enough to offer us the use of his yacht. Luckily it was readied to take him down to Blackpool, so we were able to sail fairly soon."

"We thought we spotted you near Preston, soon after we disembarked," the Reverend Langridge said around the slice of beef he was attending to.

"But we lost you," Devenish put in, "so we just kept riding south, hoping to come up with you."

Holding a bloody handkerchief to a gash in his cheek, Justin Strand said, "It occurred to us that you might decide to take ship at Liverpool, so we turned that way —"

"And followed a so-called short cut," Devenish interrupted. "Which was lucky because just before we joined the main road, Sanguinet's little covey of choirboys trotted past."

"And we let them l-lead us to you," said Bolster.

"Well, I'm dashed grateful you did," said Mitchell, straightening as Charity finished her task, and smiling up at her.

"Didn't look to me that you needed our help," Devenish said, grinning. "Five to one

394

should be child's play for a fighter like you, Redmond."

Mitchell looked at him narrowly, realized he was sincere, and flushed a little.

Justin Strand had noted the glance his sister bestowed on this notorious gentleman. He frowned and said rather grittily, "How you managed to convey my sister safely this far, this fast, I cannot guess, Redmond. But I'm forever in your debt."

Charity turned to him, surprised by the hauteur in his voice. She saw his eyes and asked quickly, "Justin, how is Guy?"

Strand hesitated. Leith said regretfully, "We don't know, I'm afraid. But I fancy you saw that the ball took him in the body. He saved my life. Tyndale was winged in our struggle, and the General carried him and Guy to Castle Drummond."

Charity's lips trembled, seeing which Devenish said gently, "He was breathing when we lifted him into the carriage, and Drummond has a daughter who's a dashed fine nurse. We can but hope for the best, m'dear."

Strand added, "The General also promised to contact the authorities at once and try to get word despatched to London." He directed a searching look at his sister. "Do sit down, poor girl. You look worn to a shade."

Her thoughts still with a very gallant gentleman of France, Charity sighed. But it was no use grieving. One could only pray. She carried her bowl to the door and handed it to the maid, who emptied it and refilled it with warm water. Returning, Charity sat at the table beside her brother and turned his cheek so that she could bathe his hurt.

Sir Harry, watching Mitchell, asked, "Mitch, are you all right? You look like the devil."

"*Merci, mon sauvage,*" said Mitchell, lightly. "Well, what next, Colonel? Are we to make a dash for Brighton at dawn?"

"I wish I could say yes. Lord knows you look as if you could use some sleep. The thing is, there's a full moon tonight. We must be on the road in an hour, I'm afraid." Leith turned to Charity. "I've asked the host for a bedchamber for you, my dear. You must be exhausted."

Her dismayed glance flashed to Mitchell, but Leith stood and reached for her hand. "Come now, Strand can finish that. I must have a word with you in private." She knew he meant to urge her to remain here, but she was too tired to argue in front of them all, and so went out with him.

Lion came in as they left. His red curls showed dark brown roots, lending him a most odd appearance, but his eyebrows were growing back so that his face no longer had the strangely naked look.

Mitchell said, "So you're still among us, are you?"

" 'Sright, guvnor," said Lion, grinning.

"What became of Little Patches?"

The Reverend said, "She jumped into the carriage when they lifted poor Guy Sanguinet inside. I think Major Tyndale allowed her to stay." He yawned. "D'you know, Harry, I believe I shall go and have a nice wash and perhaps just lie down for a few minutes."

"I'm with you, sir," said Bolster.

Harry stood. "Good notion." He glanced at his brother. "Mitch?"

Very aware that Justin Strand's blue eyes were boring at him, Mitchell said, "I'll have a word with Strand first, Harry."

Devenish glanced from one to the other. He'd give a good deal, he thought, to know what Justin meant to say to the man who had been alone with his loved sister for the better part of three days. But it was not his right. He stood, gripped hard at the table edge, then sauntered after Harry and the Reverend with only the suggestion of a limp.

Strand looked after him uneasily.

Mitchell said, "That leg's giving him hell."

Strand nodded. "God knows how he's lasted this long. Dev can run on nerve longer than any man I know."

"He's a right game 'un," said Lion. "Should I go along of him and see if I can help, sir?"

"If you please," said Strand.

Lion hurried out, closing the door behind him.

Strand finished applying sticking plaster to his cheek, then crossed to take the chair closest to Redmond. Whatever else, the poor fellow looked properly done up, and God knows, he'd done well, but . . . With somewhat strained formality, he began, "It must have been a — a devilish coil for you. I mean, having to take things easily for Charity's sake, when you —"

Redmond threw back his head and laughed uproariously. "Take things . . . easily . . . is it? Oh, egad!" He saw the bewilderment and vexation in Strand's face, and leaned across the table. "You are wondering what I've done to your sister, and God knows, you're justified. I have forced that frail girl to ride like hell hour after hour, through rain and cold and the most brutal conditions imaginable. I've dragged her out of second-floor windows, starved her until she fainted, stripped off her garments —" He saw Strand's face whiten, and went on more soberly, "I have seen her too exhausted to speak, yet riding on still; I've seen her bend a damn great cudgel over the head of a murderous scoundrel so as to save my worthless neck; I have . . . picked her up after her horse threw her, and — and thought her dead, only to have her look up at me and . . . smile." His voice became strained. He stopped speaking and put a hand wearily across his eyes for a minute.

Staring at him, astounded, Strand said an awed, "Charity? But, but she's practically an invalid! I do not see how —"

"She is incomparable," Redmond went on quietly, looking up again. "Never a word of

398

complaint, never a whimper. That dauntless, valiant little soul is the bravest lady I ever met." He met Strand's faintly aghast gaze and added gravely, "She is also — my wife."

Strand leapt to his feet, his face thunderous. "Your . . . *what?*"

Watching him coolly, Redmond nodded. "We were married at Gretna Green."

"The hell you were!" His fists clenching, Strand raged, "By God, Redmond! If you took advantage —"

Redmond drawled mockingly, "Am I to deduce I do not suit for a brother-in-law?"

"Damn your eyes! She is a complete innocent! I fancied you would have behaved like a gentleman!" White with anger, he snarled, "I've every right —"

Redmond gestured wearily. "No, do not call me out, I beg. My fault — I should not have let you run on. Only . . ." He broke off with an impatient shrug. "Shall we call it a *mariage de convenance?*"

The wind taken out of his sails, Strand sat down abruptly. "Oh, I see."

"Nothing more," said Redmond. And thought how very nearly it had become a real marriage. He felt terribly tired and discouraged suddenly and said slowly, "I have promised to procure a divorce for the lady. So soon as we're done with this."

Looking into his shadowed eyes, Strand was shocked. "I should have known," he said.

"Damned if I'm not getting hot at hand of late!" He put out his hand, standing.

Redmond stood also, and they shook hands.

Strand said awkwardly, "Thank you." And went upstairs, feeling as though he'd spat in a cathedral.

"There will be five of us," said Leith, looking around at the battered little band that stood together in the fragrant stables. "If we —"

"Don't ferget me, sir," said Lion, coming quickly to join them. "I can fight good, I can!"

"And I make seven!" The Reverend bustled into the circle of lamplight, his pudgy face indignant. "You young Bucks judge me antiquated, I collect? Well, I will not be left behind like some old codger, and so I tell you!"

Sir Harry laughed and clapped his uncle on the shoulder. "Very well, sir." He glanced at the dubious Leith, his eyes glinting. "No use, Tris. I know this gentleman too well. He'll jaw your ear off and come anyway. Might as well give up now."

Leith said sternly, "This will be a no-holds-barred race, sir. If all the mercenaries we saw on the ship disembarked at Liverpool, we may well have half a hundred of the varmints after us. They'll stop at nothing, I do assure you."

"Then why," said the Reverend patiently, "do you stand about wasting time?"

Leith's slow smile dawned. "As you will."

"Do you mean to split us, Leith?" asked Mitchell.

"It might broaden our chances of getting through," Leith answered. "Three of us could ride through Oxford and Reading, and the rest stay on this road, going south through Northampton, Wolverton, and St. Albans. But —" He broke off and glanced around. "Any better notions?"

"I have!" Devenish swaggered to join them. "If you've any notions of abandoning me here, my dastardly friends, you may be damned."

"Good God!" groaned Leith, exasperated. "Dev, you infernal idiot, you can scarce stay in the saddle. You —"

"If we were not friends, Tris," said Devenish, his eyes blazing with characteristic eagerness for this challenge, "I'd pummel your head for even thinking of shutting me out! I've a grudge to pay against our Claude, too, you know! Furthermore, I mislike the plan to split us. Divide and conquer, old lad. And it would be such a pity if Claude was to win."

"I agree," said Sir Harry. "If we've half a hundred of Claude's rogues to deal with, we shall do them no disservice do we split up, but likely render ourselves more vulnerable in a fight."

Leith refrained from the obvious comment that in a fight seven men would have little chance against fifty. "Very well. Lion, you must stay here and guard my sister." Lion groaned, but Strand muttered, "I don't like that, Leith. Not enough protection, and if Claude gets his hands on her again . . ."

From the shadows of a stall, Charity said quietly, "I shall have all the protection I could wish, gentlemen." She rode her mare into the light, a large bundle hanging from the pommel of her saddle, her cloak and hood already about her, and determination written in every line of her tired face.

"The deuce!" exclaimed Strand. "I say you shall not go, Charity!"

"It is too much to ask of any woman," Devenish protested. "And Claude is running scared now, no telling what his devils might do."

"Much better stay here and be safe and warm, dear lady," the Reverend added.

"Thank you. But I shall stay beside my husband," said Charity.

A chorus of gasps went up. Devenish, staring at Mitchell, started for him, angrily.

Strand said, "Wasn't much else they could do, Dev."

"The devil there wasn't! He stayed off the travelled highways for the most part. Likely no one saw them who'd know 'em from Adam! No need for a bolt to the Green — unless he —"

Strand caught his arm as he plunged forward. "Redmond has promised to buy a Bill of Divorcement as soon as we're done with this! Cool down, will you?"

Devenish halted, to glare, seething, as Mitchell went to look up into Charity's face.

Taking the hand she stretched down to him, Mitchell said softly, "You must be very tired, m'dear. I wish you will stay here. You'd be safer than travelling with us. And you should perhaps bear in mind that just in case anything goes awry, Rachel may stand in sore need of you."

Her grip on his hand tightened. She said intensely, "Do not ask me to stay here. I must be with you."

Her eyes were imploring. For a long moment he gazed up at her; then he nodded. "Very well, but promise me that if things look bad, you will be guided by me."

"I promise."

They rode until the moon went down and made good time until they passed through the hills north of Towcester. There, disaster struck. The storm had rolled away, but the rains started again and they were proceeding at a trot through a heavy downpour when a bridge collapsed under them. Leith and Sir Harry, who had been in the lead, were barely clear of the old structure. Mitchell heard the creaks and felt the boards shake beneath them and spurred madly, whipping Charity's horse across in the nick of time. The Reverend and Jeremy Bolster were hurled into the swollen river, and only some desperate efforts on the part of Devenish,

Lion, and Justin Strand, who waded to the rescue, saved them. Inevitably, they were delayed and had to creep cautiously through inky blackness to Towcester and an accommodating tavern where they were able to dry their clothes and hire fresh horses.

It was more than an hour before they could continue. They set out at first light, but were barely a dozen miles past the quiet village when they nearly ran into a party of Sanguinet's men. It was the Reverend who prevented a direct confrontation. He had begun to sneeze and snuffle and, fearing that he would be judged unwell, had gone off on a small detour so as to blow his nose in private. It was thus that he topped a rise, saw the group of riders, and, recognizing one of them, was able to catch up with and warn his friends in the nick of time. Leith turned westward in a wide loop, and then swung back across country towards Banbury and the Oxford road.

Again, the weather placed an infuriating check on their progress. Devenish grumbled that it was more like February than June when they were twice obliged to ford streams made treacherous by the heavy rains. They were all thoroughly soaked, and the wind came up from the east, chilling them through. It was ten o'clock before they reached Banbury, and Langridge was coughing distressfully. With stern implacability Leith decreed that he must ride no farther and they left him at a pleasant inn, the host's motherly spouse making a great business of caring for him, and the Reverend protesting between sneezes that he was perfectly able to go on.

The sun peeped through the clouds soon after they started off again; the rain ceased, and the air grew warmer. There was mud everywhere, however, and the going was slow. They did not glimpse Oxford until after noon, but Charity's heart gave a leap of hope when she saw the distant spires of the ancient town. Here, at last, they must find help and men of reason. As though in response to her thought, only moments later a troop of soldiers rode towards them.

Devenish, who was very pale and had spoken scarcely a word for the last several miles, muttered, "Any chance of enlisting their aid, d'you think, Tris?"

Leith regarded the troopers doubtfully. "Better not waste our time."

The troop passed on both sides. Suddenly, the four men bringing up the rear fanned out in front of them, and the desperate little band was surrounded.

A stern-faced Captain with magnificent black whiskers rode through his men, halted, and tossed a brisk salute. "Have I the honour to address Colonel Tristram Leith?"

Exultant, Devenish exclaimed, "Good old Smollet to the rescue! At last!"

"I am Leith," said Tristram.

"And are there also present —" the Captain drew a sheet of neatly folded paper from his pocket, spread it out, and read, "Sir Harry Redmond, Mr. Mitchell Redmond, Lord Jeremy Bolster, Mr. Alain Devenish, the Reverend Mordecai Langridge, and Mr. Justin Strand?"

The presence of all but the Reverend having been acknowledged, the Captain's whiskers seemed to vibrate with gratification. He replaced his paper, smiled, and said, "Gentlemen, you are under arrest."

With an authoritative lift of one hand, Leith silenced the angry chorus of protest. "On what charge?"

"Mr. Mitchell Redmond is charged with kidnapping and piracy on the high seas." The Captain ignored Devenish's hoot of laughter and went on formidably, "My Lord Bolster, Sir Harry Redmond, Mr. Devenish, and Mr. Strand are charged with assault, battery, and horse stealing. Colonel Tristram Leith is charged with the murder of Mr. Guy Sanguinet."

Charity's face twisted. She gasped, "Oh no! Guy is *dead!*"

The Captain's hard brown eyes flickered from her droopingly sodden cloak and hat, to her muddied boots. "You, madam," he said with a curl of the lip, "are at liberty to go. Men, *for*ward!"

The troopers turned their mounts.

Charity's frightened eyes flew to Mitchell. He said low and urgently, "You're our only hope now, Madame Mulot," and leaned to throw an arm about her and kiss her. She responded, but was slightly taken aback, under the circumstances, to feel his hand at her bosom. Something hard dug into her. She felt a chill of apprehension, then the troopers were coming between them and she had to rein back. The soldiers and their prisoners moved on. She waved in response to the shouted farewells and waves that were directed at her. Then the bridge was very empty, and she and Lion were alone.

Duly, she tidied the laces at her bosom, unobtrusively tucking Diccon's precious notebook more securely into her camisole.

"That bastard!" grated Lion furiously. "Pardin, ma'am, but that there Sanguinet wins every time. I see him push my master down and down till he wasn't nothing but dirt. Now he's won again. It ain't right!"

Charity thought wretchedly, "What shall I do without him? Without all of them?" And she said, "He's indecently rich, Lion. Much too powerful. How he would laugh." Her shoulders pulled back. She said vibrantly, "He *shall* not win! That evil man must not harm our dear land! Lion, you and I must go on! We must get to Brighton somehow . . . we *must!*"

"We will, missus," he said stoutly. "Don't you never worrit."

Nonetheless, they started off together in a mutually dismal silence, each aware of how slight were their chances. After a while, Charity reined to a halt in a pleasant copse of young birch trees. "Perhaps," she said, "if we were to go to the authorities in Oxford, we —" And she stopped, her heart giving a scared leap.

Where they had come from, she could not tell. How they could have been so swift and soundless was astounding, but lean men with dark hair and still, bronzed faces formed a wide ring about them. Several wore colourful scarves around their heads, and gold gleamed in their ears.

Lion muttered, "Gypsies. Gawd! They'll be arter our horses for sure."

Two of the men stepped forward. One was not much more than a boy, with wide, intelligent dark eyes and a proud lift to his strong chin. The other . . . Charity gave a sudden squeal of excitement and slid from her saddle.

"DiLoretto!"

"Signorina!" The Italian swept her a flourishing bow. "We again have meet. They circumstances they not-a so good, but" — his shoulders shrugged in that all-embracing gesture she remembered so well — "we make better, eh?"

Tears trembled on her lashes. She said unsteadily, "How *glad* I am to see you. But my brother and — they have been taken away and, oh, it is all so dreadful! If only you could help, but we are running out of time, and —"

"Madame," he interrupted this desperate

muddle, "tell me only this. Have you in your saddle, or about-a your person, perhaps, the crown of Charlemagne?"

"No. Gerard took it to the Regent last week."

"Mama mia!" DiLoretto struck his forehead with his clenched fist, so hard that he staggered back a step. "I must tell this to my Diccon."

"Then Diccon is alive? Thank God! Where?"

"To the west. Five miles, about. He is not-a very alive, signorina. We go quickly, now."

"No, no! We cannot. DiLoretto, listen to me! My brother and — and Mr. Redmond and their friends have been arrested. Even now they are being taken under heavy guard to Oxford. Our only hope would be to get them away before they reach the town. Oh, please, *can* you help me?"

DiLoretto looked at her thoughtfully, then he said, "Beside myself, this young-a man is called Daniel. He does not speak, but he will know."

Daniel watched Charity, his head tilted to one side. After a minute a broad grin spread across his dark features.

Thus it was that a short while later, a troop of soldiers escorting six prisoners across a bridge that spanned the swiftly flowing Cherwell River unexpectedly became embroiled with a noisily squabbling band of gypsies.

The Captain in charge of the troop, his glossy whiskers twitching with vexation at this interruption of their majestic progress, roared an

409

order for the ragtag band to clear the bridge. Instead, three caravans trundled up the far side and began to vie for the right-of-way. The argument became fierce. Voices, including that of the Captain, rose. Noses were pulled. Fists flew. Suddenly the bridge was a turmoil of flying fists, rearing, nervous horses, and angry soldiers.

Mitchell, recognizing one dark young face, caught his brother's eye and mouthed, "Daniel!" Sir Harry, following his gaze, brightened and nudged Leith. Mitchell drove home his spurs and his hack reared, neighing in fright. The line of troopers broke.

"Stop!" howled the Captain. "Stop — in the name of the King!"

Instead, six superb horsemen galloped madly down the bridge and towards a distant rise where a fair lady and a boy with flaming hair waited.

"Shoot!" roared the Captain.

The troopers strove to obey, but were hampered on every side by struggling gypsies. One man, more ambitious than his companions, fought his way clear, musket in hand, and rode in pursuit, the rest of the troop following belatedly.

The first trooper took careful aim and fired.

Bolster, bringing up the rear of the escaping band, felt his mount stagger. He jerked his feet from the stirrups and was thrown clear as the poor hack went down with a scream and a thrash of legs. Harry Redmond, glancing back, saw Jeremy getting to his feet and three troopers bearing down fast. With a whoop, Sir Harry swung around and galloped back. Bolster reached up, Sir Harry leaned down; a heave and a leap, and his lordship was mounted behind his friend. Another roar from a levelled musket. Bolster jolted and clutched at his head. His grip on Harry's waist loosened. Harry grabbed for him, but Jeremy was already falling. He landed rolling, then lay very still.

Harry dared not stop again. His face very white, he gazed back. "My God . . . Jerry . . . dear old boy. . . ." He saw a trooper stop and dismount beside that sprawled figure, and he drove home his spurs, suddenly finding it difficult to see clearly. With grief a knife blade in his breast, he rode on, whispering, "Dear old Jerry! Shot down by one of our own lads . . . our own good men. . . . My God!"

Chapter Eighteen

The sun became warmer in the afternoon, shining brightly on the lush green of the meadows and waking glittering sparkles from the stream that hurried through the woods. At the centre of the trees, seven horses grazed in a small clearing. Their seven riders, disposed about in various attitudes of weariness, felt slightly restored in body by reason of the bread, cold roast beef, and cheese that Charity had carried with her, but their spirits were low. They numbered several deep and enduring friendships among them, but Jeremy Bolster was beloved by all, and the silence was crushing.

Sir Harry, his back propped against a tree trunk, at length voiced the thought that was uppermost in all their minds. "He's not dead, of course," he said. "Old Jerry's indestructible. They couldn't kill him at Badajoz, though they gave it a jolly good . . . try. And if Boney couldn't snuff the straw-topped idiot, you cannot think that slimy little Claude . . . could. . . ." The words shredded and he said no more. Jeremy had looked dead. There had been blood on his face as he fell, and he had looked so terribly finished. . . .

Huddled on the upthrusting root of a solitary oak, Charity bowed her head into her hands. "First Diccon . . . then poor Guy. Then Major Tyndale and the Reverend Langridge. Now . . . dear Jeremy. Oh — how could they? How *could* they?" And she wept softly.

Leith said, "We cannot blame the troopers. They were only doing what they conceived to be their duty."

"I know." She sniffed and wiped fiercely at her eyes. "I'm sorry. I shouldn't . . . but it's just . . . that evil, *evil* man!"

Mitchell drawled, "Those dutiful troopers of yours, Leith, drove us in circles for the better part of an hour. I do not question your refusal to return their fire, or your evasive actions, but do you know where we are now? Damned if I do.''

Devenish, who had been stretched out with his head on his saddle, sat up and peered around. ''We've been riding north, eh, Tris?''

''I'm afraid we have. It was the only way to throw 'em off.''

''And west, dammit,'' said Strand.

''Oh, Lor'!'' exclaimed Lion. ''I'd s'posed them hills was the North Downs.''

Leith sighed. ''I wish to God they were. They're the Cotswolds.''

''And we've gone at least ten miles out of our way,'' said Sir Harry, glumly.

Leith stood, stretched, then went to help Charity from her impromptu chair. ''Can you face more riding, dear?'' he asked kindly.

She managed to smile, but she was thinking that Mitchell had been very quiet and withdrawn ever since they'd left Coventry. He had not approached her when they'd dismounted here, and it had been Justin who'd lifted her down and who had insisted she have this most comfortable of the ''seats'' they'd found. She had likely made a fool of herself with a man who was notorious for his many lights o' love.

Lion came up, leading her saddled horse. Settling herself after he threw her into the saddle, she wondered drearily if rakes were rakes because they were incapable of enduring devotion. She looked across at Mitchell, but he was engaged in an apparently grim conversation with his brother and avoided her gaze.

When they were all mounted, Leith glanced around. "Seven," he thought, "including a boy and a lady." He took out his timepiece. "Ten minutes past two 'clock . . ." he announced soberly.

Charity thought an appalled, "Two o'clock . . . *Tuesday!*" She walked her horse to Mitchell and held out her hand. He took it, his eyes sober, then glanced down at the notebook in his hand. He looked up at her. She smiled, but he stared at her sombrely and did not return the smile.

Again, they stayed clear of major roads, riding across country for the most part, heading ever south and east. They soon discovered that their clearing had been not far from Burford, their enforced detour having carried them almost twenty miles out of their way. They crossed the Thames above Abingdon and came at sunset into the high Down country. They were entering Berkshire, the fields lush and green about them, when Harry, glancing back, shouted, "Dammit! We're found again!"

This time their pursuers were greater in number, their exultant shouts leaving no doubt of their identity. The chase was on again. Leith led them at the gallop up hill and down, mile after mile, trying desperately to elude the dozen or so who strove just as desperately to come up with them. Through streams and across culverts they went, leaping ditches and racing full-tilt down slopes they would have taken with caution at any other time. After an especially mad dash down a steep hill, a village loomed up, drowsing peacefully in the sunset. Turning anxiously, Charity saw that the pursuit was far behind now. Encouraged, she started to call to Devenish, who rode beside her. By the warm crimson glow she saw that he was bowed over his horse's mane, his eyes closed, his face twisted with anguish. "Dev!" she screamed.

He looked at her dazedly. "Sorry . . . m'dear . . ." he gasped. A faint twitching smile faded fast. "Can't . . . ride no more. Awfully . . . sorry," and he slid from the saddle.

"*Tris!*" shrieked Charity.

Leith reined back, saw Devenish lying very still beside the path and shouted "Lion! Hide him!"

The youth, who had brought up the rear beside Mitchell, was already dismounting. Mitchell glanced down at Devenish, but rode on, increasing his speed so as to catch up with Leith and Charity. He could see tears on the girl's pale face. He thought, "Only five, now."

On they rode, a grim and subdued group, past villages and hamlets preparing for the evening, with open doors allowing a brief glimpse of cosy parlours or tables set for dinner in neat, whitewashed cottages. Past great manors secure behind their gates and parks, with lamps beginning to glow in many windows. Past fields and labourers coming home, bowed with weariness, yet raising a hand to wave at these five riders who came up so fast and passed with a thunder of hooves, creak of leather, and the flapping of the lady's rumpled habit. And the workers, returning to hearth and home, sat down to table and enjoyed their meal in peace and comfort. While the five who rode pushed on, desperate to elude the pursuers who clung so tenaciously mile after mile, until it was dark and the rising moon often hidden behind drifting clouds.

They passed a lonely graveyard, but Leith suddenly circled around and led the way through the tumbledown gates and in amongst the sagging headstones. And here, at last, he called a halt. They all dismounted, Strand lifting Charity down, patting her shoulder fondly as she sagged against him and leading her to where she might rest against a marble slab. Harry and Mitchell came over and sat down beside them, and Leith stood with his head slightly tilted, listening intensely.

"By God," he sighed at last, "I think we gave 'em the slip when we turned west at that last crossroads."

For a moment no one responded, each of them so exhausted as to find even the words beyond them.

Leith sank down onto the marble slab and leaned back against the headstone, closing his eyes. Charity huddled against her brother;

Harry, his head downbent, was breathing hard; Mitchell, elbows resting on his knees, wondered dully whether he would be able to mount up again and dared not close his eyes.

It was very quiet, the only sounds the hard blowing breaths of the horses who stood with heads down and shoulders splattered with foam.

After a minute, Mitchell pointed out wearily, "They're liable to be . . . waiting for us . . . up ahead."

"True," Leith acknowledged. "But if we don't stop for food . . . and rest, none of us will reach Brighton."

Looking ready to topple from his cold perch, Justin Strand said, "Stuff! We're almost there, Tris. Gad, we must be!"

"The last . . . hundred miles . . ." said Sir Harry, "is the hardest. Can we get through, d'you suppose, Leith?"

"Not unless we split up. They're all around us now."

"No choice," Strand agreed.

"You'll want to stay with Charity, Justin," said Leith.

Pulling up her heavy head, Charity mumbled feebly, "And . . . Mitchell."

Leith nodded. "Of course, dear. Now, we're just north of Farnborough and should —"

"Are we, by Jupiter!" said Strand, brightening. "Then Guildford cannot be more than twelve or so miles distant, and from there it's a straight run to Brighton!"

Very aware that the horses were close to foundering, that they all were at the edge of collapse, and that death lurked all about them, Leith asked, "Well, Sir Harry? Are you game for that straight run?"

Harry, used to forced marches, was finding it difficult to focus his eyes and wondered how poor old Mitch, who'd had by far the worst time of it, was staying awake. He replied cheerfully that he could scarcely wait to begin.

Fatigue enveloped Charity like a crushing weight. Remotely, she felt someone grip her arm and realized she was trying to sit up and making a sorry business of it. "I'm so . . . sorry," she muttered, and added a confused, "You must not stop . . . only for my sake."

They all stared at her, then at each other, and appreciative grins flickered over four weary faces.

"Please do let us stop just for a minute, love," said Mitchell, not caring whether that upset Justin Strand or not.

Charity peered at him eagerly, saw the expression in his eyes, and her heavy heart soared.

Leith said, "Strand, I want you to turn west to Basingstoke."

"The devil! It's miles out of our way!"

"Yes. You can get fresh horses there, and food. Rest until dawn, then swing gradually southeast through the Downs until you reach Brighton."

418

"Next week!" Mitchell put in indignantly. "If you don't mind, Leith, I prefer to —"

"I do not give a tinker's damn what you prefer!" growled Leith. "We are not here for you — or for me, or even for your gallant lady. We are here for England. Harry and I will make a dash for the Pavilion. If we should fail, you will be approaching Brighton from a direction Claude may not expect."

Mitchell nodded. "My apologies. We shall do as you say, of course, Colonel." He turned to his brother and put out his hand. "Good luck, *mon sauvage*."

Sir Harry pushed aside his hand and pulled him into a crushing hug. "Don't forget what I told you, halfling. And take care of your little wife."

Mitchell grinned at him. "Yes, Sir Captain."

Charity embraced Leith, and he gripped his brother-in-law's hand firmly. Then the two weary, dishevelled, but still resolute little groups mounted up, waved their goodbyes, and blended into the night.

The innkeeper was annoyed. He had waited up until eleven o'clock on the off-chance that some luxurious coach and four might pull into his yard, and no sooner had he sought out his warm bed and settled his nightcapped head onto the pillows than this scruffy lot had pounded at his door. Two gents, looking like death, and one with a bullet grazed across his head or he'd never seen one; and a lady in so sorry a condition he could only fancy they was running from something or somebody, which meant trouble with a capital T!

"I'm not at all sure as I've a room will suit," he muttered.

"We need *two* rooms," Mitchell said, managing to level a frigid glare.

The accent was Quality, the tilt of the chin was intimidating, the glint in the red-rimmed eyes was familiar. Reassured, the innkeeper said, "I've two fine chambers, sir. 'Course, me rates ain't exactly low, but —"

"We'll pay," Mitchell snapped. "My wife is very tired. Show us up, if you please, so that —"

"It's that damned dog again," Strand declared irritably.

Surprised, the innkeeper argued, "I didn't hear no dog, sir."

His arm about Charity's wilting form, Mitchell said sharply, "Strand? Wake up!"

Justin rounded on him, flushed with fury. "I didn't kill Jeremy! Do not *dare* accuse me!"

That high-pitched, querulous voice reached through the fog of exhaustion that had possessed Charity. She fought her head up. Justin's eyes glittered and at the edges of his high colour he was deathly white. "Oh, my God!" she gasped and, taking his hand, said soothingly, "It's all right, dearest. Everything is all right now."

Strand peered at her. "Lisette. . . ?" he said, puzzled.

"What the deuce. . . ?" Mitchell asked.

"Gawd!" gasped the landlord. "Only look how he shakes! I can't have him here, sir! Sorry, but —"

Strand sighed and crumpled to the floor.

The landlord gave a squeak of fright and backed away.

Kneeling beside her brother, Charity cried, "Justin! Oh, poor darling!"

"Get him away! Get him away!" shrilled the landlord.

Mitchell ignored him and slipped a hand onto Charity's shoulder. "What is it?"

"Malaria." She looked up at him in anguish. "He near died of it last year, but he's been so well, I didn't think . . . I suppose, when — when he got so cold and wet . . . ."

Mitchell stood motionless, trying to force his brain to work. "Be still, sir!" he snapped, turning angrily on the gabbling landlord. "The gentleman's illness is not catching, and you will be well paid for your trouble, I do assure you. Now, wake a servant and send him for the nearest doctor at once."

His panic subsiding when he realized there was no direct threat to his own health, the landlord hesitated.

"I am Sir Harry Redmond," lied Mitchell and, with a gleam of inspiration took Claude Sanguinet's ruby ring from his waistcoat pocket

421

and tossed it on the desk. "My wife and my brother-in-law and I were trying to win a wager, but it looks as though fate has intervened. That will secure our expenses. It's worth the price of ten inns such as this one! Now — *move!*"

The landlord jumped. This gent was Quality all right, and wasn't it just typical they'd been wagering? Cor! He snatched up the ruby. It was worth a fortune, all right. His eyes gleaming with avarice, he said eagerly. "Oh, at once, Sir Harry, anything you wish. Just ask — just ask!"

The physician came with reluctance and grumbled until he encountered Redmond's haughtily raised eyebrows and the chill, aristocratic manner that could so effectively depress pretension. The ostler who had summoned him had warned of the nature of the illness, so he had brought a supply of the invaluable quinine. He found Strand fretful and feverish, but much to Charity's relief pronounced that the attack seemed comparatively mild and would likely be of short duration. It was, however, imperative that the patient keep to his bed for several days. The decree infuriated Strand, but he had learned from bitter experience that his affliction was not to be trifled with, and he did not protest when Redmond said that he meant to snatch a few hours' sleep and press on very early in the morning. Charity, having gone out with the doctor, Strand said wearily, "How I should love to have been in at the finish." He paused, then added slowly, "You shall have to be careful. Sanguinet will have his whole crew scouring the countryside for you."

"Perhaps." Mitchell's eyes were bleak. "They'll be looking for several riders — not one man alone."

Watching him, Strand said, "You think Leith and your brother have drawn most of the action, eh?"

"You should be asleep, my friend."

Strand's head tossed fretfully. "D'you fancy they've a chance of getting through?"

Mitchell looked at him levelly. "No. No more did they." He walked to the door, then came back. "Strand," he said, staring fixedly at a bedpost, "if anything should happen to me . . . you'll take care of her?"

Strand's head was buzzing again, but he managed to point out that until now he had done so to the best of his ability.

"There are some things," Redmond went on, still concentrating on the bedpost, "I should like her to have. I'll write a few lines to Harry before I leave. I, ah, want Charity treated as befits my, er, relict. You'll deliver the letter for me?" He glanced up, his face rather red.

Shivering to a new onslaught of chills, Strand nodded and wondered with a sudden deep regret if either of the brothers would survive this mess. "H-have you told her . . . you're going on . . . alone?"

Mitchell grinned wryly. "Ain't brave enough."

It was past one o'clock before he was able to lie down, fully clothed except for his jacket, with a loaded pistol ready to hand and his boots close beside the bed. As he had requested, a maid crept in to wake him at half-past four. He was not an easy man to waken, especially when he had enjoyed less than ten hours' sleep over the past four days. The maid patted his arm, and he mumbled. She shook his shoulder, and he smiled drowsily at her and went back to sleep. In desperation, she grabbed his left arm with both hands and shoved strongly. Mitchell sprang up in bed with a muffled shout and clutched his side.

"Mercy!" cried the startled girl. "Ye said as how ye wanted to be waked now, zur!"

Breathing very fast, he gasped out, "Dreaming . . . is all. Sorry, lass."

She sighed with relief, said she had put a pannikin of hot water and shaving articles on the washstand, and crept away.

Half an hour later, washed and shaved, his garments restored insofar as was possible, and thus feeling somewhat more human, Redmond tiptoed into Strand's bedchamber. The sick man looked hot, and his head tossed restlessly against the pillows, but he was asleep. Turning to put his letter on the mantelpiece, Redmond gave a gasp. Charity was not sleeping in the trundle bed that he had ordered placed in here for her. Instead, she was curled up in a wing chair beside the bed, sleeping soundly. He propped his letter against the clock, but could not resist what he feared might be his last look at her. Her cheeks were flushed with sleep, and there were dark shadows beneath her eyes. Her hair was tangled and untidy, but the dim light of his candle awoke gleams of gold from those rumpled curls. He touched one soft strand very gently. *"Auf Wiedersehen,* Madame Mulot," he murmured, then he crept from the room.

The roan stallion chosen for him was stamping impatiently in the stableyard. The sleepy ostler holding the fiery animal regarded Redmond without affection. He was a scrawny man with a sneering mouth and a vindictive disposition. Because of this nob, he had been obliged to get out of bed and ride after the doctor. Further, because of this nob, he'd been ordered to get up only a couple of hours after he'd again crawled 'twixt the sheets, to saddle him their best horse. Well, he'd done it, and it served the nob right, may he rot!

"My, but he's a fine fellow," said Redmond, stroking the stallion admiringly.

"Said you wanted a goer," said the ostler. "Cannibal's a goer."

"Yes. I thank you." Redmond pressed a coin into the man's hand, then swung into the saddle and took the reins.

The ostler watched him. He could ride, no

doubt of that, even though he looked like he'd been swigging blue ruin for a week or two. . . . Probably had his first pony 'fore he was breeched, and his own groom along of it! Much good it might do him! The ostler grinned and slouched back into the stable.

The big roan was full of spirit and for a while Redmond indulged his eagerness to go. The powerful animal galloped with a rather jolting but untiring gait, and the miles passed swiftly. It was a fair morning with a slight breeze. The sun was coming up and Redmond rode southeast through a deserted countryside rich in wooded slopes and hills, coming at last into dear and familiar surroundings, for this was Hampshire, the county of his birth. He was soon less than ten miles from home, and the longing to turn west to Moiré Grange gnawed at him. He would be looked for there, however, and thus he schooled himself to follow Leith's orders, riding steadily southeast past quiet Alton, drowsing in the pale morning sunlight, and over dewy meadows toward Selborne. He had slowed Cannibal and when a stagecoach approached on the narrow road he'd thought it safe to follow at this hour, there was plenty of room for passing. Cannibal betrayed not a trace of nervousness until the team drew level, then suddenly plunged at the off leader, ears flattened against his head, eyes narrowed evilly, and teeth snapping at the polite bay's neck. Wrenching at the head of his carnivorous mount,

Mitchell found himself the target for streams of invective from driver, guard, and passengers, both inside and out. Cannibal was powerful and determined, and had obviously set himself to eat the bay.

In the resultant melee, the stagecoach plunged off the road and into the mud. A farmer's dray and a milk wagon drew up to watch the spectacle, and unable to escape the hostile ring of accusers, Mitchell was trapped until he resorted to digging in his spurs and setting Cannibal at the very small gap between the milk wagon and the hedge. He squeaked through and rode off, followed by infuriated vituperations. Irked because he had lost valuable time, he still supposed this to be an isolated instance. It soon became apparent, however, that the ostler's remarks had been less than all-embracing: Cannibal was aptly named. He *was* a good goer, but his idiosyncrasy, a major one, was that he yearned to eat another horse. Any horse that came within snapping distance.

Redmond left the lanes and byways, and headed across country again. The sun grew warmer, and he pushed on steadily, alone as he had never been before, for now he was haunted by the memory of a valiant companion with a gentle lilting voice, always willing to point out his shortcomings. . . . He smiled faintly and in another second was sighing because he so missed that intrepid presence, the dauntless set to her small chin, the quick way she had of entering into his moods, of understanding his silences, sharing his mirth, steadfastly enduring the hardships he endured. "My beloved Madame Mulot," he thought. The wistfulness vanished from his eyes when he caught a glimpse of scarlet uniforms on the hillside ahead. He swore and turned aside.

Twice after that he was driven from his intended route by the appearance of groups of riders he dared not risk encountering, so that it was afternoon by the time Cannibal plodded up a long rise in the Downs. A small cluster of trees offered shade, and a little brook gurgled close by. Redmond dismounted stiffly, allowed the horse to slake his thirst at the brook, then unsaddled him and secured the reins to a low shrub. Sitting with his back against a tree, Redmond stretched out his legs gratefully. Jove, but he was tired! He took out his timepiece. The hands seemed to ripple, and he had to rub at his eyes before he could focus properly. Twenty minutes past one . . . no! *two*, by gad! And still a long ride ahead. He should push on, but Cannibal must be rested and he himself ached with weariness, besides which his side was such a damnable nuisance. He propped an arm on one drawn-up knee, leaned back his head and closed his eyes, just for a moment, listening dully to the gossiping dance of the leaves. . . .

He awoke with a start when his elbow slipped from his knee. Lord! He must not do that again! The fateful ball was *tonight*, and if he once dropped off, he was liable to sleep for a week! He took off his wilted beaver and ran a hand through his damp hair, blinking at the panorama spread out before him. The velvety Downs sloped ever southwards to where lifted the distant spires of Chichester. His first tutor had lived there, and he had spent many happy hours in that lovely cathedral town known first to the Romans as Noviomagus, and afterwards as Cisseceastre. Saxon kings had walked the cobbled streets, and later, their Norman conquerors. It had seen its share of battle and death and fire, had old Chichester. But today it was green and peaceful, quietly occupying its assigned space in the present, securely rooted in its past, washed by the rains and mists that swept in from the blue reaches of the Channel. . . .

" 'This sceptred isle,' " murmured Charity, sinking down beside him. She expected him to leap up ranting and raving, but he only quoted just as softly. " 'This blessed plot, this earth, this realm, this England . . .' "

She had ridden desperately, all day, to come up with him and, not having dared hope to do so, had finally caught a glimpse of him embroiled in a dispute with a stagecoach, and guessing he meant to cut across country, had at last found him. She knelt there gratefully, watching him. He looked so tired and pale. The cut the bullet had ploughed across his scalp was visible at the hairline, and his dark hair was terribly disordered, so that she longed to tidy it, but fearing to break his mood, did not.

In a faraway voice, he murmured, "You can see the wind."

She caught her breath and, remembering what Rachel had once said of his absent-mindedness, knew that here again was the dreamy-eyed boy she had glimpsed beneath the bitter cynicism; here was the boy she could love. *Could* love? No! It was far past a possibility. She did love him. For so long as she lived, she would never love another. Tenderly, she prompted, "Tell me what you are thinking."

Still gazing to the south, he said, "It is not my thought. It was told me by a most poetical weaver named Bamford. And he was right. If you look hard enough you can — See — just above the trees there — the glow of it . . . like the aura of all those who have dwelt here before us. The effort, the courage, the pride, the suffering . . . the wind of our history. . . ." He started, glanced at her, and coloured hotly. "What fustian I'm jabbering. You must think me properly wits to let."

Perhaps for the first time, she realized how close he was to total exhaustion. She said simply, "I think you are splendid."

He stared at her. "No, how could you when you saw what a worthless craven I —" And only then did that brutal memory jolt him back into the here and now. He gasped. "My God! What the deuce are you doing here?"

"I followed you. No, it is no use to berate me, sir. My brother is resting comfortably, and the innkeeper's wife is very kind and will take proper care of him. You cannot send me away, Mitchell. My place is here. With you."

He gazed at her. How serene she was, for all that her habit was stained and creased, and the wind had blown her fair curls about under that foolish little blue hat that had once been so pert and now drooped in sadly wilted fashion. She was looking up at him as though he was some kind of god, instead of — "I'm not good enough for you," he muttered. "Don't you know that, my mouse? When I saw the look in your brother's eyes last night, I could not blame him. I'm a rake . . . a womanizing, fighting, brawling idiot. And underneath it all, I'm a rank coward. A spineless —"

"Nonsense. How could I love such a one?"

His fists clenched against the need to hold her. "You must not love a coward."

"I do not. I love a man who faced his fear and defeated it."

He sat straighter, his eyes devouring her gentle, glowing, dirty little face. "But I haven't, my darling girl. I never *will*, unless I can beat Sanguinet and so prove myself a man again."

His eyes, so full of adoration, were saying much more than the words he spoke. He was trembling, so greatly did he long to kiss her. A wave of tenderness swept Charity. She leaned to him. Mitchell sighed, tilted up her chin, and kissed her. And the Downs, the munching Cannibal, the hurrying voice of the wind, faded and were gone. They drifted together in a glory of love, joined in a long, consuming kiss that roused a new, sweet passion in Charity, so that her arms tightened convulsively.

Gasping, Mitchell jerked away.

"What is it?" she demanded. He kept his face averted for a minute, and she seized her opportunity and pounced to tear at his shirt.

"Hey!" cried Mitchell.

Charity stared, horrified, at his bared side. From the left armpit to below his waist, the skin was blackened by a great bruise, dark at the centre, purpling and greenish at the edges.

"Have you no shame?" he demanded with feigned indignation, drawing back and gingerly restoring his garments. "Dashed if ever I met a woman with such a fixation about tearing the clothes from a fellow!"

She lifted her shocked gaze to his face. "When . . . did you do that? Was it — when that brute kicked you?"

He sighed. "When I fell from the wall."

"My God! Why did you say nothing? What kind of ridiculous stoicism —"

"How could I say anything?" he intervened, reddening. "We had to get here."

"Yes, but you could have told Leith, or your

brother, when they came up with us. There was no need to —"

"And have them insist I be left behind, like poor Mordecai Langridge?"

"Of course. That is ghastly! It must hurt terribly. And — you have ridden and . . . and fought . . ." Tears glinted in her eyes. "Oh, Mitchell . . . what *madness!* What unutterably *foolish* pride!"

"No!" He caught at her hands and said desperately, "Try — please try to understand. I must do this. Don't you see? I *must!* I have never been offered the chance to do anything worthwhile for my country. And since Parnell Sanguinet shamed me, I have felt . . ." His gaze lowered. He went on painfully, "Scarcely a human being. A weak shadow of — of a creature."

She thought, "So Claude was right . . ." But she said staunchly, "And was it a weak shadow of a creature who fought his way out of Tor Keep? Were you less than a human being when you battled those louts in Coventry, or when Shotten came upon us in the stable?" And she remembered how that great brute had kicked him, and her face crumpled.

Redmond gathered her close and kissed her soft hair. "My loyal little love," he said huskily, "would you have me give up? Would you have me leave it to Leith and my brother to do this? Leave the task for somebody else?"

She looked up into the grave smile, the

faintly reproachful look. And she knew suddenly that whatever the outcome, Mitchell must run this course to its ending, even though his life be sacrificed in vain, or if Leith and Harry were already in Brighton and the Regent safely warned. And she knew she could not love him as much were he any other kind of man.

"No, my very dear," she said. "I would have you be just what you are. Always. But — please, do not *ever* leave me behind again."

Chapter Nineteen

In later years, when Charity looked back upon that fateful Wednesday in June, it remained a nightmare; an unceasing battle against fatigue and pain, and most remorseless of all, the creeping hand of Time. The wind grew ever more blustery and was soon a full-fledged gale, often startling the horses and further exhausting Mitchell, who led the way ever into the teeth of the buffeting gusts. They were almost spent when they came in late afternoon to a neat hedge tavern near Shoreham. They tried to hire a post chaise, but although Charity had brought every penny from Justin's purse, Claude's ring had been left as security for her brother's care, and now their shared funds would allow no more than feed for the horses, a sandwich, and a pot of tea. The food restored them, but they were, they admitted to one another as they crossed the stableyard, a sorry-looking pair, Charity limping and stiff, and Mitchell slightly stooped as he increasingly favoured his battered side.

They skirted the charming little coastal village, but they were able to see that there were unusual numbers of military about; keen-eyed officers leading troops of men, scrutinizing all travellers, but far more interested in riders than in carriages. Mitchell lost no time in taking to the countryside again, but was soon obliged to detour northwards to avoid a barrier across the road. They were driven ever farther from their goal, arriving at Lewes at sunset, and managing to slip into Brighton at dusk, the horses covered with sweat and dust, and Mitchell so exhausted that he sat his horse unmoving for several minutes after they had halted in a quiet lane not far from the seafront.

The wind howled between the buildings, sending a sign over a haberdasher's door flying madly on its hinges and billowing the skirts of Charity's dusty habit. At the end of the lane was a major thoroughfare; a noisy place with many people walking along despite the wind, and a great glow in the sky beyond that seemed too light to be a fire. Mitchell responded to Charity's question by saying he fancied it must be the lanterns from the Royal Pavilion. "That's the Old Steine," he said, nodding to the street at the end of the lane. "I fancy Prinny's guests are arriving. We'll leave the horses here."

He dismounted, leaning against the saddle for a brief second, then turning a haggard but smiling face as he assisted Charity down. "We're *here*, my mouse," he said jubilantly. "We've done it, by God!"

"We have." She reached up to caress his cheek. "But we must find help, my dear. You cannot —"

He shook his head. "Our time is almost gone. We'll have to get inside, somehow." He offered his arm and said flirtatiously, "Will you promenade with me, Madame Mulot?"

Her eyes misting, she slipped her hand onto his arm.

It was nine o'clock.

The Steine, a wide thoroughfare with some fine houses, a few expensive shops, and a covered walk, was crowded with an eager, jostling throng. A long procession of luxurious carriages wound along the street towards the Pavilion, and mounted guards were positioned at intervals along the route, sabres drawn, eyes intent upon the shifting mass of humanity.

Easing into the crowd, trying not to let their haste become too apparent, Charity and Redmond were swept along until they came in sight of the Pavilion itself, a breathtaking sight, like a palace of the Far East, with its graceful domes and delicate wrought iron; its balconies and cupolas and minarets, and the mighty adjoining rotunda that housed the royal stables, all glowing in the light of countless lanterns so that it seemed indeed a place of fantasy against the night skies.

Leaning to Mitchell's ear, Charity called above the tumult, "What time shall they sit down to dine, do you think?"

"At any minute, I fancy. Though to judge by this crush many will be delayed."

"Oh, Mitch! What if Claude presents his gift at the start of the meal?"

"I doubt it. Were I he, I'd have it delivered towards the end, when Prinny could quite logically be expected to suffer a seizure, and in —" He broke off, staring to the gates of the drive that wound through the lawns to the Pavilion, and the line of Household Cavalry flanking both sides of the entrance. "It looks," he said slowly, "as though we dare not approach by the direct route, m'dear."

Following his eyes, Charity gasped with fright. A tall gentleman stood conversing earnestly with one of the splendidly caparisoned officers. A dark man, who wore his black garb well and was obviously sufficiently important to be respectfully attended to. "Gerard . . ." she whispered.

"Now look a little to the right. That's Shotten, see? With the high-crowned brown beaver. Ah! And over there — two more of Claude's rogues!"

"Oh! And look on the other side of the drive, by the yellow flowers — that sullen-looking creature in the green coat — that's Clem! One

of the men who kidnapped me! Oh, Mitchell!"
She turned to clutch his arm in dismay.
"What*ever* shall we —"

An impatient group pushed past. Mitchell
winced and staggered. A shout went up, and
clinging to his arm, Charity saw a fine town
carriage of dark brown, trimmed with silver,
the crest on the door very familiar. "Vaille!"
she screamed, and pushing through the crowd,
waved desperately. *"Vaille!"*

A handsome, distinguished face appeared at
the window. The Duke of Vaille scanned the
throng, but then his coach was past and
Charity's cries were swallowed up in the roar
of acclaim as he was recognized. Two splendidly
mounted cavalrymen walked their horses forward, eyeing the girl suspiciously.

Tears of frustration in her eyes, she stretched
out her hands appealingly. They reined up and
one of the magnificent beings leaned down from
his Olympian heights. "Move along, ma'am,"
he said with firm officiousness.

"Help me," she begged. "My husband has a
message for Prince George, and —"

Shouts of laughter arose, the nearest people
eyeing her with delight.

"Oo's got *wot?*" asked a fat man with a very
red and pespiring face and a reek of gin.

"The gal's old man," explained a tall youth
wearing an atrocious red waistcoat. He pointed
to Redmond, who was striving unsteadily to
make his way to Charity's side. "He's got a

message fer our Prinny," he said with a guffaw. "A very good friend he is, I'll lay you odds. Whether he's got a hat or not!"

Another laugh was drawn from the crowd. "A lushy lad, was you to ask me, General," said the fat man, nodding up at the amused cavalryman.

"Listen to me," cried Charity, "please! If you will only —"

Angry shouts rang out somewhere along the line. The soldier straightened in the saddle, wheeled his horse abruptly, and clattered off with his comrade.

The attention of the group shifted. Redmond made his way at last to slip an arm about Charity's waist, and she leaned against him, tears of helplessness in her eyes. "Oh, Mitch! We are so *close!* How awful if we're to be beaten by indifference . . . at this stage. . . ."

The disturbance ahead had become a violent altercation. The guardsmen rode their horses ruthlessly amongst the crowd on the flagway. Shouts and screams arose. There was a splintering of glass, and people began to run. Mitchell whipped his arm about Charity and somehow forced a way back to a recessed shop door that suddenly opened.

The man about to exit carried a large bag, and a comrade beside him ducked back inside as Mitchell turned towards them. The first man with a quick movement held a glinting knife in his hand. "One sound, my cove," he snarled, his eyes narrowed and deadly.

Mitchell glanced past him into a dim interior. A small emporium by the look of it. He whispered, "Two out — two in?"

The first man grinned; the knife disappeared. "Come on then, mate," he answered softly. "Good luck to yer. But you best be quick. Our friends along the way'll be gone in a coupla winks!"

Mitchell took Charity's arm and said importantly, "Goodnight, Jenkins. See that merchandise is delivered before ten o'clock, there's a good fellow."

The two thieves passed him with deferential bows, the first man murmuring a laughing, "Garn!"

Mitchell closed the door behind them. A muffled squawking met his ears. He glanced over the top of the counter and into the wide and furious eyes of a gentleman with great white eyebrows and glaring brown eyes, who was bound hand and foot and gagged with a zephyr shawl.

"Good gracious!" gasped Charity. "Poor man! Let us —"

He drew her back. She looked at him enquiringly.

"Poor girl," he said, sighing. "How I drag you down! I believe we are become what is known as Flash Prigs. . . ."

Ten minutes later, a neat gentleman's gentleman and an equally neat lady's maid left the quiet premises and blended into the good-natured crowd.

Holding her bandbox carefully, Charity said, "Mitchell, are you quite sure that Mrs. Fitzherbert still uses her little house in the Pavilion grounds?"

He was not at all sure that the Regent's ex-wife ever came near her erstwhile home, but it was, he thought, the best chance they had. "We shall soon find out," he said. "Now, we must walk around to the tradesmen's entrance. This way, ma'am."

They hurried back the way they had come, pushing through the crowd until at last they were able to get across the street, ducking under the noses of an irate team of horses and the recipients of the comments of an equally irate coachman. Approaching the side entrance, however, they were again foiled, for several cavalrymen guarded that gate and were supplemented by three individuals looking so grim and burly that they were either Runners from Bow Street or Sanguinet's people.

Mitchell drew Charity into the shadows, fretting as the minutes crept past, wondering desperately how to bluff his way through. And then a flurry of shots rang out from the direction of the front entrance. The cavalrymen were away at the gallop, Sanguinet's men after them, and the sole remaining guard busily occupied with a cart from Gunter's. Mitchell seized Charity's arm; they walked swiftly to the far side of the cart and were past and along the path in seconds.

"I wouldn't of asked you to come, sir," the footman explained earnestly, walking downstairs beside the austere majesty of the butler, " 'cept that the manservant's a strange sort of cove — more like a gentleman than a valet, and the lady —"

"Exactly so," intervened the butler, his egg-shaped face declining in a slight nod so that the light of the chandelier in the entrance hall gleamed on his bald head. He walked ahead with sedate and unhurried steps. The young woman appeared neat enough. But the man affected too haughty an air, carrying his shoulders in so proud a way that — But here the butler's eyes drifted to the shoes, and he was aghast. One always judged by the shoes. Shoes should shine. Shabby they might be; a little. Perhaps a trifle out of the fashion, even. But shine they must. This man did not even wear shoes! The objects upon his feet were riding boots — and those a mass of mud! The butler levelled a disdainful glance at the unfortunate footman. "Gentleman, indeed!" he murmured with derision. The footman flushed and hung back as the butler descended the last three stairs, prepared to depress the pretensions of this insolent "gentleman."

Reaching the ground floor, the butler lifted his eyes and suffered a severe shock. The young woman looked completely worn out, and she watched him with a sort of tense desperation. The man was deathly pale, his handsome features haggard, his eyes red-rimmed, and an ugly gash marring his high forehead disappeared into the tumbled dark hair. But even as he stood there swaying a little unsteadily, his head was drawn back with a faint but unmistakable arrogance, and the tired grey eyes were amused as he said in a deep cultured voice, "Yes, I'm afraid we present a frightfully odd appearance. I apologize for coming to Mrs. Fitzherbert in such a way, but will you be so kind as to tell her that we must see her at once?"

Taken aback by both tone and manner, the butler reacted instinctively. "We are seldom here these days, and Mrs. Fitzherbert is not at home, sir."

In a weary voice that was as cultured as that of her companion, the girl wailed, "Oh, Mitchell! After all this!"

Charity sagged against Redmond as she spoke, and he gripped her shoulders, the smile in his eyes replaced by a glare. "A chair for my wife. At once!" he demanded crisply.

"Y-yes, sir," gasped out the butler, gesturing to his subordinate.

A triumphant gleam crept into the footman's dark eyes. He'd knowed them two was Quality the instant he'd seen 'em! Old grizzle-guts had been set down proper by the young nob! Gloating, he raced to carry over a straight-backed chair, then tore off in search of the brandy the butler ordered.

His own miseries forgotten, Redmond dropped to one knee beside Charity, took the glass the footman sped to hand him, and lifted it to her pale lips. "Just a sip, my dear," he urged.

She sipped obediently, coughed, then blinked up at the three anxious faces that watched her. "Good gracious," she said faintly, "I am a silly. Whatever must you think of us, Gilford?"

"You know my name, ma'am? Alas, I do not recall . . ."

She said distractedly, "How odd that I should recollect that at such a time. I believe Harland chanced to mention it to me, though when —"

Gilford interjected eagerly, "Do you mean the Earl of Harland, miss? Why, I served with his brother, Lord Moulton."

"I fancied you to be ex-military," said Redmond. "India, was it?"

"Aye, sir. And a more gallant officer never lived, if I may say so."

"You may. Though I fancy my brother not far behind him. I must make you known to my wife. This is Mrs. Redmond. I am Mitchell Redmond, and —"

"Sir *Harry's* brother? I'll be — Forty-third, as I recall, sir? I well remember how grieved we all were when he was listed missing. Oh my, oh my! And I keep you here in the hall with your poor lady so distressed!"

"Why, we have come such a long way, you see," said Charity, managing to conceal her rising hopes and continuing to look woebegone.

"We rode down from Scotland," said Redmond, and seeing the butler's polite interest, went on, "We left Ayrshire on Saturday."

"Cor!" gasped the footman.

Overlooking this lapse, the butler said, "Jackson, fetch refreshments into the breakfast parlour at once. Mr. Redmond, if you will just bring your wife this way, perhaps we can somehow be of assistance to you. . . ."

Redmond assisted Charity to her feet, then took the timepiece from his pocket. Twenty-three minutes past nine . . .

The footman stood in stunned silence beside the door. Gilford, his face almost as pale as Redmond's, stared blankly at the decanter of wine on the table. "God in heaven!" he muttered. "It passes belief!"

"You have put your finger on it exactly," said Redmond with a wry smile. "No one *will* believe us."

"I never could abide that there Claude Sanguinet," the footman put in, stepping forward. "Slippery damned —"

"You forget yourself, Jackson," said the butler automatically.

"Oh no I don't sir! Begging your pardon, I'm sure, but this ain't something as I can stand

445

aside and do nought! Mr. Redmond, I'm your man! If I can help in any way. Any way at all!"

Redmond stood and put out his hand. "Thank you, Jackson," he said, as the footman came eagerly to shake hands. "I wish to heaven you could!"

"If only there was *some* way we could get into the Pavilion," Charity muttered, wringing her hands as the clock struck the half-hour.

Gilford bit his lip, sat down at the table beside Redmond, causing his underling to gape with astonishment, and rested his mouth against tight-gripped hands. Mitchell waited, praying his hopes had not been in vain.

As if gathering his courage, Gilford closed his eyes a second, then looked up resolutely. "You must know, sir, that Mrs. Fitzherbert is the Regent's legal wife in the eyes of the Catholic Church. The only lady he has ever been really happy with, if I dare make so bold as to remark. When the King and all the ministers kept at him that the marriage was unlawful and that he must wed Princess Caroline of Brunswick, it fair broke his heart. But . . ." He shrugged wryly, "I've no need to tell you what you already know. His extravagances brought about his downfall. This house was one of 'em. And after they'd married him to that woman he daren't come here any more. At least," he hesitated, "not so any could see . . ."

"Then it *is* truth," exclaimed Redmond

exuberantly. "There *is* a tunnel!"

"Oh! How wonderful!" Her eyes bright with new hope, Charity asked, "Where?"

Panicking, Gilford said, "Oh, my Lord! I gave my solemn oath . . . if I am doing wrong . . ."

Seething with impatience, Redmond could not but respect the man's integrity. He said quietly, "Mr. Gilford, upon the sacred memory of the man I loved and honoured more than any other — my father — I do swear that all I have told you here is God's truth."

Gilford gazed for a long moment into those unutterably weary, yet steadfast grey eyes. Then he pushed back his chair and stood. "Thank you, sir. This way . . ."

"I'm coming too," said Charity.

Jackson pulled back her chair. "And me!"

The passage was narrow but tall enough to enable Redmond to stand erect. It was cold and clammy and shrouded with webs that indicated a lack of recent use, but it was well built, and recalling the distance from Mrs. Fitzherbert's little house to the Pavilion, Redmond thought, "It must have cost a fortune!" He walked very rapidly, so that Gilford, holding the lantern, was forced to trot to keep up. Having outdistanced the two following, Redmond murmured, "Now, when we reach the far end, Gilford, you must keep my wife back."

"You expect trouble, sir? Even inside the

Pavilion? Surely, they would not dare."

"We saw several of Monsieur Sanguinet's men outside. We know some highly placed naval and military officers are in his pocket. I'd not put anything past 'em! Tell me where we will come out."

"In the Prince's apartments, sir. There is a double wall with a deep cupboard, and behind it, steps leading to this tunnel."

"And who else knows of it?"

"So far as I am aware, until tonight only the builders, and they were sworn to secrecy, myself, and the, er, principals."

They hurried on, Redmond panting now and holding his arm pressed against the sharp anguish that tore at his ribs with every breath; the butler, his limp ever more pronounced; and Charity, tottering along, dazed with exhaustion, the footman supporting her as best he could.

Taking out his timepiece again, Redmond peered at it. It was fifteen minutes to ten o'clock. . . .

Redmond opened the cupboard door a crack. The luxurious bedchamber was deserted, the magnificent canopied bed that occupied the deep recess already turned down, and the royal nightshirt laid upon it. The chandelier hanging from the gilt-edged oval of the ceiling was a blaze of light, but several of the candelabra had been extinguished. As usual, the heat was almost overpowering. Redmond tiptoed across the room. He had instructed Gilford that when Charity and the footman came up they were to be told that he was reconnoitering and would return when he was sure the coast was clear.

He peered into the royal library, adjoining. He had once been invited to a musicale at the Pavilion but had never been in this part of the palace, and despite the desperate circumstances, could not fail to be impressed by the magnificence of the furnishings, the splendid *torchères* and carven wall lights, the recessed bookcases and everywhere the Oriental influence with dragons abounding.

He started into the library, astounded that he was thus far undetected, but heard voices close by and retreated to the bedroom again. On the far side, the dressing room was silent, but as he stepped inside he came face to face with a manservant carrying a gargantuan purple-and-gold dressing gown. The man's eyes popped, and his jaw fell. It was not time for explanations. Redmond struck hard and true, caught the servant as he sagged, and eased him to the floor.

Beyond the dressing room was an ante-room. Redmond strode to the far door and opened it cautiously. All was quiet, but distantly he could hear music and the muted hum of conversation. Had the Prince already donned the lethal crown, the sounds would be very different, but every second counted now. Somehow he must pass along the major part of the Great Corridor, but lackeys were everywhere, to say nothing of an occasional military uniform; his own quiet garb would be noticeable by its very simplicity. He hesitated, then muttered, "As well be hung for a sheep as a lamb," turned about, and hurried back to snatch up the lurid dressing gown that he had draped over the manservant. It was so large that he and Harry and Uncle Mordecai could all have fitted into it, but he wrapped it around him and tied the sash about his middle. With the addition of the garment, the heat in the rooms was almost beyond bearing and he began to perspire freely, but there was no help for it. The lackey wore a powdered wig; Mitchell borrowed it and jammed it onto his head. Glancing at himself in one of the large mirrors, he gave a gasp. The effect was astounding. So astounding that in this outrageous palace-cum-mosque-cum-pagoda he might go unnoticed. En route through the ante-room again, he noticed a very large Chinese urn tastefully painted with scenes of Waterloo and heavy with filigree and gold leaf. A card lay beside it. It was a gift to the Duke of Wellington from some potentate. Mitchell eyed the urn thoughtfully, then, the effort making him swear, he picked it up and holding it on his right shoulder, stepped into the Great Corridor and strode along deliberately.

Itself a fantasy of art and light and beauty, it was a busy place. Magnificently liveried lackeys and footmen were everywhere; splendid officers stood about in small groups, and far in the distance, a constant stream of servants was carrying trays from the Banqueting Hall, trays piled high with plates, glasses and silverware, covered tureens and platters and great dishes still containing enough food to feed many average households for a week. The meal was apparently almost over. Claude's gift would likely be presented at any moment!

His nerves taut, Mitchell marched along, the urn perched high, his head up, his stride exaggeratedly pompous. A couple of officers glanced his way and exchanged faintly disgusted grins. A splendid lackey was convulsing a cohort with what appeared to be a ribald joke. Neither paid the least attention to the vision of glory that stalked past them. At last the door to the Banqueting Room was coming closer and closer. . . . Another lackey, standing alone and decidedly bored, looked at the oncoming apparition with lack-lustre eyes. "Typical flummery nonsense . . ." he thought. His eyes drifted down that tall figure. He frowned. Now there was an odd thing. This conjuror, or juggler, or whatever he was, wore riding boots . . . very muddy riding boots. . . . "Hey!" he said, starting forward. "Just one minute!"

Of all the State Apartments in the glorious Pavilion, the Banqueting Room was surely the most awesome. It was an enormous chamber, rich with gold and crystal, the walls bright with colourful Oriental paintings, the long table set beneath a great domed ceiling more than forty feet in height. The dome, the blue of an Eastern sky, had in the centre the likenesses of long, luxuriant tree fronds, several of which were three-dimensional, being carven of copper. And from the middle of those lush plantain leaves, hanging directly above the centre of the dining table, was an enormous silver dragon, the chandelier suspended from its claws so vast and so bright that the jewelled lotus flowers and chains that festooned it dazzled the eye with their radiance. Four lesser chandeliers and eight standards created their own light so that the entire chamber was a blaze of colour and brilliance — and heat.

Since the Regent had no lady at that time to act as hostess, only gentlemen were seated at the long table, but they were an illustrious gathering. The guest of honour, of course, was the Duke of Wellington, seated at the Regent's right hand and in an expansive mood, his bray of a laugh ringing out often, his strong face relaxed into the smile that could make him seem quite handsome. Many officers who had survived the great battle were present, among them the tall and gallant Colonel Sir John Colborne of the Fighting Fifty-second, and the debonair cavalry commander, Lord Uxbridge, who had lost his leg to one of the last cannon shots fired into the fields near La Haye Sainte. Regimental reds and blues blazed around the table, but there were others not in uniform, gentlemen wearing the black and white of formal attire. And among the most elegant, a slender figure whose soft French accent contrasted with the booming voice of the Brigadier beside him.

Claude Sanguinet had not wished to be present at this banquet. It was, in fact, infuriating that it had become necessary to ensure he was invited, but after the fiasco that had resulted from Mitchell Redmond's escape, after the unforgivable ineptitude that had failed to bring about the death of that British thorn in his flesh, Claude had felt that he must be present — just in case anything went awry. His dash down the length of England had been less exhausting than that of his enemies, for he had travelled in luxuriously sprung coaches, with teams of blood horses to bear him in speed and comfort day and night, but even so, he was tired, irritated, and nervous as the moments dragged slowly past.

Because a ball was to follow, the dinner had been less than heroic in scope, but Sanguinet, not a man of large appetite, viewed the twelve *entrées* with inward disgust and was heartily glad when the covers were removed in preparation for the wine and nuts.

At last! It was time!

He smiled at a remark of the Brigadier to the effect that Prinny was in rare form tonight, and his brown eyes slanted obliquely towards the

453

Regent, a vast figure, his orders glittering on his great chest, his fat face red and perspiring, but his manner polite and amiable, betraying not the faintest sign of hauteur. "Fool," thought Claude with contempt and glanced to the doors.

He was not disappointed. Very soon a splendidly uniformed officer of the Household Cavalry ushered in a tall, black-clad gentleman who bore a small brass-bound wooden chest, carried high beneath both hands. A ripple of interest ran around the long table, and the noisy guests quieted.

"Well, now," said the Regent, his round features weathed in a benign smile, "what's all this, eh?"

The officer snapped to attention. "With your permission, sir, Monsieur Claude Sanguinet begs to be allowed to present a token of his respectful esteem on this historic occasion."

Several glances were directed at Sanguinet. The Duke of Wellington's dark eyes were expressionless; Lord Liverpool's austere countenance wore a slight frown, and Lord Castlereagh tilted his handsome head thoughtfully. The Regent, almost childishly delighted, leaned forward insofar as his bulk allowed and called down the table in French, "This then is your grand surprise, eh, Claude? The honours go to Wellington tonight, not to me. My thanks, however."

Gerard was allowed to step forward and place the little chest on the table. The Regent unfastened the clasp and swung open the lid. For a moment, he peeped inside, saying nothing. Beside him, Wellington leaned forward, and his dark brows lifted.

Almost inaudibly the Regent said, "Now . . . by Jove!" His pudgy hands lifted the crown from its purple velvet and it came into the light like a thing of glory, rich gleams darting from rubies, emeralds, and sapphires, together with the myriad sparkling hues of diamonds. Cries of admiration rang out. Prince George's pale eyes shot to Sanguinet. Obviously awed, he asked, "Is it . . . the Charlemagne?"

Sanguinet smiled and made a slightly deprecating gesture.

Across the table from the Regent, a somewhat inebriated General called, "Put it on, sir! Let us see you in't!"

"Well, I, ah, don't know . . . about that. . . ." The Regent looked rather shyly at Wellington.

Already thoroughly bored, the Duke said with a tight smile, "Why not, sir? It certainly is a splendid gift."

George grinned happily. "Well, damme, but I shall!" He lifted the crown.

Sanguinet held his breath. Gerard, his dark face unreadable, stepped back and began to drift towards the serving tables.

The Prince lowered the crown again. "A mirror! Some one of you fellows fetch me a mirror!"

A lackey slipped into the corridor, removed a large oval mirror from the wall, and carried it into the Banqueting Room.

The Regent, who had been holding up the crown of Charlemagne so that all present might exclaim over it, turned in his chair and with both hands began to lower the crown onto his head. He was frowning a little, because of a noisy commotion that had suddenly arisen in the corridor.

A loud crash and the doors burst open. There were shouts of "Stop him!" and "Warn His Highness!"

The Prince paused, his full mouth pouting, his face both dismayed and disappointed. Wellington was on his feet, his hawk gaze turned to the astonishing figure fighting his way into the room.

Mitchell's wig was gone; the urn had paid the supreme penalty when he'd aimed it at a zealous hussar in the corridor, and now he eluded those who grappled with him by the simple expedient of slipping out of the voluminous dressing gown they grasped.

Several of the waiters ran for him. Colonel Colborne sprang up to block his path, his chair going over with a crash. Many of the guests, shouting alarm, were also standing.

Desperate, Mitchell called, "Sir! The crown is —"

Sanguinet, his pale face a mask of rage, jumped up and fired a small derringer at close range, the retort shattering in that chaotic room.

Mitchell was slammed back as if by a giant hammer. He caromed into the men who pursued him and was thrown to the floor.

"Crown . . ." he gasped faintly. "Mustn't put on —"

The burly guardsman straddling him, drew back one fist with a snarl of rage.

Wellington's resonant voice pierced the uproar. *"Stop!* That's young Redmond! Let him up, I say!"

Colborne, who had also recognized this brother of his erstwhile comrade in arms, ran to pull the guardsman back.

Someone else charged through the doors — a stocky little man in the full dress uniform of a general officer, with beside him a tall ragged young giant, his dark hair tousled and the right side of his tired face badly scarred.

"Leith!" cried Wellington.

Sanguinet's face twisted with hatred. He gestured imperatively.

The bosky General who had urged the Regent to put on the crown was suddenly cold sober, another derringer appearing in his hand as he aimed at Leith and fired. Leith staggered, recovered, sprang onto a vacated chair and launched himself across that noble table. The Regent moved faster than he had been known to do for some time and was clear as Leith's long shape blurred past him. Claude snatched up the crown even as Leith's strong hands clamped about his throat. They both crashed to the floor to the accompaniment of shouts of alarm and excitement. With all his strength, Claude swung the crown and brought it smashing against the side of Leith's head. The young Colonel's hold relaxed, and he lay still.

Colborne, on one knee, his arm supporting Redmond's shoulders, asked urgently, "What is it, Mitch? Try and tell us, old fellow."

Mitchell could see only a dazzling blur. A great noise was ringing in his ears, and Colborne's words came as from a great distance. With a tremendous effort he pulled the notebook from his pocket. "Crown . . ." he whispered. "Poisoned . . . San-Sanguinet . . ." The words faded into a sigh and he was suddenly a dead weight in the Colonel's arms.

"That murdering damned weasel," snarled Wellington, snatching Diccon's notebook. He whirled about. "Sir! Do not touch the crown!"

Two shrieks rang out almost simultaneously. The first was uttered by Sanguinet, who, having struggled to his feet and grinned down triumphantly at Leith, was now frenziedly examining a small scratch on the middle finger of his right hand. The second scream issued from Charity's lips as she ran into the room and saw Mitchell lying unconscious in John Colborne's arms. Falling to her knees beside him, she sobbed out his name and, clutching his unresponsive hand, looked imploringly into Sir John's startled face.

"Mais non! Mais . . . non!" The shrill wail, unutterably desolate, keened through the uproar. Claude Sanguinet, his face ashen, raised clenched fists and shook them in the air in an agony of frustrated fury. Another sound escaped his writhing lips. Neither scream nor shout, it died into a terrible, strangling sob. Before the collective gaze of that stunned gathering, Monsieur Claude Sanguinet sank to the floor. One hand, in a last convulsive grab, fastened onto the tablecloth, dragging it downwards. The crown of Charlemagne fell with it, to lie beside — but not on — the head of the man who had schemed and murdered and plotted for so many years and at the end had contrived only to bring about his own death.

Chapter Twenty

Mitchell's first awakening was hellish. His left side was on fire, his right shoulder made breathing an agony, he ached from head to foot, and — worst of all — she was not at his side. Whenever he dared open his eyes, he peered through the mists, but she was not here. He knew that he was in a strange room of great size and richness; he knew that kind hands tended him; he fancied to have seen Harry a time or two; and somehow he knew that

England was safe. But she was not here. Why did she not come? Was she hurt? Or ill? Or had she decided he was beneath contempt after all. . . ? Had that ghastly confrontation at Tordarroch so disgusted her that, now it was all over, her sensibilities had righted themselves and she did not want to see him again? Hot, miserable, and pain-racked, his head began to toss, which made the pain worse. And so he lay there, increasingly fretful and despairing, calling for her, in vain.

The next time he awoke, he thought for a wonderful moment that she had come, but his vision clearing, he saw that it was an older lady in a starched white apron, sitting in the chair beside his bed, tatting, her thin fingers flying, and thread somehow shaping itself into an intricate little square. Mitchell stared at it until his eyes began to blur. He heard the door open and turned eagerly, then clutched wildly at the coverlet, biting back a cry of pain. Things became a trifle dim, but suddenly the disembodied face of a very fierce-looking man loomed over him. A gentle voice said, "Easy, lad — easy. We will bring her to you, just as soon as we can. Try to sleep now."

But they did not bring her, and the weary hours dragged past until he slid gratefully into darkness. . . .

Sir Harry Redmond sat at a black japanned escritoire in the small but elaborate ante-room, writing industriously. A vivid bruise along the right side of his forehead, extending downwards into an equally vivid black eye, made his efforts a trifle tedious, and he was turning his head to squint awkwardly at the paper when a large hand clapped on his shoulder, causing him to toss the pen into the air and give a little jump of shock.

Tristram Leith smiled down at him and murmured a conciliatory, "Sorry, old boy. Didn't realize your nerves was in such a state."

"Well, what the deuce would you expect?" exclaimed Sir Harry indignantly. "Only look at what you've made me do! Ink all across the blasted thing, and it's my third attempt to write to my wife. By George, if you didn't carry your arm in that stupid sling, I —" He checked, his green eyes becoming narrower than usual, and asked sharply, "What news, Tris?"

Leith threw one long leg irreverently across the end of a long Egyptian-style sofa with griffin's feet and said laconically, "A groom just brought word that my wife goes along nicely." His dark eyes softened. "Thank God! She sent me a letter. . . . What of your brother? Awake yet?"

Sir Harry's lips tightened. "Several times. But he's drifted off again, fortunately."

Leith nodded, having weathered such a storm himself. "It's not a coma, I hope?"

"No. But for the most part he's out of his head, poor old fellow. The doctor says he's

461

completely exhausted and may sleep for several days. Do you know, Leith, that blasted idiot has a bruise on his side you'd not believe. Rode all the way from Hadrian's Wall with three cracked ribs and said not a word about it!"

"Did he, by God! You must be very proud of him, Harry. Has —" And Leith interrupted himself to shout a glad, "Dev! Jupiter, but I thought you'd never get here!"

Leaning heavily on the arm of Lion, whose hair was now half-brown and half-red, Devenish hobbled to grip Leith's outstretched hand, be pounded on the back by Sir Harry, who had also sprung up to greet him, and to remark with considerable indignation that he'd never have come had he known what he was letting himself in for. "Did you know," he said, casting a wary eye towards the closed door, "that Wellington himself is in the Saloon? He told me that England could be proud of us and gave me a clap on the back that damn near knocked me into the fireplace!"

Leith and Sir Harry exchanged uneasy glances. Leith muttered, "The old fire-eater didn't say as much to John Colborne after he'd right-shouldered his Fifty-second out of that blasted cornfield at Waterloo and pretty well saved the day!"

Devenish shook his head glumly, then said, "Lord, what a cawker I am! How does your brother go on, Harry? I hear he was a trifle knocked up."

"Sleeping now. Claude's shot broke his collarbone, and the doctor had a devilish time digging the ball out, but we think he'll make a good recovery."

"Glad to hear it," said Devenish. "When the Duke said they'd call in Lord Belmont, I was afraid —"

Whitening, Harry sprang to his feet. "Called in — who?"

"Belmont. Didn't you know?"

"Be damned if I did. Why? Do you know about this, Leith?"

"No," said Tristram, adding in his calm fashion, "but I shouldn't fly into a pucker. Prinny's so blasted grateful to all of us that he likely feels obliged to provide the finest. I'm getting dashed tired of having him wring my hand ten times a day, I don't mind telling you."

"Good God!" said Devenish. "Knew I shouldn't have come! How's our battling invalid?"

Leith chuckled. "She sat by Mitchell's bed not saying a single word after they'd hauled him into that Sultan's tent of a bedchamber day before yesterday. I didn't realize until they were finished with Mitch that Charity was fast asleep. She hasn't stirred since."

Harry shook his head. "Who'd have guessed that tiny, frail little creature could ride all this way . . ."

"If you d-describe me, Harry, you c-can —"

463

The rest of that rather shaken utterance was drowned as the three friends turned, whooping, to greet the pale man, a bandage wrapped around his fair head, who tottered to join them.

"Jerry! You confounded idiot — you're alive!" cried Harry, overjoyed.

"If you say so," said his lordship, sinking gratefully into the chair Leith whipped around for him.

" 'Course he's alive, you dolt," said Devenish, beaming. "Don't you see that the ball took him in the head? Only place it could do no damage."

When the badinage and laughter that covered their relief had died down, Harry asked, "How the devil did you get here? I wonder they let you leave your sickbed."

"Pr-Prinny sent a d-damned great state coach for me. With two outriders, six horses, liveried coachman, a guard, and two footmen! Blessed if ever I saw such a commotion! They've got grooms r-riding hell for leather in all directions to noti-noti-noti-tell our families and find those of us who dropped along the w-way — did you know it?"

Amused, Leith said, "Justin will shrivel up, poor fellow. Or perhaps he'll be so fortunate as to remain hidden."

"Oh no, he won't," said Bolster. "They're to fetch him tomorrow, I was t-told. Serve him right, silly clunch! And y-your uncle's on his way, Harry."

"I don't suppose," Devenish put in gravely,

"anyone knows yet — about Guy?"

There was a brief silence. His eyes sad, Leith murmured, "How could two brothers be so unlike, I wonder? Guy so thoroughly decent. And Claude —"

"The late unlamented," interposed Devenish dryly.

"So thoroughly —" Leith went on.

"B-b-b-b, rotten," finished Bolster. "Well, let me tell you, Dev —" But he did not do so, because the door opened and Charity ran in.

"Oh, my poor . . . poor dears!" she said, half laughing, half crying, as the battered group stood to welcome her. "But you are *alive*, Jeremy! Oh, how *grateful* I am!" She flew to kiss him very gently, and he blushed and stammered and shyly kissed her back, while Devenish grinned and grumbled that the rest of them might as well have expired for all the attention *they* received and only because his lordship had all the rank. Whereupon, of course, Charity turned to embrace him and then fluttered about like a bright butterfly in her pretty peach muslin gown, sympathizing with their hurts, praising them, her great eyes reflecting her deep affection for them all, but holding also an underlying anxiety that wrung Harry's heart and made him dread the moment when she should come to him.

"A fine sister-in-law you will think me," she said, as she gave him her hands, "to leave you to the last. It is only that you seem the least damaged, you see."

"What — with this dreadful wound?" he protested, bending his dark head so that she might exclaim over his bruises.

She smiled, stood on tiptoe, and kissed his forehead lightly, asking how he came to suffer such afflictions.

"Why, it was when we'd come at last to the Pavilion after the most hair-raising series of brushes with our Claude's rogues," he said. "Properly set upon we were and had to run for our lives."

"Ah," she said intently, "so that was the shot we heard? It was because Gerard and Shotten and the soldiers all went rushing around to discover the cause that Mitchell and I were able to get past the gate."

"Is that so? Then it was worth it, though the ball came devilish close to making a widow of Nanette." Sir Harry pulled down his collar, disclosing a deep graze across his neck.

"Good heavens! But — you did escape?"

Leith said, "No. We were caught. Luckily, one of the officers chanced to be an old friend of mine, Miles Cameron. It was through Miles's intervention that I was able to get my hands on Sanguinet." He sighed. "However briefly. Well — it's all over now. And how are you feeling, my dear?"

"Well rested, thank you," she said, her voice a trifle too nonchalant. "They tell me I have slept for two days. They also tell me that my

— that Mitchell is — here. Is he conscious yet?"

Her eyes searched Harry's face. He longed to say the words she so obviously prayed to hear and instead answered very gently, "Not at the moment, Charity. Sound asleep."

"He has not spoken . . . at all?"

Sir Harry bit his lip and yearned to be elsewhere. "Not, ah, well, he has been a trifle feverish, you know. Not, er, lucid, exactly."

Her heart twisted. So he had not asked for her. It was logical, of course. They had survived a nightmare of danger and because they had fought their way through together, she had dared to hope . . . But that gallant, handsome, altogether adorable gentleman would not want a plain little dab of a girl. Not once their terrible . . . wonderful idyll was done.

They all saw the light go out of her eyes, and they rallied around at once, exclaiming at her long sleep, marvelling at her endurance and bravery, teasing her, loving her. She responded somehow, longing to see *him*, to be assured that he would live, that he was not suffering too dreadfully. And instead she laughed with these dear friends who tried so hard to ease her sorrow.

Another gentleman stamped to join them. A tall, grey-haired, irascible-appearing individual with a rasp of a voice, a lantern jaw, black eyes deep-sunken under great bushy eyebrows. "How the deuce," he said, ignoring protocol completely, "do you expect me to get this damnable fever down when no one will *cherchez la femme?*"

Charity gave a hurt little gasp.

"Your pardon, madam," he snarled, scowling at her. "My manners are deplorable, I'm told. I am Belmont." Without waiting to hear who she was, he demanded, "Is the boy's brother here? Oh, it's you, is it? Well, why ain't you out searching for the woman instead of standing here, fooling about? Do you *want* him to die?"

Terror-stricken, Harry mumbled, "I did not think — I mean, surely there's no thought of *that,* my lord?"

"Good God, man! Are you daft? That young fool rode and fought his way for — what is it? three hundred miles? — in a state when anyone with half a brain would have taken to his bed! How it is his lung ain't pierced, I don't know, but he is beyond exhaustion, that I *do* know, and he cannot rest. He has a smashed shoulder, is battling a high fever besides, and is half out of his mind for the woman he loves. And you ask if he might die! 'Fore God, I've lost patients for half as much! Fretting and worrying will kill men quicker than any bullet. *Find* the woman! And fast! Else we very well may lose the lamebrain!"

Frantic, Harry stammered, "But, but I don't know who she *is!*"

"He's your *brother* and you don't know his *chères amies?*"

Throwing an anguished look at Charity's

pale, stricken face, Harry blurted, "Well, Mitchell's been abroad for — for nigh a year. The, er, lady is French, I know, but —"

"Any fool knows that! What is *your* name, if I may ask, ma'am?"

In a frozen croak of a voice, Charity managed, "I am . . . Mr. Redmond's wife, sir," and she wondered if this was how it felt to die of grief.

For all his harsh manners, Lord Belmont was not an unkind man. He heard the note of pathos in that cracked little voice, and his heart plummeted. "Oh, ecod! I am indeed sorry, Mrs. Redmond." He turned a dismayed face to Harry. "I shall take my clumsy mouth away at once. My humblest apologies." He fled, but turning at the door added, "I assure you, the case is really becoming quite desperate. Try and find this Madame Mulot, or —"

"*What?*" screamed Charity, spinning to face him, her face shining with a great joyous light. "*What* did you say?"

"Jupiter!" thought Sir Harry. "To think I ever judged her plain. . . !"

Mitchell really did not want to wake the third time. It was all too wearying and painful, and he was so very hot and without hope. But then a gentle hand was stroking his hair, a soft, broken, beloved voice murmured, "Wretched, most odious rake, oh, *why* must you call for me by *that* name?"

His eyes shot open. He turned his head, not

caring how remorselessly the pain clawed through him. And she was there, her tanned, beautifully boned face close to his, her great eyes liquid with love, her cool hand touching his cheek.

It was all right, then.

He gave a deep sigh. "My little mouse," he whispered, and with a faint but contented smile fell asleep.

Wellington said grimly, "We think we got 'em all, gentlemen. Most of the ringleaders, at all events. Gad, but that murdering little weasel had his web spun from Dinan to Paris to Vienna to the Hebrides and points south to Brighton!" He leaned back in his chair in the privacy of one of the visitor's apartments and looked from General Smollet, whom he detested, to Leith, whom he had always thought a splendid officer. "Had it not been for you and your friends —"

"One in particular," interjected Smollet, recklessly.

The Duke did not care to be interrupted and turned upon the General a look that froze Leith's blood and had been known to make men's knees knock like castanets.

Bristling, the sturdy little Smollet thought, "Devil fly away with him!" and his grey eyes, fierce under their beetling brows, darted sparks. "Had it not been for a very gallant gentleman named Diccon," he persisted, "these fine young fellas would never have had their chance, sir. Nor the Regent his life. For more than five years that poor devil —"

"I am well aware of Major Diccon Paisley's record," interpolated Wellington.

Surprised by the new name, Leith's dark brows twitched upwards.

His chin aloft and his eyes cold, Wellington continued, "He knew the chances he took when he entered the Intelligence Service."

"He paid the price willingly," growled Smollet. "And got precious little thanks for it."

"I doubt he asked any, sir!" But the Iron Duke liked an officer who stood by his men, and he thought suddenly that Smollet put him in mind of poor old Picton. The height in his manner vanished. With a mischievous twinkle, he added, "He'll likely continue to pay the price until he finds the sense to enter a less nerve-racking business."

Leaning forward, Leith asked eagerly, "Then he *has* survived, sir?"

"Where that gentleman is concerned, it's a case of 'least said, soonest mended.'" Wellington smiled. "As will be the case with you, Colonel, and your magnificent efforts for England."

Smollet, who had found it necessary to blow his nose, now exclaimed, "My lord! You cannot keep such a matter quiet!" He had said "my lord" instead of "your grace!" Oh, well, too

471

late now! He went on rather feebly, "Too many knew of it."

"The people who knew of it have already taken an oath to keep silent. Good God, man! Have a little sense. To publish such a desperate affair can only inspire some other group of fanatics to try the same thing! With England in the throes of this accursed economic shambles, and the Regent as popular as —" He bit off that sentence, finishing grimly, "It must *never* become public knowledge! The best service one can render to those who would prevail by threat and terror is to make their deeds known. Stifle 'em, and you destroy 'em!"

General Smollet nodded, but muttered, "Then poor young Redmond will never receive the honours he deserves." He glanced to Leith. "How is the boy?"

"Much better, sir. Since we brought his lady to his side, his recovery has been remarkable. I doubt he will want to leave here, though, he's been so pampered these last two weeks."

"You have *got* to get me away from here, *mon sauvage*," said Mitchell imploringly, gazing at his brother's amused countenance.

"Ungrateful clod." Harry stretched comfortably on the end of the bed, his back against the carven bedpost. "Here's our poor Prinny doing all he can to show his gratitude, and —"

"No, but he scares me to death! I woke up

yesterday afternoon and there he was again, peering at me for all the world like some doting parent. The minute he saw my eyes open, he jumped up and started babbling all sorts of rot, and then came at me with a sword that must have been used in the Crusades! For a minute I thought my last hour had come, I don't mind telling you!"

"The devil!" said Harry, straightening. "He never did!"

Bolster, straddling a nearby chair, chuckled. "So you're knighted, are you, Mitch? That'll put you in your pl-place, Harry!"

Feigning indignation, Harry said, "Of all the impudent mushrooms! I suppose you fancy yourself quite my equal now, halfling?"

"Er, not exactly," said Mitchell, staring very hard at the coverlet.

"And what, dare I ask, may that mean?"

Slanting a glance up at this brother he had always loved and admired, Mitchell said with the old gentle humility that was delighting Harry, "I could never be that, you know."

"True," said Harry, winking at Bolster.

"And besides," said Mitchell, hesitantly, "Prinny did not name me a baronet exactly."

Outraged, Harry snarled, "Why, that ungrateful — Then, why the sword?"

"It seems I am now . . . the, er, first Baron Redmond of Moiré. . . ."

"What?" Leaping to his feet, Harry howled, "Why, you damned insolent puppy! Do you

mean to tell me that flabby — that Prince George — Do you say you are a *Baron* and I a mere *Baronet?*"

Mitchell threw back his head and laughed so hard he wrenched his shoulder. Harry and Bolster laughed with him.

Wandering around the book room, tapping his whip against one gleaming topboot, Mitchell glanced at the crowded shelves, admired the beautifully wrought reference table, and peered out of broad windows to a sweep of lawns and the distant blue loom of the Surrey hills, bathed in the sunlight of this warm July afternoon. "What d'you think of the estate, m'dear?" he asked.

Charity, who had been watching him lovingly, said, "It seems very large for a single man. Has Guy a lady somewhere, do you suppose?"

"Every man has a lady somewhere." He grinned. "Taking his time about coming. Tris *did* say he was better, didn't he?"

"He said Guy was sufficiently recovered for us to come and see him. Mitch, I'm so glad he has decided to live down here close to us, so that —" She stopped, her breath catching in her throat.

The doors had opened, and Guy Sanguinet was on the threshold. A tall, angular, cross-looking woman pushed the invalid chair, and Guy, a gaunt, white-faced shadow of himself, smiled gladly as he saw them, extending a very thin right hand. "My dear friends," he said, pressing Charity's hand to his pale lips, "how very good of you to come and see me. *Merci*, madame. You can be so kind as to the tea things bring."

Mitchell gripped Charity's hand steadyingly as Guy's dark head turned to his attendant. She bit her lip and fought for self-control, vexed because Leith had not prepared her.

Mrs. Nayland slanted a grim look of warning at Mitchell, then stamped out, slamming the door behind her.

"How are you now, my dear fellow?" asked Mitchell, wheeling the chair closer to the sofa and then seating himself beside Charity.

"Much better, I thank you. Leith have come to see me — did you know it? Ah! And I have forget the thing *très importante!* My congratulations! How happy I am for your marriage."

"You must come to our wedding," said Mitchell, grinning broadly.

Guy stared.

Charity explained, "The announcement of our betrothal went to the newspapers last week. We are to have a formal ceremony, you see, Guy. Although I am sure the gossips are having a glorious time with all the rumours."

"But you are secretly married — no? And thus I shall claim my privilege."

Charity stood and bent down to be kissed.

Guy regarded her with fond concern. "You must not weep for me, little one. Only look —"

475

He lifted that thin right hand again and flexed the fingers. "I am fortunate, most. At first, they say I never shall move either hand again. Now — see!"

She was quite unable to say anything sensible and tried desperately to smile despite the painful constriction in her throat.

"And your legs?" asked Mitchell bluntly.

Guy shrugged. "Oh, *une chose si petite.* . . . How much more pleasant is it to be wheeled about and — Ah, little one! Do not! Do not!"

"Oh, Guy!" gasped Charity, disappearing into her handkerchief. "Oh, my dear! You have known so very much . . . of sorrow! It is not *fair!*"

Mitchell said with unwonted sternness, "Madame Mulot!"

She blinked, wiped her eyes, and said in a thready voice, "I know. I am behaving very badly. I'm sorry."

"It is not 'bad' for this French fellow to know he is loved," said Guy, smiling steadily. "And marriage, my dear, have suit you very well. You are the lucky man, Mitchell."

"I am, indeed." Squeezing his wife's trembling hand, Mitchell asked, "Is there anything you wish to know, Guy? About Claude?"

Just for an instant, a bleak look came into the clear hazel eyes. Guy said tersely, "No." Then he added, "Ah, here is my good helper and our tea."

Charity poured, of course, and they enjoyed

tea and little cakes, while chattering about the Reverend Langridge's return to health and Bolster's joyous reunion with his Amanda and of how furious Lisette had been when she learned her beloved Justin had suffered a recurrence of the malaria she fought so determinedly.

"How fortunate he is, to have the lady to watch over him," said Guy, and because they all knew such a blessing could never be his, he at once went on hurriedly, "Tell me of your so beautiful sister, Charity. How is Rachel?"

"Very well. She fairly radiates health and happiness, thank heaven."

"And, you will pardon, but there is the chance, perhaps . . . for me to be told when the babe arrives?"

"Most assuredly," said Charity, then laughed. "I can only hope poor Tristram's nerves will survive it all. You knew, of course, that Major Tyndale came down and was presented to Prinny?"

"Yes. Is a fine gentleman, that one. And what of our young hothead? How is the so intrepid Devenish? That leg was the big nuisance during your wild ride, *n'est-ce pas?*"

"You'll never get him to admit it," said Mitchell. "The boy took care of him. Lion."

"And Josie takes very good care of Dev," Charity put in. "She is a most dutiful daughter. And bullies him dreadfully."

"*Bon*. But this boy, the Lion. He will be

placed in an orphanage, or working house, do you call it? This would not be good."

Charity sighed. "I have been worrying about him, I'll own. He has been helping out in the stables at Silverings. Best says he's willing, and a hard worker. But . . ." She hesitated, reluctant to speak of the high ambition the boy had once confided to her. "I know you will think me silly, but I cannot think that is the place for him."

"I agree," said Mitchell, misunderstanding. "Lion is growing like the proverbial weed. He's got a fine pair of shoulders. Might be quite a fighting man some day."

"You men and your fighting!" scolded Charity. "Haven't we had enough?"

"More than enough," Guy agreed, laughing. "I wonder now, do you suppose this ferocious child might possibly be willing to come to me? It, er, would be company for me, and I could see that he had some sort of education. . . ?"

Charity clapped her hands with delight. "How perfect that would be! Mitchell, what do you think? He has no family, I know. This is such a beautiful estate — is there any reason he should not be allowed to come?"

Mitchell hesitated. The boy was crude and untutored. However, Mrs. Nayland had not impressed him as being a model of gentle concern either. He said slowly, "I should think it would be a jolly good solution. Guy? Are we tiring you?"

Sanguinet, who had been looking rather furtively out of the window, apologized at once. "I beg you will forgive my manners of the most poor. And if that is the hint you must be upon your way — pray do not. I had hoped you might stay at least overnight."

They assured him they would be delighted to do so, but the grim look in the eyes of Mrs. Nayland had been properly interpreted, and Mitchell pleaded an unbreakable prior engagement. Guy looked so genuinely disappointed that Charity asked anxiously, "You are not alone here, surely?"

"No, no. I have friends who come often to see me. Good neighbours, you know. And a companion I had hoped would return so that you might — Ah! Here she comes!"

A familiar shape sprang lightly in at the open window. A small voice said a friendly, "Purrrttt?" And Little Patches ran to jump upon Charity's lap, butt against her chin, submit to a few caresses, repeat the process with Mitchell, and then race to occupy Guy's lap.

Watching the cat as she turned around and around preparatory to settling herself, Charity exclaimed, "Oh, how she has *grown!* Guy, you cannot call her Little Patches any longer!"

Guy stroked the cat, his eyes very soft as he watched her. "She is my most faithful friend. How glad I am you have allow me to keep her, Charity. So very much she brighten my days."

Mrs. Nayland came in to take the tray and levelled another steady stare at Mitchell.

"Guy," he said, promptly, "we must be on our way, I'm afraid. But before we leave, I would like to ask you something . . . if it is not too personal a matter. I, er, have wondered for some time —"

"What it was that my brother hold over me — no?" Guy nodded, caressing Little Patches, but with his eyes frowning into the past. "You have hear," he said slowly, "my brother address me as the bastard. This was truth, but not quite in the way you may think. Claude and Parnell have the same mother, you see, Papa's first wife. My mama was a very gentle lady who died soon after I was born. Her mother, my grandmère, was most beautiful, but very proud. She had loved her daughter deeply, and because they were fine aristocrats but poor, had — how you say this? — had bragged a little, telling her friends how well her Lorraine have marry, how fine is her home, how devoted her husband. My grandmère, you must know, was very dear to me. Always, she was kind. And I" — he shrugged and said in a deprecating fashion, "well, I was a rather lonely little boy. One day, Grandmère was sleeping in her small house in Paris, and the wind it blow one of her pretty scarves too near the candle. The room catch fire, and my poor grandmère was very badly burned. Papa made some small provision for her, but there are many bills for very much.

After my father died, Claude, *naturellement*, was head of the house. He find out quite soon that he can make me do what he want, by threatening to withhold the funds for Grandmère. She was —" His right hand clenched suddenly. "She was blind, and in much pain. And I was all she have, do you see?"

Mitchell muttered something under his breath.

"My God!" whispered Charity. "How savage he was!"

Guy said quietly, "And so it go on, and I am made to stay because I have the head for figures and detail and am useful to Claude. Only when I learn he have deceive your sister, little one, and means to force her to wed him so as to have the highly born English wife, I tell him — no more! Grandmère and I, we will survive, somehow! But then . . ." He paused, a little pulse beginning to twitch beside his mouth.

"Never mind, Guy," said Mitchell. "I had no right to upset you. It is of no importance and —"

Guy lifted his hand. "I am all right. You will hear it all, and you may not then, I hope, despise me so badly. Claude told me, you see, that contrary to my grandmère's beliefs, my father had never married Mama. He knew how proud Grandmère was, how deeply religious she was, and that such news would break her heart and her spirit." He put a trembling hand across his eyes and because he was still far from well, his voice broke. "I — could not, you see.

I just — could not . . ."

Appalled, Mitchell stared at him.

Charity knelt beside Guy's chair and clasped his hand. "Is — is your dear grandmama still living?" she asked.

"No. She went to be with Mama some months ago. Claude did not tell me of it."

Pressing his thin hand to her cheek, Charity murmured, "My dear, oh, my dear! I am so sorry. But how could you think we despised you? Always, Rachel and I thought you kind and honourable. Always, we knew that whatever the hold Claude had over you, it must be something very strong indeed, to keep you bound to him."

"*Merci. Merci, ma chérie.*" Guy kissed her hand and with a rather shaken laugh added, "You will not call me out, Mitchell, for speaking so to your lovely wife? I know you are the very dangerous duellist."

Mitchell stood and helped Charity to her feet. "My duelling days are done, friend. This little rascal" — he tugged one of Charity's bright curls — "would have my ears did I dare think of such a thing!"

They left soon afterwards, Mitchell tossing Charity into her saddle, then swinging astride his big bay, and both of them turning at the top of the drivepath to wave at the man who sat there in his chair, waving gaily, bravely, back at them.

As they watched, a small tricolour shape tore

from the house, raced three times around the chair, then flung itself onto the man's lap and ran to butt a small head against his chin.

Epilogue

The sunset was glorious, painting the river scarlet as it meandered past the beautiful old half-timbered structure that was Moiré Grange and brightening the blush on Charity's cheeks. She lay in her husband's arms on top of the hill, shivering deliciously because of the kisses that, having progressed down her throat, were now moving lower, and — "Mitchell!" she gasped, slapping his hand.

"What's this?" he demanded, persisting.

"Oh! How naughty you are! And our wedding day yet a month away!"

"I wonder you did not remind me of that fact last night," he murmured, drawing the golden chain from her bosom.

Her blush deepened and her lashes drooped before his adoring gaze. "Wicked, wicked rake! How ungallant in you to remind me of my . . . disgraceful abandonment."

"Your glorious abandonment," he corrected, bending to kiss her soft lips and then add wickedly, "In the event, beloved, that you very logically present me with *un petit paquet,* we

485

may have to offer considerable explanations some time next March . . ." And laughing into her shy eyes, he said, "Good God! Why do you keep this miserable thing?"

Her fingers at once clamped over the old wedding ring he had bought for her in Carlisle. "Do not *dare* to steal it from me, sir!"

"Devil I won't! I shall buy you a far more suitable ring when —"

"No! Please, darling, no ring in the world could be more suitable than this one. . . ." Kissing the little ring and tucking it back under her bodice, she added saucily, "Even though you did trick me into wearing it."

Mitchell forgot the ring, leaning to her worshipfully, and Charity reached to pull down his dark head, whispering, just as his lips claimed hers, "Oh, Mitchell . . . my love . . . my —"

"Enough of that, my girl!" exclaimed Mitchell, sitting up abruptly after a heavenly interval and running what he mistakenly believed to be a tidying hand through his rumpled locks. "I'll not be responsible, else! To the more mundane aspects — what do you think of Moiré? Now that Harry has deeded it over to me, we should live here, eh?"

"But of course," she said, rearranging her dress with rather belated propriety. "You love it, and I think it a delightful old house."

He sighed. "Trouble is, the old place is so large. Costs a veritable fortune to keep up, you know. And we" — he hesitated — "well, we're not exactly poor, but —"

"Poor! But you are Baron Redmond of Moiré, and —"

"And that's the sum total of it." He nodded glumly. "Prinny gave me the title, but there are no funds or additional lands or whatever! *En effet,* I am baron of my own estate. Sorry, love."

She stared at him, then gave a ripple of laughter. "Oh, but how very ridiculous! Well, we can live at the Hall, then. Justin has often told me it is mine when I marry, and you do not object to the house, do you, love?"

"Object to it! I think it a splendid old place. But there's not a great deal to choose between them for size."

Charity smiled and, refraining from pointing out that she was a considerable heiress, said, "But then you have married a lady who knows how to hold household, my lord."

Dismayed, he said, "I must get used to that form of address, I collect. Perhaps we can keep the title secret so they'll not know."

"So who will not know?"

"Why, my tutor and the fellows up at Oxford. They're sure to give me the very devil if —" He saw that she was staring at him in a shocked way. It had been a sly means of breaking it to her, and he said repentantly, "My beloved, shall you mind very much? I really would like to go back and try for a fellowship."

"Well! If ever I heard the like! So I'm to be married to some stuffy professor of ancient history and live surrounded by musty old tomes and bothersome students, am I?"

He said, eyeing her askance, "Not if you really object, of course. Only I thought — Well, you love history too, and — and —"

She chuckled and snuggled closer against him. "Foolish creature."

Relieved, he hugged her. "Poor girl, such a life you will lead. When I begin to study again, you will find me to be a most irritating fellow, apt to forget everything but my research, and always with my head stuck in a book."

She drew back and looked up at him. The acid twist to the fine mouth was gone. The hauteur in the grey eyes was replaced by a warm tenderness that made her heart beat faster. She thought, "How blessed I am," and said, "My consolation will be to dream of seeing you take your seat in the House."

Mitchell gave a start. "By Jove! You're right." He gazed at the distant Home Wood and murmured thoughtfully, "I'll have a say in how the old homeland is run. . . . I wonder . . ."

Charity reached up and began to twist a strand of his hair into an elf lock. When he remained silent, she probed curiously, "Wonder what, dear?"

"Well . . ." He glanced at her rather

diffidently. "You know how I feel about the Black Country. Do you suppose — I mean, if I stood up and spoke like a sensible man — do you think they might . . . listen to me?"

"Oh, Mitch! I think it a superb notion! Why not? You might be able to stop the factory owners from so wounding the land. And the people. Or at least — *try!*"

"I shall!" he said, his eyes glinting. "By God! This is a heaven-sent opportunity! If I could start them to thinking about the decent people now so abused and exploited; about the helpless children . . ."

She saw the spark of anger return to his eyes, and she knew that he would fight. "They will hate him for it," she thought. And that very thought deepened her love and her pride.

Glancing down at her, the visionary light faded from Mitchell's eyes. "My main task in life must be to make you happy, my most valiant love," he said tenderly.

She smiled and said on a sigh, "There is just one difficulty, my dearest dear . . ."

"No — what is it?" he asked, holding her ever nearer.

"I cannot but wonder," said Charity demurely, "whether an ignorant warthog with tall feet could possibly find happiness with . . . a fieldmouse. . . ."

Lord Mitchell Redmond, ex-rake and duellist, promptly bent his full and not inconsiderable expertise to convincing his bride that this most unlikely union could be a very happy one indeed.

A note on the text
Large print edition designed by
Lyda E. Kuth.
Composed in 16 pt Plantin
on a Mergenthaler Linotron 202
by Modern Graphics, Inc.